WHY WE TOOK THE CAR

WOLFGANG HERRNDORF

Translated by Tim Mohr

ARTHUR A. LEVINE BOOKS
An Imprint of Scholastic Inc.

Originally published as *Tschick* by Wolfgang Herrndorf, copyright © 2010 by Rowohlt.Berlin Verlag GmbH

Translation by Tim Mohr copyright © 2014 by Scholastic Inc.

Library of Congress Cataloging-in-Publication Data

Herrndorf, Wolfgang, 1965–
    [Tschick. English]
    Why We Took the Car / Wolfgang Herrndorf ; Translated by Tim Mohr. — 1st American ed.
    p. cm.
    Summary: Mike Klingenberg is a troubled fourteen-year-old from a dysfunctional family in Berlin who thinks of himself as boring, so when a Russian juvenile delinquent called Tschick begins to pay attention to him and include Mike in his criminal activities, he is excited — until those activities lead to disaster on the autobahn.
    ISBN 978-0-545-48180-9 (hardcover : alk. paper) 1. Russians — Germany — Berlin — Juvenile fiction. 2. Immigrants — Germany — Berlin — Juvenile fiction. 3. Automobile theft — Juvenile fiction. 4. Juvenile delinquents — Germany — Juvenile fiction. 5. Self-esteem — Juvenile fiction. 6. Friendship — Juvenile fiction. 7. Berlin (Germany) — Juvenile fiction. [1. Russians — Germany — Berlin — Fiction. 2. Immigrants — Fiction. 3. Automobile theft — Fiction. 4. Juvenile delinquency — Fiction. 5. Self-esteem — Fiction. 6. Friendship — Fiction. 7. Berlin (Germany) — Fiction. 8. Germany — Fiction.] I. Title.
    PZ7.H43222Why 2014
    833.92 — dc23

2012044118

10 9 8 7 6 5 4 3 2 1   14 15 16 17 18

First edition, January 2014

Printed in the U.S.A.   23

Book design by Christopher Stengel

The translation of this work was supported by a grant from the Goethe-Institut, which is funded by the German Ministry of Foreign Affairs.

To my friends

The first thing is the smell of blood and coffee. The coffee machine is sitting over on the table, and the blood is in my shoes. And if I'm being completely honest, I have to admit it's not just blood. When the old guy said "fourteen," I pissed my pants. I'd been sitting there slumped in the chair, not moving. I was dizzy. I tried to look the way I imagined Tschick would look if someone said "fourteen" to him, and then I got so scared I pissed myself. Mike Klingenberg, hero. I have no idea why I'm freaking out now. It was clear the whole time that it would end this way. And you can be sure Tschick wouldn't piss his pants.

Where is Tschick, anyway? I'd last seen him on the side of the autobahn, hopping into the bushes on one leg. But I figure they must have caught him too. You're not going to get far on one leg. Obviously I can't ask the police where he is. Better not bring it up at all in case they hadn't seen him. Maybe they really hadn't seen him. There's no way they're going to find out about him from me. Even if they torture me. Though I don't think German police are allowed to torture people. They only do that on TV. And in Turkey.

But sitting in your own piss and blood in a highway police station and answering questions about your parents isn't exactly the greatest thing ever. In fact, maybe getting tortured would be preferable — at least then I'd have an excuse for freaking out.

The best thing to do is to keep your mouth shut. That's what Tschick said. And that's exactly how I see it too. Especially now, when it doesn't matter anyway. Nothing matters to me at this point. Well, almost nothing. Tatiana Cosic still matters to me, of course. Despite the fact that I haven't thought about her in quite a while now. But as I'm sitting there in the chair and the autobahn is rushing past outside and the older policeman has spent the last five minutes fumbling around with the coffee machine, filling it with water and emptying it out again, flipping the power switch on and off, and looking at the bottom of the machine, when it's obvious to any moron that the extension cord isn't plugged in, I find myself thinking about Tatiana. Even though she had nothing to do with the whole thing. Is what I'm saying here hard to follow? Yeah, well, sorry. I'll try again later. Tatiana isn't even part of the story. The prettiest girl in the world isn't part of the story. Throughout the entire trip, I'd imagined that she could see us. How we'd gazed out from the high point of that field of grain. How we'd stood on top of that mountain of trash with our bundle of plastic hoses, like the last idiots left on Earth . . . I'd always imagined Tatiana was standing behind us, seeing what we saw, smiling when we smiled. But now I'm happy that I only imagined that.

The policeman pulls a green paper towel out of a dispenser and hands it to me. What am I supposed to do with it? Wipe the floor? He grabs his nose with two fingers and looks at me.

Aha. Blow my nose. I blow my nose and he smiles helpfully. I guess I can forget about the whole torture thing. But where should I put the paper towel now? I scan the room. The entire floor of the station is covered with gray linoleum, exactly the same stuff as in the hallways of our school gymnasium. It smells a bit similar too. Piss, sweat, and linoleum. I picture Mr. Wolkow, our gym teacher, sprinting down the hall in his tracksuit, with seventy years of workouts behind him: "Let's go, people, hop to it!" The sound of his footsteps smacking the floor, distant giggles from the girls' locker room, Wolkow turning to look in that direction. I picture the tall windows, the bleachers, the rings that never get used dangling from the ceiling. I picture Natalie and Lena and Kimberley coming in through the side entrance of the gym. And Tatiana in her green sweats. I picture their blurry reflections on the floor of the gym, the sparkly pants the girls all wear these days, their tops. And how lately half of them show up for gym in thick wool sweaters and another couple have doctor's notes. Hagecius Junior High School, Berlin, eighth grade.

"I thought it was fifteen," I say, and the policeman shakes his head.

"Nope, fourteen. What's with the coffee machine, Horst?"

"It's broken," says Horst.

I want to talk to my lawyer.

That's the sentence I probably need to say. It's the right sentence in the right situation, as everybody knows from watching TV. And it's easy to say: I want to talk to my lawyer. But they'd probably die laughing. Here's the problem: I have no idea what this sentence means. If I say I want to talk to my lawyer and they ask me, "*Who* do you want to talk to? *Your* lawyer?" what am I supposed to answer? I've never seen a law-yer in my life, and I don't even know what I need one for. I don't know if there's a difference between a lawyer and an attorney. Or an attorney general. I guess they're like judges except on my side. I guess they know a lot more about the law than I do. But I guess pretty much everyone in the room knows more about the law than I do. First and foremost the police-men. And I could ask them. But I'll bet that if I ask the younger one if I could use some kind of lawyer right about now, he'll just turn to his partner and yell, "Hey, Horst! Horsty! Get a load of this. Our hero here wants to know if he needs a lawyer! Bleeding all over the floor, pissing himself like a champ, and wants to talk to *his lawyer*!" Ha, ha, ha. They'd laugh them-selves silly. And I figure I'm bad enough off as it is. No reason to make an even bigger ass of myself. What's done is done. Nothing else is going to happen now. And a lawyer can't change that. Whether or not we caused some bad shit is a ques-tion only a lunatic would try to argue. What am I supposed to say? That I spent the entire week lying next to the pool, just ask the cleaning lady? That all those pig parts must have just fallen from the sky like rain? There's really not much more I can do. I could pray in the direction of Mecca, and I could take a crap in my pants, but otherwise there aren't many options left.

The younger officer, who actually looks like a nice guy, shakes his head again and says, "Fifteen? No way. Fourteen. You're criminally accountable at fourteen."

I should probably have feelings of guilt at this point, remorse and all that, but to be honest I don't feel a thing. I'm just unbelievably dizzy. I reach down and scratch my calf, except that down where my calf used to be, nothing's there. My hand is streaked with violet red slime when I pull it back up. That's not *my* blood, I'd said earlier when they asked. There was enough other slime in the street for them to worry about — and I really didn't think it was my blood. But if it isn't my blood, I ask myself now, where is my calf?

I lift my pant leg and look down. I have exactly one second to think. If I had to watch this in a movie, I think to myself, I would definitely throw up. And sure enough I'm getting sick now, in this oddly calming highway police station. For a split second I see my reflection on the linoleum floor coming toward me, then it smacks into me and I'm out.

The doctor opens and closes his mouth like a carp. It takes a few seconds before words come out. The doctor is yelling. Why is the doctor yelling? He yells at the small woman. Then someone in a uniform steps in, a blue uniform. A policeman, one I don't know yet. The cop shouts at the doctor. How do I even know he's a doctor? He's wearing a white coat. So I guess he could also be a baker. But in the pocket of the coat is a metal flashlight and some kind of listening device. What would a baker need something like that for — to listen for a heartbeat in a bread roll? It's got to be a doctor. And this doctor is pointing at my head now and shouting. I feel around under the sheet where my legs are. They're bare. Don't feel like they're covered in piss or blood anymore. Where am I?

I'm lying on my back. Above me everything is yellow. Glance to the side: big dark window. Other side: white plastic curtain. A hospital, I'd say. The doctor would make sense then too. And, oh yeah, the small woman is also wearing scrubs and carrying a notebook. What hospital — Charité? No, no. I have no idea. I'm not in Berlin. I'll have to ask, I think to myself, but nobody is paying any attention to me. The policeman doesn't like the way the doctor is shouting at him, and he's shouting back. But the doctor just shouts even louder, and interestingly enough you can see who is calling the shots here. The doctor apparently has the authority, not the policeman. I'm worn out and also somehow happy and tired; it feels as if I'm bursting from within with happiness, and I fall back to sleep without saying a single word. The happiness, I find out later, is called Valium. It's administered with big needles.

When I next wake up, it's all bright. The sun is shining in the big window. Something is scratching at the soles of my feet. Aha, a doctor, a different one, and he has another nurse with him. No police. The only unpleasant thing is the doctor scratching at my feet. Why is he doing that?

"He's awake," says the nurse. Not exactly a genius.

"Ah, aha," says the doctor looking at me. "And how do you feel?"

I want to say something, but the only thing that comes out of my mouth is, "Pfff."

"How do you feel? Do you know your name?"

"Pfff-fay?"

What the hell kind of question is that? Do they think I'm crazy or something? I look at the doctor and he looks at me; then he leans over me and shines a flashlight in my eyes. Is this an interrogation? Am I supposed to confess my name? Is this the torture hospital? And if it is, could he just stop lifting up my eyelids for a second and at least pretend he's interested in my answer? Of course, I don't answer anyway. Because, while I'm deciding whether I should say Mike Klingenberg or just Mike or Klinge or Attila the Hun — that's what my father says whenever he's stressed, when he's gotten nothing but bad news all day; he drinks two shots of Jägermeister and answers the phone as Attila the Hun — I mean, as I'm deciding whether to say anything at all or to skip it altogether given the situation, the doctor starts saying something about "four of these" and "three of these" and I pass out again.

There's a lot of things you can say about hospitals, but you can't say they're not nice. I always love being in the hospital. You do nothing all day long, and then the nurses come in. They're all super young and super friendly. And they wear those thin white outfits that I love because you can always see what kind of underwear they have on underneath. Just why I think that's so cool, I'm not sure. Because if they wore those outfits on the street, I'd think it was stupid. But inside a hospital it's great. I think so, anyway. It's a little like those mafia movies, when there's a long silence before one gangster answers another, and they just stare at each other. "Hey!" A minute of silence. "Look me in the eyes!" Five minutes of silence. In regular life that would be stupid. But when you're in the mafia, it's not.

My favorite nurse is from Lebanon and is named Hanna. Hanna has short dark hair and wears normal underwear. And that's cool: *normal underwear*. Other kinds of underwear always look a bit sad. On most people. If you don't have Megan Fox's body, it can look a little desperate. I don't know. Maybe I'm weird, but I like normal underwear.

Hanna is actually still studying to be a nurse. This is her residency or whatever. Before she comes into my room she always pokes her head around the corner and then taps on the door frame with two fingers. Which I think is very thoughtful. And she comes up with a new name for me every day. First I was Mike, then Mikey, then Mikeypikey — which I thought sounded like some old Finnish name. But that wasn't the end. I was Michael Schumacher and Attila the Hun, then pig killer, and finally *the sick bunny*. For that alone I'd love to stay here in the hospital for a year.

Hanna changes my bandages every day. It hurts pretty bad, and I can see from the look on her face that it hurts her to cause me pain too.

"The most important thing is for you to be comfortable," she always says when she's finished. And then I always say I'm going to marry her one day or whatever. Unfortunately she already has a boyfriend. Sometimes she just comes by and sits on the side of my bed because I don't really get any other visitors, and we have great conversations. Real adult conversations. It's so much easier to talk with women like Hanna than with girls my age. If anyone can tell me why that is, I'd love to hear it, because I sure can't figure it out.

CHAPTER FOUR

The doctor is less talkative. "It's just a piece of flesh," he says. "Muscle," he says. "No big deal, it'll grow back, there'll just be a little indentation or scarring," he says. "It'll look sexy." And he says this every day. Every day he looks at the bandages and tells me the same thing — there'll be a scar, that it's no big deal, that it'll look as if I fought in a war. "As if you've been to war, young man, and women like that," he says, and he says it in a way that's supposed to sound somehow profound. But I don't understand whatever the deep meaning is. Then he winks at me, and I usually wink back even though I don't understand. The man has helped me out, after all, so I can help him out too.

Later on, our conversations improve, mostly because they become more serious. Though actually it's just one conversation. Once I'm able to limp around, he takes me to his office — which, oddly enough, has only a desk and no medical devices — and we sit across the desk from each other like a couple of CEOs closing a deal. On the desk is a plastic model of a human torso with removable organs. The large intestine looks like a brain, and the paint on the stomach is peeling.

"I need to talk to you," says the doctor, which has got to be the stupidest beginning to a conversation that I can possibly imagine. I wait for him to start talking, but unfortunately when someone begins a conversation that way they never start talking right away — somehow *I need to talk to you* and not talking always go together. The doctor stares at me and then drops his gaze and opens a green folder. He doesn't throw it open; he carefully opens it the way I imagine he would peel open the stomach of a patient on the operating table. Cautiously, deftly, very seriously. The man is a surgeon after all. Congratulations on that, by the way, I'm sure someone's real proud.

What comes next is less interesting. Basically he wants to know how I got my head injury. Also where I got my other injuries — from the autobahn, as I had already explained, okay, okay, he knew that already. But the head injury, yeah, well, I fell off my chair at the police station.

The doctor puts the fingers of his hands together. Yes, that's what it says in the report: Fell from chair. At the police station.

He nods. Yes.

I nod too.

"It's just us here," he says after a pause.

"I see that," I say like an idiot, and wink first at the doctor and then for good measure at the plastic torso.

"You don't have to be worried about saying anything here. I'm your doctor, and that means our conversations are completely confidential."

"Okay," I say. He'd said something similar to me a few days before, and now I understand. The man is sworn to secrecy and he wants me to tell him something that he can keep secret. But what? How unbelievably cool it is to piss your pants out of fear?

"It's not just a question of misconduct. It's also a question of negligence. They shouldn't have taken you at your word, do you understand? They should have examined you and called a doctor immediately. Do you know how critical your condition was? And you say you *fell off the chair*?"

"Yes."

"I'm sorry, but doctors are a skeptical bunch. I mean, they wanted something from you. And as your attending doctor . . ."

Yeah, yeah. For God's sake. Confidentiality. I get it. What does he want to know? How someone falls off a chair? Sideways, down, and plop. He shakes his head for a long time; then he makes a small gesture with his hand — and suddenly I understand what he's trying to figure out. My God, I'm so slow sometimes. So damn embarrassing. Why didn't he just ask?

"No, no!" I shout, waving my hands wildly in the air like I'm swatting a swarm of flies. "It was all legit! I was sitting in the chair and I lifted up my pant leg to look at it, and when I did I got all dizzy and fell over. There were no *external factors*." Good phrase. Learned it from a police show.

"Are you sure?"

"I'm sure, yes. The police were actually really nice. They gave me a glass of water and tissues. I just got dizzy and fell over." I straighten myself up in front of the desk and then demonstrate like a talented actor, twice letting myself slump to the right until I nearly fall over.

"Very well," says the doctor slowly.

He scribbles something on a piece of paper.

"I just wanted to know. It was still irresponsible. The blood loss . . . they really should have . . . and it did look suspicious."

He closes the green folder and looks at me for a long time. "I don't know, maybe it's none of my business, but I'd really be interested to know — though you don't have to answer if you don't want to. But what did you want — or where were you trying to go?"

"I have no idea."

"Like I said, you don't have to answer. I'm only asking out of curiosity."

"I would tell you, but if I did, you wouldn't believe me anyway. I'm pretty sure."

"I'd believe you," he says with a friendly smile. My buddy.

"It's stupid."

"What's stupid?"

"It's just . . . well, we were trying to go to Wallachia. See, I told you you'd think it was stupid."

"I don't think it's stupid, I just don't understand. *Where* were you trying to go?"

"Wallachia."

"And where is that supposed to be?"

He looks at me curiously, and I can tell I'm turning red. We're not going to delve any deeper into this. We shake each other's hands like grown men, signaling an end to the conversation, and I'm somehow happy that I didn't have to push the bounds of his confidentiality.

CHAPTER FIVE

I've never had any nicknames. In school, I mean. Or anywhere else, for that matter. My name is Mike Klingenberg. Mike. Not Mikey or Klinge or anything like that. Always just Mike. Except in the sixth grade, when I was briefly known as Psycho. Not like that's the greatest thing either, being called Psycho. But it didn't last long and then I was back to being Mike again.

When someone doesn't have any nicknames, it's for one of two reasons. Either you're incredibly boring and don't get any because of that, or you don't have any friends. If I had to decide between one or the other, I'd have to say I'd rather have no friends than be incredibly boring. I mean, if you're boring you won't have any friends anyway, or you'll only have friends who are even more boring than you are.

But there is one other possibility: You could be boring *and* have no friends. And I'm afraid that's my problem. At least since Paul moved away. Paul had been my friend since kindergarten, and we used to hang out almost every day — until his dumbass mother decided she wanted to live out in the country.

That was about the time I started junior high, and it didn't make things any easier. I hardly saw Paul at all after that. His new place was half a world away, at the last stop of one of the subway lines and then six more kilometers by bike from there. And Paul changed out there. His parents split up and he went nuts. I mean really crazy. Paul basically lives in the forest with his mother and just lies around brooding. He always had a tendency to do that anyway. You really had to push him to do anything. But out there in the middle of nowhere, there's nobody to push him, so he just stews. If I remember right, I visited him three times out there. He was so depressed every time that I never wanted to go again. Paul showed me the house, the yard, the woods, and a hunting blind in the woods where he'd sit and watch animals. Except, of course, that there were no animals. Every few hours a sparrow flew by. And he jotted down notes about that. It was early in the year, right when *Grand Theft Auto IV* came out, though Paul wasn't interested in that kind of thing anymore. Nothing interested him except wild critters. I had to spend an entire day up in a tree, and then the whole thing just became too idiotic for me. Once I also secretly flipped through his notebook to see what else was in it — because there was a lot in it. Things about his mother, things written in some kind of secret code, drawings of naked women — terrible drawings. Nothing against naked women. Naked women are awesome. But these drawings were not awesome. They were just messed up. And between the sketches, in calligraphy, observations about animals and the weather. At some point he'd written that he'd seen wild boars and lynxes and wolves. There was a question mark next to the word *wolves*, and I said to him, "This is the outskirts of Berlin — lynxes and wolves, are you sure?" And he grabbed the book out of my hand and looked at me as if *I* was the crazy one. After that we didn't see each other very often. That was three years ago. And he'd once been my best friend.

I didn't get to know anybody in junior high at first. I'm not exactly great at getting to know people. And I never saw it as a major problem. Until Tatiana Cosic showed up. Or at least until I noticed her. She'd been in my class the whole time. I just never noticed her until the seventh grade. No idea why. But in seventh grade she suddenly popped up on my radar — and that's when all my misery began. I guess at this point I should probably describe Tatiana. Because otherwise the rest of the story won't make sense.

Tatiana's first name is Tatiana and her last name is Cosic. She's fourteen years old and her parents' last name is also Cosic. I don't know what their first names are. They're from Serbia or Croatia, you can tell from their last name, and they live in a white apartment building with lots of windows. Yadda, yadda, yadda.

I could blather on about her for ages, but the surprising thing is that I actually have no idea what I'm talking about. I don't know Tatiana at all. I know the things that anyone in her class would know about her. I know what she looks like, what her name is, and that she's good at sports and English. And so on. I know how tall she is because of the physical exams they gave us on health day. I found out where she lives from the phone book. And other than that, I know basically nothing. Obviously I could describe exactly what she looks like and how her voice sounds and what color her hair is and everything. But that seems to me unnecessary. I mean, everyone can imagine what she looks like: She looks great. Her voice sounds great too. She's just great all around.

CHAPTER SIX

I guess I never explained why they called me Psycho. Because, as I mentioned, I was known as Psycho for a while. No idea what the point was. I mean, obviously I know it was supposed to suggest that I had a screw loose. But as far as I'm concerned, there were several other people who deserved the name more than I did. Frank could have been called Psycho, or Stobke, with his lighter. They're both way crazier than I am. Or the Nazi. But then again, the Nazi was already called Nazi, so he didn't need another name. And of course there was a reason that I got the name instead of anyone else. It was the result of an assignment in Mr. Schuermann's German class, sixth grade, a word prompt story. In case you don't know what a word prompt story is, it goes like this: You get four words, like "zoo," "ape," "zookeeper," and "hat," and you have to write a story that includes all of the words. Real original. Totally moronic. The words Mr. Schuermann thought up were "vacation," "water," "rescue," and "God." Which was definitely more difficult than zoo and ape. The main difficulty was God, obviously. We only had ethics classes, not religion, and there were sixteen kids registered as atheists in the class, including me. Even the Protestants in the class didn't really believe in

God. I don't think. At least, not the way people who *really* believe in God believe. People who don't want to harm even an ant, or who are happy when someone dies because that person is going to heaven. Or people who crash a plane into the World Trade Center. Those people really believe in God. That's why the writing assignment was tough. Most of the students grabbed on to the word "vacation." A little family is paddling around off the Côte d'Azur and are taken totally by surprise by a terrible storm and yell "oh, God" and are then rescued or whatever. And I could have written something like that too. But as I sat down to write the story, the first thing that occurred to me was the fact that we hadn't been on vacation for three years because my father had been preparing for bankruptcy. Which didn't bother me — I never particularly liked going on vacation with my parents anyway.

Instead, I spent last summer squatting in our basement carving boomerangs. One of my elementary school teachers taught me how to do it. He was an expert in the boomerang department. Bretfeld was his name, Wilhelm Bretfeld. He'd even written a book about boomerangs. Two books actually. But I didn't realize that until after I'd finished elementary school. I ran into old Bretfeld in a field. He was basically standing right behind our house in the cow pasture throwing his boomerangs, homemade boomerangs he'd carved himself. It was yet another thing I had never realized really worked. I thought the things only came back to you in the movies. But Bretfeld was a pro, and he showed me how to do it. I was blown away. Also because he'd made them himself. "Anything that's round in front and sharp at the back will fly," said Bretfeld. Then he looked at me over the frames of his glasses and asked,

"What's your name again? I can't remember you." The thing that most blew my mind was the long-distance boomerang. He'd developed it himself. It could fly for ages — and he had *invented* it. All over the world today, when someone throws a boomerang and it stays in the air for five minutes, setting some record, and a picture is taken of it, it's always there: *based on a design by Wilhelm Bretfeld*. He's world renowned, Bretfeld. And he was standing in the field behind our house last summer and showed me how to do it. A really good teacher. Though I never noticed it in elementary school.

In any event, I spent the entire summer break sitting in the basement whittling. And it was a great summer break, much better than going somewhere on vacation. My parents were almost never home. My father drove around from creditor to creditor and my mother was at the beauty farm. And that's what I wrote the assignment about: *Mother and the Beauty Farm*, a word prompt story by Mike Klingenberg.

The next class, I got to read it aloud. Or I had to. I didn't want to. Svenja was first up, and she had written one of those nonsense stories about the Côte d'Azur, which Schuermann thought was great. Then Kevin read basically the same story except that instead of the Côte d'Azur it was the Baltic coast. Then it was my turn. Mother at the beauty farm. It's not really a beauty farm. Though my mother does always look better when she comes back from it. It's actually a clinic. She's an alcoholic. She's drunk booze for as long as I can remember, but the difference is that it used to be funnier. Everyone is normally funny when they drink, but when a certain line is crossed people get tired or aggressive. And when my mother started walking around our place with a kitchen knife again, I was standing upstairs with my father as he called down, "How about another trip to the beauty farm?" That's how the summer started at the end of sixth grade.

I like my mother. I have to add that, because what I'm about to say might not cast her in the best light. But I always liked her, and still do. She's not like other moms. That's what I've always liked best about her. She can be really funny, for instance, and you can't say that about most mothers. Calling the clinic the beauty farm was one of her jokes.

My mother used to play a lot of tennis. My father too, but not very well. The ace in our family was my mother. When she was still in shape, she won the tennis club championship every year. She even won it with a bottle of vodka in her system, but that's another story. Anyway, as a kid I was always at the courts with her. My mother sat on the terrace at the tennis club and drank cocktails with Frau Weber and Frau Osterthun and Herr Schuback and the rest of them. And I sat under the table and played with Matchbox cars as the sun shone down. In my mind the sun was always shining at the tennis club. I looked at the red clay dust on five sets of white tennis shoes and collected bottle caps — you could draw on the insides of the caps with a ballpoint pen. I was allowed to have five ice creams a day and ten cans of Coke and could just tell the waiter to add it to our tab. And then Frau Weber said, "Next week at seven again, Frau Klingenberg?"

And my mother: "Sure."

And Frau Weber: "I'll bring the balls next time."

My mother: "Sure."

And so on and so forth. Always the same conversation. Though the joke was that Frau Weber never brought balls — she was too cheap.

Once in a while there was another version. It went like this:

"Again next Saturday, Frau Klingenberg?"

"Can't do it. I'll be away."

"But doesn't your husband's team have a league match?"

"Yes, but he's not going to be away. I am."

"Aha. Where are you going?"

"To the beauty farm."

And then somebody at the table who didn't know the phrase yet always, always, always, threw out the unbelievably clever quip, "You certainly don't need any help in that department, Frau Klingenberg."

Then my mother would knock back the rest of her Brandy Alexander and say, "That was only a joke, Herr Schuback. It's actually a rehab facility."

Then we would walk home hand in hand because my mother was no longer capable of driving. I carried her heavy racquet bag and she said to me, "You can't learn much from your mother. But two things you can learn: First, you can talk about anything. Second, what people think doesn't mean shit." That was enlightening. Talk openly. Screw what other people think.

My doubts crept in only later. Not doubts about the ideas in principle. But doubts about whether my mother really didn't care what other people thought.

Anyway, the beauty farm. I don't know exactly what went on there. Because I was never allowed to visit my mother. She didn't want me to. But whenever she came home from the place she told the craziest stories. The therapy apparently consisted of talking a lot and not drinking. And sometimes exercise as well. But most of them couldn't really do much exercise. For the most part they talked while tossing a ball of yarn around in a circle. The person allowed to speak was the person with the ball of yarn. I had to ask about the ball of yarn five times because I wasn't sure whether I'd heard it right or whether maybe it was a joke. But it was no joke. My mother didn't think this detail was so funny or fascinating, but to be honest I found it incredibly fascinating. Just try to imagine it: ten adults sitting in a circle and throwing a ball of yarn around. Afterward, the entire room was full of yarn, but that wasn't the point of the whole thing, even if it's fair to think so at first. The point was to create a *web of communication*. Which tells you that my mother wasn't the craziest person in the place. There must have been considerably crazier ones too.

But anyone who thinks the ball of yarn must be the strangest thing at the clinic hasn't heard about the cardboard boxes. Every patient had a cardboard box. It hung from the ceiling in each room, with the open side facing up. You had to throw notes into the box, basketball style. Notes where you wrote your aspirations, wishes, resolutions, prayers, or whatever. Whenever my mother wished for something, made a resolution, or scolded herself, she wrote it down on a piece of paper, folded it up, and then basically did a Dirk Nowitzki and slam-dunked it in the cardboard box. And the insane thing about it was that nobody ever read them. That wasn't the point. The point was just writing it down so it was there and you could see it — *my desires and wishes and all that crap are hanging right there in that box.* And because the cardboard boxes were so important, you had to give them names. The name was written on the box with a felt-tip marker, so basically every drunkard had a box named "God" hanging from the ceiling with all his or her aspirations inside it. Because most people just called their box God. That's what the therapists suggested — just call it God. But you were allowed to call it whatever you wanted. Some old lady called hers "Osiris" and somebody else "Great Spirit."

My mother named her box "Karl-Heinz," and as a result a therapist came and peppered her with questions. The first thing he wanted to know was whether it was her father. "Who?" she asked, and the therapist pointed at the box hanging from the ceiling. My mother shook her head. Then the therapist asked just who he was, this Karl-Heinz. And my mother said, "That cardboard box." So then the therapist asked what the name of her father was. "Gottlieb," she said, to which the therapist said, "Aha!" It was supposed to sound clever, as if the therapist had just figured something out. Gottlieb, aha! My mother had no idea what the therapist had figured out, and he never said. And that's the way it went the entire time. They all tried like crazy to act as if they had things figured out, but they never gave away what they knew. When my father heard about it — the thing with the cardboard box — he nearly fell out of his chair laughing. He kept saying, "My God that's sad," though he was laughing. So I had to laugh too, and my mother decided it was funny as well, at least in retrospect.

And I put all of that into my school essay. And in order to get the word "rescue" in, I added the scene with the kitchen knife. And since I was on a roll, I even added a bit about how she mistook me for my father when she came down the stairs one morning. It was the longest assignment I'd ever written — at least eight pages long — and still I could have written a Part Two, a Part Three, and a Part Four if I'd felt like it. Though as I found out, Part One was more than enough.

The class totally lost it while I was reading it aloud. Schuermann told everyone to quiet down and then said, "Nice, very nice. How much longer is it? Still so much to go? That'll do for now, I'd say." I didn't have to read the rest. Schuermann had me stay after class so he could read the rest of it on his own, and I stood there next to him feeling very proud — first because it had been such a success and second because Schuermann wanted to read the whole thing personally. Mike Klingenberg, author. And then Schuermann closed the notebook I'd written my assignment in and shook his head. I took it as an appreciative shake of the head, the kind that signals, *How can a sixth grader write such an incredibly great essay?* But then he said, "Why are you grinning like an idiot? Do you think this is funny?" And it slowly dawned on me that it hadn't been such a success after all. At least not as far as Schuermann was concerned.

He got up from his desk, walked over to the window, and stood there looking out at the schoolyard. "Mike," he said, turning around again to face me. "That's your *mother*. Did you ever stop to think about that?"

Obviously I'd made a huge mistake. I just didn't know what it was. But it was clear from Schuermann's reaction that I'd committed an absolutely massive error with my assignment. And that he thought it was the most embarrassing essay the world had ever witnessed. But I couldn't figure out why this was the case — he never said, and to be honest I don't know why to this day. He just kept repeating that it was my *mother*, until he suddenly started getting very loud and said my assignment was the most sickening, unsavory, and shameless one he'd encountered in fifteen years of teaching — blah, blah, blah — and that I should immediately rip the pages out of my notebook. I was totally devastated, and of course I reached straight for my notebook, like a moron, to rip out the pages. But Schuermann grabbed my hand and shouted, "I don't mean literally rip it out. Don't you understand anything? What you need to do is think hard about what you've done. Really think!" I thought for a minute about it, but to be honest I just didn't get it. I still don't get it. I mean, it's not as if I made any of it up or anything.

After that I was called Psycho. For almost a year, everyone called me that. Even in class. Even when the teacher was there. "Come on, Psycho, pass the ball! You can do it, Psycho! Chill out, Psycho!" And it only stopped when André landed in our class. André Langin. Handsome André.

André had been held back. He had a girlfriend by the end of his first day in our class. And he had a new one every week after that. These days he's with a Turkish girl who looks like Salma Hayek. He was sniffing around Tatiana for a little while too, and it drove me nuts. For a few days they were talking to each other constantly — in the hall, in front of school, in the schoolyard. But in the end they didn't get together, I don't think. That would have killed me. At some point they stopped talking to each other, and shortly afterward I heard André explain to Patrick why men and women don't get along — crazy scientific theories about the Stone Age, saber-toothed tigers, and childbirth and all that. I hated him for that too. I hated him from the very first moment, though it wasn't easy for me. For one thing, even though André's not the brightest bulb, he's not a complete waste of space. He can be nice too, and he's pretty laid-back. And, like I mentioned, he's decent looking. But he's still an asshole. And just to make it worse, he lives only a block away from me, at 15 Wald Street. The house is full of assholes, by the way. The Langins have a giant place. His father's a politician, city councilman or something. Of course. And my father says, "Langin thinks he's Mr. Big Man!"

But to get back to the story I meant to tell, when André was brand-new in our class, we took a field trip to go hiking somewhere south of Berlin. Just a standard nature walk in the woods. I trailed way behind the others and actually tried to take in the nature. This was around the time we had planted an herb garden, and I was genuinely interested in nature for a while there. Interested in *trees*. I was thinking of becoming a scientist or something. But not for long, and it probably had something to do with that field trip, where I hung back so I could examine the leaf patterns and growth forms in peace. That's when it suddenly occurred to me that I didn't give the slightest crap about leaf patterns and growth forms. Ahead of me everyone was laughing and having fun, and I could make out Tatiana Cosic's laugh from the rest; two hundred meters behind, Mike Klingenberg was traipsing through the forest looking at fucking leaf patterns in nature. Which wasn't even really nature. It was just some crappy woods with educational plaques posted every ten meters. Hell.

At some stage we stopped at a three-hundred-year-old white beech tree that had been planted there by Frederick the Great. The teacher asked who knew what kind of tree it was. Nobody knew. Except me, of course. But I wasn't so crazy as to admit in front of the whole class that I knew it was a white beech. I might as well have said, "My name is Psycho and I have a problem." It was depressing that we were all standing around the tree and not a single person knew what it was. I'm getting to the point now. Beneath this white beech tree Frederick the Great had also put a few tables and benches so people could sit and picnic. Which is exactly what we did. By coincidence I ended up at a table with Tatiana Cosic. Opposite me was André, handsome André, with his arms stretched out right and left around the shoulders of Laura and Marie. As if he were best friends with them. Except that he wasn't friends with them at all. He'd been in our class for maybe a week at that stage. But the two of them didn't object. On the contrary, they seemed to be frozen with excitement and didn't move a muscle. It was as if they were afraid his arms would, like skittish birds, get spooked if they moved their shoulders. André didn't say anything at all. He just looked around with his bedroom eyes. And then he glanced at me and, after thinking for a while, said to nobody in particular but definitely not to me, "Why is this guy called Psycho anyway? He's totally boring." Laura and Marie laughed themselves silly over this top-quality joke, and since it had been such a success, André repeated it: "Seriously, why is this walking sleeping pill named Psycho?" And ever since then, I've been Mike again. And it's even worse than before.

There are a lot of things I'm no good at. But if there's one thing I can do, it's the high jump. I mean, okay, I'm not an Olympic athlete, but I'm still pretty close to unbeatable at high jump and long jump. Even though I'm one of the shortest kids, I get as high as Olaf, the tallest kid in our class. Early in the year I set a record for our age group, and I was really proud. We were standing at the high jump bar, and the girls were all sitting around on the grass nearby, where Frau Bielcke was giving them a lecture. Frau Bielcke blathers on and the girls just sit there scratching their ankles. They don't constantly run around the track like we have to with Mr. Wolkow.

Wolkow is our gym teacher, and he loves to give us lectures too. Every gym teacher I've ever had has let the words fly. With Wolkow, Mondays are reserved for the soccer results, pretty much the same on Tuesdays, Wednesdays he talks about the Champions League, and by Friday he's already looking forward to that weekend's soccer matches and all the analysis surrounding them. In summer he airs his opinions on the Tour de France, but once he starts talking about doping he quickly comes back around to the much more important topic of soccer and the happy fact that there's no doping in that sport.

Because it's of *no use* in soccer. That is Wolkow's honest opinion. But nobody cares anyway because of one basic problem: Wolkow talks only while we're running. He's in insane shape. He must be seventy, and yet he's always out in front of us, loping comfortably and gabbing on and on. And then he always says, "Men!" Then he's silent for about ten meters. Then, "Dortmund." Another ten meters. "Haven't got a chance." Ten more meters. "Home field advantage. Am I right or am I right?" Twenty meters. "And that old fox who coaches Bayern Munich. It's not going to be a walk in the park." Giddyup, giddyup. "What do you all think?" Thirty seconds of silence. Obviously nobody says anything because we've already run like a million loops around the track. Once in a while Hans, the Nazi, who's a knuckle-dragging soccer fan and who is always lagging behind the rest of us, sweating his ass off, yells, "Hey, ho, let's go, Hertha Berlin!" And that's too much even for Wolkow, the old windbag, and he slows down so Hans can catch up, then lifts his pointer finger and yells in a voice quivering with rage, "Joe Simunic! The cardinal sin!" And Hans yells back, "I know, I know." Then Wolkow speeds up again and mumbles to himself, "Simunic, my God! The foundation of the franchise! Never trade the franchise player! And now they've tanked."

Just the fact that we're not forced to listen to him blather is reason enough to get excited about the high jump. Maybe we did the high jump only on days when Wolkow had such a heavy chest cold that he couldn't run and talk at the same time. When he's fighting a normal cold, he still manages to babble, just a bit less than usual. When he's dead, class is canceled. But when he's really sick, he runs silently around the track.

During the high jump he jotted down our results in his black notebook and croaked about how we had managed to clear a few centimeters more the previous year. The girls, like I said, were sitting next to the high jump setup listening to Frau Bielcke. In reality, none of them were listening, of course, and were actually looking over at us.

Tatiana was with her best friend, Natalie, at the outer edge of the group of girls. They crouched down and whispered to each other. It was as if I were sitting on hot coals. I desperately wanted to jump before Frau Bielcke finished her sermon. Luckily Wolkow suddenly made it a contest: The bar was put at one meter and twenty centimeters and anyone who couldn't clear it was out. Then it would be raised in five centimeter increments for each new round. At one meter twenty only Heckel failed. Heckel has a fat gut, has had it since he was in fifth grade. And he has toothpicks for legs. It's no great surprise that he can't get far off the ground. He's not very good in any school subject, but he's particularly crap at sports. He's dyslexic too, which means his spelling doesn't count against him in German class. He can make as many mistakes as he wants. All that counts is the content and the style because dyslexia's like a disease and he can't do anything about it. But I keep thinking that the same is true for his matchstick legs — there's nothing he can do about them. His father is a bus driver and looks exactly the same: a tub on stilts. So really Heckel is high-jump dyslexic too, and how high he gets shouldn't be counted, only his style. But it's not a recognized disease, so he fails gym and all the girls giggle when the tub of lard shields himself from the bar with both hands and falls with a whimper on his face. Poor bastard. Though I have to admit it does look funny. Because even if height were discounted for Heckel, his style is still an F.

By the time we reached one meter forty centimeters, the field began to dwindle. At one meter fifty, the only ones left were Kevin and Patrick, and, with great effort, André. And me, of course. Olaf was sick. When André squeaked over the bar, the girls cheered and celebrated, and Frau Bielcke looked at them sternly. At one meter fifty-five, Natalie shouted, "You can do it, André!" Such a stupid way to cheer him on, since there was no way he could do it. On the contrary, he actually went *under* the bar, which often happens in the high jump when you bite off more than you can chew. He crawled off the back of the cushion and tried to compensate by making a joke as if he was going to throw the bar like a spear. But it's an old joke. Nobody laughed. Next they cheered on Kevin. Kevin the math genius. But he couldn't clear one meter sixty. Then I was the only one left. Wolkow set the bar at one meter sixty-five, and even as I approached it I could just feel that today was my day. It was Mike Klingenberg Day. I could feel a rush of triumph even as I leapt. I didn't jump so much as sail over the bar like an airplane. I hung in the air, I floated. Mike Klingenberg, star of track and field. I think that if I could have given myself a nickname just then, it would have been something like Aeroflot. Or Air Klingenberg. Or the Condor. But unfortunately you can't give yourself nicknames. As my back sank into the soft landing pad, I could hear restrained applause from the side where all the boys were gathered. But from the side where the girls were I heard nothing. As the mat rebounded and I bounced back up, I immediately looked over at Tatiana. And Tatiana was looking at Frau Bielcke. Natalie was looking at

Frau Bielcke too. They hadn't even seen my jump, the stupid cows. None of the girls had seen my jump. They had no interest in what the psychotic sleeping pill had managed to clear. Aeroflot my ass.

It really pissed me off the entire day. Though to be fair it hadn't interested me either. As if the fucking high jump would interest me for even a second! But if André had managed to clear one meter sixty-five — or even if he had managed to get to the point where he could have *attempted* one sixty-five — the girls would have run around the track with pom-poms. For me, on the other hand, not a single one even watched. I'm of no interest. And I just can't help wondering: Why doesn't anyone watch when Air Klingenberg flies over the bar to set a new school record, while everyone watches when some airhead submarines his way under the bar? But that's the way it was. That was what the whole crappy school was like, that was what the girls were like, and there was no way around it. At least that's what I always thought before I met Tschick. That's when things started to change.

Right from the start, Tschick rubbed me the wrong way. I couldn't stand him. Nobody could stand him. Tschick was trash, and that's exactly what he looked like. Mr. Wagenbach dragged him into class after Easter break, and when I say he dragged him into class, I really mean it. It was the first period after the break — history. The students were sitting in their chairs as if stapled in place, because if anyone is an authoritarian asshole, it's Wagenbach. Although asshole is a bit of an overstatement. Wagenbach's okay, actually. He lectures okay and he's not as stupid as most of the rest of them — like Wolkow. At least with Wagenbach it doesn't take a lot of effort to pay attention to what he's saying. And it's a good thing to pay attention, too, because Wagenbach can really rip you to shreds. Everybody knows it. Even kids who've never had him for a class. Before fifth graders even enter Hagecius Junior High they know: Watch out for Wagenbach! You can hear a pin drop in his class. In Schuermann's class, you hear cell phones ring about five times a day. Patrick even managed to change his ringtone during Schuermann's class — he tried out six, seven, eight different ringtones one after the next until finally Schuermann asked for *a little quiet*. And even then he didn't have the nerve to glare at Patrick. If somebody's phone were to ring in Wagenbach's class, whoever it belonged to would definitely not live to see recess. There's even a rumor that Wagenbach used to keep a hammer on his desk to smash cell phones that went off in his class. But I don't know if that's true.

Anyway, as usual, Wagenbach came in wearing a bad suit and carrying his shit-brown briefcase, and behind him he was dragging this kid who looked half-comatose. Wagenbach slammed his briefcase down on his desk and turned around. He waited with a scowl on his face until the boy was standing next to him and said, "We have a new classmate. His name is Andrej . . ."

Then he looked down at a notepad, and at the kid again. Apparently, he wanted the new student to pronounce his own name. But the boy just stood there with his eyes half-closed and stared into the distance without saying anything.

Perhaps it's not worth mentioning what I thought the moment I saw Tschick for the first time, but I want to anyway. I had an extremely bad feeling about him the second I saw him next to Wagenbach. He seemed like just another asshole. Even though I didn't know him at all and had no idea whether he really was an asshole. He was Russian, it turned out. He was average height, had on a dirty white shirt that was missing a button, bargain basement jeans, and misshapen brown shoes that looked like dead rats. He also had extremely high cheek-bones and slits instead of eyes. His eyes — these narrow slits — were the first thing you noticed about him. They made him look Mongolian and you could never tell where he was looking. He had his mouth open a little on one side — like he was smoking an invisible cigarette. His forearms were huge and there was a big scar on one of them. His legs were skinny, and the top of his head was kind of squared off.

Nobody giggled. Nobody ever giggled in Wagenbach's class. But I had the impression that even if we'd been in somebody else's class nobody would have giggled. The Russian just stood there and looked who-knows-where out of his Mongolian eyes. And he completely ignored Wagenbach. It was quite an accomplishment to ignore Wagenbach. It was practically impossible.

"Andrej," Wagenbach said, staring again at the notepad and silently moving his lips. "Andrej Tsch . . . Tschicha . . . tschoroff."

The Russian mumbled something.

"Excuse me?"

"Tschichatschow," said the Russian without looking at Wagenbach.

Wagenbach inhaled through his nostrils. That was one of his quirks. Inhaling through his nostrils.

"Great, Tschischaroff. Andrej. Could you tell us a little bit about yourself? Where you're from, which school you attended previously?"

This was standard. Whenever new students arrived in school, they had to say where they were from or whatever. And now for the first time since he entered the room, Tschick's expression changed. He turned his head slightly toward Wagenbach as if noticing him for the first time. He scratched his neck, turned back toward the class, and said, "No." The room was deathly quiet.

Wagenbach nodded seriously and said, "You don't wish to say where you're from?"

"No," said Tschick. "Who cares?"

"Fine. In that case I will tell the class a bit about you, Andrej. Out of politeness, I would like to introduce you to the class."

He looked at Tschick. Tschick looked at the class.

"I take your silence as consent," said Wagenbach. He said it with an ironic tone the way all teachers do when they say something like that.

Tschick didn't answer.

"Or do you have something against it?" asked Wagenbach.

"Go right ahead," said Tschick with a wave of the hand.

Somewhere a couple of girls started to giggle. *Go right ahead!* Insane. He pronounced each syllable distinctly, with a strange accent. And he was still just staring at the back wall of the classroom. His eyes might even have been closed. It was tough to tell. Wagenbach gave the class a look. And it was absolutely silent again.

"Right," he said. "Andrej Tschicha . . . schoff is the name of our new classmate, and as you can no doubt discern from his name, our guest has come from far away. The boundless Russian expanses, which Napoleon conquered in 1812 and, as we'll see, was soon expelled from again. Just as Charles XII had been before him and Hitler would be after him."

Wagenbach inhaled through his nostrils. The introduction had no impact on Tschick. He didn't move.

"In any event, Andrej came to Germany four years ago with his brother, and . . . Wouldn't you rather explain this yourself?"

The Russian made some sort of sound.

"Andrej, I'm talking to you," said Wagenbach.

"No," said Tschick. "And by no I mean, No, I would not rather tell it myself."

Suppressed laughter. Wagenbach nodded awkwardly.

"Fine, then I will do it, if you have no objection. But this is most unorthodox."

Tschick shook his head.

"It's not unorthodox?"

"No."

"Well, *I* find it unorthodox," insisted Wagenbach. "I think it's admirable to introduce oneself. But in the interest of time, we'll keep this short. Our friend Andrej is from a family of German origin, but his native language is Russian. He's a great communicator, as we can see, but he first learned German when he arrived here in Germany, and as result should be granted understanding in certain . . . in certain areas. Four years ago he started in a special education program. Then he transferred because his grades permitted him to enter a standard school. But he didn't stay there long either — next up was a year at a vocational school and now he's joining us. And all of this in just four years. Is that right so far?"

Tschick rubbed the back of his hand across his nose, then looked at his hand. "Ninety percent," he said.

Wagenbach paused to see if Tschick was going to say anything more. But he didn't. The ten percent discrepancy remained unexplained.

"Alright," said Wagenbach in a surprisingly friendly tone. "No doubt we're all interested to hear the rest of the story, but unfortunately you can't stand up here forever, as enjoyable as it is talking with you. I would like to suggest that you sit at the free desk in the back there, since it's the only one available. Yes?"

Tschick lumbered down the aisle like a robot. Everyone stared at him. Tatiana and Natalie put their heads together, whispering.

"Napoleon!" said Wagenbach. Then he paused dramatically to pull a pack of tissues out of his briefcase and blow his nose at length.

Tschick arrived in the back of class in the meantime, and down the aisle where he had walked wafted a scent that almost knocked me over. A vapor trail of alcohol. I was three seats from the aisle and I could have put together a list of the drinks he'd had in the last twenty-four hours. That was how my mother smelled when she had a bad day. Maybe that was the reason Tschick hadn't faced Wagenbach or opened his mouth — he was worried about the booze on his breath. But Wagenbach had a cold. He couldn't smell anything anyway.

Tschick sat at the free desk in the back row. Kallenbach, the class clown, had started the year there, but he'd been moved to the front row before the end of the first day of school so the teachers could keep him under control. And now, instead, this Russian was sitting in the back row, and I'm sure I wasn't the only one thinking that it hadn't been such a great idea to move Kallenbach now that the Russian was going to end up back there. He was on a totally different level from Kallenbach — that was obvious. And that's why everyone kept turning around to look at him. After his performance with Wagenbach you just knew something was going to happen. This was going to be interesting.

But then nothing happened the rest of the day. Each new teacher who came in greeted Tschick and he had to spell his name at the beginning of every period. But everything went smoothly. The next day was quiet too. It was a major disappointment. He always wore the same ratty shirt to school, didn't participate in class, said "Yes," "No," or "Don't know" whenever he was asked anything, and didn't disturb things. He didn't become friends with anyone. He didn't even try to make friends with anyone. He didn't reek of alcohol the second day, but you still got the impression when you looked at him in the back row that he was somehow out of it. The way he slumped in his chair with his eyes barely open, you never knew whether he was asleep, wasted, or just really laid-back.

But about once a week he would smell like booze again. Not as bad as on that first day, but still obvious. There were some kids in class — myself not included — who had already gotten drunk or high, but for somebody to show up to school in the morning drunk? That was new. Tschick chewed really strong-smelling mint gum whenever he was drunk, so everyone figured out how to tell what state he was in.

But otherwise nobody knew much about him. It was absurd enough that someone would transfer from a special ed program to a school like ours. And then there were his clothes. But there were people who defended him, saying he actually wasn't stupid at all. "At least not as stupid as Kallenbach," I said one time — I was one of the people who defended him. But the only reason I defended him, to be honest, was because Kallenbach was standing next to me and he always got on my nerves. From the things Tschick said, you really couldn't tell whether he was smart or stupid or somewhere in between.

Of course there were also rumors about him and his background. Chechnya, Siberia, and Moscow all came up. Kevin said Tschick and his brother lived in a camping trailer on the outskirts of the city, and that his brother was a weapons dealer. Somebody else said he knew for a fact the brother was a pimp and there was talk of a forty-room mansion where the Russian mafia had orgies. Another kid said Tschick lived in one of the old high-rise apartment buildings out toward the big lake, Mueggelsee. The truth was that all of it was a load of crap. And the only reason he generated so many rumors was because Tschick himself never talked to anyone. But for the same reason, he was slowly forgotten. Or at least forgotten as much as someone who comes to school in the same awful shirt and cheap jeans everyday and sits in the class clown's seat can be forgotten. At least the dead animal shoes were replaced by a pair of white Adidas, which, of course, somebody *knew* had just been stolen. And maybe he had stolen them. But the number of rumors surrounding him kept dwindling. The last thing was a nickname for him, which was Tschick. And for those who thought that was too simple, there was also "special ed." And with that, the topic of the Russian was pretty much exhausted. Inside our classroom, at least.

Out in the parking lot he remained a topic of conversation a bit longer. In the morning, kids from the adjacent high school hung out in the parking lot. Some of them already had cars. And they found the Mongolian incredibly interesting. Guys who'd been held back five times and liked to stand in the open doors of their cars, just so everybody could see they were the owners — owners of cars that were hunks of junk, but which were tuned and modified. They made fun of Tschick. "Wasted again, Ivan?" Every morning. Especially one guy with a yellow Ford Fiesta. I didn't know for a long time whether Tschick realized they were making fun of him, but one day he stopped in his tracks at the edge of the parking lot. I was locking up my bike and heard them all loudly taking bets on whether Tschick would manage to make it through the door to the school the way he was staggering. Or as they put it, the way the fucking Mongolian was staggering. And Tschick stopped and went back toward the parking lot and up to the guys doing the talking. They were all a head taller than he was and several years older, and they grinned as the Russian walked up to them — and then past most of them. He went straight up to the Ford Fiesta guy, who was the loudest of all, put his hand on the car door and said something to him so quietly that nobody was able to hear what it was. The grin on the Ford guy's face slowly disappeared and Tschick turned around and went into our school building. After that, nobody made any comments when he walked past.

I wasn't the only one who saw this happen, and from that point on there was no stopping the rumors about his family being in the Russian mafia. Nobody could imagine any other way he could have managed to silence the idiot with the Ford with a couple of sentences. But of course that was baloney. Mafia. Bunch of baloney. That's what I thought, anyway.

CHAPTER TEN

Two weeks later we got our first math assignments back. First, Mr. Strahl put the results on the board to scare us. This time there was one A, which was unusual. Strahl's favorite sentence was: "As are reserved for God." Horrifying. But Strahl was a math teacher, after all, meaning he was a madman. There were two Bs, loads of Cs and Ds, no Es. And one F. I had a slight hope that I'd earned the A — math was the only subject I ever managed to score an A in once in a while. But it turned out I had a B−. Still, not bad. In Strahl's class a B− was practically an A. I looked around discreetly to see who was celebrating having gotten an A as the papers were passed back. But nobody showed any sign of celebrating. Not Lukas or Kevin or any of the other math wizards. Instead, Strahl held on to one assignment, walked it personally to the back row, and handed it to Tschichatschow. Tschick was sitting there chewing intently on strong peppermint gum. He didn't look at Strahl. He just stopped chewing and breathing. Strahl bent down, wet his lips, and said, "Andrej."

There was practically no reaction. His head turned ever so slightly — like in a gangster film when somebody hears the click of the hammer when a gun is put to his head.

"Your assignment. I don't know what it is," said Strahl, leaning a hand on Tschick's desk. "I mean, if you didn't have this at your old school, you'll have to repeat math class. You didn't even . . . you don't seem to have even attempted to solve the problems. All the stuff written here" — Strahl leafed through the pages of Tschick's assignment and lowered his voice, though you could still hear him fine — "these *jokes*. I mean, if you haven't studied it before, I'll take that into account, of course. I had to give you an F, but the grade is, shall we say, not written in stone. I would suggest that you turn to Kevin or Lukas. Have a look at their assignments. Go over their notes from the last two months. Ask them any questions you have. Because the way things are going now, there's just no point."

Tschick nodded. He nodded in a very understanding kind of way, and then it happened. He fell off his chair, right at Strahl's feet. Strahl flinched and Patrick and Julia jumped up. Tschick lay on the floor as if he were dead.

We all figured the Russian was capable of a lot of things, but passing out because he was so sensitive about getting an F on his math homework was not one of them. But as it turned out, it had nothing to do with any sensitivity on his part. He hadn't eaten anything all morning and had obviously drunk a lot of alcohol. In the school nurse's office he filled the sink with puke and then was sent home.

Still, it didn't help his reputation much. Nobody ever found out what the jokes were that he put in his notebook instead of the math problems, and I can't remember who ended up having the A. But what I do know and will probably never forget, is the look on Strahl's face when the Russian keeled over at his feet. Holy crap.

45

The annoying thing about the whole story, however, wasn't that Tschick fell out of his seat or that he got an F. The annoying thing was that two weeks later he got a B. And then an E after that. And then another B. Strahl was going bananas. He said things like, "Your studying paid off," and "Don't let up now," but even a blind person could see that his Bs had nothing to do with whether he was studying or not. All it had to do with was whether he was drunk or not.

This slowly dawned on the teachers as well, and Tschick was reprimanded and sent home a few times. There were discussions with him behind closed doors too, but the school didn't do much about it at first. Tschick had had a difficult time in life or whatever, and in the wake of recent education system scandals everyone wanted to prove that even a low-class, drunken Russian would be given a fair shake in the German school system. So there were no real consequences. And after a while, the situation got calmer. Nobody knew what had been bothering Tschick, but after a while he got by okay in most subjects. He chewed less and less peppermint gum in class. And he didn't create any disturbances. If it wasn't for his occasional bender, you might even have forgotten he was there.

CHAPTER
ELEVEN

"*A man who has not seen Herr K. in a long time greeted him with the words, 'You haven't changed at all.' 'Oh,' said Herr K., turning pale.* Now that was an agreeably short story."

Mr. Kaltwasser took off his jacket as he walked in and threw it over the back of his chair. Kaltwasser was our German teacher, and he always entered the class without saying hello. Or at least, you never heard a greeting because he started the lesson before he even walked in the door. I have to admit that I didn't really know what to make of Kaltwasser. Besides Wagenbach, Kaltwasser was the only other staff member who actually did a decent job of teaching. But while Wagenbach was an asshole — as a person — you couldn't really tell what Kaltwasser was like. I couldn't, anyway. He came in like a machine and just started talking. That went on for precisely forty-five minutes. And then Kaltwasser left again. You never had any idea what to think of him. I couldn't say what he was like as a person. I couldn't even say whether I thought he was nice or not. Everyone else seemed to think he was about as nice as a frozen turd, but I'm not so sure. I could imagine that, outside school, he might be okay in his own way.

"Agreeably short," Kaltwasser repeated. "And I'm sure some of you thought you could keep an interpretation of the story just as brief. But of course it's not that simple. Or did someone here find it that simple? Who would like to begin? Volunteers? Come on, people. The back row seems to be catching my eye."

We turned and followed Kaltwasser's glance to the back row. Tschick had his head on the desk and you couldn't tell whether he was looking at his book or sleeping. It was sixth period.

"May I be so bold as to disturb you, Mr. Tschichatschow?"

"What?" Tschick's head rose slowly. The ironic formality of Kaltwasser's question set off alarm bells.

"Are you there, Mr. Tschichatschow?"

"On the job."

"Did you do your homework assignment?"

"Of course."

"Would you be so kind as to read it to us?"

"Uh, okay." Tschick looked quickly around, spotted his bag on the floor, plunked it down on his desk, and began looking for his notebook. As always, he hadn't unpacked his things at the beginning of the period. He kept pulling more and more notebooks out and seemed to be putting real effort into finding the right one.

"If you didn't do the assignment, just say so."

"I have the assignment — where is it? Where is it?" He put a notebook down on his desk, shoved the rest back into his bag, and started paging through the one on his desk. "Here it is. Shall I read it?"

"I insist."

"Right, I'll get started. The assignment was the *Stories of Herr K.* Here we go. Interpretation of the *Stories of Herr K.* The first question you have, of course, when you read Precht's stories . . ."

"Brecht," said Kaltwasser. "Bertolt Brecht."

"Aha." Tschick fished a ballpoint pen out of his bag and scribbled in his notebook. He put the pen back in the bag.

"Interpretation of the *Stories of Herr K.* The first question you have, of course, is who this mysterious person behind the letter *K* might be. Without overstating things, it's possible to say that it is a man who avoids the spotlight. He hides behind a letter — the letter *K*. It is the eleventh letter of the alphabet. Why is he hiding? Because in actuality, Herr K. is a weapons dealer. Along with other murky figures (Herr L. and Herr F.), he founded a criminal organization that considers the Geneva Convention a joke. He's sold tanks and fighter jets and made billions, but nowadays avoids getting involved in the actual dirty work. Instead, he cruises the Mediterranean on his yacht, where the CIA came after him. So Herr K. fled to South America and had his face altered by the renowned plastic surgeon Dr. M. And now he is taken aback that someone has recognized him and thus turns pale. It goes without saying that both the man who has recognized him on the street and the renowned plastic surgeon will soon find themselves in very deep water wearing cement shoes. That's it."

I looked at Tatiana. Her brow was furrowed and she had a pencil in her mouth. Then I looked at Kaltwasser. There was nothing to read in his face. Kaltwasser seemed to be tense, but more the kind of tension you show when you're interested in something. Nothing more. He didn't give Tschick a grade. Next Anja read the proper interpretation, the one that Google gives. Then there was a long discussion about whether Brecht was a communist. And then the period was over. All this happened shortly before summer break.

Now I have to talk about Tatiana's birthday. Tatiana's birthday fell during summer break, and there was going to be a huge party. Tatiana had announced the party way in advance. Word was that she was going to celebrate her fourteenth birthday out in Werder, near Potsdam, just southwest of Berlin, and that everyone would be invited to stay overnight and everything. She asked all her best friends about their schedules because she wanted to make sure they'd be able to come. And since Natalie was leaving for the summer on the third day of break, the whole thing had to be pushed forward to the second day of summer break. Which is why all the details came out so early.

The house in Werder belonged to an uncle of Tatiana's and was right on a lake. The uncle was willing to basically hand it over to Tatiana, and there wouldn't be any other adults around except for him. The party was going to go all night and everyone was supposed to bring their sleeping bags.

Obviously it was a big topic of conversation in class, for weeks in advance. I kept thinking about the uncle. I'm not sure why I found him so fascinating, but I figured he must have been a pretty interesting guy — I mean, he was willing to hand over his house for a party, not to mention that he was related to Tatiana. Anyway, I was excited to meet him. I pictured myself talking to him in the living room, standing next to the fireplace, having a great conversation. Though I didn't even know if there was a fireplace in the house. I wasn't the only one excited about the party. Julia and Natalie had been thinking for ages about what they were going to give Tatiana — you could read that in the notes they passed to each other in class. That is, I could read it because I sat in a chair that was in the direct line between the two of them and had to pass the notes. I was electrified by their gift ideas, and couldn't think about anything except what I could give Tatiana for her birthday. Julia and Natalie had finally decided to give her the new Beyoncé CD. Natalie had to check something from a list Julia made that looked something like this:

- *Beyoncé*
- *P!nk*
- *the necklace with the [illegible]*
- *make a list with more suggestions*

Natalie put a check next to the top item. Everybody knew Tatiana loved Beyoncé. Which at first was a bit of a problem for me, because I always thought Beyoncé was shit. At least musically. She looked great, of course, and actually there was definitely some similarity between the way she looked and the way Tatiana looked. So after a while, I didn't think Beyoncé was so shit after all. On the contrary. I began to like Beyoncé. I even liked her music suddenly. No, wait, that's not right. I thought her music was *fantastic*. I bought her last two albums and listened to them nonstop while thinking of Tatiana and wondering what I was going to show up at her party with to give her for her birthday. There was no way I could give her a Beyoncé album. Julia and Natalie and probably thirty others had already come up with that idea — Tatiana was going to get thirty Beyoncé CDs and would have to exchange twenty-nine of them. I wanted to give her something special but couldn't think of anything. Until that note with the multiple choice question crossed my desk.

I went to the store and bought an expensive fashion magazine with Beyoncé's face on the cover and started sketching it. Using a ruler, I drew evenly spaced lines vertically and horizontally across the photo until the whole thing was divided up into little squares. Then I took out a huge piece of paper and penciled in a set of squares five times larger than those on the magazine cover. I learned this method from a book. *The Old Masters* or something like that. You can use the method to make a large picture based on a small one. You just recreate it square by square. You could do it on a copy machine too. But I wanted it to be a drawing. I guess I wanted people to be able to see that I put real effort into it. If you show a lot of effort, people can figure out the rest. I worked on the drawing every day for weeks. I worked really hard. With just a pencil. And I just got more and more worked up while working on the drawing, thinking about Tatiana and her party and the supercool uncle I was going to have such a witty conversation with next to the fireplace.

There may be a lot of things I'm no good at, but drawing isn't one of them. It's like the high jump. If drawing Beyoncé and doing the high jump were the most important disciplines in the world, I would be way ahead. Seriously. But unfortunately nobody gives a damn about the high jump, and as for drawing I was beginning to have my doubts. After four weeks of hard work, Beyoncé looked almost like a photo — a giant pencil Beyoncé with Tatiana's eyes — and I probably would have been the happiest person in the universe, if only I had then gotten an invitation to Tatiana's party. But I didn't get one.

It was the last day of school, and I was a little nervous because the classroom was bursting with thoughts of the party. Everyone was talking nonstop about Werder, but no invitations had been passed out. At least I hadn't seen any. Nobody knew exactly where the party house was, and Werder isn't so tiny that you couldn't miss it. I had already memorized the map of Werder. I figured Tatiana would tell everyone the address on the last day of school. But that's not what happened.

Instead, two rows in front of me, I spotted a small green card in Arndt's pencil case. It was during math. I saw Arndt show the little card to Kallenbach, who frowned. I could see there was a little map in the middle of the card. And then I looked around and realized everyone had these green cards. Almost everyone. Kallenbach didn't have one, given the way he was staring at Arndt's like an idiot. Though he always looked liked an idiot. He was an idiot. That's probably why he wasn't invited. Kallenbach bent down to look closely at the writing on the card — he was nearsighted but for whatever reason never wore his glasses. Then Arndt pulled it away from him and shoved it into his bag. As I figured out later, Kallenbach and I weren't the only ones who didn't get invitations. The Nazi didn't get one, Tschichatschow didn't get one, and neither did one or two others. Of course. Boring kids and losers weren't invited — Russians, Nazis, and idiots. I didn't have to think for long to figure out what Tatiana thought of me. Because I wasn't a Russian or a Nazi.

Otherwise pretty much the entire class was invited, along with people from some of the other classes. Probably a hundred people. But I wasn't invited.

I kept hoping right until the last period of the day and the distribution of our final report cards. I hoped that it was all a mistake and that when the final bell rang Tatiana would come over to me and say, "Psycho, man, I forgot to give you one of these! Here's the invite! I hope you can make it — I'd be terribly disappointed if you, of all people, weren't able to come. Have you thought about what you're giving me for a present? Of course, I can depend on you! Okay, see you there. I really hope you can make it! My God, I can't believe I almost forgot to give you one!" Then the bell rang and everyone went home. I packed up my things slowly, to give Tatiana every opportunity to realize her mistake.

Out in the hall, the only people still standing around were the fat kids and nerds, all talking about their grades and crap like that. As I walked out of the building, maybe twenty meters from the door, someone grabbed my shoulder and said, "Awesome jacket." It was Tschick. His eyes were narrowed even more than usual as he smiled, and I saw both rows of his teeth. "I'll buy it. The jacket. Hold up a minute."

I didn't stop, but I could hear that he was still following me.

"It's my favorite," I said. "Not for sale." I'd found it at a thrift shop and bought it for five Euros, and it really was my favorite jacket. Made in China, with a white dragon printed on the chest. Supercheap-looking, but also supercool. The perfect jacket for a low-class tough. Which is why I liked it so much — at first glance you couldn't tell that I was exactly the opposite of a low-class tough: a rich scaredy-cat totally unable to defend himself.

"Where can I get one? Hey, wait up! Where are you going?" He shouted across the entire parking lot and thought it was funny. It sounded as if he'd had more than just alcohol. I turned onto a side street.

"Did you get held back?" he continued.

"What are you shouting about?"

"Did you fail?"

"No."

"You look like you were failed."

"What do you mean?"

"You look like you just found out you got held back, that you'll have to repeat."

What did he want from me? I caught myself thinking that Tatiana had made a good decision not to invite him.

"Bunch of Ds, though, eh?"

"No idea."

"What do you mean, 'No idea'? If I'm bothering you, just say the word."

I was supposed to tell him he was bothering me? And then he'd punch me in the face, or what?

"I don't know."

"You don't know if I'm bothering you?"

"No, whether I got a bunch of Ds."

"Seriously?"

"I didn't look yet."

"At your report card?"

"Nope."

"You didn't look at your report card yet?"

"Nope."

"Really? You got your report card and didn't even look at it? How cool is that?" He was gesturing wildly as he talked, and as he walked next to me I realized he wasn't actually any taller than me. Just more stocky.

"So you won't sell me the jacket?"

"No."

"What are you up to now?"

"Going home."

"And then?"

"Nothing."

"And after that?"

"None of your damn business." Now that I realized he wasn't going to mug me, I felt braver. That's the way it always is, unfortunately. When somebody is hostile to me, I'm so nervous that I can barely keep my knees from buckling. But if they are even the slightest bit friendly, I immediately start insulting them.

He walked silently beside me for another hundred meters or so, then tugged on my sleeve and said again what a cool jacket he thought it was. Then he slipped through some bushes along the side of the road. I watched him trudge off across the grassy wasteland in the direction of the high-rise apartment blocks, with the plastic grocery bag he used as his school knapsack hanging over his right shoulder.

CHAPTER
THIRTEEN

After a while I stopped and sat down on the curb. I didn't feel like going home. I didn't want it to turn into just another day. It was a special day. An especially crappy day. I took forever getting home.

When I opened the door, nobody was there. A note was on the table: *Dinner's in the fridge.* I unpacked my things, looked at my report card, put on the Beyoncé CD, and crawled under my blanket. I couldn't decide whether the music comforted me or made me even more depressed. I think, actually, it depressed me even more.

A few hours later I went back to school to pick up my bike. I'd forgotten it. Seriously. It was about two kilometers to my school, and some days I walked. But I hadn't walked that day. I'd been so deep in thought when Tschick started talking to me that I had unlocked and then relocked my bike, and then just marched off. It really was a horrible day.

So I followed the route for the third time of the day, past the piles of dirt and the playground at the edge of the wasteland. I climbed up the lookout tower of the play fort and sat down. It was a wooden tower with a fence built partway around it so little kids could play cowboys and Indians. If there'd been any little kids around. But I'd never seen a little kid there. Or even an older kid or adult for that matter. Not even junkies slept there. I was the only one ever there, sitting up in the tower when I felt crappy, where nobody could see me. To the east you could see the high-rises of Hellersdorf. To the north, Weiden Lane wandered off beyond the bushes, and farther on was a colony of little summer cabins. But around the playground was absolutely nothing, just a wide open wasteland that had originally been a construction site. It was supposed to have been the site of a brand-new town house development — you could still see a description of the development on the big weather-beaten sign that had fallen over on the side of the street. COMING SOON: 96 BEAUTIFUL NEW TOWN HOUSES. Below that was something about what lucrative investments they'd make, and somewhere at the bottom it said KLINGENBERG REAL ESTATE & DEVELOPMENT.

But one day they'd found three extinct bugs, a frog, and a rare grasshopper, and ever since the environmentalists have been suing the developers and the developers have been suing the environmentalists and the lot has been left empty. The court battle has gone on for ten years now, and if my father is to be believed, it'll take another ten years to be settled — because there's no way to beat the environmental fascists. That's my father's term: "environmental fascists." And these days he drops the word "environmental" from the phrase too, because the court battle has ruined him. A quarter of the land in the development site belonged to him, and all the suits and countersuits landed him right in the toilet. If an outsider were to listen to our dinner table conversation sometime, he wouldn't understand a single word. For years, all my father has talked about is shit, assholes, and fascists. For a long time I wasn't sure how much he'd lost and how it would affect us. I always thought my father would figure a way to get out of the whole thing with some legal loophole — and maybe he thought so too. At least at first. But then he'd thrown in the towel and sold his share. He took a huge loss, but he figured the loss would be even bigger if he kept going back to court with the rest of the developers. So he sold his share in the project to the assholes. That's what he calls the people he worked with. The assholes continued to fight in court for the right to build. That was a year and a half ago. And for a year now, it's been clear: That was the beginning of the end. My father tried to make up for the losses on the Weiden Lane development by playing the stock market, and now we're broke, our vacation's off, and the house we own doesn't belong to us anymore. That's what my father says. And all because of three caterpillars and a grasshopper.

The only thing left of the development is the playground, which was built at the very beginning to demonstrate how child-friendly the area was. But it was all for nothing.

I'll also admit there was another reason I hung around that playground. From up there on top of the tower you could see two white apartment buildings. The buildings are behind the colony of summer cabins, somewhere beyond the woods. And Tatiana lives in one of them. I never knew where exactly, but there's a window at the top of the building on the left where you can see a green light whenever the sun starts to go down. For whatever reason, I just decided that was where she lived. So sometimes I just sit on the lookout tower and wait until I see that green light go on. When I'm on the way from soccer practice or an afterschool class. I peer through the cracks between the boards and carve letters in the wood with my keys — if the green light comes on I get a warm feeling in my heart, and if it doesn't, it's always a huge disappointment.

But that day it was much too early, so instead of waiting I headed back toward school. My bike was there, lonely and alone in the bike stand that looked as if it stretched for miles. The flag was hanging limp on the flagpole, and there was nobody left in the building. The only person around was the janitor, who I saw pulling two trash cans out to the street. A convertible blasting Turkish hip-hop steamed past. This is how the place would be for the rest of the summer. No school for six weeks. No Tatiana for six weeks. I pictured myself hanging from the playground lookout tower by a rope.

Back home I didn't know what to do. I tried to fix the headlight on my bike, which had been broken for a long time. But I didn't have the replacement part I needed. I put on *Survivor* by Destiny's Child and started rearranging the furniture in my room. I pushed the bed to the front of the room and the desk to the back. Then I went back downstairs and fiddled around some more with the bike light. But it was pointless, so I tossed my tools in the flower garden, went back upstairs, threw myself onto the bed, and started screaming. It was the first day of summer vacation and I was already going crazy. At some point I pulled out the drawing of Beyoncé. I looked at it for a long time, then held it up in front of me with two hands and began to tear it in half, very slowly. When I'd ripped it as far as Beyoncé's forehead, I stopped. That's when I started to cry. And what happened after that I can no longer remember. All I know is that at some stage I dashed out of the house and into the woods and up a hill, and then I started to run. You couldn't really say I was going for a run because I was wearing normal clothes, but I did pass about twenty runners per minute on the trails through the woods. I just ran through the trees screaming, and I was incredibly pissed off at everyone else who was running in the woods because they could *hear* me. When I saw a guy walking with ski poles coming toward me, I could barely keep myself from grabbing his stupid poles and beating his ass with them.

When I got home again I stood in the shower for hours. I felt a bit better afterward — like somebody who's been floating around the Atlantic in a lifeboat for weeks and finally sights a ship only to have the ship come alongside and toss him a can of Red Bull and keep on going. That's about how I felt.

Downstairs I heard the front door open.

"What's all that stuff lying around outside?" yelled my father.

I tried to ignore him, but it was difficult.

"Do you plan on leaving it there?"

He meant the tools I'd been working on my bicycle with. After checking in the mirror to see if my eyes were still red, I headed downstairs again. When I got outside there was a taxi driver standing in front of the house scratching his crotch.

"Go up and tell you mother it's time to go," said my father. "Have you even said good-bye? You forgot, didn't you? Go on upstairs! Go!"

He hustled me up the stairs. I was pissed. But unfortunately my father was right. I'd completely forgotten about the whole thing with my mother. I'd known for the past few days, but somehow in all the excitement I'd forgotten. My mother had to go off again to rehab for a month.

She was sitting in a fur coat in front of the mirror in their bedroom, and she was tanked. There wouldn't be anything available at rehab, after all. I helped her up and carried her suitcase down. My father carried the suitcase to the taxi, and the taxi had barely pulled away before he called her — as if he was terribly worried about her. But that wasn't the case, as soon would be clear. My mother hadn't been gone for half an hour before my father came into my room with a clownishly somber face on, and in a clownishly somber voice said, "I'm your father. And we need to talk about something serious. Something that won't be pleasant for you or for me."

It was the same face he put on a few years earlier when he said he needed to talk to me about sex. It was the same face he put on when he told me that because of some sort of cat allergy, we had to put not only our cats but also my turtle and the two rabbits I kept in the garden to sleep. That was the face he looked at me with now.

"I just found out I have a business meeting," he said, as if he himself was baffled by the whole thing. He grimaced for extra effect. He babbled on a bit more, but the upshot was simple. He was going to leave me alone for fourteen days.

I made a face meant to signal that I needed to put in some very serious thought about whether I'd be able to handle such a tragic situation. Could I handle it? Fourteen days all alone in a cruel air-conditioned world consisting only of swimming in our pool, eating delivery pizzas, and watching videos projected on the wall? Yes, I nodded sorrowfully, I could give it a try, and yes, I'd probably survive somehow.

His furrowed brow and downward-turned mouth relaxed a little. I guess I overdid it.

"And don't you dare get yourself into any stupid shit! Don't think you can misbehave. I'm going to leave two hundred Euros — it's already downstairs on the table, and if there's any problem, call me immediately."

"At your *business* meeting."

"That's right, at my *business meeting*." He looked at me angrily.

He made another call to my mother, pretending he was worried, and while he was on the phone his assistant arrived to pick him up. I went straight downstairs to see whether it was still the same one. Because she's extremely hot, and only a few years older than me — probably nineteen or so. And she always laughs. It's almost unbelievable how much she laughs. I had met her for the first time about two years earlier when I visited my father at his office. And she had run her fingers through my hair and laughed when I used the copy machine to make images of the right and left sides of my face, my hands, and my bare feet. She doesn't do that anymore, unfortunately. Run her fingers through my hair, I mean.

She hopped out of the car wearing shorts and a skintight sweater, and it was immediately clear what sort of business meeting this was going to be. The sweater was so tight you could see every detail. I decided it was okay that my father hadn't bothered to put on a big show of hiding the whole thing. He didn't need to. Both of my parents knew the score. My mother knew what my father was up to, and my father knew what my mother was up to. And when they were alone together, they screamed at each other.

The thing I didn't understand for a long time was why they didn't just get separated. For a while I thought I was the reason.

Or money was the reason. But eventually I decided they actually liked screaming at each other. That they liked being unhappy. I read about it in a magazine somewhere — that there were people who liked being unhappy. People who were actually happy when they were unhappy. Though I have to admit that I didn't entirely understand the article. I mean, on the one hand a light went on in my head, but on the other I didn't really get it.

Still, I've never come up with a better explanation for the way my parents are. And I've thought about it a lot. So much sometimes that I get a headache thinking about it. It's like when you look at those 3-D pictures, where you have to stare at a pattern until an invisible shape pops out. Other people were always better at that than I was — with me, I could barely get it to work at all. And as soon as I was able to see the invisible shape — usually a flower or a deer or whatever — it disappeared again immediately and I'd get a headache. That's exactly how it is when I try to figure out what the deal is with my parents: I just get a headache. So I don't think about it anymore.

While my father packed his suitcase upstairs, I made conversation with Mona downstairs. That's her name, Mona. The assistant. The first thing she said to me was how warm it was and how it was supposed to get even warmer in the next few days. The usual. But when she heard I'd have to spend my summer vacation alone, she looked at me with such a sad face that my own tragic fate nearly brought tears to my eyes. Abandoned by my parents, God, and the world! I thought about asking her to run her fingers through my hair again like she had next to the copier that time. But I was too shy to ask. Instead, I stared the whole time at her skintight sweater while pretending to be looking past her and studying the landscape, out the window, as she jabbered on about what a highly responsible man my father was, blah, blah, blah. Getting older had its pluses and its minuses.

I was deeply engrossed in studying the landscape when my father came down the stairs with his suitcase.

"Don't feel sorry for him," he said. He gave me the same warnings he had given me before, told me for the third time where he had left the two hundred Euros, then put his arm around Mona's waist and walked out with her to the car. He could have spared me that. Putting his arm around her, I mean. I think it's fine that they don't put on some sort of show of secrecy, but he could at least wait to put his arm around her until they're off our property. That's my opinion. I slammed the door, closed my eyes, and stood there silent and still for a minute. Then I threw myself down onto the tile floor and started to sob.

"Mona!" I cried. My throat tightened. "I have to confess something to you!" My voice echoed ominously in the empty foyer, and Mona, who already seemed to have sensed that I needed to confess something to her, put her hands to her mouth in horror.

"Oh, God, oh, God!" she cried.

"You can't take this the wrong way," I sobbed. "I'd never work for the CIA voluntarily! But they've got us by the throat — do you understand?" Of course she understood. She collapsed next to me, crying.

"But what are we supposed to do?" she cried frantically.

"There's nothing we can do!" I answered. "We just have to play along with their game. The most important thing is to keep up the façade. You have to keep reminding yourself that I'm an *eighth grader*, and that I *look* like an eighth grader, and that we have to live our lives as if everything's normal — we have to pretend for another year or two that we don't even know each other!"

"Oh, God, oh, God!" cried Mona, throwing her arms around my neck. "How could I ever doubt you?"

"Oh, God, oh, God!" I cried, pressing my forehead onto the cold tile floor and doubling over. I cried on the floor for about half an hour. And after that I felt better.

CHAPTER
FOURTEEN

I cried until the Vietnamese woman showed up. She normally comes three times a week. The Vietnamese woman is pretty old — about sixty, I guess — and can't really speak German. Without a word, she shuffled past me into the kitchen and came back out with the vacuum cleaner. I watched her working for a while; then I went over to her and told her that she didn't need to work the next two weeks. I wanted to be alone. I told her that my parents would be away during that time, and that if she just came by two weeks from Tuesday and whipped things into shape, that would be great. It was tough to put it in a way that she understood. I thought she'd drop the vacuum out of pure joy, but that's not what happened at all. At first she didn't believe me. So I showed her the list of chores my father had left for me to do, and all the things he'd stocked up on for me, and then I showed her the calendar where my father had circled in red the Wednesday he'd be back. But she still didn't believe me, so I showed her the two hundred Euros he had left. And that's when I realized why she was so stubbornly clinging to her vacuum cleaner. Because she thought she wouldn't get paid if she didn't work. So then I had to explain that she'd get paid anyway. Man, I was so embarrassed. Nobody will notice, I told her. It took a lot of effort to get it across to her because she doesn't speak German. But at some point she did leave — after we'd gone back to the calendar and both pointed several times at the Tuesday in two weeks and looked in each other's eyes and nodded. I was worn out by the time she left. I never know what to say in these situations. We had an Indian working as a gardener for a while too, though he was let go to save money. But it was the same with him. It's so embarrassing. I want to treat them like regular people, but they act like they're servants who are there just to move the dirt out of your way — which, granted, is why they're there. But I'm only four-teen! My parents don't have a problem with it. And if they are around it's no problem for me either. But when I'm alone in a room with the Vietnamese woman I feel like Hitler. I always want to grab the rags out of her hand and clean everything up myself.

I walked her out, and I would like to have given her some-thing too. But I didn't know what. So I just waved like an idiot as she walked off, and was incredibly relieved once I was finally alone again. I gathered up the tools that were still lying in the flower garden and then stood there in the warm evening air and took a few nice deep breaths.

Diagonally across the street the Dyckerhoffs were barbe-cuing. The oldest son waved with the grill tongs in his hand. Like all our neighbors he's an incredible asshole, so I quickly looked away. And that's when I saw a creaky bicycle cruising down the street. Though cruising down the street is overstat-ing it a bit. And to call it a bicycle is also a stretch. It was the frame of an old girls' bike, but it had two different-sized wheels in the front and back. In the middle was a tattered old leather seat. There was also a hand brake dangling down from the handlebars. It looked like a broken antenna. The back tire was flat. And riding the contraption was Tschichatschow. With the exception of my father, he was pretty much the last person I wanted to run into right then. Though to be honest, other than Tatiana, everyone was the last person I wanted to run into. But the expression on his Mongolian-looking face told me he didn't feel the same way.

"*Kablam!*" Tschick said, smiling as he steered his bike onto the sidewalk in front of me. "You know what happened? I was riding over there — and *kablam*. This is where you live? Hey, is that a flat-tire repair kit? How cool is that! Can I use it?"

I didn't feel like talking. I gave him all the tools and told him just to leave them there when he was done. I was busy, I said, I had to get going. Then I went straight inside and listened through the closed door to see if he was maybe going to take off with the tools. After a little while I went upstairs, lay down in my room, and tried to think about something else. But it wasn't so easy. I could hear the clang of the tools downstairs as he tinkered with his bike. He was singing in Russian too. Really badly. And somebody in the neighborhood was mowing their lawn. But when things finally quieted down around the house, it made me uneasy. I looked out the window and saw somebody walking around our backyard. Tschick walked all the way around the pool, then stood shaking his head in amazement next to the aluminum ladder while scratching his back with a screwdriver he was carrying. I opened the window.

"Awesome pool!" yelled Tschick, smiling up at me.

"Yeah, awesome pool, awesome jacket. Now what?"

He just stood there. So I went downstairs and we chatted a little. Tschick couldn't get over the pool. He wanted to know what my father did, so I told him. I wanted to know what he'd said to get the Ford Fiesta dude to stop bothering him. He shrugged his shoulders. "Russian mafia." He grinned. And I could tell that wasn't the real answer. But he wouldn't tell me what he'd really said, despite my pestering him for a while. We talked about this and that and eventually — inevitably — we made our way over to the PlayStation and started playing *GTA*. Tschick didn't know how, and we didn't get far. But still, this was better than lying in the corner and screaming.

"And you really didn't get held back?" he asked at some point. "I mean, did you end up looking at your report card? I still don't get that. Man, you're on vacation, you'll probably go somewhere cool with your parents, you can go to that party, you've got an awesome . . ."

"What party?"

"Aren't you going to Tatiana's?"

"Nah, don't feel like it."

"Seriously?"

"I have other plans for tomorrow," I said, pushing madly on the triangle button of the game controller. "And besides, I'm not invited."

"You didn't get invited? That sucks. I thought I was the only one."

"It'll be boring anyway," I said, running over a few people with a tanker truck.

"Maybe if you're gay. But for a guy like me that party is the ultimate. Simla will be there. And Natalie. And Laura and

Corinna and Sarah. Not to mention Tatiana. And Mia. And Fadile and Cathy and Kimberley. And sweet-ass Jennifer. And that blonde from the other class. And her sister. And Melanie."

"Huh," I said, staring blankly at the TV screen. Tschick was staring blankly at the screen too.

"Let me try the helicopter," he said.

I handed him the controller and we didn't talk any more about the party.

When Tschick headed home, it was almost midnight. I heard the bike creak off toward Weiden Lane, and then stood alone in front of our house for a minute. Above, stars in the night sky. And that was the best thing about the entire day: that it was finally over.

Things were better the next morning. I woke up as early as I normally did for school. Couldn't change my inner alarm clock that quickly. But the silence in the house reminded me: I'm all alone and it's summer break, the place belongs to me, and I can do whatever I feel like.

The first thing I did was carry some CDs downstairs and crank the stereo in the living room all the way up. I put on the White Stripes. Then I opened the back door and lay down by the pool with three bags of chips, a Coke, and my favorite book and tried to put all the bad shit out of my mind.

Even though it was still early, it was already ninety degrees in the shade. I dangled my feet in the water, and Count Luckner began to talk to me. That's my favorite book: *Count Luckner, The Sea Devil*. I've already read it at least three times, but I figured another time couldn't hurt. Count Luckner is a pirate during World War I and sinks one English ship after another. But he does it in a gentlemanly way. Meaning he doesn't kill anyone. He scuttles their ships but saves all the crewmen and takes them ashore, all in the service of His Majesty, the Kaiser. And the book's not made up, it all really happened. The coolest part is when he's in Australia. He works as a lighthouse keeper and a kangaroo hunter. I mean, he was *fifteen*. He didn't know a soul down there. He jumped ship, joined the Salvation Army, then ended up working at the lighthouse and hunting kangaroos. But I haven't gotten that far yet this time through.

The sun was beating down, so I opened up the patio umbrella. The wind blew it over. So I put it upright again and laid some heavy things on the base. Then everything was peaceful. But I couldn't read. I was suddenly so excited about the idea that I could do anything I wanted that I did nothing at all. I'm completely different from Count Luckner in that regard. I sat back and went through all the crap with Tatiana again in my mind. Then I realized that the lawn needed to be watered. My father had forgotten to tell me to do it, so I could have gotten away with not doing it. But I did it anyway. It would have bugged me if I had to do it, but now that the house basically belonged to me and the yard was *my* yard, I kind of enjoyed watering the lawn. I stood on the steps in front of the house and sprayed with the hose. I had cranked the faucet all the way open and the water must have shot fifty meters through the air. Still, I couldn't reach the farthest corner of the front yard, despite my trying out all kinds of tricks and messing with the nozzle. Because I had to do it without leaving the front stoop. I'd made that a rule. The White Stripes were cranked up in the living room, the door was open, and there I stood, barefoot, with my pants rolled up and a pair of sunglasses on top of my head, the lord of the manor spraying his acreage. And I could do this every morning! I didn't really want to be seen doing it, but I didn't see anybody around. It was 8:30 on the second day of vacation, and everybody was sleeping in. Two blue tits chirped in the yard. The pleasantly pensive and recently fallen-in-love Lord von Klingenberg tarried all alone, surveying his estate. Well, not entirely alone. Jack and Meg were visiting, as they often did when they were looking to get away from the constant crush of paparazzi, and putting on a little jam session in the back room. The lord of the manor would soon join them and play along to a few rocking tunes on his recorder. The birds chirped, the water rained down on the grass . . . nothing pleased Lord von Klingenberg more than these mornings filled with birdsong as he watered his lawn. He crimped the hose, waited ten seconds for the pressure to build up, then shot a sixty meter surface to surface missile of water at the rhododendrons. *In the cold, cold night*, sang Meg White.

A rickety car came limping down the street. It was a Lada, a small Russian car shaped a little like a jeep. It slowed in front of our house and pulled into the driveway. For a minute, the light blue Lada stood in front of our garage with the engine still running. Then it shut off. The driver's side door opened and Tschick got out. He put his elbows on the roof and watched me spraying the lawn.

"Huh," he said. Then he was silent for a while. "Is that fun?"

CHAPTER SIXTEEN

I kept waiting for his father or his brother or somebody else to get out of the car, but nobody else appeared. And the reason was that nobody else was in the car. It was just tough to see that through the dirty windows.

"You look like some kind of queer, or like you just discovered that somebody shat in your garden last night. You want me to drive you somewhere, or would you prefer to just keep sprinkling water around?" He smiled his broad Russian grin. "Hop in, man."

Obviously I didn't get in. I wasn't completely crazy. I went over and sat down in the passenger seat, with my feet still out of the car. I didn't want to stand there all conspicuously in the driveway.

The Lada looked even worse inside than it did outside. There were a bunch of wires hanging out beneath the steering wheel, and a screwdriver was jammed up under the dashboard.

"Are you out of your mind?"

"I just borrowed it. It's not stolen," said Tschick. "I'll take it back. We've done it a million times."

"Who is *we*?"

"Me and my brother. He found it. It just sits on the street like garbage. You can borrow it. The owner never notices."

"What about all that?" I pointed to the jumble of wires.

"You can shove it back in."

"You're crazy. What about fingerprints?"

"Fingerprints? Is that why you're sitting so funny?" He pulled at my arm, which I had scrunched up against my chest. "Don't wet your pants. That's just police show bullshit. Fingerprints. Look, you can touch anything. Go ahead, touch whatever you want. Come on, let's take a spin."

"Not me." I looked at him and didn't say anything more at first. He really was crazy.

"Didn't you say yesterday that you wanted to get out and experience things?"

"By that I didn't mean prison."

"Prison? You're not criminally accountable — you're a minor."

"Do whatever you want. But I'm not going." To be honest, I had no idea how old you had to be to get charged as an adult. And I wasn't sure what "criminally accountable" meant. I mean, sort of. Basically. But not really.

"Nothing can happen to you. My brother always says to me that if he were my age, he'd rob a bank. They can't do anything to you until you're fifteen. My brother's thirty. In Russia, they beat the shit out of you anyway. But here! Nothing. And besides, nobody gives a crap about this car. Seriously. Not even the owner will miss it."

"No way."

"Just once around the block."

"No."

Tschick let up the emergency brake, and I can't really say why I didn't hop out. Normally I'm a scaredy-cat. Maybe for that reason I wanted not to be a scaredy-cat just once. With his left foot he stepped on the far left pedal, and the Lada rolled silently backward down the driveway. Then he stepped on the middle pedal with his right foot and the car stopped. Then he grabbed the wires hanging from the base of the steering wheel and the engine started. I closed my eyes. When I opened them again, we were gliding down Ketschendorf Way, and then we turned right into Rotraud Street.

"You didn't use your blinker," I said meekly, my arms still pressed to my chest. I was so nervous I thought I was going to keel over. Then I started grabbing for the seat belt.

"There's no reason to be scared. I drive like a champ."

"Put your blinker on like a champ."

"I've never blinked."

"Please."

"Why? Anyone can see where I'm turning. And there's nobody around anyway."

That was true. The street was empty. It remained true for about another minute. By then Tschick had turned twice more and we were on the Avenue of Cosmonauts. There are four lanes on the Avenue of Cosmonauts. I started to panic.

"Okay, okay. Let's go back now."

"I make Formula One drivers look like chumps."

"Yeah, you said that already."

"Isn't it true?"

"No."

"Seriously. Don't I drive well?" asked Tschick.

"*Super,*" I said. And when it struck me that this was my mother's standard answer to my father's standard question, I added, "Just super, dear."

"Don't blow a gasket."

Tschick didn't drive like a Formula One champion, but he didn't drive too badly either. Not much better or worse than my father. And he had now started to head back in the direction of our neighborhood.

"Can't you follow the rules of the road? That's a double line you just crossed."

"Are you gay?"

"What?"

"I asked if you were gay."

"Have you lost your mind?"

"You called me *dear.*"

"I called you . . . what? That's called irony."

"Okay, so are you gay?"

"Because of my use of irony?"

"And because you're not interested in girls." He looked me directly in the eyes.

"Keep your eyes on the road!" I screamed. I have to admit I was getting a bit hysterical at this point. He was driving without even looking where he was going. My father did the same thing sometimes, but my father was my father and he had a driver's license.

"Everybody in the class is nuts for Tatiana. Absolutely nuts."

"Who?"

"Tatiana. There's a girl in our class named Tatiana. You never noticed her? Tatiana Superstar. You're the only one who never checks her out. So are you gay? I'm just asking."

I thought I was going to fall over and die.

"I don't have a problem with it," said Tschick. "I have an uncle in Moscow who runs around in leather pants with the ass cut out of them. He's totally cool otherwise. Works for the government. And he can't do anything about the fact that he's gay. There's really nothing wrong with it."

Holy crap. I mean, I don't have a problem with it if somebody's gay either. Though that's not how I pictured things in Russia — people running around in ass-less chaps. But that I acted like Tatiana Cosic didn't exist — that had to be a joke, right? Because *of course* I acted as if she didn't exist. How else could I act around her? For a complete nobody, a walking sleeping pill, that was the only way not to make a fool of myself in front of her.

"You're an idiot," I said.

"I'm cool with it. As long as you don't try to mess with my asshole."

"Cut it out. That's disgusting."

"My uncle . . ."

"Screw your uncle! I'm not gay, man. Can't you see I'm in a shitty mood?"

"Because I'm not putting my blinker on?"

"No, you idiot, because I'm not gay!"

Tschick looked at me, totally confused. He was silent. I didn't want to explain it. I hadn't meant to say a word about it, but it had slipped out. I'd never talked to anyone about something like this before, and I didn't want to start now.

"I don't understand," said Tschick. "Am I supposed to understand? You're in a shitty mood because you're not gay? Huh?"

I looked out the window, wounded. At least I didn't care when two old people stared at us through the dirty windows when we stopped next to them at a red light — they'd probably call the police. But at that point I hoped the police would pull us over. At least then there'd be some action.

"Okay, shitty mood . . . but why?"

"Because today is *the day*, man."

"What is today?"

"The party, idiot. Tatiana's party."

"You don't have to pretend now just because you're sexually disoriented. Yesterday you said you didn't want to go."

"As if I could."

"I really don't think there's anything wrong with it," said Tschick, putting a hand on my knee. "I don't give a crap about your sexuality problems, and I won't tell anyone, I swear."

"I can prove it," I said. "Shall I show you?"

"You want to show me that you're not gay? Oooo-kay," he said, swatting away invisible flies.

We were already close to home. This time Tschick didn't park in front of our house. He parked on a little side street, an alley where nobody would see us get out of the car. When we got upstairs and Tschick was still looking at me as if he'd found who knows what out about me, I said, "Don't blame me for what I'm about to show you. And don't laugh. If you laugh . . ."

"I won't laugh."

"You know Tatiana is crazy about Beyoncé, right?"

"Yeah, of course. I would have stolen a CD for her if she'd invited me to her party."

"Yeah. Anyway. Check this out."

I pulled the drawing out of a drawer. Tschick took it and held it up with his arms stretched out in front of him. At first he didn't pay as much attention to the drawing itself as to the backside, where I'd repaired the rip with clear tape so that you could barely see the rip from the front. He studied the rip and then looked at the drawing again. Then he said, "You have *feelings* for her."

He said it very seriously, without any crap. It was really strange. And it was the first time that I thought this guy wasn't so stupid after all. Tschick took one look at the rip and knew exactly what the story was. I don't know many people who could figure it out so quickly. Tschick looked at me with a solemn expression on his face. I liked that about him. He was somebody who could definitely play the fool. But when the chips were down, he didn't play around. He took things seriously.

"How long did this take you? Three months? It looks like a photo. What are you going to do with it now?"

"Nothing."

"You have to do something with it."

"What am I supposed to do with it? Am I supposed to go to Tatiana's and say, 'Hey, happy birthday, I have a little something for you here — and, oh, it doesn't bother me a bit that you didn't invite me even though you invited every other idiot, it's no problem, really. And it's actually just a coincidence that I was passing by. Anyway, hope you enjoy the drawing that I worked my ass off on for three months!'"

Tschick scratched his neck. He put the drawing on my desk, looked at it, shaking his head, then looked at me again and said, "That's exactly what I would do."

"Seriously, you have to do something. If you don't, you're crazy. Let's drive there. Who cares if you think it's embarrassing? Nothing is embarrassing in a stolen Lada. Put on your awesome jacket, grab your drawing, and get your ass into the car."

"Never."

"We'll wait until it's getting dark, and then you get your ass into the car."

"No."

"Why not?"

"I'm not invited."

"You're not invited! So what? I'm not invited either. And you know why? Because of course the Russian idiot doesn't get invited. But do you know why *you* weren't invited? See — you don't even know. But I do."

"Then say it, oh, Wise One: because I'm boring and ugly."

Tschick shook his head. "You're not ugly. Or maybe you are, I don't know. But that's got nothing to do with it. The reason is because there's no reason to invite you. You don't stand out. You have to get noticed, man."

"How am I supposed to stand out? Come to school drunk every day?"

"No. My God. But if I were you and looked like you and lived here and had clothes like yours, I'd have gotten a hundred invitations."

"Do you need clothes?"

"Don't change the subject. As soon as it gets dark, we're driving down there."

"No way."

"We're not going to go to the party. We're just going to drive past."

What an idiotic idea. Or, to be more precise, there were three ideas, and every single one of them was idiotic: show up without an invitation, drive a stolen Lada all the way across Berlin, and — craziest of all — take the drawing with us. Because one thing was clear: Tatiana would surely figure out the score when she saw the drawing. There was no way I was going.

While Tschick was driving me to Werder, the town where the party was, I kept muttering that I didn't want to go. At first I said that he should turn around, that I'd had a change of heart. Then I said that we didn't have the exact address. Then I swore that there was no way I would get out of the car when we arrived.

I kept my hands folded under my arms for the entire trip. This time it wasn't because I was afraid of leaving fingerprints but because I was shaking. Beyoncé was sitting on the dashboard in front of me and shaking too.

Despite my anxiety, I realized that Tschick was driving more carefully than he had earlier in the day. He avoided roads with multiple lanes and eased his foot off the gas as we approached red traffic lights so we wouldn't be sitting at any intersections letting people look into the car. At one point we had to pull over to the side of the road because there was a brief rain shower and the windshield wipers didn't work. But we were nearly out of the city by then. It poured, but only for five minutes. A passing thunderstorm. Afterward the air smelled fantastic.

As we started off again, I peered through the windshield and watched as the wind pushed the water droplets apart. It suddenly occurred to me how strange it was to be cruising in a car that didn't belong to us through the evening streets of the city, then along the tree-lined boulevards of West Berlin, past a lonely gas station, and then on little roads outside the city toward Werder. Eventually the red sun disappeared completely behind dark clouds. I didn't say another word, and Tschick was silent as well. And I was happy that he was so determined to get to the party that I supposedly didn't want to go to. I hadn't thought of anything else for three months — and now here it was and I was about to come across as the biggest loser ever, right in front of Tatiana.

It turned out the house wasn't hard to find. We probably could have found it if we'd just driven on the streets along the lake, but instead, as we passed the sign announcing we'd entered Werder, we spotted two kids on mountain bikes with sleeping bags strapped onto them — it was André and some other idiot. Tschick followed them but drove far enough behind them that they didn't notice. And then we saw the house. Redbrick, with a front yard full of bikes, and lots of noise coming from the backyard, which faced the lake. A hundred meters ahead of us. I slid down from my seat into the footwell as Tschick rolled down his window and hung his arm casually out of the car and drove past the scene at a snail's pace. There were about a dozen people in front of the house, standing around in the yard and in the open doorway — people with glasses and bottles in their hands, talking on phones, smoking cigarettes. There were loads more in the back. Familiar and unfamiliar faces, girls all tarted up. And like the sun, right in the middle, Tatiana. She may not have invited the biggest losers or the Russian, but she seemed to have invited everyone else with a pulse. We slowly passed the house. Nobody had seen us, and it occurred to me that I didn't have any idea how I was going to give the drawing to Tatiana. I began to think seriously about the idea of just tossing it out the window. Somebody would find it and take it to her. But before I could do something stupid, Tschick had stopped the car and hopped out. I watched him, horrified. I don't know if it's always so embarrassing to have a crush on somebody. Apparently I'm not very good at it. As I was debating whether to remain in the footwell and pull my jacket over my head or to get back into my seat and put an it-wasn't-my-idea look on my face, fireworks started going off behind the redbrick house, exploding red and yellow in the sky, and almost everyone ran into the backyard. The only people left out front were André and Tatiana, who'd come to say hi to him.

And Tschick.

Tschick was standing directly in front of them. They stared at him as if they didn't recognize him — and it's entirely possible they didn't recognize him. Because Tschick had my sunglasses on. And he was also wearing a pair of my jeans and my gray jacket. We'd spent the day going through my closet

and I'd given Tschick three pairs of pants, a couple of shirts, a sweater, and a few other things. As a result he no longer looked like some hopeless Russian hardship case, but more like a soap opera star. And that's not meant to sound like an insult. But he just didn't look like himself anymore — he'd even put gel in his hair. I saw him start talking to Tatiana and saw her answer. She looked pissed. Tschick motioned to me behind his back. As if in a trance, I got out of the car and as for what happened next, don't ask me. I have no idea. I was suddenly next to Tatiana with the drawing in my hand and I think she looked at me with the same pissed-off look she'd glared at Tschick with. But I didn't notice.

I said, "Here."

I said, "Beyoncé."

I said, "A drawing."

I said, "For you."

Tatiana stared at the drawing, and before she had looked up from it I heard Tschick say to André, "Nah, no time. We have something to take care of." He nudged me and went back to the car. I followed. Then the engine fired up. I pounded my fist on the dashboard as Tschick shifted into second gear and crept toward the end of the cul-de-sac.

"Want to see something cool?" he asked.

I didn't answer. I couldn't.

"Want to see something cool?" Tschick asked again.

"Do whatever you want!" I yelled. It felt as if a wei been lifted from my shoulders, such a feeling of relie'

Tschick revved the engine and raced toward th' cul-de-sac. Then he yanked the steering wheel fir and then the left and pulled the emergency bra

time. The car did a 180 right in the middle of the street and I nearly flew out the window.

"That doesn't always work," Tschick said proudly. "Doesn't always work."

He accelerated past the redbrick house and I saw out of the corner of my eye the people on the sidewalk. Time seemed to be standing still. Tatiana stood there with the drawing in her hand, André with his mountain bike, and Natalie had just run around from the side of the house.

The Lada sped into the curve in the road and I pounded on the dashboard.

"Step on it!" I shouted.

"I am."

"Faster!" I yelled, watching my fists pound the dash. Relief does not begin to express the way I felt.

I walked down the dark, narrow corridor. I could hardly make out a thing. Then I went left into the tunnel where the rails ran and pressed my back to the wall. I could see the two barrels and an open door. I saw Tschick looking around a corner. I was right on his heels now and even from behind I could tell that he had no idea what he was doing. But he kept walking around like an idiot for another couple minutes, never realizing I was there. Then he stopped right out in the open. I raised my shotgun and blasted him in the back. A fountain of blood sprayed out of him. He dropped to the ground and didn't move. "Shit," he said, "where do you keep coming from? I never see you." I switched to the chain gun, obliterated his corpse, and hopped around.

"Okay, okay, that'll do. You don't have to rub it in, man." Tschick pressed START AGAIN, but it was hopeless. He just couldn't figure out the lay of the land. You could follow him for hours and he never noticed. And I just destroyed him every time. I was like a world champion at *Doom*, and he didn't have a clue.

He went and got himself another beer.

"What if we just took off?" he asked.

"What?"

"Go on vacation. We don't have anything else to do. We could just go on vacation like normal people."

"What are you talking about?"

"Hop in the Lada and go."

"That's not exactly how *normal* people do it."

"But we could."

"Nah. Push START."

"Why not?"

"Nah."

"If I kill you," said Tschick. "Let's say, if I kill you once in the next five games. Or, no, make it ten."

"You couldn't kill me if I gave you a hundred chances."

"Ten."

He was concentrating hard. I shoved a handful of chips in my mouth and waited until he had picked up a chain saw. Then I let him chop me to bits.

"Seriously," I said. "Suppose we did."

We'd pissed away almost the entire day. We'd gone swimming twice. Tschick had told me about his brother. And then he'd discovered the beer in the fridge and helped himself to three bottles. I tried to drink one too. I've tasted beer lots of times, but I never like it. It didn't taste any better this time. I managed to choke down three quarters of the bottle anyway, but it didn't have any effect on me.

"What if they tell on us?"

"They're not going to tell on us. If they were going to, they would have done it by now and the police would have been here already. They have no idea that the Lada was stolen. They only saw us for ten seconds. They probably just thought it belonged to my brother or whatever."

"Where do you want to go, anyway?"

"I don't care."

"You know, if you go somewhere, it's helpful to know where you're going."

"We could go visit my relatives. I have a grandfather in Wallachia."

"Where does he actually live?"

"What do you mean? In Wallachia."

"Does he live near here?"

"What?"

"Or somewhere far away, in the middle of nowhere?"

"Not somewhere, man. In Wallachia."

"It's the same thing."

"What's the same thing?"

"The middle of nowhere and Wallachia is the same thing."

"I don't understand."

"Wallachia is just a word, man," I said, polishing off my beer. "It's just an expression! Like East Bumfuck or the sticks."

"It's where my family is from."

"I thought you were from Russia?"

"Yeah, but part of my family is from Wallachia. My grandfather. And my great-aunt and great-grandfather and . . . what's so funny?"

"It's like having a grandfather in Hickville or BFE."

"And what's the joke?"

"There's no such place as Hickville! BFE means Bumfuck, Egypt. And Wallachia doesn't exist either. When you say somebody lives in Wallachia it means they live in the boondocks."

"And the boondocks don't exist either?"

"Nope."

"But my grandfather lives there."

"In the boondocks?"

"You're getting on my nerves. My grandfather lives in some dipshit town in a place called Wallachia. And we're going to drive there tomorrow."

He'd gotten serious again, and so had I. "I know a hundred and fifty countries in the world and the names of all their capital cities," I said, grabbing Tschick's beer and taking a swig. "There's no such place as Wallachia."

"My grandfather's cool. He always has a cigarette tucked behind each ear. And only one tooth. I was there when I was five or something."

"What are you, anyway? Russian? Or Wallachian or something?"

"German. I have a passport."

"Yeah, but where are you from?"

"A city called Rostov. It's in Russia. But my family is from all over — Volga Germans, ethnic Germans. Danube Swabians, Wallachians, Jewish Gypsies . . ."

"What?"

"What what?"

"Jewish Gypsies?"

"Yeah, man. And Swabian and Wallachian . . ."

"No such thing."

"As what?"

"Jewish Gypsies. You're talking shit. You're talking nothing but shit."

"Not at all."

"A Jewish Gypsy would be like an English French. There's no such thing."

"Of course there's no such thing as English French," Tschick said. "But there are French Jews. And there are Gypsy Jews."

"Gypsy Jews."

"Exactly. They wear a funny thing on their head and drive around Russia selling carpets. You know what I'm talking about — the things on their heads. Coverings. Coverings on their heads."

"Coverings on their asses, more like. I don't believe a word you are saying."

"You know that movie with what's-his-name?" Tschick really wanted to prove it to me.

"Movies are not real life," I said dismissively. "In real life you can only be one or the other — a Jew or a Gypsy."

"Gypsy isn't a religion, man. Jewish is a religion. A Gypsy is just someone without a home."

"People without homes are Berbers."

"Berbers are carpets," said Tschick.

I thought about it for a while longer, and when I asked Tschick one last time whether he was *really* Jewish Gypsy and he nodded solemnly, I believed him.

What I still didn't believe was the crap about his grandfather. Because I knew for a fact that Wallachia was just a made-up word. I tried a hundred different ways to prove to Tschick that there was no such place as Wallachia. But I noticed the only time my words made any impact at all was when I made a couple of grand arm gestures as I talked. Tschick mimicked the gestures. Then he went to get more beer. He asked whether I wanted another one too. But I just wanted a Coke.

I was really wound up. And as I watched a fly flitting around the table, I had the feeling that the fly was wound up too — because I was. I'd never had such a good time before. Tschick put two bottles of beer down on the table and said, "You'll see. My grandfather and my great-aunt and my six cousins — four of them are girls, and they're as pretty as orchids. You'll see."

My mind was soon occupied with thoughts of the cousins. But Tschick had no sooner left the house than the images of his cousins and everything disappeared into the ether, leaving only a feeling of misery. It had nothing to do with Tschick. It had to do with Tatiana. It had to do with the fact that I had no idea what she thought of me now, and that I might never find out. And at that moment I would have given anything to be in Wallachia or anywhere else in the world but Berlin.

Before I went to bed, I opened my laptop. I had four e-mails from my father complaining that I'd switched off my cell phone and wasn't answering the landline. I had to think up some excuse and would need to write him an e-mail back saying that everything was going great here. Which it was. And since I didn't feel like writing the e-mail and couldn't think of a good excuse, I looked up Wallachia on Wikipedia. That's when my mind *really* started to race.

Early Sunday morning. Four o'clock. Tschick had said that would be the best time. Four A.M., dead of night. I had barely slept at all, just dozed on and off a little, and I was instantly wide awake when I heard footsteps on our terrace. I ran to the door and there was Tschick, standing in the darkness with a duffel bag. We whispered even though there was no reason to whisper. Tschick threw his duffel down in the hall and we set off to retrieve the car.

When we'd driven back from Werder, he'd parked the Lada where it was normally parked, which was about a ten-minute walk from my house. A fox crossed the sidewalk right in front of us, heading in the direction of downtown. A garbage truck whooshed by us and we passed a coughing old lady walking in the opposite direction. We actually stood out more in the middle of the night than we would have during the day. About thirty meters from the car, Tschick gave me the signal to wait. I stood in some bushes and felt my heart racing. Tschick pulled a yellow tennis ball out of his duffel bag. He pressed it on the door handle of the Lada and hit it with the flat of his hand. I couldn't imagine what good it would do, but Tschick rasped, "Professional on the job!"

The door opened. He waved me over.

Inside he fiddled with the wires and the engine fired up. He hit the bumpers of both the car in front of us and the one behind us as he tried to get out of the parking spot. I huddled down in the passenger seat and examined the tennis ball. It was a normal tennis ball with a finger-sized hole cut into it.

"Does that work on all kinds of cars?"

"No, not all of them. But ones with central locking — it creates a vacuum." He scraped his way out of the parking spot as I pressed and squeezed the tennis ball in my hand. I just couldn't see how it worked. Russians!

Ten minutes later we were loading up the Lada. There's a door directly from our house to our garage, so we carried everything we thought we needed out that way. First off was bread — along with crackers and various spreads and a couple jars of jam. We figured we'd want to eat at some point. And to do that we also needed plates and knives and spoons. We threw in a three-man tent, sleeping bags, and sleeping mats. Then we took out the mats and replaced them with air mattresses. Half the household ended up in the car after a while, and then we started taking stuff back out again. Most of it you don't really need. There was a lot of back and forth. We fought about whether we'd need Rollerblades, for instance. Tschick said that if we ran out of gas, one of us could Rollerblade to a gas station. But I figured we might as well just throw in the foldable bicycle for that. Or just go by bike instead of car. We were nearly done when we decided to bring a case of bottled water, and that turned out to be the best idea of all. Or rather the only good idea at all. Because everything else proved useless: badminton racquets, a huge stack of manga, four pairs of shoes, my dad's toolbox, six frozen pizzas. One thing we didn't take were cell phones. "So the cocksuckers can't tell where we are," said Tschick.

And also no CDs. The Lada had big speakers in the back but only an old lint-stuffed cassette player bolted under the glove box. But to be honest I was just as happy not to have to listen to Beyoncé in the car. And of course we took the two hundred Euros as well as what money I had of my own. I wasn't sure what we would use it for. In my mind we'd be driving through unpopulated wastelands — practically deserts. I hadn't studied Wikipedia enough to have seen what it looked like down closer to Wallachia. But I definitely couldn't imagine there was much going on there.

CHAPTER
TWENTY

I had hung my arm out the window and put my head down on it. We were driving at a leisurely pace through pastures and fields as the sun slowly rose somewhere beyond Rahnsdorf. It was the weirdest and most beautiful thing I'd ever experienced. I can't pinpoint what was so weird about it, because it was just a car ride, and that was nothing new. But there's a difference between sitting in a car with adults who are talking about construction-grade concrete and Angela Merkel, and being in a car with no adults and no chitchat. Tschick had hung his arm out the window too and was guiding the Lada up a little hill with his right hand. It was as if the thing was driving itself through the fields. It was a totally different sort of car ride, a totally different world. Everything seemed bigger, the colors brighter, the noises as if they were in surround sound. It wouldn't have surprised me a bit if all of a sudden Tony Soprano or a dinosaur or a spaceship had appeared on the road in front of us.

We took the most direct route out of Berlin, leaving the early-morning bustle behind us, and then wound our way through the villages on the outskirts of town on back roads and quiet country lanes. Which is where we realized we hadn't brought a map. All we had was a map of Berlin.

"Maps are for pussies," said Tschick. And he was right, of course. But there was an obvious problem with that logic: How would we ever find our way to Wallachia when we couldn't even find Rahnsdorf? So we decided just to head south. Wallachia was in Romania, and Romania was south.

The next problem was that we didn't know which way was south. There were already storm clouds in the sky that morning, and you couldn't see the sun. It was sweltering outside; much hotter and more humid than the day before.

I had a little compass on my keychain — got it out of a gumball machine one time. It didn't seem to point south inside the car and when I tried it outside the needle spun all over the place. We stopped just to try it out, and when I got back in the car I noticed there was something under the mat in the footwell. It was a cassette — *The Solid Gold Collection*, by Richard Clayderman. But it wasn't real music. It was just some tinkling on the piano, Mozart or something. We didn't have anything else to play, and we thought maybe something else had been taped over it, so we listened to it all the way through. Forty-five minutes. The idiot. Though I have to admit that even after Richard and his piano had made us puke, we flipped it over and listened to the other side, which had exactly the same kind of crap on it. Better than nothing. Seriously, though, I didn't tell Tschick at the time and I'm not proud saying it now, but the minor-key stuff really took the wind out of my sails. I kept thinking about Tatiana and the way she had looked at me when I gave her the drawing. And then we were rattling down the autobahn to "Ballade pour Adeline."

Somehow we'd strayed onto a road that dumped us onto the autobahn. Tschick could drive okay, but he had never experienced anything like a German autobahn. Dealing with it took all he had. When he was supposed to merge, he stepped on the brakes, hit the gas, braked again, and then weaved along the shoulder at a snail's pace before he finally managed to swerve left into the lane. Luckily nobody rammed us from behind. I was pressing my feet against the floorboard with every ounce of my strength. And I thought if we died, Richard and his piano would be to blame. But we didn't die. The rattling in the Lada kept getting louder and louder and we decided we'd get off at the next exit and stick to little local roads. There was another problem with the autobahn too: A man in a black Mercedes pulled up alongside and looked across at us, making wild gestures. He was flashing numbers with his fingers and held up his cell phone and seemed to be trying to write down our license plate number. I was scared shitless, but Tschick just nodded as if to thank the guy for telling us we still had our lights on. Then we lost him in traffic.

Tschick did look older than fourteen. But no way did he look eighteen — old enough to drive. Though we had no idea what he looked like at full speed through the filthy windows of the Lada. We decided to do a few experiments on a dirt road after we'd gotten off the autobahn to see how he could best come across as an adult. I stood on the side of the road and Tschick drove past me about twenty times. He started by sitting on top of our sleeping bags and putting my sunglasses on top of his head. He tried smoking a cigarette. He ripped some pieces of duct tape and stuck them on his face to simulate a goatee. But he just looked like a fourteen-year-old with duct tape on his face. Then he took the tape off except for a little strip under his nose. He looked like Hitler that way, but from afar it actually made him look older. And since we were now out in the politically backward state of Brandenburg, nobody would take offense.

So the only thing we still had to deal with was our lack of orientation. But we saw a sign to Dresden, and Dresden was definitely south of Berlin. So we went that way. Whenever we had a choice of roads we took the smaller, less trafficked option. And along those roads the signs only indicated the next tiny town rather than Dresden. How did you know whether Burig or Freienbrink was farther south? We flipped coins. Tschick loved flipping coins to decide. He said we should make all our decisions on the route that way. Heads we turned right, tails left, and if it stayed upright on its edge we would go straight. But obviously it never stayed upright so we never made any forward progress. So we quickly abandoned the coin flip and just went right-left, right-left. That was my suggestion, but it was no better. In theory, if you keep turning right and then left, you'll never drive in a circle. But we managed to drive in a circle. When we passed a sign for the third time that said Markgrafpieske to the left and Spreenhagen to the right, Tschick came up with the idea of only going toward places that began with the letter *M* or *T*. But there were too few of them. I suggested looking at how far away places were according to what was listed on the signs and heading to ones where the distance was a prime number. But at a sign that said BAD FREIEN-WALDE 51 KILOMETERS we mistakenly turned that way and by the time we realized it was three times seventeen we were already at another crossing.

Eventually the sun came through the clouds. The road forked in the middle of a cornfield. To the left the road was cobblestone. To the right, dirt. We fought over which way was south. The sun wasn't quite in the middle. It was a few minutes before eleven o'clock in the morning.

"That's south," said Tschick.

"No, that's east."

We got out and ate a couple chocolate-coated cookies that were already partly melted. The bugs in the cornfield were making an overwhelming buzz.

"You know an ordinary watch can show you the points of a compass?" Tschick took off his watch. It was an old Russian model, the kind you have to wind. He held it out between us, but I didn't know how the trick worked, and he didn't either. I think you're supposed to aim one hand at the sun, and then the other one will point north. Something like that. But if we aimed one hand at the sun at eleven in the morning, both hands pointed in the same direction — and that was definitely not north.

"Maybe it points south?" said Tschick.

"What — and half an hour from now south is that way?"

"Or maybe it's because of daylight savings? It doesn't work in summer. I'll turn it back an hour."

"What will that change? The hands turn completely around in the space of an hour, but north and south aren't constantly shifting around."

"Yeah, but if a compass spins — maybe it's a gyrocompass."

"A gyrocompass?"

"You've never heard of a gyrocompass?"

"A gyrocompass has nothing to do with a gyroscope. It doesn't spin," I said. "It works with alcohol — there's alcohol inside it."

"You're pulling my leg."

"I know that from a book about a ship that capsizes. One of the sailors is an alcoholic, and he breaks open the gyrocompass to drink the fluid inside. And they have no way to orient themselves."

"Doesn't sound like a true story."

"It's true. The book is called *The Sea-Bear* or *The Sea-Wolf*, I think."

"You mean Steppenwolf. That's also about drugs. That's the kind of stuff my brother reads."

"Steppenwolf is a *band*," I say.

"Well, I'd say if we don't know which way is south, we should just take the dirt road," said Tschick, strapping his watch back on his wrist. "Less likely to see other cars."

As always, he was right. It was a good decision. We didn't come across another car for an hour. We were someplace where there weren't even any houses on the horizon. In one field there were pumpkins as big as medicine balls.

The wind picked up, and the wind died down again. The sun disappeared behind dark clouds, and two raindrops fell on the windshield. The drops were so big that they wet almost the entire windshield. Tschick drove faster as tall trees bent in the wind. Suddenly a gust of wind blew our car practically across the street. Tschick turned into a bumpy track that cut between two fields of wheat. The tinkling piano seemed more dramatic now. And then, after one kilometer, the farm road just stopped, right in the middle of the field.

"I'm not driving back now," said Tschick, rumbling forward without even braking. The stalks of wheat crackled against the fenders and doors. Tschick let the vehicle coast in the field, downshifted, and stepped on the gas. The engine revved and the grille of the Lada parted the sea of golden wheat like a snowplow. Though the Lada was making strange noises, it plowed through the field effortlessly. But it was tough to tell which way we were going. You couldn't see over the stalks of wheat. No horizon to aim for. Another drop of rain fell on the windshield. The field started to slope gently upward. We must have meandered and turned because we came across a section of grain we'd already plowed a path through. I told

Tschick we should try to write our names in the field — somebody in a helicopter could read them. Or maybe we could see our names on Google Earth. But we lost our sense of direction when we were crossing the first T. We just drove around, then went up a hill again and when we got to the top the wheat suddenly ended. Tschick braked at the last second. The back of the car was still in the grain. The front of the Lada peeked out at the landscape. A lush green cow pasture sloped steeply away below us, giving us a wide-open view over endless fields, groups of trees, farm roads, hills and ridges, mountains, meadows, and woods. Clouds were lined up on the horizon and you could see lightning hitting the steeple of a distant church, but you couldn't hear any thunder. It was dead quiet. The fourth raindrop plopped down on the windshield. Tschick turned off the engine. I turned off the cassette player.

We just sat there looking out over the landscape for a few minutes. Smaller white clouds floated along below the dark storm clouds. Blue-gray mist swirled around the distant ridges and some ridges closer by. The dark clouds swelled and billowed toward us.

"*Independence Day*," said Tschick.

We pulled out bread and jam and a couple of Cokes, and as we were setting up for a picnic in the car, it got very dark. It was early afternoon, but it was suddenly as dark as night outside. Just then I saw a cow fall over in one of the meadows. At first I thought I was seeing things, but Tschick saw it too. All the other cattle had turned their butts into the wind, but the one just fell over. Then the wind stopped as quickly as it had started. For a moment, nothing happened. It was so dark you couldn't read the labels on the soda bottles. Then it sounded like a bucket of water had splashed onto our windshield and the rain hit us like a wall.

It lasted for hours. It crashed and thundered and poured. A tree bough as thick as my arm and covered with foliage went flying across the valley below us as if some kid was flying it like a kite. When it finally stopped raining that evening, the entire wheat field behind us had been matted down, and the pasture in front of us had been turned into a swamp. It would have been impossible to drive in any direction. We were stuck. So we spent our first night sleeping in the car on top of that hill. It wasn't terribly comfortable, but given the mud all around us, there wasn't any alternative.

I didn't sleep much, but luckily that meant that at first light I saw the farmer driving his tractor through the valley below us. I didn't know whether he'd seen us, but I woke up Tschick and he immediately started the car. We inched backward through the wheat, more coasting than driving down the hill, and at some point hit the road again. Off we went.

The chocolate cookies were edible again, and after we ate them for breakfast, Tschick tried to teach me how to drive in a meadow next to some woods. I wasn't crazy about the idea at first, but Tschick said it was embarrassing to steal cars when you couldn't even drive. He also accused me of being scared, which I was.

Tschick did a practice run so I could watch exactly what he was doing — which pedals he was pushing and how he shifted. I'd seen my parents drive a million times, but I never really paid attention to how they did things. I didn't even know which pedal was which.

"The clutch is on the left. You let that up very slowly and step on the gas pedal at the same time — see? See?"

Of course I didn't see a thing. Let the pedal up? Step on the gas? Tschick showed me.

When you start, you put it in first gear. But you have to stand on the clutch and also, with your right foot, tap the gas pedal. Then you have to let up the clutch and give it gas at the same time. That's the most difficult part — getting the car going when it's standing still. It took me twenty tries before I got the Lada rolling, and then when I finally did I was so surprised that I pulled up both my feet — and the car jumped and then the engine cut out.

"Just step on the clutch and you won't stall. The same thing when you brake — push the clutch at the same time or else the engine will stall."

It took a while before I could brake properly. You're supposed to push the brake pedal with your right foot, but I couldn't get that through my head at first. For whatever reason, I kept stepping on it with both feet. Once I'd finally mastered everything and got the car rolling, I cruised around the meadow in first gear and it was amazing. The Lada actually did what I wanted it to do. When I got going a little faster, the engine really started to whine and Tschick told me to step on the clutch for three full seconds. I stood on the pedal and Tschick shifted into second gear for me.

"Now step on the gas!" he said, and suddenly I shot off. Fortunately the meadow was huge. I practiced for a few hours. That's how long it took before I could get the car going and shift up to third gear and back down again without constantly stalling. I was drenched with sweat, but I didn't want to stop. Tschick was sunning himself on the air mattress at the edge of the woods. The only people we saw all day were two walkers who passed by without even noticing us. At some point I skidded to a stop next to Tschick and asked how he hotwired the car. Now that I could drive, I wanted to know about everything else too.

Tschick pushed his sunglasses onto the top of his head, hopped into the driver's seat, and rummaged around in the mess of wires beneath the steering wheel. "You have to connect this wire, the steady-plus wire, number thirty, which is connected to the battery, to the one that runs power to the car's electrical system when the key is turned — number fifteen. See, thirty to fifteen. The duct tape is holding them together. You have to wrap it around there real thick. Once they are connected, the ignition system has power. Then you just touch the starter relay wire — this one, the number fifty — to those two wires. Done."

"And that works for any car?"

"I've only ever tried it on this one. But my brother says it'll work on any car. Fifteen, thirty, and fifty."

"And that's it?"

"The only other thing you have to do is break the locking pin on the steering column. The rest is easy-peasy. To free up the steering wheel, you put your foot here, and boom, done. And obviously you have to bypass the fuel pump."

Obviously. Bypass the fuel pump. I didn't say anything for a minute. We'd learned about electrical currents in physics class. That there was plus and minus, and that the electrons flowed through wires like water and all that. But that seemed to have nothing to do with what was happening in our Lada. Steady-plus? It sounded as if a completely different sort of electricity was flowing in this car than in the wires in physics class. Like we'd landed in some alternate reality. But maybe physics class was the alternate reality. Because the fact that Tschick's system worked showed he must be right.

Tschick drove back onto the road. After we'd passed a bakery in a little village, we both got the itch for a coffee. We parked the car in some bushes outside town and walked back to the bakery. There we bought coffee and fresh rolls topped with cheese and cold cuts. And just as I was about to bite into my roll, somebody behind me said, "Klingenberg, what are you doing here?"

Lutz Heckel, the tub of lard on stilts, was sitting at a table behind us. Sitting next to him was an even bigger tub of lard on stilts and a not quite as big tub of lard on more solid columns.

"And the Mongolian's here too," Heckel said, surprised, but also in a tone that left no doubt as to what he felt about Mongols in general and about Tschick in particular.

"Visiting relatives," I said and turned quickly away. It didn't seem like a good time for an extended conversation.

"I didn't know you had relatives around here."

"I do," said Tschick, raising his cup of coffee like he was making a toast. "There's a detention center in Zwietow."

I couldn't remember seeing Heckel at Tatiana's party, but

110

the next thing he asked us was *how* we'd gotten here. Tschick made up something about a bicycle tour.

"Schoolmates of yours?" I heard the big tub of lard ask, and then I didn't hear much of anything for a while. At some point I heard car keys rattle on the table behind us and the chairs were pushed back. Daddy Heckel walked past us on his stilts and went back up to the counter. He came back with an armload of rolls, put four of them down on our table, and said, "Gotta make sure our bikers have enough energy out there on the road!" Then he rapped his knuckles on the table as a good-bye, and the tub of lard family walked off across the town square.

"Uh," Tschick said.

I didn't know what to say either.

We sat in front of the bakery for a good long time. We'd really needed the coffee. And the bread.

Every half an hour a bus packed with tourists rolled into the town square. There was a little castle somewhere in town. Tschick was sitting with his back to the square, where the buses stopped and let people off, but I had to look at the senior citizens spilling out of the buses. Because the tourists were all old. They were all wearing brown or beige clothing and stupid-looking hats, and when they passed the spot where we were sitting — which was slightly uphill from where the buses stopped — they were huffing and puffing like they'd just finished running a marathon.

I could never imagine becoming so old, being all beige like that. All the old men I knew looked like that. And the old women. They were beige. It was incredibly difficult to conceive of the fact that these old women must have once been young. That they had once been the same age as Tatiana, and that they had gotten dressed up and gone out to dance at places where people referred to them as "hot dishes" or whatever they said fifty or a hundred years ago. Not all of them, of course. Some of them were dull or ugly even then, no doubt. But even the dull and ugly ones probably had dreams about how their lives would pan out. They must have had plans for the future. Even the totally normal ones had plans for the future. And what I guarantee was not in those plans was becoming a beige senior citizen. The more I thought about these old folks who kept climbing out of the buses, the more depressed I got. The thing that got to me the most was the thought that even among the people on these bus tours, there must have been some who weren't boring or dull when they were young. Some had been attractive. Some were the prettiest girls in their class even — the ones everybody had a crush on. And seventy years ago some kid probably sat in a playground fort and got excited when he saw the light go on in some of these old ladies' rooms. But those girls had become beige senior citizens too, and you couldn't tell them apart from the rest. They all had gray skin and fleshy noses and ears now, and it made me so depressed that I practically threw up.

"Psst," said Tschick, looking past me. I followed his gaze and spotted two policemen walking along a row of parked cars looking at every license plate number. Without a word, we took our paper cups and sauntered casually back to the bushes where we had parked the Lada. Then we drove back the way we had come that morning, back along a country road, out of there like a shot. We didn't have to talk long about what we would do next.

In a wooded area not far away, we found a parking lot where people parked to go hiking. We started looking for a license plate we could unscrew, but it wasn't easy to find one. Most of the plates weren't even attached with screws. Fortunately there were quite a few cars there. And finally we found an old VW Beetle with Munich plates. We attached our plates to the VW in the hopes that the owner wouldn't immediately notice his were gone.

Then we drove a few miles on dirt paths that crisscrossed fields before taking a little road into a forest and then pulling over at an abandoned sawmill. We stuffed our backpacks and hiked off into the woods.

We weren't planning to ditch the Lada, but despite switching the license plates we weren't too confident about the whole situation. It seemed like the smartest thing to do was to keep it off the road for a while. We could spend a day or two in the woods. That was the plan. Though we didn't have a real plan. We didn't really know if they were looking for us or not. And whether they would give up after a few days if they were looking for us.

We hiked up a trail, and as we rose higher on the ridge the woods thinned out a bit. Eventually we came to an observation platform with a cool view out over the area. But even better than the view was the fact that there was a snack stand there selling water and candy and ice cream. So we wouldn't starve. And we decided to stay near the snack stand. Not far below the scenic lookout was a steep meadow. We found a quiet spot there below a giant elderberry bush. We lay down in the sun and snoozed the day away. Late in the day we loaded ourselves up with Snickers and Cokes and crawled into our sleeping bags and listened to the crickets start to chirp. During the day, hikers, bikers, and buses had come and gone constantly to the observation platform, but when it started to get dark we had the entire mountain to ourselves. It was still warm, almost too warm, and Tschick, who had managed to get the owner of the snack stand to sell him two beers at the end of the day, popped them open with a lighter.

More and more stars appeared in the sky above us. We lay on our backs and watched as the spaces between the stars filled with smaller stars, and then even tinier stars came into view between the smaller stars. The blackness kept retreating.

"It's amazing," said Tschick.

"Yeah," I said. "It is amazing."

"It's way better than TV. Though TV's good too. You ever seen *Star Wars*?"

"Of course."

"You seen *Starship Troopers*?"

"Is that the one with the monkeys?"

"No, bugs."

"And a brain bug at the end? A giant brain with — with slimy things sticking out of it?"

"Yeah!"

"That's an amazing movie."

"Yeah, it is amazing."

"Can you imagine? Somewhere up there, on some star — that's what's happening! Actual bugs are taking over some planet, slaughtering all the inhabitants, and nobody even knows about it," I said. "Except for us."

"Right, except for us."

"But we're the only ones who realize it. And the bugs don't know that we know."

"Seriously? Do you really think so?" Tschick rose to his elbows and looked at me. "Do you think there really is something out there? I mean, not necessarily bugs. But something?"

"I don't know. I heard one time that you can calculate the probability of there being other life in the universe. The chances are very slim, but since the universe is infinitely large, if you multiply even the slimmest odds by infinity you get a number — a number of planets where there's probably life. It worked here, after all. So somewhere out there I guarantee there are giant bugs."

"That's exactly what I think, exactly what I think!" Tschick lay back down on his back and looked intensely at the sky. "Amazing, isn't it?"

"Yeah, amazing."

"It just blows me away."

"And just imagine: The bugs go to the bug movies! They make movies on their planet and they're sitting in some bug cinema watching a movie set on Earth — it's about two kids who steal a car."

"And it's a horror film!" says Tschick. "The bugs think we're disgusting because we're *not* slimy."

"But they all think it's just science fiction, and that we don't exist in reality. People and cars — what a load of crap! Nobody watching the movie thinks it could be true."

"Except for two young bugs! They think it could be real. Two young school bugs who have just stolen an army helicopter. They're flying around the bug planet thinking the same thing we are. They think we exist because we think they exist."

"Crazy!"

"Yeah, crazy."

I looked up at the stars extending out into incomprehensible infinity and was somehow frightened. I was moved and frightened at the same time. I thought about the bugs. I could almost see them up there in some flickering little galaxy. Then I turned to Tschick and he looked at me, looked me right in the eyes, and said that everything was amazing. And it was. It was truly amazing.

And the crickets chirped the entire night.

When I woke up in the morning, I was alone. I looked around. There was a light fog clinging to the meadow and no sign of Tschick. But since his air mattress was still there I didn't think much of it. I tried to go back to sleep, but at some point my uneasiness got the better of me. I went up to the observation platform and looked in every direction. I was the only person on the mountain. The snack stand wasn't open yet. The sun looked like a red peach in a bowl of milk, and with the first beams of sunshine came a group of cyclists riding up the road. Not even ten minutes later, Tschick came tromping up the hill too. He had walked down to the sawmill to check on the Lada and see if it was still there. It was still there. We went back and forth for a while on what to do, and then decided that we would go back down now and drive on after all. Waiting around made no sense.

While we were talking, the group of bicyclists had spread out and sat down on a low wall near the observation deck — a dozen kids our age and one adult. They were eating breakfast and talking quietly among themselves, and there was something really weird about them. The group was too small to be a school class or summer camp, too big to be a family, and too well dressed to be from a loony bin or orphanage. Something was off about them. Their clothes were strange. They weren't brand-name clothes, but they didn't look cheap either. On the contrary. They looked expensive — but uncool. And they all had really clean faces. I don't really know how to describe it, but their faces were somehow cleaner than normal. The weirdest one of all was the chaperone. He talked to them like he was their boss. Tschick asked one of the girls what institution they'd escaped from and she said, "We're not from an institution. We're Mobile Nobles. We're riding from manor house to manor house." She said it very seriously and very politely. Maybe she was putting us on and this was a bike tour organized by the local clown school.

"And you guys?" she said.

"What about us?"

"Are you also on a bicycle tour?"

"We're motorists," Tschick said.

The girl turned to the boy next to her and said, "You were wrong. They are motorists."

"And you guys are what exactly? Mobile Nobles?"

"What's so strange about that? Is *motorist* somehow less weird?"

"Yes, but *mobile nobles*?"

"And you guys are the proletariat in a chariot?"

Man, they were mean. Maybe the stash of cocaine had gone missing at the local clown school. We never figured out what those kids were really doing up there on the mountain, though we did come across them a little while later on the road. We passed them in the Lada and the girls waved and we waved back. Don't know about the nobility, but at least the mobility was true. For some reason we felt unbelievably confident again from that point on. And Tschick also suggested that if we needed to use code names, he would be Count Tschickula and I would be Count Lada.

The problem we had that morning, however, was that we had nothing to eat.

We'd brought some cans of stuff but no can opener. There were a couple crackers but nothing to put on them. And the six frozen pizzas were thawed and absolutely inedible. I tried to use a lighter to grill a piece of one of them, but it didn't work. In the end, six Frisbees flew out of the Lada like UFOs fleeing the burning death star.

Relief came a few kilometers down the road. A sign pointed left to a little village, and on the same signpost was an ad for a supermarket one kilometer away. We took the left and you could see the huge store from a long way off, sitting there like a shoe box plopped down in the landscape.

The adjacent village was tiny. We drove through and parked by a big barn, where nobody would see us, and then walked back into town. Even though the entire village consisted of maybe ten streets that all met at a fountain in the town square, we couldn't figure out which direction we needed to go to get to the supermarket. Tschick thought we needed to go left. I thought we should go straight. And there was nobody on the street to ask. We wandered through totally empty village streets until finally a boy on a bike appeared. It was a wooden balance bike with no pedals. He had to move his legs like he was running in order to push the thing along. He was probably twelve, meaning he was about ten years too old for the bike. His knees dragged on the ground. He stopped right in front of us and gaped at us with huge eyes — like a mutated frog or something.

Tschick asked him where the supermarket was and the kid smiled — a smile that said that he was either confident or clueless. He had huge gums.

"We don't shop at the supermarket," he said decisively.

"Interesting. But where is it?"

"We shop at Froehlich's market."

"Aha, at Froehlich's." Tschick nodded at the kid like a cowboy who didn't want to have to hurt another cowboy. "What we're really interested in is how to get to the supermarket."

The boy nodded eagerly, lifted a hand to his head as if he was going to scratch himself, and then motioned indistinctly with the other hand. Finally he stuck out his pointer finger and aimed it between two houses. There, on the horizon, was a farmstead set among tall poplar trees. "There's Froehlich's! That's where we always shop."

"Fantastic," said Tschick. "And now, one more time, where is the supermarket?"

His gums made it clear that we probably weren't going to get an answer. But there was nobody else on the street we could ask.

"What do you guys want to do there?"

"What do we want to do there? Mike, Mikey — what do we want to do at the supermarket again?"

"Do you want to get stuff or just have a look around?" asked the boy.

"Look around? Do you go to the supermarket to look around?"

"Come on, let's go," I said. "We'll find it." And to the boy, "We want to buy some food."

There was no point in making fun of the boy with the frog eyes.

Just then a tall, very pale woman stepped out of a house and called, "Friedemann! Come inside, Friedemann, it's noon!"

"I'm coming," answered the boy, and his voice had changed. He had taken on the same singsong tone as his mother.

"Why do you want to buy food?" he asked. Tschick had already walked over to the woman to ask the way to the supermarket.

"To the what?"

"The supermarket," said Friedemann.

"Oh, the big store," said the woman. She had a strange-looking face. Emaciated but not unhealthy looking. She said, "We don't shop there. We shop at Froehlich's."

"So we've heard." Tschick put on his most polite smile. He was good at it. Though I had the feeling he overdid it a little sometimes. Still, the fact that he looked like a Mongolian invader balanced things back out.

"Why would you want to go there?"

Oh, Christ, was the entire family like this? Didn't any of them know what you do at a supermarket?

"Go shopping," I said.

"Shopping," said the woman, drawing her arms to her chest as if to keep herself from accidentally pointing the way to the supermarket.

"Food! They want to buy food," squealed Friedemann.

The woman looked at us suspiciously and then asked if we were from around here and what we wanted here. Tschick told her a story about a bicycle tour, crossing East Germany, and the woman looked up and down the street. Not a bike in sight.

"And we have a flat," I said and, like Friedemann, gestured vaguely in no particular direction. "But we really need to do some shopping because we haven't had breakfast. . . ."

Nothing in her facial expression or her manner changed, but she said, "We have lunch at noon and you are very welcome to join us, you young men from Berlin. You will be our guests."

Then she showed her gums too — not quite as much as Friedemann, but a lot. Friedemann spun his balance bike around and shot toward the house, letting out a sound that was apparently a scream of excitement. There were now three or four smaller children standing at the door to the house all staring at us with big frog eyes.

I didn't know what to say, and Tschick didn't know either.

"What's for lunch?" he finally said. They were having something called Risi Bisi. Whatever that was. I scratched my head and Tschick went for a grand finale. He opened his eyes wide, bowed slightly, and said, "That sounds fantastic, ma'am."

Oh, Christ, I couldn't believe it. That must have been lesson two from the German classes they give to immigrants.

"Why did you do that?" I whispered as we headed inside behind the woman. Tschick waved his arms as if to say, "What else was I supposed to do?"

Before we could follow her into the house she nodded to Friedemann, who took us by the hands and led us around the side of the house into the backyard. I didn't like the situation. It also made me uneasy that, when Friedemann looked away for a second, Tschick made a sign with his finger that Friedemann was crazy.

In the backyard was a big white wooden table with ten chairs around it. Four of them were already taken by Friedemann's siblings. The oldest one was a girl who was maybe nine, and the youngest was a boy of about six. And all of them looked alike. The mother brought out the food in a huge pot. Apparently this was Risi Bisi: rice in a yellowish goop, with little chunks and green herbs floating in it. The mother served everyone a bowl with a soup ladle, but nobody touched their food. Instead, they all lifted their arms as if on command and joined hands. And since the entire family was looking at us now, we also lifted our hands. I linked hands with Tschick and Friedemann, and the mother lowered her head and said, "Okay, maybe we don't necessarily have to do this today. We welcome our guests, who have traveled from far away, to the day's festivities and give thanks for everything that is bestowed upon us. *Guten Appetit.*"

Then everyone shook hands and we ate. Say what you will, but the goopy rice tasted fantastic.

When we were finished, Tschick pushed his empty bowl away with both hands and, in the woman's direction, said that it had been a scrumtrulescent meal. The woman reacted by furrowing her brow. I scratched my head and added that it had been ages since I had eaten so well. Then Tschick said it had been super scrumtrulescent. The woman showed a little of her gums and cleared her throat in her fist, and Friedemann looked at us with his big frog eyes. And then came dessert. Holy crap.

I'd rather not even tell the next part. But I will anyway. Florentine, the nine-year-old, brought the dessert out on a tray. It was something foamy and white topped with raspberries. There were eight individual bowls of it. Eight different-sized bowls. I figured there'd be a fight over the biggest bowl. But I was wrong.

The eight bowls sat huddled together in the middle of the table and nobody touched them. Everyone just shifted in their chairs and looked at the woman.

"Quickly, quickly!" said Friedemann.

"First I have to think," she said and closed her eyes for a moment. "Okay, I have it." She cast a friendly look at me and Tschick and then looked around the table again. "What did Merope Gaunt get for Slytherin's locket when she . . ."

"Twelve galleons!" shouted Friedemann, jumping in his seat and shaking the table.

"Ten galleons," said all the others.

The mother pensively rocked from side to side and then smiled. "I believe Elisabeth was first."

Elisabeth coolly grabbed the biggest bowl with the most raspberries. Florentine protested because she thought she'd shouted the answer at the same time, and Friedemann pounded on the table shouting, "Ten! I'm an idiot! Ten!"

Tschick kicked me under the table. I shrugged. Slytherin? Galleons?

"You've never read Harry Potter?" asked the mother. "Oh well, it doesn't matter. We're changing subjects now."

She thought for another moment and while she did, Elisabeth took a little spoonful of her dessert, held it to her lips, and waited. She waited until Friedemann looked at her; then she slowly put the spoon into her mouth.

"Geography and science," said the mother. "What was the name of the research vessel Alexander von Humboldt . . ."

"Pizarro!" cried Friedemann as his chair fell backward. He immediately took the second biggest bowl, put his nose to the rim, and whispered, "Ten, ten. How did I ever come up with twelve?"

"That's not fair," said Florentine. "I knew the answer too. It's just because he yelled."

Next the mother asked what was celebrated on Pentecost. I probably don't have to tell you how the game played out. When the two smallest bowls were left, the mother asked who had been the first president of the Federal Republic of Germany. I said Adenauer and Tschick said Helmut Kohl. The mother wanted to give us our desserts anyway, but Florentine was against that. And so were the rest of the children. I would happily have forfeited my dessert at that point. Jonas, the youngest of all the children, about six years old, rattled off the names of all the presidents of the Federal Republic of Germany, starting with the correct answer, Theodor Heuss, and then took charge of the game himself. He asked us what the capital of Germany was.

"Uh, I would say Berlin," I said.

"That's what I would have said, as well," said Tschick, nodding earnestly.

Say what you will, but the dish once again was fantastic. I swear I've never tasted such delicious foam with raspberries.

Afterward we thanked the family for the excellent meal and were about to leave when Tschick said, "I have a question for you. How do you figure out which way is north with a watch when it's . . ."

"You aim the hour hand at the sun! Then you wind the minute hand to twelve and it is pointing south!" yelled Friedemann.

"Correct," said Tschick, pushing him his bowl with the last few raspberries in it.

"I knew that too," said Florentine. "It's just because he always yells."

"I might have gotten that," said Jonas, sticking his finger in his ear. "But maybe I wouldn't really have known that. I'm not sure. Would I have known that?" He looked quizzically at his mother, and his mother patted his head lovingly and nodded as if to say he would surely have known the answer.

CHAPTER TWENTY-SIX

They all walked us to the gate to say good-bye, and they gave us a huge pumpkin to take with us. It was just sitting there, a huge pumpkin, and they said we should take it in case we got hungry. We took it but didn't know what to say. They waved good-bye for a long time as we wandered off.

"Cool people," said Tschick. I wasn't sure whether he was serious or not. I didn't think he could be serious since he'd made the twirling-finger this-kid-is-crazy sign when we'd walked in. But his facial expression made it clear he was serious. I guess he was serious about both things. He was serious that the kid was crazy and that he thought they were "cool people." He was right too: They were cool, crazy people. They were nice and they were nuts, they made great food and knew a lot of stuff — just not the location of the supermarket. That they didn't know.

But we finally found it anyway. Later, as we turned into the street where the Lada was parked, carrying two huge bags of groceries and a giant pumpkin, I put the pumpkin down on the curb and went behind a bush to take a piss. Tschick trudged on without turning around — I'm only describing all of this in such detail because it proved important.

When I came out of the bushes, Tschick was about a hundred meters ahead of me and just a few steps from the Lada. I picked up the pumpkin and at the same moment a man carrying a bicycle came out of a driveway between me and Tschick. He lifted the bike up, flipped it over, and put it down on its seat and handlebars. The man was wearing a yellow shirt, greenish pants, and clip-in shoes. On the bike rack was a white hat that fell off when he turned it upside down. It was only when I looked at the hat on the ground that I recognized it as a policeman's cap. I also noticed something else we hadn't seen when we'd parked on the street: On the little brick house in front of the barn was a sign hanging with the green and white logo of the police. It was the town sheriff's place.

The town sheriff had yet to notice us. He cranked the pedals of his bike, pulled some tools out of his bag, and tried to wrestle his chain back on the sprocket wheel. He was having a hard time. He looked down at his dirty fingers and rubbed them together. Then he saw me. Fifty meters away: a boy with a giant pumpkin. What was I supposed to do? He could see that I was walking in his direction, so I just kept going. The pumpkin belonged to me, after all. My legs began to tremble, but it seemed to have been the right decision: The town sheriff's gaze returned to his bike. Then he looked up again and saw Tschick. Tschick had just gotten to the car, had thrown his bag of groceries in the backseat, and was about to climb into the driver's seat. The policeman stopped rubbing his hands together. He stared in Tschick's direction, took a step toward the car, then stopped again. There's nothing inherently suspicious about a boy getting into a car. Even when he opens the driver's door. But if Tschick were to start the engine, I knew what would happen next. I had to do something. I lifted the pumpkin up above my head and yelled, "Don't forget to bring the sleeping bag!"

I couldn't think of anything better. The policeman turned back to me. Tschick turned to me too. "Dad says to bring the sleeping bag! The sleeping bag!" I yelled again. When the cop turned again toward Tschick, I gestured at my head and my hip — meant to be a policeman's hat and gun — to try to telegraph the man's profession to Tschick. Without his hat on, and in those green cycling pants, it wasn't easy to tell. I must have looked like an idiot, but I couldn't think of any other way to signal that it was a cop. Tschick seemed to understand what was going on. He disappeared into the car and came out again with a sleeping bag in his hands. Then he closed the door and pretended to lock it (Dad gave me the keys, I just had to grab something), and came back toward me and the policeman with the sleeping bag. But he stopped after about ten steps. I wasn't a hundred percent sure why he stopped. But I think something in the cop's facial expression must have given away the fact that our clever move wasn't the greatest piece of acting he'd ever seen.

Tschick started backing up. Then he started to run. The policeman ran after him, but Tschick was already at the wheel. He backed onto the street at lighting speed and the policeman accelerated like a track star. Not because he could catch the car — there was no way he'd be able to do that — but so he could read the license plate number. Holy shit. A town sheriff who could run like a gold medalist. I stood there the whole time like an idiot, pumpkin in hand. As the Lada headed for the horizon, the sheriff finally turned back toward me. Don't ask what I did next. Normally, with any thought at all, I would never have done it. But nothing was normal anymore, and maybe it wasn't so stupid anyway. I ran to the cop's bicycle. I threw the pumpkin down and ran to the bike. I was significantly closer to it than he was at this point. I flipped it right side up and climbed onto the seat. The cop yelled, but fortunately he was yelling from a fair distance. I stepped on the pedal. Up to that second it had all been a blur, but now it became a vivid nightmare. I stepped with all my might on the pedal and didn't budge. It must have been in the highest gear, and I couldn't find the shifter. His shouts were getting closer. I had tears in my eyes and my thighs felt as if they were going to explode. But just as it seemed he would be able to reach out and grab me, I got the bike going and sped away from him.

I flew through the village on its cobblestone roads. It didn't take me longer than a minute and a half to reach the town square, but I knew how risky it was since the cop had probably already gotten to a phone. If he wasn't stupid — and he didn't give any indication of being stupid — he would have called someone who could grab me as I sped through the center of town. Maybe there was more than one policeman in this village. I raced between gray houses and around corners and finally onto a path that led out into the fields.

As it started to get dark, I lay in the woods alone, wheezing and anxious. The policeman's bike was hidden under some dense brush. I wracked my brain as I waited. I was more and more unsure of what to do. I was a hundred or maybe two hundred kilometers south or southeast of Berlin in some forest, while Tschick was driving around somewhere in a light blue Lada with Munich plates on it, a car every cop in the area was on the lookout for, and I had no idea how we were going to find each other. Normally I guess you'd try to meet up where you'd lost each other. But that wouldn't work in this case — it was right in front of the town sheriff's place.

Another possibility would have been to go to Friedemann's

house and leave a message for Tschick. Or hope that he had left one for me. But for whatever reason, it seemed highly unlikely that he would have done that. The village was small, the people all knew each other, and Tschick would never have driven through town again in the Lada. The only chance was that he would try to sneak into town after nightfall, but even that was risky given the probability that everyone there had already heard about the whole thing. It also seemed unlikely to me because all of a sudden I thought of something much more likely.

If you couldn't meet where you'd last seen each other, you could still meet in the last *safe* place you'd been together — the observation platform, the snack stand, and the spot hidden by the elderberry bush.

It seemed somehow logical. At least it seemed logical as I lay there with my face in the muck. It was the easiest solution, and the more I thought about it the more convinced I was that it would occur to Tschick too. Because it occurred to me. And besides, the platform was in a good location — far enough away from town but close enough for me to reach by bike. Tschick must have seen me take off on the bike. So I cowered in the bushes through the night and then started off at first light. I rode way out around the village, going through the woods and fields. It wasn't hard to find my way, but it was much farther than I'd thought. I could see the ridgeline shrouded in fog in the distance, but it never seemed to get any closer. It didn't take long before I was extremely thirsty. And hungry. Off to the right of the field I was in, there were a few houses clustered around a little brick church, so I headed that way. The "village" consisted of three houses and a bus stop. The street signs were in a foreign language and I thought for a second I was already in the Czech Republic. But that was impossible. I hadn't seen anything like a border.

There was a funny little shop, but it was closed and didn't look like it was going to open up anytime soon. The shop windows were so dirty that they were practically opaque, but inside I could see half a loaf of bread and a faded pack of gum on a table, and behind that a shelf stacked with East German laundry detergent.

There was a crazy guy standing at the bus stop. He was pissing in the middle of the street, tottering around with his dick in his hand like he was having a grand old time. There was nobody else around, and the angled rays of the morning sun made the cobblestones of the road look as if they were coated with red enamel. I thought about ringing one of the doorbells and asking whoever answered to sell me something. But once I actually rang the bell at a house where a light was on — the name on the door was Lentz, I remember that clearly — I lost my nerve and just asked the man who opened the door if I could have a glass of water. The man was half-naked. He was wearing gym shorts and was sweating. He was young and clearly worked out, and had bandages on his wrists. "A glass of water!" he bellowed. He stared at me for a second and then pointed to a faucet on the side of the house. As I drank from the faucet he asked if I was okay. I told him I was doing a bike tour. He laughed and shook his head and asked again if everything was okay. I pointed to his bandages and asked if everything was okay with him. He suddenly got very serious, nodded, and the conversation was over.

When I arrived at the observation platform, I was alone atop the mountain and it was still early in the morning. Behind the sawmill I'd seen only a lone black car, and the snack stand up here was still covered by a locked grate. I walked down to the elderberry bush. Our garbage was still on the ground, but there was no sign of Tschick. I was incredibly disappointed.

For hour after hour, I sat up there and waited. And I got more and more distraught. People came and went, and tour buses came and went, but the Lada never appeared. It didn't seem like a good idea to ride anywhere else. If Tschick was driving around, he needed to be able to find me someplace. If we both ended up driving around, we'd never find each other. At some point I became convinced they must have caught him, and I resigned myself to spending the night under the elderberry bush. But then my gaze fell on a garbage can. It was filled with candy bar wrappers, empty beer bottles, and wine corks, and it occurred to me that we too had thrown away all of our trash in that very garbage can. We hadn't left anything under the elderberry bush. I ran like a madman back down to the bush — and found an empty Coke bottle. Looking at it more closely, I discovered a rolled-up note crammed into the neck of the bottle. I pulled it out and it read, *I'm in the bakery where we ran into Heckel. Come at six. — T* But that had been crossed out and another message was written beneath it: *Count Tschickula is working at the sawmill. Stay here and I'll pick you up at sunset.*

I sat happily at the observation platform until evening. Then I got more and more upset. Because Tschick didn't show up. There were no more tourists either, just a black car driving around in circles at the back of the parking lot. It had been there since dusk, and I'm not sure how blind you can be — because it wasn't until the car pulled right up to the platform and a man with a Hitler mustache opened the door that I realized it was a Lada. Our Lada.

I hugged Tschick, then punched him, then hugged him again. I couldn't calm down.

"Man!" I shouted. "Man, oh, man!"

"How do you like the color?" Tschick asked. Then we barreled down the hill with the pedal to the metal.

I told him everything that had happened to me since we'd lost each other. But what Tschick had to tell was much more interesting. As he was fleeing the scene he had accidentally come across the bakery where we'd met Heckel and had parked the car not far from there. He figured it was too risky to keep driving around. He sat in front of the bakery for the entire day and had seen nothing but police cars go by.

Then he'd walked to the observation platform, which was only a few kilometers away. He had waited for me there. But since I didn't show up — as I was sleeping in the woods — he left the note in the bottle about the bakery and went back to the car. On the way he'd passed a home improvement store and stolen masking tape and a case of spray cans. Since he hadn't seen any more cops on the street, he had put the spray paint in the car and driven back to the observation platform. But I still wasn't there, so he left the second note and parked the car at the sawmill and painted it. He had thought of everything: The car had new license plates now too.

When I told Tschick about the man with the bandages and the other one pissing in the street, he said he'd noticed that there were a lot of crazy people out here. As for the signs written in another language, he didn't know what the story was.

"It certainly isn't Russian," he said as we looked at a strange sign lit up by the first few streetlights to blink on.

The next day we were back on the autobahn. And this time not by accident. We were feeling confident, we wanted to make headway, and we did. For about fifty kilometers. Then Tschick pointed to the fuel gauge, which was already well into the red.

"Shit," he said.

We hadn't thought about the fact that we would need to get gas. At first it didn't seem like a huge problem. There was a rest stop two kilometers up the road and we had money. But then I realized that two eighth graders in a car might not look right to the gas station employees. I should have realized that before.

"Here's fifty, keep the change!" said Tschick, laughing hysterically.

We pulled off at the rest stop anyway. It was shortly before noon and the place was jammed. Tschick pulled past the diesel pumps and parked between two tractor-trailers where nobody could see us. We looked around sadly. Tschick said we'd never be able to get gas there, and I suggested we use the tennis ball to grab a different car.

"Too many people around," said Tschick.

"We'll just wait until it's less busy."

"Let's just wait until evening," he said. "Then one of us can go to the farthest pump and get it all ready, and the other can pull the Lada around on the outside — fill it up and go. That way we'll save money too."

Tschick thought it was a brilliant plan — as good as Hannibal marching over the Alps. And I might have agreed with him if I had known how a gas pump worked. But I'd never held a gas pump in my hand, and eventually I realized that he never had either. There's not only a trigger in the handle of the pump but some other lever to lock it or something. I'd seen my father do it a million times, but I never paid close attention.

We bought ice cream bars at the rest-stop shop, sat down on the curb opposite the pumps, and watched people fill up their tanks. It didn't look so difficult. It just took forever to fill up. And there were always people standing around, and an attendant watching everything from the panoramic window of his booth. Of course, we could have just put a few liters in and sped off, but then we'd be in the same jam by the time we reached the next rest stop.

"Don't you still have the tennis ball?" I asked. I pointed at the parking lot — so many nice cars.

"We can't steal a new car every time we run out of gas."

"But you still have the ball, right?" I looked at Tschick. He had his arms wrapped around his knees and his head buried.

"Yeah, yeah, yeah," he said. But he said that we wanted to take the Lada back, and that we couldn't steal a hundred cars one after the next. I found this all very enlightening. But what if it meant the end of our trip?

A red Porsche pulled up to a gas pump and a young woman with sleek blond hair got out and grabbed the handle with pink-polished fingernails. And that's when it hit me — I knew how we could get gas. We just had to siphon it out of another car! It was easy, I told Tschick. All we needed was a hose. You stick that in the gas tank, suck on it for a second, and the gas flows right out. I'd seen it in a book I got as a present when I started school. It was a book that explained the entire world — for six-year-olds. Obviously six-year-olds aren't taught how to steal gasoline. But I remembered an illustration of a bucket on top of a table. There was water in the bucket, and the water was flowing smoothly up and out of the rim of the bucket in a hose. It works because of some physics principle.

"What are you telling me? That the water flows up?"

"You have to suck on it to get it started."

"Haven't you ever heard of gravity? It won't flow up."

"It runs down once it gets started. Overall it's flowing downward."

"But the gas doesn't know that it will eventually be flowing downward."

"It's a law of physics. There's a name for it. Something with force and tube. The something-force rule."

"Bullcrap," said Tschick. "The bullcrap-sandwich rule, more like."

"Haven't you ever seen it in a movie?"

"Yeah, but that's *in a movie*."

"I know it from a book," I said. I didn't say it was a book for six-year-olds. "I think the name is something with a C — like capital force or whatever."

"Capital crap, man."

"No, wait, that's not it. I know! Capillary! Capillary action is the name of the principle."

Tschick didn't say anything for a moment. He still didn't believe it. But the fact that I'd thought of the name of the force had taken the wind out of his sails. I told him that capillary action was strong enough to allow liquids to flow against gravity and all that. Mostly I kept at it just to make an effort — and because I didn't want our trip to be over. I mean, I'd never actually seen anyone do the trick with the hose.

We ate another round of ice cream bars and then another. And when we still didn't have a better idea, we decided to give it a try.

The problem, of course, was that we didn't have a hose. We looked all around the rest stop first, the area behind the gas station, the brush nearby, an adjacent field, and then farther and farther away. We found hubcaps, plastic tarps, bottles, loads of beer cans, and even a five-liter canister without a top. But nothing we could use as a hose. We looked for almost two hours, and while we did we cooked up all sorts of other plans for how we'd get out of there. But the plans got more and more ridiculous and that somehow made us more and more frustrated. No damn hose anywhere. No pipe, no tube, no cable. It was the kind of thing you always saw lying around when you didn't need one.

Tschick went into the rest-stop shop and looked in the auto parts section and anywhere else he thought he might find a hose of some sort. But there was nothing. Instead, he came out with a handful of drinking straws. We tried to connect the straws into a long tube, but with one glance at the rickety result even a brain-dead three-year-old could have seen it wasn't going to work.

And then Tschick had an idea. He remembered seeing a dump along the road. I couldn't remember seeing a dump, but

Tschick was sure. On the right-hand side of the road a few kilometers before the rest stop he'd seen giant mounds of garbage. And if there was a place we could definitely find a hose, that was it.

We took a dirt path that ran next to the guardrail alongside the highway, then cut through some woods and walked through fields and over fences, keeping the autobahn in view the whole time. It was just as hot as it had been the day before, and clouds of insects hung like fog at the edge of the woods. We walked for more than an hour without coming across the dump, and I was fed up and ready to ditch the idea of siphoning gas. But Tschick was completely convinced now that siphoning gas was the answer and didn't want to go back without a hose. While we were arguing, we came across a huge blackberry patch. And though most of the berries weren't ripe yet, there was a section that must have gotten more direct sun, because all the berries were ripe. And they tasted fantastic. I don't know if I've mentioned this, but there is nothing in the world I like better than blackberries. We stayed there for a while and gorged ourselves. Afterward it looked as if we were wearing makeup — our entire faces were purple.

I felt great again after that, and had no objection to walking another few hours in search of a hose. Which is good, because it did in fact take two hours before we caught sight of the dump. Giant mountains of garbage, hemmed in by the autobahn on one side and woods on the rest. We weren't the only ones poking around there. We could see an old man bent over collecting electrical wire. And there was a girl our age there too, covered in filth. And two children. But they didn't seem to be together.

I started working through a mound of household trash and picked up two photo albums to show Tschick. One was a family album full of pictures of a father, mother, son, and dog all smiling in every picture, even the dog. I flipped through it, then decided to throw it away after all — it made me depressed. It made me think of my mother and how badly things were going for her and how much more distress I was probably going to cause her when she found out about all of this. Then I slipped on a slick plank of wood and fell into a pile of rotten fruit.

Tschick had climbed onto another mound and found a big brown plastic canister with a filler cap. He beat the canister like a drum and then held it over his head. It was great. But as for a hose — negative.

I kept an eye out for washing machines, but in all the ones I found, the drum had been ripped out and the hose removed. As the hunched man wandered past me, I asked him if he had any idea why the hoses were missing from all the washing machines. He barely looked up and just pointed to his ears, as if he were deaf. The girl shot past me like a quick little animal at one point too, but she didn't even look at me. She was barefoot and her legs were blackened with dirt all the way up to her knees. She had on rolled-up army pants and a filthy T-shirt. She had small eyes, bulging lips, and a flat nose. And her hair — it looked like the clippers had gotten fouled up while she was having a haircut. I decided not to try to talk to her. She had a wooden box under her arm, but I wasn't sure if she'd found it here or had brought it to carry things, and it wasn't clear what she was looking for anyway.

After a while I went up and met Tschick on top of the biggest mound. Neither of us had found anything except for the ten-liter canister Tschick had. But what use was that? This was a dump with no hoses. We sat down on a gutted washing machine on top of the mountain of garbage. The sagging sun had already reached the tops of the trees. The sound of the autobahn was quieter, and the old man and the children were no longer in sight. The only person left was the girl, who sat on top of another mound looking across at us. Her legs hung from the open door of an old wardrobe. She yelled something in our direction.

"What?" I yelled back.

"You're idiots!" she called.

"Are you crazy or something?"

"You heard me, moron. Your friend's an idiot too!"

"What the hell kind of asshole is that?" said Tschick.

For a long time all we could see were her legs, dangling out of the wardrobe. Then she sat up and started to put on a pair of boots that were sitting next to her in a drawer. She looked across at us.

"I've got something!" she yelled, though it was clear she didn't mean the boots. "Do you?"

"Shove it up your ass!" shouted Tschick.

She stopped tying the boots for a second. Then she bent forward and stretched out her legs and called, "You're so dumb you couldn't even fuck!"

"Shove it up your ass and shut your mouth!"

"Russian bastard!" She'd made out his accent.

"I'm going to come over there!"

"Oooh, the big bad man is going to come over here. What are you going to do? Come on! Come over here, you pussy! I'm *so* scared."

"I don't think she's right in the head," said Tschick.

The mounds were so steep that it would have taken several minutes to get over there.

It was quiet for a few minutes, and then she called, "What were you looking for?"

"A pile of shit," said Tschick.

"Hoses!" I shouted. All the cursing was beginning to bug me. "We were looking for hoses. You?"

A crow swooped over the mound and skidded down on a piece of sheet metal. The girl didn't answer. She lay back down in the wardrobe again.

"What about you?" I shouted.

For a while all you could see were her filthy calves. Then a hand came into view.

"Hoses are over there."

"What?"

"Over there."

"She's just pretending she knows," said Tschick.

"I heard that!" yelled the girl.

"So?"

"Dirty bastard!"

"Where over there?" I called.

"Where am I pointing?"

You could see her knee and her hand, but to be honest it looked as if her hand was pointing at the sky. It was quiet for a few minutes. Then I climbed down from our mound and up the one she was on.

"Where?" I asked, catching my breath as I approached her wardrobe.

She lay there without moving and stared at my neck. "Come here. Come on."

"Where?" I said, and suddenly she hopped up. Surprised, I staggered back a few steps and nearly fell. Behind me was a ten-foot drop. "Do you know where the hoses are or not?"

"You're the queer with the dirty Russian boyfriend, yeah?" She wiped a piece of fruit off my shirt that I hadn't noticed. Then she picked up her wooden box, tucked it under her arm, and started off. Up the next mound, then the next, and then she stopped and pointed down, "There!"

At the foot of this mound was a smaller mound of scrap metal and behind it a huge pile of hoses. Long hoses, short hoses, all sorts of tubes and hoses. Tschick, who had followed us, had already scrambled down and grabbed a thick washing machine hose. "Built-in angle!" he called. He wouldn't look at the girl.

"No, an angle is no good," I said. I disconnected a hand-held showerhead from its hose.

"What do you need it for?"

"An angle is always good," said Tschick, running the angled end into his canister.

"Hey, I asked you something," said the girl.

"What was the question?"

"What do you want it for?"

"It's a birthday present for my father."

Oddly enough she didn't curse at me. She just put an annoyed look on her face and said, "I showed you where the crap was, so now you can tell me what you want it for."

Tschick was kneeling among the hoses, examining the various washing machine hoses and shoving them into the canister.

"Why do you want them?"

"We stole a car," said Tschick. "And now we need to steal gasoline for it."

He looked at the girl through a big tube.

She pelted him with about a hundred curse words. "I should have known. You retards. Even though I showed you the damn things. Typical. Do whatever you want." She wiped her face with her T-shirt and sat down with her wooden box on a tractor tire. I held up my shower hose and gave Tschick the signal to quit looking. With three hoses and a canister we headed off.

"What are you really going to do with them?" the girl yelled.

"You're getting on my nerves," Tschick said.

"Do you have anything to eat?"

"Do we look like we do?"

"You look like retards."

"You're repeating yourself."

"Do you have any money?"

"For you?"

"You wouldn't have found them without me."

"Go fuck yourself."

Tschick and the girl continued to insult each other until we were nearly out of earshot. He kept turning around and yelling insults at her, and she shouted insults back at him from a mound of garbage. I stayed out of it.

But then she started to run after us. For some reason I had a funny feeling about the whole thing when I saw *how* she was running after us. Normally, girls don't run right — they run awkwardly. But this girl could *run*. She ran like it was a matter of life or death — and with the wooden box under her arm no less. I wasn't exactly afraid of her, the way she hurtled toward us, but I definitely thought she was weird.

"I'm hungry," she said, catching her breath. She was looking at us as if she was staring into the distance.

"There are blackberries over there," I said.

She drew a circle around her mouth with her finger and said, "And here I was thinking you were queer. Because of the lipstick."

Tschick and I walked on, and he whispered to me that she wasn't right in the head.

We hadn't gotten far when we heard her yelling again.

"Hey!" she called.

"What?"

"Where are the blackberries, man? Where are the blackberries?"

The way back seemed to go a lot faster than the way there. Maybe it was because the girl talked nonstop. At first she had walked behind us, then between us, and then on the other side of the path. Tschick held his nose at some point and looked at me, and it was true. She stank. She smelled horrible. You didn't notice it while in the dump, because the whole place stank. But she was giving off a serious stench. If she'd been in a cartoon, flies would have been buzzing around her head. And she talked nonstop. I don't remember exactly what she was talking about, but she kept asking us stuff like where we lived and where we went to school, whether we were good at math. That seemed particularly important to her — whether we were good at math. She asked if we had siblings, whether we knew Cantor's theorem of infinity and on and on. But whenever we asked why she wanted to know all of this, she never answered. She wouldn't even tell us what she was looking for at the dump.

Instead, she told us that she wanted to work at a TV station one day. Her dream was to be the host of a quiz show. "Because you look good and you work with words." She had a cousin who worked in TV and said it was a super job except that you had to work nights.

After she'd talked for long enough about TV, she came back to the joke about us stealing a car and said that Tschick was a funny guy, and that she had laughed inside when he'd told the joke about stealing the car. Tschick scratched his head and said that, yeah, she was right, he was a funny guy sometimes, which was exactly why he planned to give his father a hose for his birthday.

"And you're more the quiet type," said the girl, poking me in the shoulder and asking me again if I *really* went to school. I hope we reach the blackberries soon, I thought, or we'll never get rid of her.

I figured she would turn around and go back at some stage, but she walked the three or four kilometers to the blackberry patch. I was hungry again too, and so was Tschick, so we all plunged into the berry patch.

"We have to get rid of her somehow," whispered Tschick. I looked at him as if he had said we shouldn't saw off our feet.

Then the girl started to sing. Very quietly at first, in English, broken by pauses when she was chewing berries.

"Now she's singing some crap too," said Tschick. I said nothing, because for one thing she wasn't singing crap. She was singing "Survivor" by Destiny's Child. Her pronunciation was ridiculous. She must not have spoken English — it sounded as if she was just imitating the sounds. But she sang unbelievably well. I gingerly grabbed a thorny branch with my thumb and pointer finger and pulled it aside to have a look through the leaves at the girl singing and humming and munching berries there in the bushes. Add to that the taste of the blackberries in my own mouth, the orange-red sunset, and the background sound of the autobahn, and I found myself in an extremely weird mood.

"We're going to head off on our own now," said Tschick when we were standing on the path again.

"Why?"

"We have to get home."

"I'll go with you. I'm going that way too," said the girl.

And Tschick said, "This isn't the way you were going."

He told her a thousand times that we didn't want her to come with us, but she just shrugged her shoulders and kept walking along behind us. Finally Tschick faced her and said, "Do you know how bad you stink? You smell like a pile of crap. Get out of here."

As we walked on, I could tell she was still following us. But she started walking slower and slower, and soon enough we could no longer see her. Darkness started to creep between the trees. We heard some noise in the bushes at one point, but it was probably just an animal.

"If she follows us, we're screwed," said Tschick.

Just to be safe, we walked faster and then, after rounding a sharp turn, hid in some bushes and waited. We waited at least five minutes, and when the girl didn't appear, we walked the rest of the way back to the rest stop.

"You didn't have to say all that stuff about her smelling bad."

"I had to say something. And anyway, man, she did stink! She must live in that dump."

"She sure did sing nicely," I said after a while. "And there's no way she lives in the dump."

151

"Why did she ask us for food?"

"Yeah, okay, but this isn't Romania. People don't live in dumps here."

"Did you catch a whiff of her?"

"We probably smell just as bad."

"I'm telling you, she lives there. Ran away from home. Seriously, I know people like that. She's messed up. Nice body and all, but she's a homeless nut-job."

To the left, above the autobahn, you could see the first stars. It was getting tough to see the path and stay on it. I suggested we walk along the shoulder of the autobahn. I was afraid we'd lose our way otherwise. It was a stupid argument since we could hear the rush of the autobahn from the woods anyway. But to be honest, I was getting a little afraid in the dark woods. I have no idea why. It couldn't have been the fear of running into criminals — we were definitely the only criminals running around in those woods. In fact, maybe that's what made me uncomfortable. I guess I finally realized that's what we were. I was happy when we could see the neon lights of the rest stop through the trees.

The first thing we did was buy ice cream and Cokes. We hid the canister behind a guardrail and walked through the parking lot with our ice creams, eyeballing the gas tanks of parked cars. None of them could be opened. I was beginning to have doubts when Tschick finally found an old VW Golf with a broken gas tank door.

We waited until it was really dark and nobody was anywhere in sight, and then got to work.

The washing machine hose was so inflexible that we might as well have thrown it out. But we got the shower hose into the tank with no problem. We just couldn't get the gas to start flowing. Even though the tank was full. The end of the hose was all wet with gasoline.

After I'd tried sucking on the tube about ten times with no luck, Tschick tried. After he'd sucked a bunch of times he looked at me and said, "What the hell kind of book was it you saw this in? Where'd you get it?"

I had no desire to tell him what kind of book it was. I tried sucking on the tube again. I could tell the gas was coming up the tube. Once I had it almost to my lips. But no more than three drops came out. We squatted between the parked cars and looked at each other.

"I know how it works," Tschick finally said. "Fill your mouth and then spit it out. That'll work for sure."

"Why me?"

"This wasn't my idea."

"I have a better idea. Do you still have the tennis ball?"

"Oh, man," said Tschick. "I can't. No way."

"It's pitch-black out here. Nobody will see us."

"I *can't*," Tschick said with a pained look on his face. "You didn't really believe that, did you? You can't open a car lock with a tennis ball. Otherwise everybody would steal cars. The Lada was open the whole time. Didn't you notice? The lock is busted or maybe the owner just never locks it — I mean, who's going to steal a rust bucket like that anyway. My brother realized it was always open and . . . don't look at me like that! My brother pulled the same prank on me with the tennis ball. Oh, man. *Don't turn around.*"

"What's wrong?"

"Get your head down. There's somebody over there. By the Dumpsters."

I leaned up against the Golf and tried to carefully look over my shoulder.

"They're gone. There was a shadow over there by the recycling bin."

"So let's get out of here."

"There he is again. I'll have a smoke."

"What?"

"Camouflage."

"Forget camouflage, let's get out of here."

154

Tschick stood up and kicked the container and hose under the Golf. It made a loud scraping noise. I stood up too. Something moved behind the Dumpsters. I saw it out of the corner of my eye.

"Could be goats," murmured Tschick. He lit up a cigarette in his mouth, standing right next to the gas tank door.

"Why don't you just throw a match in there while you're at it."

He took a few puffs and started stretching. It was the least convincing acting job of all time.

Then we went slowly back to the Lada. As we walked away I nudged the gas tank door of the VW closed with my hip.

"You idiots!" yelled someone behind us.

We looked into the darkness in the direction the voice had come from.

"Screwing around for half an hour without getting a drop. Idiots. Real pros."

"Maybe you can say it a little louder," said Tschick.

"And smoking on top of it!"

"Can't you shout any louder? We want the whole parking lot to know."

"You guys are too dumb to fuck."

"True. And now could you please piss off?"

"Don't you know you have to suck on the hose?"

"What do you think we were doing the whole time? Get out of here!"

"Shhh!" I said.

Tschick and I ducked behind a car. The girl didn't care. She looked around the parking lot.

"There's nobody around, you scaredy-cats. Where's the hose?"

She took our equipment out from under the VW. She stuck one end of the hose into the gas tank and the other — along with a finger — into her mouth. She sucked ten, fifteen times like she was gulping down the air; then she pulled the hose out of her mouth with her finger over the end.

"Right. Where's the canister?"

I pulled it out from under the car and set it down. She stuck the hose into the mouth of the container and gas rushed out of the tank. All by itself. And it didn't stop.

"Why didn't it work for us?" asked Tschick.

"The end of the hose has to be below the level of the gas in the car," said the girl.

"Aha," I said.

"Oh," said Tschick. We watched as the canister filled up. The girl kneeled down, and when the flow of gas stopped, she screwed the gas cap back on and shut the tank door.

"Below what level?" whispered Tschick.

"Ask her, you idiot," I said.

That's how we met Isa. With her elbows on the backs of the two front seats she watched closely as Tschick started the Lada. We still had no desire to take her along, but after the whole gasoline thing it would have been tough not to. She wanted to come with us, and when she heard we were from Berlin she said that was exactly where she was heading. And then when we explained that we weren't going toward Berlin right now, she said that was perfect. She kept trying to find out where we were going, but since she wouldn't tell us where she was going, we didn't tell her either. We just said we were heading south, at which point she remembered she had a half-sister in Prague she really needed to go see. And we had to go right past Prague anyway. Plus, like I said, it would have been tough not to take her with us since she was the only reason we had any gas.

Once we were rolling down the autobahn again, we opened all the windows. It still stank, just not as badly. Tschick had adapted to driving on the autobahn by this point. He drove like Hitler in his heyday, and Isa sat in back and jabbered on and on. She was suddenly full of energy and shook the backs of our seats as she talked. Not that it was normal behavior, but it was preferable to the streams of obscenities she'd been scream-ing earlier. And the things she talked about weren't entirely uninteresting. I mean, she wasn't stupid. And even Tschick held his tongue after a while and nodded as he listened to her.

But the two of them still hadn't entirely settled their differ-ences. When Isa stuck her head between the front seats Tschick motioned to her hair and said, "There's things living in there."

Isa sat back immediately and said, "I know." And a few kilometers later she asked, "Do you guys happen to have a pair of scissors? I need to cut my hair."

With the help of the exit signs, we tried to figure out where we were. But none of us recognized the names of the towns. I began to suspect we hadn't gotten far on all those dinky coun-try roads. But it didn't matter. At least not to me. The autobahn didn't seem to be heading south anymore, and at some point we exited and started following the sun along country roads again.

Isa asked to hear our lone cassette tape. Then after one song, she asked us to throw it out the window. A ridge of mountains came into view on the horizon — we were heading straight for them. They were really tall, with jagged bare tops. We had no idea what mountain range it could be. There was no sign. Definitely not the Alps. Were we still in Germany? Tschick swore there were no mountains in East Germany. Isa said there were, but the tallest were only a thousand meters high. In geography, we'd just studied Africa. Before that we'd learned about America, and before that the Balkans. We hadn't gotten any closer to Germany than that. And now, here was a mountain range that wasn't supposed to be there. At least we all agreed it didn't belong there. It took about half an hour before we reached the foot of the mountains, and then we began the serpentine climb up them.

We had sought out the dinkiest road we could find, and we had to put the Lada in first gear and fight our way up. To our left and right the fields hung like towels from the steep hillsides. Then came a forest. And when we emerged from the forest we were sitting at the top of a gorge with a crystal clear lake in it. A small lake. Half of it was bordered by pale gray cliffs, with a concrete and metal structure on one side. The rest was ringed by a dike of some sort. And we were the only people around. We drove down and parked the car near the edge of the lake. From the concrete dam you could look down toward the valley below and across at the rest of the mountains. A few hundred meters below the dam was a little village. This was an ideal spot to spend the night.

The lake looked too cold for swimming. I stood on the dam next to Isa and took a deep breath. Tschick went over to the car, grabbed something, and walked back with it casually hidden behind him. We'd apparently both had the same thought. With a nod from Tschick, we picked Isa up and tossed her into the water. A fountain of water shot up as she went under, and another one shot up as she surfaced with her arms flailing. It was at that moment that I realized we had no idea if she could swim. She screamed and splashed — though she overdid it enough that you could tell she knew how to swim. She also started treading water and wasn't sinking an inch. She shook her wet hair, swam a little breaststroke, and cursed us out. Tschick threw her the bottle of shower gel he'd gotten from the car. And as I was trying to figure out if that was funny or if I should feel bad for her, I got a poke in the back and fell into the water too. It was colder than cold. I screamed as soon as my head was out of the water. Tschick stood on the side and laughed as Isa alternately laughed and cursed.

The concrete structure was too tall to climb up, so we had to swim across the lake to a part where the bank was at water level. While we swam, Isa let an unending stream of curses fly, kicked me underwater, and said that I was an even bigger moron than my boyfriend. We got into a tussle. As this was going on, Tschick strolled to the car, put on his bathing suit, and came to the lakeside with a cigarette in his mouth and a towel over his shoulder.

"This is how a gentleman goes swimming," he said, making what was supposed to be an elegant face. Then he dove headfirst into the lake.

We cursed him in tandem.

When we got back on land, Isa immediately took off her shirt and pants and everything else and began to soap herself up. That was just about the last thing I had expected.

"Lovely," she said. She was standing in knee-deep water, gazing out at the landscape, and washing her hair. I wasn't sure where to look. I acted like I was looking all around. She really did have a great body and her skin was covered with goose bumps. I had goose bumps too. Tschick swam to the bank freestyle, and oddly enough there was no more chitchat. Nobody said anything, nobody cursed, and nobody made any jokes. We just washed ourselves, shivered from the cold, and dried ourselves off with the same towel.

With a mountain view and fog beginning to creep into the valley below, we ate a package of gummy bears we had left over from our visit to the supermarket. Isa had on one of my

T-shirts and shiny Adidas shorts. Her stinky clothes were lying on the edge of the dike — and stayed there, forever.

That night we tried to figure out where she was from and where she was trying to go, but the only thing we could get out of her were crazy stories. It was clear she wouldn't tell us what she was doing in the dump or what she had in her wooden box even to save her own life. The only thing she told us was her last name, Schmidt. Isa Schmidt. At least, that was the only thing she told us that we believed.

Early the next morning, Tschick set off alone to go buy food in the village down in the valley. I was still half-asleep on the air mattress, looking out over the dimly lit landscape. Isa had the back of the Lada open and asked again if we happened to have scissors and if I would cut her hair.

I did find a little pair of scissors in the first aid kit, but I'd never cut hair before. She didn't care, and she wanted it all cut off except for a row of bangs in front. She sat down on the side of the dike, took off her T-shirt, and said, "Go ahead."

After a few seconds she turned to me and said, "Why haven't you started? I don't want the T-shirt to get covered in hair."

So I started cutting. At first I tried not to touch her head too much while I was cutting her hair, but it's difficult to give someone a haircut with tiny scissors without bracing yourself on their head. And it's even more difficult not to keep looking at naked breasts when they're right in front of you.

"Look, he's jacking off," said Isa. I looked toward the edge of the woods and saw an old man standing there — not even behind a tree — with his pants around his ankles spanking it.

"Oh, man," I said, taking the scissors away from her head.

Isa jumped up, picked up some rocks, and, with lightning speed, started running toward the old man. She shot up the hill and started throwing rocks as she ran. She was throwing the rocks fifty meters, easy — and dead straight, like laser beams. And somehow it didn't surprise me. Anyone who could run like her could obviously throw well too. At first the old man kept stroking, but when Isa got a bit closer he whipped up his pants and staggered into the woods. Isa followed him, yelling and waving her arms wildly. But I could see that she had stopped throwing rocks. When she reached the edge of the woods she stopped. She came back out of breath and sat down in the exact same spot as before.

I must have stood there like a statue for a while because at some point she tapped my thigh and said, "Go on."

The only thing missing was the bangs. I kneeled in front of Isa to be able to make a straight line. And I gave it everything I had to avoid taking even the tiniest glimpse anywhere except at her forehead. I held the scissors perfectly level and made a tentative initial trim. Then I leaned back and surveyed it like a real artist and cut a bit more. The hair fell past her small eyes and on down.

"It doesn't have to be perfect," Isa said. "The rest of it's a mess anyway."

"Not at all. It looks great," I said. And in my mind, *You look great.*

I didn't say anything more. When I was done, Isa wiped the hair away and we sat next to each other on the dike, looked out at the view, and waited for Tschick to come back. Isa still hadn't put her T-shirt back on. In front of us the mountains were still shrouded in a bluish morning mist that also hung in the valleys. I asked myself why it was so beautiful. I wanted to say how beautiful it was, or how beautiful I thought it was and why — or rather, how beautiful it was and that I couldn't explain why it was so beautiful. But at some point I figured it wasn't necessary to explain.

"Have you ever had sex?" asked Isa.

"What?"

"You heard me."

She had put her hand on my knee and my face felt as if someone had thrown boiling water on it.

"No," I said.

"Well?"

"Well what?"

"Do you want to?"

"Do I want to what?"

"You understand what I'm saying."

"No," I said.

My voice was suddenly high and squeaky. After a bit Isa took her hand away and we sat silently for at least ten minutes. There was still no sign of Tschick. Suddenly the mountains and the view seemed totally uninteresting. What had Isa just said? What had I answered? It was only a few words — what did they mean? My mind was racing, and it would take five hundred pages to write down all the thoughts that went through my head in the next five minutes. I'm sure none of it was too fascinating anyway — it's only fascinating in the moment, when you're in a situation like that. I kept asking myself whether Isa was serious. And whether I was serious when I said I didn't want to sleep with her, if that really was what I'd said. Though it was true that I didn't want to sleep with her. I mean, I thought she was amazing and all, but at that moment, on that misty morning, I thought it was perfect just sitting there next to her with her hand on my knee. And it was incredibly disappointing when she took her hand away. It took an eternity before I was able to form a sentence. I practiced saying it in my head about ten times and then said it aloud in a voice that made it sound as if I were about to have a heart attack. "But I like having your . . . um, uh . . . hand on my knee."

"Oh yeah?"

"Yeah."

"Why?"

My God. Why? Another heart attack.

Isa put her arm around my shoulder.

"You're shivering," she said.

"I know," I said.

"You don't know much."

"I know."

"We could kiss. If you'd like."

And at that exact moment, Tschick came into view carrying two bags from a bakery. There was no kissing.

Instead, we went up the mountain. We had never planned out what we wanted to do, but as we ate breakfast we kept looking around at a mountain that looked like the tallest mountain on earth. At some point it became obvious we had to go up it. The only question was how. Isa wanted to hike up. I agreed. But Tschick thought going on foot was absurd. "If you want to fly, you use an airplane," he said. "If you want to wash your clothes, you use a washing machine. And if you want to go up a mountain, you use a car. We're not in Bangladesh."

We drove through the woods toward the mountain, but it was difficult to figure out which turns to take. Only beyond the mountain did we find a road snaking its way toward the top, and we crept along cliffs until we reached a pass. From there the road went back down again, so we had to walk to the peak after all.

Either we were going up some route the tourists didn't use, or we were the only ones there that morning. In any event we didn't come across anyone except a few sheep and cows. It took two hours to reach the very top, but it was worth it. The view looked like a really great postcard. There was a giant wooden cross at the highest point, and below that a little cabin.

The entire cabin was covered with carvings. We sat down there and read some of the letters and numbers cut into the wood: CKH 4/23/61, SONNY '86, HARTMANN 1923.

The oldest one we could find was: ANSELM WAIL 1903. Old letters cut into old, dark wood. And then the view and the warm summer air and the scent of hay wafting up from the valleys below.

Tschick pulled out a pocketknife and started carving. As we talked and basked in the sun and watched Tschick carve, I kept thinking about the fact that in a hundred years we'd all be dead. Like Anselm Wail was dead. His family was all dead too. His parents were dead, his children were dead, everyone who ever knew him was dead. And if he ever made anything or built anything or left anything behind, it was probably dead as well — destroyed, blown away by two world wars — and the only thing left of Anselm Wail was his name carved in a piece of wood. Why had he carved it there? Maybe he'd been on a road trip, like us. Maybe he'd stolen a car or a carriage or a horse or whatever they had back then and rode around having fun. But whatever it was, it would never again be of interest to anyone because there was nothing left of his fun, of his life, of anything. The only people who would ever know anything at all about Anselm Wail were the people who climbed this mountain. And the same thing would be true of us. Suddenly I wished Tschick had carved our full names in the wood. Though it took him almost an hour just for the six letters and two numbers he did carve. He did a nice job, and when he was finished it said: AT MK IS '10.

"Everyone'll think we were here in 1910," said Isa. "Or 1810."

"I think it looks nice," I said.

"I like it too," said Tschick.

"And if some joker comes and carves a few letters in between it will say ATOMKRISE '10," said Isa. "The famous atomic crisis of 2010."

"Oh, shut up," said Tschick, but I thought it was pretty funny.

The fact that our initials were there with all the others — alongside initials carved by dead people — really did my head in.

"I don't know how you guys feel," I said, "but all the people here, the dates — I mean, death." I scratched my head and didn't know what to say. "I guess what I'm trying to say is that I think it's cool that we're here. I want you to know that I'm happy to be here with you. And that we're friends. But you never know how long — I mean, I don't know how long Facebook will exist, but I'd still like to know what becomes of you fifty years from now."

"Google us," said Isa.

"You can Google Isa Schmidt?" said Tschick. "Aren't there a hundred thousand of them?"

"I was going to suggest something different, actually," I said. "What do you say to meeting here again in fifty years? In this exact spot, in fifty years. On July 17, 2060, at five o'clock in the afternoon. Even if we haven't had any contact in thirty years. Everyone will come here, regardless of whether you're a manager at Bosch or living in Australia or whatever. Let's swear on it and then never mention it again. Or is that stupid?"

No, they didn't think it was stupid. We stood next to the carved initials and swore. And I bet we all thought about whether it was possible that we'd still be alive in fifty years and be back here. And wondered whether we'd be pathetic old people, though I didn't think that was possible. Figured it would probably be difficult for us to get up the mountain at that age. That we'd all have our own stupid cars, that inside we'd still be the same people, and that thoughts of Anselm Wail would still hit me like a ton of bricks, just as they had today.

"Let's do it," said Isa.

Tschick wanted us all to cut our fingers and daub blood on the initials, but Isa said we weren't Winnetou or whatever. So we didn't do it.

As we were walking back down we saw two soldiers below. At the pass, where we'd left the Lada, a couple of tour buses were parked. Isa ran over to one of them. The side of the bus had illegible writing on it, no idea what it said, but Isa went right up and started talking to the driver. Tschick and I watched from the Lada. Then Isa sprinted back and called, "Do you have thirty Euros? I can't pay you back right now, but I will sometime, I swear. My half-sister has money, and she owes me — and I need to go to her place."

I was speechless. Isa grabbed her wooden box out of the back of the car, looked at me and Tschick, cocked her head to one side and said, "I'll never make it there with you guys. Sorry."

She hugged Tschick; then she looked at me for a second, and then she hugged me and kissed me on the mouth. She turned and looked at the tour bus. The driver waved. I pulled thirty Euros out of my pocket and gave them to her silently. Isa hugged me again and ran toward the bus. "I'll get in touch! You'll get the money back!"

I knew I'd never see her again. Or at least not for fifty years.

"You didn't fall in love again, did you?" asked Tschick as he picked me up off the pavement. "Seriously, though, you have the touch with women."

The sun beat down and the asphalt looked like liquid metal as it receded into the distance. We were out of the mountains and were coming up on an intersection where cars were standing still. They looked as if they were quivering in the afternoon heat, like they were underwater. It didn't look like construction. More like an accident. And suddenly we saw a car with a flashing blue light on its roof.

Tschick swerved to the right and turned onto a road through a field lined with tall electrical transmission towers. The road was wide enough that a truck could have driven it, but it was grown over with grass and looked as if it hadn't been used in a long time. The police didn't seem to have noticed us. But we could see the police car for only a few more seconds before the road wound its way into a birch forest. There were birch saplings beneath the bigger birches so you couldn't see more than a few meters in any direction. The only place you could see anything was above, where the sky shone through the tops of the trees and transmission towers were visible now and then. The road kept getting narrower and didn't really give the impression that it was leading anywhere. It finally ended at a lopsided wooden gate hanging awkwardly from its hinges. Beyond the gate were marshy lowlands, and those marshy lowlands looked so different from the rest of the landscape that we looked at each other with the same thought: *Where on Earth are we?* We deliberated for a few minutes, and then I got out and yanked the gate open. Tschick drove through and I shut it again.

Flat mounds of light-colored earth were separated by dark swampy patches that were purplish green. And scattered in the swamps were concrete blocks with metal rods sticking out of them — and each rod had some kind of yellow flag on it. At first there were only a few of the concrete blocks, but the farther we drove, the more of them there were, until the entire landscape consisted of the blocks with yellow flags stuck in them. One every few meters as far as you could see. The Richard Clayderman tape would have been the perfect soundtrack because the view was just so tragic — like a sad tinkling piano. The road was getting swampy too, and Tschick crept along in first gear through soft potholes, the transmission towers always next to us. I was sweating. Four kilometers. Five. The terrain began to change, rising slightly. The row of transmission towers ended and the wires hung down from the last one like hair. Ten meters beyond, the world ended.

You had to have seen it: The landscape just stopped. We got out and stood by the last clump of grass. At our feet the ground had been steeply cut away, dropping at least thirty or forty meters down. And below was a moonscape. The ground was whitish gray and pockmarked with craters so big entire buildings could have fit in them. Off to our left was a bridge that led out over the abyss. Although bridge is probably not the right word. It was more like a trestle made out of wood and steel — like a giant scaffold running dead straight out across the pit to the other side, which was maybe two kilometers away. Maybe more. It was impossible to gauge the distance. You couldn't tell what was on the other side either. Maybe trees and shrubs, but who knew. Behind us the massive swamp, in front of us the void. And even if you listened closely, you heard absolutely nothing. No crickets, not a single blade of grass rustling, no wind, no flies, nothing.

We wracked our brains for a while trying to think what this place could be. Then we walked over to look at the trestle. It was wider than it looked from a distance, and was covered with thick wood planks. There didn't seem to be any other way around the abyss. And since we didn't want to drive back the way we'd come, Tschick went and got the Lada. He rolled a few meters onto the trestle — or bridge, or causeway, or whatever it was — and said, "It'll work."

Still, I didn't like the look of it. I got back in the car, and, even slower than a walking pace, we drove out along the wooden planks. The noise the planks made was so hollow and eerie that I got back out so I could walk ahead of the car. I kept an eye out for broken planks, tested suspicious looking spots with my feet, and looked through the cracks down into the depths. Tschick rolled along a few car lengths behind me. Anyone who had come upon us would have thought we looked like old people, creeping along. On the other hand, this wasn't exactly a street with an express lane.

When we had gotten far enough out that we could barely see the spot where we'd started but still couldn't really see the far side either, we took a break. Tschick grabbed Cokes out of the car and we sat on the edge of the plank road. Or tried to, anyway. The wood was so hot you couldn't sit on it until you stood there and cast a shadow for a while on the spot where you wanted to sit. We stared out at the crater landscape. And once I'd looked at the crater landscape for long enough, I thought about Berlin. It was suddenly difficult to imagine that I had once lived there. I could hardly imagine that I'd gone to school there. And I also couldn't possibly imagine that I would go back again.

On the other side of the abyss were scraggy bushes and some grass and a sort of village. A crumbling road meandered between derelict buildings. The windows were nearly all broken, the roofs caved in. No signs, no cars, no vending machines, nothing. The fences around the gardens had long since fallen apart. Weeds grew from every crack.

We went inside an abandoned farmhouse and looked through the rooms. Moldy wooden shelves leaned against one wall. In a kitchen, an empty jam jar and a plate. A newspaper from 1995 on the floor with a report on strip mining. Once we were sure there were no people in the entire area, we went through a few more houses. But we didn't find anything interesting. Old clothes hangers, worn out rubber boots, a couple of tables and chairs. I had expected at least one skeleton. Though we didn't venture down into the dark basements.

We drove on through the town. The windows of one two-story ruin had been covered with plywood, and someone had painted symbols and numbers in white paint on the wood. There were white symbols and numbers painted all over the place — on rocks to the left and right of the road, on fence posts. And then in the middle of the road a huge pile of scrap wood and planks. There were car tracks going around it, and as Tschick approached it warily, shifting down to first gear, we heard an incredible blast. Then a creaking sound. We looked at each other. The Lada was standing still now, and then came another blast that sounded like someone had taken a sledge-hammer to the car's body panels. Or had thrown a big rock at it. Or shot at it. Tschick turned his head, and then we realized the entire back window was cracked in a spiderweb pattern.

I sprang out of the car. I don't know why, but I jumped into some grass behind the car. And I don't remember the next few seconds. What I do know — because Tschick told me after-ward — is that he threw the car into reverse and shouted at me to get in. But I had crawled alongside the car and was waving both of my arms above the hood. I was also carefully peeking at the ruin on the opposite side of the road, scanning the bombed out windows until I saw just what I expected: In one of the window frames was somebody holding a rifle aimed at us. I looked at the muzzle for a second, but then he raised the barrel and put down the gun. It was an old man.

He was standing on the second floor of the house with white writing on it. He was shaking, but not, as far as I could tell, the same way I was shaking. In his case it looked to be old age making him shake. He put a hand up to shield his eyes against the blinding sun as I continued to wave like an idiot.

"What are you doing? Get in!" Tschick yelled. But I had stood up and started walking — still waving my arms and showing my hands — toward the building.

"We don't want anything! We just got lost. We're leaving!" I called to the old man.

He nodded. He picked up the rifle by the barrel, shook it in the air, and shouted, "No timetable! No map and no timetable!"

I stayed there in the yard in front of his house and tried to express with my body language how right he was.

"Never go into the field without a map!" he yelled. "Come on in. I have sodas. Come on in."

Obviously that was the last thing I wanted. To go in there. But he insisted. And in the end it wasn't a very difficult decision. He could easily still shoot us. It was tough getting around all the wood, but the old man didn't seem to be too crazy. I mean, at least he spoke like a normal person.

His living room — if you could call it that — wasn't in much better condition than the rooms we'd searched in other houses. You could tell it was occupied, but it was incredibly dark and dirty. A bunch of black-and-white photos hung on one wall.

We had to sit on a sofa and the old man, now apparently in a festive mood, brought a half-full bottle of Fanta orange soda. "Drink," he said. "Go ahead and drink out of the bottle."

He sat across from us in a comfy chair and started sipping some kind of moonshine out of an old jam jar. The rifle was between his knees. I had figured he'd ask us about the Lada first off, or ask where we were trying to get to. But it turned out he wasn't itching to know any of that stuff. As soon as he heard we were from Berlin, he was most interested in whether the city had really changed as much as they said, and whether you could walk on the street without being attacked. After we told him about ten times that violence was unheard of in our school, he suddenly asked, "Do you have sweethearts?"

I was going to say no, but Tschick answered more quickly.

"His is named Tatiana, and I'm crazy about Angelina," he said. I realized why he said it right away, but the answer didn't seem to satisfy the old man.

"Because you are two very handsome boys," he said.

"No, no," said Tschick.

"At your age, you don't know in a lot of cases which way you might lean."

"Nah," said Tschick, shaking his head. I shook my head too, sort of the way a Lionel Messi fan would shake his head if you asked him if he didn't really think Cristiano Ronaldo was the greatest soccer player of all time.

"So you guys are in love with these girls, yeah?"

We said yes. It made me kind of queasy the way he kept dancing around the topic. He just kept talking about girls and love and the fact that the most beautiful thing in the world was the alabaster body of adolescence.

"Believe me," he said. "One day you close your eyes and the next you open them to find withered flesh hanging in tatters. Love, love! Carpe diem."

He got up, took two steps over to the wall, and pointed at one of the many little photos. Tschick shot me a worried look, but I got up immediately, put on my best overly respectful smile, and examined the photo his wrinkled finger was hovering near. It was a passport photo, and in one corner you could see a quarter of a stamp and a quarter of a swastika. The photo was of a handsome young man in uniform with a slightly sullen look on his face. Apparently the old man himself. As I was looking at the picture, his wrinkled finger wandered over to indicate the next photo to the right.

"And that's Elsa. She was my sweetheart."

The picture showed a sharp-featured face, and at first glance I couldn't tell if it was a boy or a girl. But "Elsa" was wearing a different uniform from the soldier or Hitler Youth member next to her. So it might have been a girl.

He asked whether he should tell the story of his relationship with Elsa, and since he'd picked up the rifle again — without thinking, as if it was just an extension of his body or a part of his history — we could hardly say no. So we listened to his story.

It wasn't a proper story. At least it wasn't told the way people normally tell a story about the love of their life.

"I was a communist," he said. "Elsa and I were communists. Devoted communists. And not just after 1945 like all the rest of them. We'd always been communists. That's how we met — in a resistance group named after Ernst Roehm. Nobody would believe it all now, but that was a different time. And I had no equal when it came to marksmanship. Elsa was the only girl in the group, very reputable, from a good family, and she looked like a boy. She had translated lots of forbidden literature. She had translated that Jew Shakespeare. She'd translated Ravage. She could speak English exceptionally well, and not many people could back then. And I typed it up for her on a typewriter — yeah, that's how it was back then. Love of my life, fire of my loins. In the concentration camp they gassed Elsa right away. I was conscripted into a penal battalion and sent with my rifle to the Battle of Kursk. I could pick off an Ivan from four hundred meters."

"A what?" asked Tschick.

"An Ivan. A goddamn Russian," said the old man, pausing to think. He didn't look at me or Tschick, and Tschick and I were able to exchange a quick glance. Tschick didn't seem particularly uneasy, and I wasn't anymore either.

"I thought . . ." I said. "Weren't the Russians also some kind of communists?"

"Yes."

He thought silently again. "And I could hit one in the eye from four hundred meters. Horst Fricke, the best sharpshooter in his unit. I had more oak leaf clusters on my chest than an entire damn forest. I picked them off like clay pigeons. They were crazy. Or rather, the commanders were crazy. They drove the hordes at us. Private Sinning cleaned things up at the front with a machine gun, and Fricke was the rear guard. Sometimes it was Fricke alone versus Ivan. And they were armed too. Think about that before you ask such stupid questions. Talking about morals and all that crap. It was me or them! That was the only question. More Ivans every day, youthful flesh tumbling toward us. An ocean of flesh. They had a lot of it. All that living space out east. There were just too many Russians. And behind every line the Cheka, the counterrevolutionary police, shooting anyone who wouldn't run into our barrage of fire. Everyone thinks the Nazis were so bad. But compared to the Russians? Pissants. And that's how they finally overran us. With flesh. They never would have managed it with machines. One Ivan and another Ivan and another Ivan. I had a callus on my trigger finger as big as a grape. Look."

He held up both of his pointer fingers. And sure enough, the one on his right hand had a bulge near the first knuckle. Of course, I had no way of knowing if it really came from shooting Ivan.

"This is all a bunch of crap," said Tschick.

Oddly enough, the man didn't really react to this. He kept talking for a while, though we never did find out what it all had to do with the love of his life.

"There's one thing you need to understand, my doves," he said, finishing up. "Everything is meaningless. Love too. Carpe diem."

Then he pulled a little brown glass bottle out of his pants pocket and handed it to us as if it was the most precious thing on Earth. He made a big fuss about it, but he didn't want to say what was in the bottle. The label was yellowed and the bottle looked as if it had been in his pocket since he fought in the Battle of Kursk. We should open it only in case of an emergency, he said, only if the situation was so dire that we no longer knew what to do. Not before that point. And this stuff would help us. Actually he said *save*. It would save our lives.

We took it with us and walked out to the car. I held the bottle up to the light but couldn't tell what it was. Some viscous liquid and something solid.

Once in the car, Tschick tried without luck to decipher what was left on the label. And when he finally opened it, the car started to reek of rotten eggs and he tossed it out the window.

The road petered out at the edge of town, and we had to go cross-country. The chasm we'd crossed was off to the left somewhere. A long gravel embankment fell away to the right. In between was a forty- or fifty-meter-wide berm — like a small plateau. I turned around and in the distance I saw the village, the two-story house where sharpshooter Fricke lived, and — that a police car was pulled up in front of the house. It was tiny from this distance, barely visible, but it was unmistakable — the cops. The car seemed to be turning. I pointed it out to Tschick and we took off across the dirt. The berm kept getting narrower and the cliff edge kept getting closer. Then we saw the autobahn running below as it snaked around the gravel embankment. I could see a little rest area with two picnic benches, a Dumpster, and an emergency call box. We could probably drive straight onto the autobahn there — if we could find a way down. We were at the end of the damn plateau. I looked frantically out the back window as Tschick aimed the car at the embankment, a forty-five-degree slope covered with gravel and boulders.

"Down?" he yelled. I didn't know how to answer. He hit the brakes one last time, and then we were over the brink and that was it — we were hurtling down the embankment.

We probably could have made it if we had driven straight down. But Tschick tried to go sideways and switch back and there was no stopping the Lada at that point. We started skidding, got hung up on something, and flipped over. We rolled over three, four, five, six — I don't know how many times — and came to rest upside down. I wasn't sure what had happened. What I was sure of, though, was that the passenger door was open, so I tried to climb out. But I couldn't. It took about half an hour before I realized the reason I couldn't get out wasn't because I was injured but because I hadn't unbuckled my seat belt. Then I was finally out and I noticed the following things: a green Dumpster directly in front of me, an overturned Lada with steam coming out of the hood and hissing, and Tschick crawling along the ground on all fours. He hoisted himself up, stumbled for a few steps, and yelled, "Come on!" and started to run.

I didn't run. Where were we going to run? Behind us was the plateau and most likely the cops, in front of us was the autobahn, and beyond the autobahn were fields stretching to the horizon. Not exactly the ideal topography to escape from the law. There were a few trees and bushes around the rest area, and off across the fields was a big white box — probably a factory.

"What's going on?" Tschick yelled. "Are you hurt?"

Was I hurt? No, apparently not. Maybe a few bruises.

"Is something wrong?" he asked, coming back toward me.

I wanted to offer an explanation for why I thought it was such a stupid idea to try to escape on foot. Then there was a rustling of leaves and cracking of branches, and a hippo came through the bushes in front of us. Somewhere in Germany, right on the side of the autobahn, in the middle of a wasteland, a hippo came out of the bushes and rushed at us. It was wearing a blue pantsuit, had a curly blond perm, and was carrying a fire extinguisher in its hand. Four or five rings of fat jiggled around its waist. It had two barrels sticking out of the bottom of the pantsuit, and it stomped across the ground, stopped in front of the overturned Lada, and held up the fire extinguisher.

Nothing was burning.

I looked at Tschick and Tschick looked at me. We looked at the woman. Because that's what it was. A woman, not a hippo. Nobody said a word and I was thinking that a jet of white would shoot out of the fire extinguisher and bury us beneath a mountain of foam.

The woman waited a while for the car to explode in flames so she could put her fire extinguisher to use. But the Lada was just as underwhelming in death as it had been in life. There was only a hissing from the engine compartment. One of the back wheels was still spinning, getting slower and slower, and then it stopped.

"Are you boys okay?" the woman asked, still looking warily at the hood of the car.

Tschick tapped his finger on the fire extinguisher. "Something burning?" he said.

"Oh my God," the woman said lowering the extinguisher. "Did anything happen to you?"

"Nothing," said Tschick.

"You're not hurt?"

I shook my head.

"Where is your father? Or your mother? Who was driving?"

"I was driving," said Tschick.

"You just got the car from . . ."

"It's stolen," said Tschick.

If the doctor who later examined me was right, I was in shock during this time. When you're in shock all the blood rushes to your legs and there's basically no more blood in your head and you can't think straight. At least, that's what the doctor said. He also said it was a reaction from caveman times — when the Neanderthals were wandering through the woods and a mammoth suddenly appeared, they went into shock, and all the blood in their legs allowed them to run away faster. Thinking wasn't so important back then. Sounds odd to me, but that's what the doctor told me. Maybe Tschick had been right to try to run away and maybe I was stupid not to, but hindsight is twenty-twenty. And here was a woman standing in front of us with a fire extinguisher — and she was shocked too. Because even though I was in shock, and Tschick was in shock, this woman was in much worse shape. It would have been enough just to see the car flip down the hill or to have Tschick tell her it was a stolen car. She was shaking really bad. She looked at Tschick, pointed to a trickle of blood running down his chin, and said, "Oh my God." Then the extinguisher fell from her hand and onto Tschick's foot. He immediately fell to the ground, lifting his leg, grabbing it with his hands, and screaming.

"Oh my God!" the woman screamed again, kneeling next to Tschick in the grass.

"Shit," I said. I took a quick look at the ridge above us — still no cops.

"Is it broken?"

"How should I know?" screamed Tschick, rolling around in pain.

So this was the situation: We'd driven hundreds of miles around Germany, ridden over an abyss on a scaffold, been shot at by Horst Fricke, had gone off the end of an embankment and rolled the car a half-dozen times, and come through it all basically unscathed — and then a hippo charged out of the bushes and destroyed Tschick's foot with a fire extinguisher.

We leaned down over his foot but had no idea if it was broken or just bruised. One thing was clear — Tschick couldn't stand on it.

"I'm so sorry!" said the woman. And she really did feel bad, you could tell. She seemed more pained than Tschick, at least judging by their faces. But while my head was still reeling and Tschick was rolling around on the ground moaning, she was the first one to get herself together. She felt Tschick's chin again and then lifted his lower leg in the air. "Ouch," she said as she twisted his ankle this way and that, and Tschick whimpered.

"You need to go to the hospital" was her conclusion.

"Hang on," I wanted to say, but the hippo had already shoved her front hooves under Tschick and lifted him up as easily as if he were a piece of toast.

Tschick screamed, but more out of surprise than pain. She disappeared through the bushes as quickly as she had come. I ran after them.

Beyond the shrubs was a green BMW 5 Series. The woman tossed Tschick into the passenger seat. I got in the back. When she climbed into the driver's seat, the car sunk two feet on her side and Tschick bounced up in his seat. Crazy, I thought, but it turned out I should have saved that word for what happened during the next few minutes.

"We have to hurry!" said the woman gravely, though when she said it presumably she wasn't thinking about fleeing from the police.

I was the only one who kept turning around and noticed that the police car must have managed to find a way down the embankment — because in the far distance the car was fighting its way through the scrub brush at the base of the slope.

"Buckle up," said the woman, stepping on the gas pedal. The BMW was doing a hundred kilometers an hour in two seconds. As she went around bends, I was thrown around the backseat like a paper airplane. Tschick was moaning.

"Put your seat belt on," she repeated.

I clicked my seat belt.

"What about you?" said Tschick to the woman.

Through the back window, I could see the traffic behind us recede. Somewhere in the distance you could hear a police siren, but not for long. And no wonder — we were up to two hundred and fifty kilometers an hour. Neither the woman nor Tschick seemed to have heard the siren. They were still talking about seat belts.

"It's not my car," said the woman. "I need a belt two meters long." She giggled. She spoke in a normal voice, but when she giggled it was squeaky, like the sound a little girl would make while being tickled.

When we came upon any obstacles, the woman honked her horn or flashed her lights. And if that didn't work she just calmly blew past them in the service lane as if she was pulling through the McDonald's drive-in. She'd obviously gotten over her shock.

"It's permitted in an emergency," she said. Then she giggled again. "So you guys were driving that car?"

"We're on vacation," said Tschick.

"And you stole it?"

"Borrowed, actually," said Tschick. "Or stolen. But we were going to take it back. I swear."

The BMW barreled along. The woman didn't respond. What could she have said? We had stolen a car and she had dropped a fire extinguisher on Tschick's foot. Studying her in the rearview mirror, I couldn't tell what kind of look flashed across her face, if any look flashed across her face at all. She certainly didn't seem hysterical.

She passed two tractor-trailers, and then she said, "So you guys are car thieves."

"If you say so," said Tschick.

"I say so."

"What are you?"

"This car belongs to my husband."

"No, I mean, what do you do for a living? And do you know where there's a hospital?"

"The hospital's not far from here. And I'm a speech therapist."

"What does a speech therapist do therapy on?" asked Tschick. "People's language?"

"I teach people to speak."

"Babies or what?"

"No. Children sometimes. But mainly adults."

"You teach adults to talk? Illiterate people or something?" Tschick grimaced, totally focused on the woman. I think he was basically trying to keep his mind off the pain in his foot, but the topic of conversation really did seem to grab him.

As the two of them were talking up front, I spent the whole time looking out the back. I probably missed some parts of the conversation. And like I said, I was in shock. But what I caught was the following:

"Vocal formation," said the woman. "Singers, people who do a lot of public speaking, people who mumble. Most people don't speak properly. You don't speak properly, actually."

"But you can still understand me."

"It's about your voice. You need to project your voice, it needs to resonate. See, your voice comes from here," she said, indicating her throat. Probably without even noticing it, she had let up on the gas a little once they had started talking. We were only going about a hundred and eighty now. I tapped Tschick on the shoulder, but he was deep into the conversation.

"I talk with my mouth."

"Normal speech has nothing to do with being able to project your voice. A good, resonant voice comes from here, from the core. But when you talk it comes from here. It needs to come from here." As she said the last "here," she hit herself twice beneath her breasts, making a sound something like *hee-R-R*.

"From hee-R-R?" said Tschick, hitting himself on the chest the same way.

"You have to think of it like athletics. The whole body is involved. The diaphragm, the abdominal muscles, the pelvis, it takes all of them. Two-thirds comes from the diaphragm versus only one third from the lungs."

Now we were down to a hundred and sixty kilometers an hour. If this kept up, she'd bring the car to a halt with her speech therapy.

"The important thing is to get to the hospital quickly," I said.

"It's okay," said Tschick. "It doesn't hurt so bad anymore."

I buried my head in my hands.

"When you talk from here," said the woman, "you get nothing but a little croaking sound. The air comes out of your throat — *uh, uh*. It has to come from here." She opened her mouth into a big O, held her hands in front of her gut, and lifted them as though she were hoisting an invisible box. She had to let go of the steering wheel to do it. Tschick reached across and steadied the wheel.

"From here," said the woman, calling, "Oooo!"

It scared me. But Tschick was all excited. I tried again to gesture to him, but he didn't understand it. Or he wasn't paying attention. Or maybe the woman's state of mind had infected him. The speedometer said one hundred and forty kilometers an hour. Still no sign of the cops.

"Oooo! Oooo! Oooo!" went the woman.

"Uh! Uh!" went Tschick.

"More in the middle, and move it down," said the woman, stepping on the gas again. "The human body is like a tube of toothpaste — when you squeeze it, something comes out the top. Oooooo! Ooooo!"

"Uh! Uh!" went Tschick.

"Better. Oooooooaaaaaaah!"

"Ooaaah!"

That's seriously how it went — all the way to the hospital.

We catapulted down the off-ramp, made two hard rights, and two minutes later we pulled up in front of a huge white building in the middle of nowhere. No cops in sight.

"An excellent hospital," said the woman.

"I don't have any health insurance," said Tschick.

The woman looked briefly upset. Then she leaned across Tschick and opened the door for him. "Don't worry. I'm the one who hurt you, and I'll pay for it, of course. Or my insurance will. Or whatever. Keep your chin up."

There was a lot of activity in the emergency room. It was Sunday night, and there were at least twenty people waiting around. At the check-in desk, a man wearing stone-washed jeans was puking into a bucket he was held under one arm while holding out his insurance card with the other arm.

"Please wait outside," a nurse said to us.

Tschick and I sat down on two free plastic chairs. After we'd been waiting for a while, the speech therapist went to the vending machines to buy drinks and candy bars. While she was away, we were called. Tschick couldn't stand on his foot, so I went up to the desk to explain the situation.

"And what is his name?"

"André." I said it the French way. "André Langin."

"Address?"

"Fifteen Wald Street, Berlin."

"Insurance?"

"DDK."

"You mean DBK?"

"Yep, that's it." DBK. I'd heard André bragging about it during his physical on health day. How great it was to have such top-notch health coverage. What an asshole. Though of course now I was happy about it too. My voice was cracking a little. Guess I should have done a bit of speech therapy in the car too.

I was mostly nervous about what all they would ask me next. I'd never been to an emergency room before.

"Birth date?"

"Thirteenth of July, 1996." I had no idea when André's birthday was. I was just hoping they wouldn't be able to check it too quickly.

"And what's wrong with him?"

"A fire extinguisher fell on his foot. And he might have hit his head too. It's bleeding. The woman there" — I pointed to the speech therapist, who was walking back toward Tschick with an armful of candy bars — "can confirm everything."

"Don't talk my ear off," said the nurse. She'd had her eye on the man with the bucket the entire time and seemed constantly on the verge of standing. In fact, during the minute I was standing there talking to her, she got out of her chair twice, like she was going to go over there and take away the bucket, but she sat back down both times.

"The doctor will call you."

The doctor will call us. It was that easy.

The speech therapist was somewhat surprised I'd taken care of the health insurance issue. She looked at me with her head cocked to the side.

"I just gave them my name," I said.

She sat with us, waiting for us to be called. We told her she didn't have to, but I think she felt guilty. For hours, she talked to us about speech therapy, video games, movies, girls, and car thieves. She was really nice. When we told her about trying to write our names in the wheat field with the Lada, she giggled the whole time. And when we told her we were probably going to take the train back home to Berlin when we got out of the hospital, she believed us.

They kept rushing people with blood streaming down them through the emergency room waiting area. And when it was almost midnight and they still hadn't called us, the woman finally said good-bye. She must have asked us a thousand times if there was anything else she could do for us. She gave us her address in case we needed it to get reimbursed for the medical bills, and gave us two hundred Euros to pay for the train tickets. I was a little embarrassed, but I wasn't sure how to turn it down. And then she said something weird when she was leaving. She looked at us, after having done everything anyone in her position could possibly do, and said, "You two look like potatoes." Then she walked away. She pushed her way through the revolving door and was gone. I found it unbelievably funny. To this day, I still laugh every time I think of it: You two look like potatoes. I don't know if anyone will understand it, but she really was the nicest of all.

Tschick finally got to see the doctor. A minute later he came back out. We had to go upstairs for an X-ray. I was getting more and more tired. At some point I dozed off on a bench in the hall, and when I woke up, Tschick was standing in front of me on crutches. His foot was in a cast. A real plaster cast, not some plastic splint.

A nurse put a few painkillers in his hand and told us we had to wait because the doctor needed to look at his foot again. I wondered who had put the cast on if it wasn't the doctor. The janitor? The nurse took us to an empty room where we could wait. There were two freshly made beds in the room.

The mood was no longer a happy one. Our trip was over. Even if nobody except us knew about it. We were pretty miserable. I had no desire to go anywhere on the train. Tschick's pills took a while to work. He lay in bed moaning. I went to the window and peered out. It was still dark out, but when I pressed my nose against the glass and put a hand on each side of my face, I could make out the coming dawn. I saw a hint of light and . . .

I told Tschick to turn off the light. He used one of his crutches as a remote control. The landscape became much more visible. I saw one lonely phone booth along the hospital driveway. I saw a sole concrete block. I saw a desolate fence, and a field. Some open land. Something about this area seemed familiar. As it got lighter, I could make out three vehicles on the other side of the strip. Two cars and a giant tow truck with a crane on it.

"You are not going to believe what I'm looking at."

"What is it?"

"I'm not sure."

"What is it?"

"Have a look."

"I'm not looking at shit," said Tschick. And then, after a pause, "What is it?"

"Seriously, you really have to see it for yourself."

He groaned. I heard him fiddle with the crutches. Then he pressed his face to the glass next to mine.

"It can't be," he said.

"I know," I said.

We stared out over the plowed field we had seen a few hours before from the other side. There'd been a white box on the horizon then. We were in that white box now. The speech therapist had driven in a big loop.

The sun had yet to break over the horizon, but you could already see the black Lada in the rest area next to the autobahn. It was upright now, resting on its wheels. They must have turned it back over. The trunk was open and three men were walking around the car, standing next to it, walking around it some more. One was in uniform, two in the overalls typical of sanitation workers. At least that's what it looked like from a distance. The crane on the tow truck was being maneuvered over the Lada, and somebody was putting chains around the wheels. The uniformed man closed the trunk, opened it again, then shut it again. Then he went over to the cab of the tow truck. Then two people went back over to the Lada. Then one went over to the truck again.

"What are they doing?" asked Tschick.

"Can't you see?"

"No, I mean, what are they *doing*?"

He was right. They were just walking back and forth doing this or that, doing the same things over and over again, but really doing nothing. Maybe they were looking for clues or something. We watched for a while longer, then Tschick lay back down in bed, moaning, and said, "Wake me up if anything happens."

But nothing happened. One of the men tested the chains, one went back over to the tow truck, one smoked.

Suddenly the view disappeared because the light went on in our room. The doctor was standing in the doorway, breathing loudly. In one of his nostrils was a blood-soaked cotton ball hanging down to his upper lip. He slowly shuffled over to Tschick's bed.

"Lift up your leg," he said. He had a voice like a war-movie general.

Tschick hoisted the cast. With one hand the doctor jiggled the cast, while with the other he held the wadding in his nose. He grabbed an X-ray out of a folder and held it up to the light. Then he threw it onto the bed next to Tschick and shuffled back out. He turned around in the doorway and said, "Contusion, hairline fracture, fourteen days." Then he rolled his eyes. Then, like he was steadying himself, he leaned against the door frame. He took a deep breath and said, "It's no big deal. Fourteen days off your foot. Consult your own doctor once you're home." He looked at Tschick, gauging whether he'd understood him, and Tschick nodded.

The doctor closed the door behind him as he left. But two seconds later he threw it open again, now seemingly wide awake. "A joke!" he said, smiling first at Tschick, then at me. "What's the difference between a doctor and an architect?"

We didn't know. So he gave the answer. "A doctor buries his mistakes."

"Huh?" said Tschick.

The doctor swatted the air with his hand. "If you get tired, there's coffee in the nurse's station. You can help yourselves. Good ol' caffeine."

He closed the door again. I had no time to wonder why the doctor was so weird because I went straight to the window. Tschick shut off the light with one of his crutches, and I just caught sight of the police driving off on the autobahn. The tow truck was already gone. The Lada was all by itself in the parking lot of the rest area. Tschick didn't believe me.

"Did the tow truck break down or something?"

"No clue."

"Well, it's now or never."

"What?"

"What do you mean, *what*?" He hit a crutch against the window.

"There's no way it'll still drive," I said.

"Why not? And if it won't, who cares. We at least need to get our stuff out of it. Even if it can't be driven . . ."

"There's no way you can still drive it."

"Still drive what?" asked a nurse, switching on the light. She had Tschick's — or rather André's — file in one hand and two cups of coffee on a tray in the other.

"Your name is André Langin," I whispered while rubbing my eyes like I was blinded by the light. Tschick said something about how we needed to get home. And unfortunately, that was exactly the reason the nurse wanted to talk to us.

CHAPTER FORTY

Berlin was pretty far away, she said — where were we headed now? I told her we were staying in the area with an aunt and that it was all no problem. I shouldn't have said that. The nurse didn't ask where the aunt lived, but she took me to the nurse's station and put a phone in my hand. Tschick suppressed his pain, staggered out on his crutches, and said that we could go by foot. The nurse said, "Go ahead and try her first. Or don't you know the number?"

"Of course I do," I said. I saw a phone book on the table and didn't want that shoved into my hands next. So I dialed a random number hoping nobody would answer. Four in the morning.

I heard it ring. The nurse probably heard it too, since she was standing right there next to us. The smart thing would have been to call my own house, because it was a sure bet that nobody would answer there. But to do that I would have had to dial the Berlin area code first, and the nurse already looked suspicious enough as it was. It rang once, twice, three times, four. I was getting ready to hang up and say our aunt must still be asleep and that we could just walk . . .

"Errm, uh, Reiber residence," said a man's voice.

"Oh, hi, Aunt Mona!"

"This is the Reiber residence," said the man sleepily. "No aunt. No Mona."

"Did I wake you?" I asked. "Of course, stupid question. Here's the deal." I gestured to the nurse that everything was taken care of so she could get back to work if she needed to.

Apparently there was no work to be done, because she stayed as still as a statue.

"You must have the wrong number," I heard the voice say. "This is Mr. Reiber."

"Yeah, I know. I hope you didn't . . . yeah, oh yes," I said, signaling to Tschick and the nurse how surprised and worried Aunt Mona was to get a call from us at this hour.

The silence on the line now was almost as annoying as the throat-clearing and coughing had been.

"Yeah, no, well, something happened," I continued. "André had a little accident. Something fell on his foot. No, no. We're at the hospital. They put a cast on him."

I looked at the nurse. She still didn't budge.

There were some unintelligible noises from the other end of the line, and then the voice was there again. He didn't sound so sleepy anymore. "I get it," said the man. "We're having a pretend conversation."

"Yes," I said. "But it's no big deal. It's not too serious — just a hairline fracture or whatever."

"And I am Aunt Mona."

"No — I mean, yes, yes, exactly."

"There's somebody next to you, listening." The man made a noise of some sort. I wasn't sure, but I thought he might be quietly laughing.

"Yep, yeah . . ."

"And if I shout really loud right now, you'd have a major problem on your hands, right?"

"Please, no, uh . . . no. You really don't need to worry. Everything's all taken care of."

"It's not taken care of," said the nurse. "She needs to pick you up."

"Do you need help?" asked the man.

"What?"

The nurse looked as if she was going to grab the phone from me any second to speak to Aunt Mona herself.

"You have to pick us up, Aunt Mona. Can you? Yes?"

"I don't really understand what this is about," said the man on the phone, "but it sounds like you're in real trouble. Is someone threatening you?"

"No."

"I mean, a broken ankle, making a fake call at four in the morning, and you sound like you can't be a day over thirteen. You must be in trouble."

"Well, yeah."

"And obviously you can't say what it is. So one more time: Do you need help?"

"No."

"Are you sure? This is the last time I'm going to offer."

"No."

"Okay, I'll just listen, then," said the man.

"In any event, if you could maybe pick us up in the car," I said, sounding embarrassed.

"Not if you don't want me to," the man said, chuckling. And that threw me off. If he had hung up or yelled at me, I would have understood that at four in the morning. But the fact that he was amused and offered to help us, that was crazy. Ever since I was a little boy my father had told me that the world was a bad place. The world is bad and people are bad. Don't trust anyone, don't talk to strangers, all of that. My parents drilled that into me, my teachers drilled that into me, even TV drilled that into me. When you watched the local news — people were bad. When you saw primetime investigative shows — people were bad. And maybe it was true, maybe ninety-nine percent of people were bad. But the strange thing was that on this trip, Tschick and I had run into almost only people from the one percent who weren't bad. And now here I was, getting a random stranger out of bed at four A.M., for no good reason, and he was super nice and even willing to help us. Maybe they should tell you about things like that in school too, just so you're not totally surprised by it. I was so surprised that all I could do was kind of stutter.

"Yeah, twenty minutes, great, yeah. You'll pick us up. Good." For the grand finale of my performance, I turned to the nurse and asked, "What's the name of this hospital again?"

"Wrong question!" hissed the man immediately.

The nurse furrowed her brow. My God, was I an idiot.

"Virchow Hospital," she said slowly. "It's the only one within *fifty* kilometers."

"Exactly," said the man.

"Ah, she just said the same thing," I said, pointing to the phone.

"So you're also not from around here," said the man. "You must have really gotten yourselves into some shit. I hope I can read about it in the paper tomorrow."

"Yeah, me too," I said. "Definitely. We'll be waiting."

"Okay, good luck," said the man.

"Thanks!"

The man laughed again and hung up.

"Was she *laughing*?" said the nurse.

"This isn't the first time we've made her worry," said Tschick, who had only gotten half of the conversation. "She's been through this before."

"And she thinks it's funny?"

"She's *cool*," said Tschick, emphasizing the word "cool" in a way that said not everyone in the room was cool.

We stood by the phone for a few minutes; then the nurse said, "You're a couple of rascals."

Then she let us leave.

We sat down in front of the hospital entrance and acted as if we were keeping an eye out for Aunt Mona. Once we were sure nobody was watching us anymore, we took off. I ran and Tschick hobbled. There was a fence at the edge of the field. Tschick threw his crutches over and then threw himself over. A few yards into the field he got stuck. The field was freshly plowed and the crutches sank into the dirt like a hot knife in butter. It wasn't going to work. He started swearing, left the crutches sticking up, and hopped along with one arm around my shoulders. When we had made it across about a third of the field, we turned around. The landscape was blue. Light from the sun, which was still hidden behind the hospital building, shone through the mist and the tops of trees. The crutches, still sticking up, though one had drooped to the side, looked like a cross. In one of the windows of the upper story of the hospital building — maybe even the same window we'd looked out and seen the Lada — there was a shape in white scrubs looking out at us. Probably the nurse thinking about what a couple of nutjobs she'd just taken care of. If she had realized how crazy we really were, she probably wouldn't have been standing there, just watching.

205

But she must have seen where we were heading, and she probably also saw us arrive at the car. The roof and the passenger side were dinged up, but not so badly that you couldn't sit comfortably inside. The passenger door couldn't be opened, but you could slide across from the driver's side. The interior looked like a dump. The accident, being flipped over, and then being flipped back up, had sent everything flying all over the place — all our supplies, jam jars, gas canister, empty bottles, sleeping bags. The Richard Clayderman cassette was stuck between the seats. The hood of the car was slightly buckled, and the part of the roof where the car had been lying upside down was smeared with sand-covered oil. "That's it," I said.

Tschick squeezed himself into the driver's seat but couldn't get his plaster-covered foot onto the gas pedal — the cast was too wide. He put the car in neutral, squirmed in the seat a little, and tapped the gas with his left foot. The engine fired right up. Tschick shifted into the passenger seat. I said, "You must have lost your mind."

"All you have to do is push the gas and steer," he said. "I'll shift."

I sat down at the wheel and told Tschick it wasn't going to work. There was half a tank of gas, and the motor was idling smoothly, but when I looked at the autobahn and saw the cars going by at two hundred kilometers an hour, I knew it wasn't going to work.

"I have to tell you a secret," I said. "I'm the biggest coward in the world. The most boring person on the planet and the biggest coward. We'll have to walk. Maybe I could give it a try on a dirt track or something. But not on the autobahn."

"Why would you possibly say you were boring?" asked Tschick. So I asked him if he realized why I had even agreed to go with him to Wallachia in the first place. Namely, because I was boring — so boring, in fact, that I didn't get invited to a party that everyone else got invited to. So I had decided for once in my life *not* to be boring. Tschick said I was nuts and that he hadn't been bored for a single second since he had gotten to know me. That on the contrary this had been the coolest and most exciting week of his entire life. Then we talked about the coolest and most exciting week of our lives — and it was hard to accept that it was now over.

Tschick looked at me for a long time and said it wasn't true that Tatiana didn't invite me because I was boring, and it wasn't true that she didn't like me for that reason either.

"Girls don't like you because they're afraid of you. That's what I think. Because you don't pay them attention and because you're not a kiss-ass like André Langin. You're not boring, you idiot. Isa liked you right away. Because she's not as stupid as she looks. She actually has a brain — unlike Tatiana."

I looked at Tschick. I think my jaw must have been hanging open.

"Yeah, yeah, you're in love with Tatiana. And she's good looking, for sure. But seriously, compared to Isa she's a total moron. And I'm a good judge of that, unlike you. Because — can I tell you a secret?" Tschick gulped, and looked as if he had a cannonball stuck in his throat. He was silent for at least five minutes. Then he said he could judge them because he wasn't interested in them. Girls. Then he was silent again for a while. He had never told anyone, he said, and now he had told me, but I didn't need to worry about it. He wasn't looking for anything from me, he knew I was into girls and all that, but that he just wasn't that way and there was nothing he could do about it.

You can think what you want about me, but I wasn't that surprised. I really wasn't. I didn't know it for a fact, but I guess I had a feeling. Really. When he talked about his uncle in Moscow the very first time we were in the car, the whole thing about my jacket, the way he treated Isa. I mean, obviously I didn't know for sure. But in retrospect it seems as if I had some idea.

Tschick rested his head on the dashboard. I put a hand on his back. We sat there and listened to "Ballade pour Adeline," and I thought for a few minutes about what it would be like to be gay. It could really have been the solution to all my problems. But it wasn't going to work. I mean, I really liked Tschick, but I knew I liked girls. Then I put the Lada into first gear and started to move. It had been so sad sitting in the hospital all night thinking about the fact that the trip was over. And it was so fantastic to be looking out the windshield again with the steering wheel in my hand. I practiced a little in the parking lot. I was still having trouble shifting, but when Tschick took over that duty, leaving me just to push the clutch, it was okay. So we accelerated onto the on-ramp. Then I pulled into the emergency lane and stopped.

"Take it easy," said Tschick. "Easy does it. Let's try it again."

We waited for another gap in traffic. And by that I mean we waited until there wasn't another car in sight. Then I stepped on it again and accelerated.

"Shift!" shouted Tschick, and I stepped on the clutch pedal as he put it into second gear.

I was sweating like crazy.

"It's all clear, merge!" Tschick put it into third gear and then fourth, and I slowly relaxed.

I flinched again when the first fat Audi zoomed by doing five hundred kilometers an hour or whatever, but after a while I got used to it and realized driving on the autobahn was actually easier than on smaller roads where you're constantly braking and shifting and accelerating. Here I had a lane to myself and just had to go straight. I watched the lane markers racing toward me like in a video game — but it looked totally different in the driver's seat of a real car. There's just no way to imitate it with PlayStation graphics. Sweat was still streaming down me, and my back clung to the seat. Tschick stuck a piece of black duct tape on my upper lip, and then we drove and drove.

Clayderman tinkled the ivories, and between him tinkling, the partially collapsed roof of the car, Tschick's messed-up foot, and the fact that we were doing a hundred in a rolling Dumpster, I was overcome with a strange feeling. It was a feeling of bliss, a feeling of invincibility. No accident, no authority, no law of nature could stop us. We were on the road and we would always be on the road. And we sang along to the music, at least as best as you can sing along to tinkling instrumental music.

CHAPTER
FORTY-TWO

We drove until it started to get dark, then turned off the autobahn onto a country road somewhere deep in the middle of
nowhere. I drove in third gear, winding along between the fields.
Everything was quiet. The evening was quiet and the fields were
yellow and green and brown, and the color was seeping from the
landscape as the light faded. Tschick had his arm out the window and his head on his arm. I had my arm out the window too,
the way you do in a boat when you dip your fingers in the water.
I felt tree leaves and plant stalks graze my hand as my other
hand guided the Lada through the darkened landscape.

The last beams of light disappeared from the horizon. It
was a moonless night, and I remembered the first time I saw
what nighttime looked like, or at least the first time I realized
what nighttime was. I was eight or nine and I have Herr Klever
to thank. He lived in the apartment block across the street. We
lived in an apartment block too, and at the end of the street
was a big field of barley. I used to play with a girl named Maria
in that barley field in the evening. We would crawl through the
grain on all fours, making paths, creating a giant maze. And
one night Herr Klever, an old man, showed up with his wiener
dog and a flashlight. He lived on the third floor and was always

shouting at us. He hated kids. He trudged around with his dog, shining his flashlight into the field and shouting that we were ruining the crops. He shouted that we had to come out immediately and that he was going to call the police and have us arrested and that we would have to pay a thousand Euro fine. We were eight or nine, like I said, and didn't know this was just the typical stupid crap old people say. In a panic we ran out of the field. Maria was smart and ran toward our apartment block. But I went the other way first, and the old man was there with his dog blocking the way. He stood his ground, fiddled with his flashlight, and kept shouting. So I ran in the opposite direction, back into the field.

I ran through the field and into Hogenkamp Road because I thought I might be able to go all the way back around. I knew the way from having done it during the day. But now the Hogenkamp was dark and seemed to be hemmed in by scrub brush. Just beyond was Hogenkamp playground — we never went there because there were older kids there. But at night, of course, it was empty. The giant zip line wasn't being used. It was a funny feeling. I could have had the whole place to myself, could have done whatever I wanted, but I didn't stop — I just kept running and running. There wasn't a single person any-where around. Lights were on in front of little houses, and I kept running down another street, where there was also not a soul. It was a huge detour, making an arc out around the field of several miles. But back then I could run like a champ. And after a while I actually liked it — running through this dark, empty world. I wasn't even sure if I was still scared, and I stopped thinking about Herr Klever.

Obviously I'd been out at night other times, earlier in my

life. But it hadn't been the same. That had always been with my parents or in a car on the way home from a relative's house or whatever. This was a whole new world, a completely different world than it was during the day. It felt as if I'd just discovered America. I didn't see a single person the entire way. Then suddenly I saw two women. They were sitting on the steps in front of a Chinese restaurant, and I couldn't figure out what they were doing there. One of them was crying and shouting, "I'm not going in there! I'm not going in there again!" The other one was trying to calm her down, but to no effect. Above them, Chinese characters in yellow and red lit up the night. There were dark trees around the building. And in the foreground, an eight-year-old was jogging past. I was annoyed. The women were probably annoyed too, and also wondering what the heck an eight-year-old was doing out running at night. We looked at each other, them crying and me running. I have no idea why that made such a strong impression on me. I guess I'd never seen grown women crying before, and I thought about it a lot afterward. Anyway, this was a night like that.

I leaned my head to the side and looked out the window as the Lada quietly took the curves of the road through the blue-green grain fields of summer. At some point I said I wanted to stop, and I stopped. The countryside was dark, and we stood and looked out over a field where in the distance you could see the black shape of a farm. I was about to say something when off to our left a light went on in the window of another farmhouse. I didn't say anything after all. Then Tschick put his arm around my shoulders and said, "We've got to get going."

We got back in the car and drove on.

The next day we were back on the autobahn. A huge tractor-trailer passed us. It looked as if it was made out of pig stalls. A couple of wheels, a rusty cab, and license plates from Albania or something. It was only with a second glance that I saw that what looked like pig stalls actually were pig stalls. The cages were stacked next to each other and on top of each other, and out of every one peeked a pig.

"What a shit life," said Tschick.

The road slanted slightly uphill in this section, and it took the truck ages to pass us. When we could finally see its rear wheels, it started to drop back again. After a minute, the cab reappeared next to us. Somebody rolled down the window of the passenger door.

"Did he see you?" asked Tschick. "Or is he looking at the dents on our roof?"

I let up on the gas pedal to make it easier for him to get by us. The truck put its blinker on, swerved into our lane, and then started going slower.

"What the hell kind of idiot is this guy?" said Tschick.

We slowed way down.

"Pass him."

I went into the left lane. The truck swerved back into the left lane in front of us.

"Pass him on the right, then."

I steered back into the right lane. The truck got in the middle, straddling the two lanes, and to this day I don't know if he was trying to slow us down or if he was just a moron. Tschick said I should wait for another car to come along and then follow it past the truck. But no other cars came along. The autobahn was completely empty.

"Should I use the emergency lane?"

"Maybe if we can get a running start," said Tschick. "If you think you can do it. You'll have to shift."

We fell back, I stepped on the clutch, and Tschick put it in third. The engine whined.

"Now step on it — it'll take off like a rocket."

Rocket turned out not to be the best description. More like the shifting of a sand dune. We had fallen about a hundred and fifty or two hundred meters behind the truck, and even with the pedal to the metal it took about a minute before we got back up behind it. And the tachometer was quivering in the red by then. I pulled up right behind the truck so I'd be invisible to the driver. He was swerving back and forth, and I wasn't sure which side to pass him on.

"Swerve with him," said Tschick. "Then at the last second, zip by!"

I still had my foot all the way down on the gas pedal. I should point out that I wasn't nervous at that moment. I'd swerved like this a million times in video games. It came more naturally than driving straight. And the pig transporter was just the sort of obstacle you had to go around in driving games.

I pulled right up behind the truck so I could shoot around it in the emergency lane. And that's exactly what I would have done if Tschick hadn't been there. If Tschick hadn't been there, I wouldn't have survived.

"HIT THE BRAKES!" he screamed. "BRAAAAAKE!"

My foot stepped on the brake pedal even before I heard and understood his scream. My foot braked automatically because I was used to doing what he said to do when I was driving. So he shouted "brakes" and I braked — without knowing why. Because as far as I could tell there was no reason to brake.

There was space between the truck and the guardrail for at least five cars, and it would have been ages before I had realized that the truck hadn't made way but rather had *skidded* out of the way. The rear end of the trailer had slid sideways, and even though we were right behind the trailer I suddenly saw the cab directly in front of me in the middle of the road — and I saw the trailer overtaking the cab. The eighteen-wheeler was transforming itself into a barrier — and that barrier was skidding in front of us, across the entire width of the autobahn, as we skidded toward it. The scene was so strange that later I had the feeling it had taken several minutes to unfold. In reality, it didn't even last long enough for Tschick to scream "brake" a third time.

The Lada turned sideways. The barrier in front of us drifted backward, tipped over with a crash, and left us faced with eighteen rotating wheels. Thirty meters in front of us. In absolute silence we glided into those wheels, and I thought, *Okay, we're going to die.* I thought I would never get back to Berlin, I would never see Tatiana again, and I would never know whether she liked my drawing or not. I thought I needed to apologize to my parents and I thought, *Crap, I forgot to save the game.*

The other thing I thought was that I should tell Tschick that I'd nearly decided to become gay because of him. I was going to die sometime, so it might as well be now, I thought as we finally slid into the truck — and nothing happened. In my memory I didn't even hear a crash. Though there must have been an incredible crash. Because we rammed straight into the truck.

CHAPTER FORTY-FOUR

I didn't feel a thing for a minute. The first sensation I had was the feeling that I couldn't breathe. The seat belt was cutting me in half and my head was practically on the gas pedal. Tschick's cast was also somewhere near my head. I sat up. Or at least I turned my head. Above the cracked windshield was a truck tire obscuring the sky. It was turning silently. There was a dirty lightning bolt sticker on the hub of the wheel — a red bolt on a yellow background. A fist-sized clump of gunk dangled from the axle, slowly detached itself, and then splattered on the windshield.

"So much for that," said Tschick. He had survived.

Thunderous applause broke out. It sounded like a huge crowd was shouting, whistling, hooting, and stomping their feet, and it didn't seem completely unjustified — for an amateur driver, my braking performance had been top notch. At least that was my opinion, and it didn't surprise me that others thought so as well. It's just that there was actually no crowd there.

"Are you okay?" asked Tschick, shaking my arm.

"Yeah. You?"

The passenger side of the car next to Tschick had been crushed inward about a foot, but very evenly. There were shards of glass everywhere.

"I think I cut myself." He held up a bloody hand. The audience was still roaring and whistling, but those sounds were mixed with grunts now.

I extricated myself from the seat belt and fell onto my side. The car was apparently lying at an odd angle — I had to climb out the side window. I immediately fell over something in the street. I tried to get up but fell over again and landed in a pool of bloody sludge. A dead pig. A few yards behind us a red Opel had come to a stop. Inside the car were a man and a woman, both pushing down the door locks. I sat down on the hood of their car and grabbed the radio antenna. I wasn't able to stand anymore, and the antenna felt good in my hand. I never wanted to let go of it. For the rest of my life. "Are you okay?" Tschick called again when he had climbed out of the Lada.

At that moment, a screeching pig came running around the end of the overturned trailer. And then a bunch more. The lead pig ran, bleeding, across the autobahn and into some bushes. Some of the others ran after it, but most of them just stood there surrounded by dead pigs and battered stalls and screeched hysterically. Then I saw the police on the horizon. At first I wanted to run, but I knew there was no point. And the final two images that I can remember are of Tschick hobbling off into the bushes with his cast, and of the trooper standing next to me with a friendly look on his face, taking my hand off that antenna and saying, "It'll be okay without you."

I've already told you the rest.

"He doesn't understand."

My father turned to my mother and said, "He just doesn't understand. He's too stupid."

I was sitting on a chair and he was on another one facing me. He was bent over so far that his face was directly in front of mine and his knees were pressing against mine. I could smell his aftershave with every single word he shouted. Aramis. A gift from my mother for his hundred and seventieth birthday.

"You really screwed up. Is that clear?"

I didn't answer. What would I say? Of course it was clear. And he wasn't saying it for the first time. More like the hundredth time that day. I had no idea what he wanted to hear from me.

I looked at my mother. My mother coughed.

"I think he gets it," she said. She stirred her Amaretto with a straw.

My father grabbed me by the shoulders and shook me. "Do you understand what I'm saying? Kindly say something!"

"What do you want me to say? I've already said yes. Yes, I understand. Yes, it's clear."

"You don't understand a thing! Nothing is clear to you. He thinks this is just about saying the words. What an idiot!"

"I'm not an idiot just because for the hundredth time . . ."

Bam. He smacked my face.

"Josef, don't." My mother tried to stand up but lost her balance and let herself sink back into the armchair next to the bottle of Amaretto.

My father got right in my face. He was shaking with rage. Then he crossed his arms on his chest and I tried to put on a face creased with worry — because my father probably expected that, and because I knew his arms were only crossed because he was about to smack me again. Up to that point I had just said what I thought. I didn't want to lie. This face was the first lie that I trotted out — to speed things along.

"I know that we screwed up big-time, and I know . . ."

My father started to move his arms and I flinched. But this time he just yelled: "No, no, no! It's not *we* who screwed up, you idiot. It's your piece of trash Russian friend who screwed up. And you're so stupid that you let yourself get dragged into it. You're too stupid even to adjust a rearview mirror!"

My face showed my annoyance, because I'd already told him a thousand times what really happened — even if he didn't want to hear it.

"Do you think you're an island? Don't you realize this is going to fall on us? How do you think this makes me look? How can I sell somebody a house when my son might steal their car?"

"You aren't selling any houses anymore anyway. Your company is . . ."

Bam. The sound of his hand hitting my face made a crack. I fell to the floor. Moron. In school we were always told that violence is never the answer. My ass. When you get a smack in the face, you know damn well it's an answer.

My mother screamed, I got up, my father looked at my mother and then away again, and then he said, "Sure, sure, it doesn't matter anyway. Sit down. I said sit down, you idiot. You listen to me and you listen good. You've got a good chance of getting away with just a slap on the wrist. I know that from Schuback. Unless you act as idiotically as you are right now and you tell the judge how great you are at hotwiring cars with this and that wire and all that crap. They love doing that in the juvenile justice system — they bring charges against somebody so they will testify against others. And obviously that's what they plan to do to you too, except that you're too goddamn stupid. But you can be sure of one thing: Your Russian friend is not as stupid as you. He knows how it works. He's already got a criminal past — robbing stores with his brother, fraud, fencing stolen goods. Yeah, I see the look on your face. That's how those types of people operate. Of course he didn't tell you about it. He also doesn't have a nice home like this to show the court. He's living in a hole right now. In some closet-sized shit-hole. Where he belongs. He'll be lucky if he gets to stay in a juvenile detention center. Schuback says they could also deport him. And tomorrow he'll pay any price to save his own skin — do you understand? He already gave his statement and he put all the blame on you. It always works that way — every idiot tries to blame the others."

"And that's what I'm supposed to do too?"

"You're not just *supposed* to do it, you *will* do it. Because they'll believe you. Do you understand? Lucky for you the agent from Child Welfare was impressed with our place. How the house looked. You should have seen him looking at the pool. He said it straight out — that this was the right sort of house to raise a child in, with all the bells and whistles." My father turned to my mother and my mother stared into her glass. "You were dragged into it by that low-class Russian bastard. And that is exactly what you will tell the judge — regardless of what you told the police. Got it? Got it?"

"I'll tell the judge what happened," I said. "He's not stupid."

My father stared at me for approximately four seconds. That was the end. I saw a flash in his eyes; then I didn't see anything for a while. The blows struck me everywhere, and I fell off my chair and squirmed around on the floor with my forearms in front of my face. I heard my mother scream and fall over and shout "Josef!" By the end I was lying on the floor in such a way that between my arms I could see out the window to the backyard. I still felt the kicks, but they were coming more slowly. My back hurt. I saw the blue sky above the garden and sniffled. I saw the sides of the umbrella swaying in the wind above the lounge chair. Next to the chair was a brown man fishing leaves out of the pool with a dip net. They'd rehired the Indian.

"Oh, God, oh, God," said my mother, coughing.

I spent the rest of the day in bed. I lay on my side and toyed with the blinds, swinging in the afternoon sun above me. The blinds were ancient. I'd had them since I was three. We'd moved five times and still they'd always been there. That occurred to me for the first time as I played with them. I could hear my parents' voices outside in the backyard. Now they were giving an earful to the Indian. He must have missed a waterlogged leaf in the pool. It was my father's big day of yelling. Later I heard birds in the yard and the sun began to set. It got peaceful.

I lay there as it got darker and darker, stared at the blinds, and wondered how long things would be like this. How long could I lie here, how long we'd live in this house, how long my parents would still be married.

And I looked forward to seeing Tschick again. That was the only thing I looked forward to. I hadn't seen him since the accident on the autobahn, and that was four weeks ago now. I knew they'd taken him to a juvenile detention center. But it was a place where you weren't allowed to have any outside contact — you couldn't even get a letter.

CHAPTER FORTY-SIX

Then came the court proceedings. I was dying from nervousness. The rooms alone were terrifying. Giant staircases, columns, statues on the wall like in a church. You also can't tell from watching courtroom TV shows that you have to wait around for hours and hours in a place that feels like a funeral home. I felt like I was waiting for my own funeral as I sat there. And I also thought to myself that I would never so much as steal a pack of gum again.

When I entered the courtroom, the judge was sitting behind his desk and pointed to the place I was supposed to sit down — at a table, kind of like at school. The judge was wearing a black poncho, and there was a woman sitting next to him who seemed to be surfing the Internet the whole time. At least that's what it looked like. She typed now and then, but she didn't look up from the computer for all the hours we were in the courtroom. Off to the left was another guy in a black poncho. That turned out to be the prosecutor. The black clothes were apparently an integral part of court cases. Out in the halls of the courthouse there were more people running around in black outfits, and the whole thing made me think of the white scrubs and lab coats of the hospital — and of nurse Hanna —

and I was glad at least that you couldn't see people's underwear through the black outfits.

Tschick wasn't there yet, but he came in about a minute later, escorted by someone from the juvenile detention center. We hugged each other and nobody tried to stop us. But we didn't have much time to chat. The judge got started right away. I had to say my name and address and all that, and then Tschick had to do the same. Then the judge basically repeated all the questions the police had already asked us. Not sure why, since he already knew our answers from the court documents. And as far as the facts of the case, there was no dispute. I told more or less the truth, the same as I did when the police asked me the questions. I mean, I left out a few tiny details — like the fact that we had used André Langin's name at the hospital. But that kind of stuff was okay to sweep under the rug — nobody cared about it. The main thing the judge wanted to know was *when* we first took the car, *where* we went with it, and *why* we did it. That last part was the only difficult question: Why? The police had kept asking us the same question, and now the judge, too, wanted to know. But I didn't know how to answer. Luckily he offered us potential answers — were we just trying to have fun? Fun. Well, yeah, fun, that seemed to me the most probable explanation even if I wouldn't have put it exactly that way. I couldn't really say what I was hoping to find in Wallachia. I had no idea. And I wasn't sure whether the judge would be interested in the whole Tatiana Cosic story. That I'd made a drawing for her and that I was afraid I might be the most boring person on Earth, and that for once in my life I didn't want to act like a coward. So I just said that his fun theory was right.

It also occurs to me that I lied about something else. It had to do with the speech therapist. I didn't want her to get into any trouble because of us, since she'd been so incredibly nice. So I just never mentioned her and the fire extinguisher. I said the same thing I'd told the police — that Tschick had broken his foot when the Lada flipped over coming down the embankment next to the autobahn, and that we had walked across the field to the hospital. Not a word about the speech therapist.

An okay lie, really. But even when I said it to the cops, it occurred to me that I'd probably get caught for it. Because Tschick would probably make up some other explanation when they asked him. And they would ask him. But oddly enough, the truth never came out because Tschick had exactly the same thought I did — he didn't want to drag the speech therapist into it either. And as it emerged in court that day, he had used the same explanation I had — that he'd broken his foot when the car went over the embankment and we'd limped through the field to the hospital. It never occurred to anybody that our story defied logic. Because when you end up in the middle of nowhere, in a place you've never been before, and you get into an accident, and all you can see are fields all around you and, in the distance, a white building with a couple of trees in front of it, how in the world would you know it was a hospital?

Anyway, like I said, the judge was more interested in other things.

"What I'd like to know is which of you initially had the idea to take this trip?" He addressed the question to me.

"The Russian of course!" came a voice from the gallery. My father, the idiot.

"The question is addressed to the accused," said the judge. "If I wanted your opinion, I would ask you."

"*We* had the idea," I said. "Both of us."

"No way," piped Tschick.

"We just wanted to drive around a little," I said. "Take a vacation, like normal people . . ."

"Not true," Tschick interjected.

"It's not your turn," said the judge. "Wait until I get to you."

The judge was strict. The only person allowed to speak was the one he spoke to. And when he got to Tschick, Tschick immediately said that it was his idea to go to Wallachia and that he'd had to practically drag me into the car. He explained that he knew how to drive and how to hotwire cars, and that I was so clueless I didn't know the gas pedal from the brake. He was talking complete nonsense, and I told the judge it was nonsense. And the judge said it wasn't my turn anymore, and I could hear my father groaning in the background.

After we had talked for long enough about the car, we came to the worst part — people talking *about* us. The man from the juvenile detention center testified about Tschick's background, talking about him as if he wasn't even there, basically saying his family was nothing more than trash — even if he didn't use that word. Then the guy from Child Welfare talked about his visit to my house, about what a filthy rich family I came from, how I was left unsupervised and neglected, and in the end he characterized my family as a kind of trash too. And when the verdict was read, I was surprised I wasn't given life in prison. Tschick had to stay in the detention center where he was already being held. And as for me, I was issued a directive to do community service. Seriously, that's what the judge said. Fortunately he explained what that meant — and in this case it meant I had to spend thirty hours wiping old people's asses. And then the whole thing finished up with an interminable lecture on morality, though what he said was actually okay. Not the kind of stuff my father says, or what you hear in school — it was more stuff that made you see things in terms of life and death, and I actually found myself listening closely to the judge because he didn't seem like a complete moron. On the contrary. He seemed pretty sensible. And his name was Burgmuller in case anyone is interested.

So that was the summer. And then it was time for school to start again. Instead of 8C, 9C was now posted on the door of the classroom. Nothing else had changed. Same seating chart. Everyone in the same spots as the previous year, except in the back row, where there was an empty seat. No Tschick.

First class on the first day of school: Mr. Wagenbach. I was a minute late, but for some reason I didn't get chewed out. I was still limping a little, and still had a few cuts on my face here and there. Wagenbach lifted one eyebrow and wrote the word "Bismarck" on the blackboard.

"Your classmate Tschichatschow will not be in class today," he said as an aside, but either he didn't know the reason for his absence or he didn't say. I don't think he knew the reason.

I was a little sad when I saw the empty seat, and sadder still when I glanced over at Tatiana, who was sitting there all tan, with a pencil in her mouth. She was listening to Wagenbach, and it was impossible to say if she was the proud owner of a pencil sketch of Beyoncé or if she had just crumpled it up and tossed it in the garbage. She looked so hot that morning that I had difficulty not constantly looking over at her. But with an iron will I kept myself from doing that.

I was trying to muster a little interest in Bismarck when Hans put a note on my thigh. I held it in my fist for a minute because Wagenbach was looking in my direction. Then I looked at it to see who I needed to pass it on to. But it said Mike. I couldn't remember getting a single note the previous school year. Except for the kind that everyone got — the ones that said stuff like *Don't look up, there are footprints on the ceiling* or other elementary school crap like that.

I waited another minute and then unfolded it and read. I read it five times straight. It wasn't such a complicated note — in fact, there were just ten words — but I still had to read it five times to understand it. It said: *My God, what in the world happened to you?!? Tatiana.*

I just couldn't get the last word through my head. I didn't look around.

The chance that somebody was trying to make an ass of me was relatively high. It was a common trick in the past — to send a fake note saying something like *I love you* or whatever. But you could usually tell who had really sent it because the person was trying to secretly watch you.

I looked in the direction the note had come from — which was also where Tatiana sat. Nobody seemed to be watching me. I read the note a sixth time. It was Tatiana's handwriting. I knew it well. The *A* with the rounded top, the curlicue of the *G*. I could imitate it perfectly. And of course if I could, so could everyone else. But just suppose — suppose — that it really was from her? Suppose the girl who didn't invite me to her party really wanted to know what had happened to me?

Wow. How should I answer? Assuming I did answer, that is. Because, after all, a lot had happened, and it would take hundreds of pages to explain it all. Though I would love to have done just that — written hundreds of pages. How we'd driven around, how we'd flipped the car, how Horst Fricke had shot at us. The moonscape we discovered, the whole debacle with the pigs, and a thousand other things. And how I'd dreamed that Tatiana was seeing it all. But I was pretty sure she didn't really want to know all the details. That the note was more out of politeness. I thought for a little while longer, and then I gathered myself and wrote, *Ah, nothing special*, and sent the note back.

I didn't look at Tatiana as she read it, but thirty seconds later it was back. This time there were only nine words. *Come on, tell me! I really want to know.*

She really wanted to know. I needed an eternity for my response. Despite the fact that again it wasn't very detailed. Of course, I secretly wanted to write my novel-length version for her. But there's not too much space on a piece of scrap paper. I put a lot of thought into it. Class was almost over when I wrote Tatiana's name on the outside again and handed it back to Hans. Hans passed it to Jasmin. Jasmin let it sit next to her for a while like she didn't care about it. Then she flipped it to Anja. Anja tossed it across the aisle onto Olaf's desk, and Olaf, who was as dumb as a box of rocks, was handing the note over André's shoulder just as Wagenbach turned around.

"Oh!" said Wagenbach, picking up the note. André made no effort to keep it from him.

"Top secret dispatches!" Wagenbach said, holding it up. The class laughed. They were laughing because they knew what was coming next, and I knew too. I wished I had Horst Fricke's rifle in that instant.

Wagenbach got out his reading glasses and read aloud: "Mike — Tatiana. Tatiana — Mike." He looked up first at Tatiana and then at me.

"I value your active participation in class. But if you had questions about the details of Bismarck's foreign policy, you should have just asked," he said. "There's no need to write your questions on tiny slips of paper in the hope that I accidentally find them."

This wasn't the first time he'd made this joke. He made it every time. But the class didn't care. They loved the whole charade.

There was no hope that he would stop there. There were teachers who just tore up notes, teachers who threw them in the trash or tucked them into their pockets, and then there was Wagenbach. Wagenbach was an asshole. He was the only teacher in the whole school who would read an entire text-message history when he confiscated a cell phone. It didn't matter if you begged or cried, Wagenbach read *the whole thing* aloud.

He unfolded the note solemnly, and I hoped for a miracle — like a meteorite falling from the sky and squishing Wagenbach. Or at least the bell ringing for the end of class. That would have done the trick. But of course the bell didn't ring, and of course no meteorite fell from the sky. Wagenbach's gaze swept over the class and he straightened his posture. I think he would have loved to have been an actor or cabaret performer. But he only managed to become an asshole. I mean, if only it had just been a normal old note about the usual crap. But this note contained the first meaningful words I'd ever exchanged with Tatiana — and perhaps the last — and Wagenbach had no right to read them aloud for all the world to hear.

"So, Miss Cosic writes" — and here Wagenbach paused and nodded his chin at Tatiana as if we didn't know who she was — "the budding literary talent Miss Cosic writes: *My God!*" He said these words in a high-pitched squeak.

"My God," Wagenbach squeaked, *"what in the world happened to you?"*

"Jackass," I said, but it went unheard as everyone yucked it up. Tatiana stared at her desk. Her gaze never shifted. Wagenbach turned to me.

"And what did Mr. Klingenberg answer?"

He put his chin to his chest and spoke in a voice like a stupid cartoon bear. *"Ah, nothing special."*

The class was howling. Even Olaf, who had screwed the whole thing up, was laughing now. I could hardly stand it.

"What polished repartee," said Wagenbach. "But will the intellectually curious Miss Cosic be satisfied with this answer? Or will she crave more?"

Squeaking again: *"Come on, tell me! I really want to know."*

Stupid cartoon bear: *"Well, it was like this."*

Behind his glasses, Wagenbach squinted his eyes. He could hardly believe what he was about to read. Tatiana raised her head a little because she didn't know my answer yet either. I stared out the window and wondered what Tschick would do in this situation. Probably put a completely blank look on his face. He was better at that than I was.

Wagenbach was getting into his cartoon bear act so much that he must not have even realized what he was reading.

"Tschick and I drove around with the Lada. We were planning to drive to Wallachia, but then we flipped the car after somebody shot at us." Wagenbach paused and then continued in a normal voice. *"Then there was a police chase, a trip to the hospital. Then I crashed into an eighteen-wheeler full of pigs and my leg got all cut up . . . but anyway, no big deal."*

A few people were still laughing. Especially the three people who hadn't been at Tatiana's party. The ones who had seen me and Tschick in the Lada were more or less silent.

"Well, what do you know," said Wagenbach. "Mr. Klingenberg, the magician! Accidents, chases, gunfights. What, no murder? I guess you can't have it all."

He obviously didn't believe a word of what he had read. I guess it didn't sound very believable. And I wasn't too hot to enlighten him.

"The thing I like best about Mr. Klingenberg's exciting life isn't the cops and robbers material or that he included a chase involving — if I'm not mistaken — an *automobile* and Mr. Tschichatschow. No, no, my favorite part of this is the artful language. How concise and descriptive! How does he wrap up the whole escapade again?" He looked at me, then at the class, and then said, *"No big deal."*

Wagenbach brandished the note in front of Jennifer and Luisa, who were unlucky enough to be sitting in the front row.

"No big deal!" he repeated, starting to laugh. He probably hadn't had so much fun in a long time. Someone who was not enjoying herself at all was Tatiana. You could see it on her face. And not just because she had written me the note. She had probably figured out that my story was no made-up tall tale.

Up to this point, Wagenbach had just had fun at our expense. What we still had to look forward to was the humiliation portion of the program. The sermon. The idiotic shouting. Everyone knew it was coming, everyone was waiting for it. And when Wagenbach held up his hand, signaling for everyone to quiet down — for some reason there was no shouting, no sermon, no punishment. Instead, a meteorite really did fall from the sky. There was a knock at the door.

"Yes!" said Wagenbach.

Voormann, the principal, opened the door.

"Sorry to have to interrupt," he said. He scanned the room with a serious look on his face. "Are the students Klingenberg and Tschichatschow here?"

"Just Klingenberg," said Wagenbach.

Everyone had turned to the door, and Voormann was standing in the door frame. But you could see two uniformed officers behind him in the hall. Broad-shouldered cops in full gear, with handcuffs and pistols and all.

"Then Mr. Klingenberg needs to come with me," said Voormann.

I stood up as casually as I could — as casually as you can when your legs are shaking — and gave Wagenbach a last look. His stupid grin was gone. He actually looked a bit like a dim-witted cartoon bear, though if this were really a cartoon they would have to give him crosses for eyes and a squiggly line for a mouth now. I felt awesome despite the wobbly knees. And the shaking stopped as soon as I was outside facing the police officers.

Voormann apparently didn't know what to say. Both police-men had blank looks on their faces. One was chewing gum.

"Do you want to speak to him alone?" asked Voormann. The one chewing gum looked with surprise at Voormann, stopped chewing for a second, and shrugged. As if to say, "We don't care."

"Do you want a room where you won't be disturbed?" said Voormann.

"It won't take long," said policeman number two. "It's not a summons. We just stopped by."

Silence. Blinking. I scratched my head.

"I was in the middle of a call," Voormann finally said, tentatively. And as he walked off, "I hope everything gets cleared up."

Then it began. Number one asked, "Mike Klingenberg?"

"Yeah."

"45 Nauen Street?"

"Yeah."

"You know Andrej Tschichatschow?"

"Yes, he's a friend of mine."

"Where is he?"

"In Bleyen — the facility there."

"The juvenile detention center?"

"Yeah."

"I told you," said number two.

"How long has he been there?" asked number one, looking at me.

"Since the trial — actually before the trial."

"Have you had contact with him?"

"Has something happened to him?"

"The question was, have you had contact with him?"

"No."

"I thought he was your friend?"

"Yes."

"So?"

What on earth were they getting at? "It's a facility where you're not allowed to have any outside contact for several weeks. You're cut off from the world. You guys should know better than me."

Number one was chewing with his mouth open. This was a great relief after dealing with Wagenbach.

"What's happened?" I asked.

"A Lada," said number two. He let it sink in. A Lada. "A Lada disappeared from Annen Street."

"Kersting Street," I said.

"What?"

"We took it from Kersting Street."

"Annen Street," said the cop. "Day before yesterday. Old pile of junk. Hotwired. Found again last night near the end of one of the subway lines. Totaled."

"Yesterday," said number one. He chomped down on his gum twice. "Found it yesterday. Stolen the day before."

"So you're not talking about our Lada?"

"What do you mean by *our* Lada?"

"You know what I mean."

The gum smacked in his mouth. "We're talking about the one from Annen Street."

"What do I have to do with it?"

"That is the question."

And that's when it dawned on me that Tschick and I would be on the hook for every damn car hotwired in northeastern Berlin for the next hundred years.

But I couldn't have been the one who stole the car on Annen Street because I'd spent the day looking after old people and the evening at soccer practice. It also wasn't hard to convince the cops that Tschick couldn't have done it from a secure facility. Oddly enough, it seemed as if they had already sensed we had nothing to do with it. Especially number two, who kept saying they just wanted to spare themselves the trouble of a summons by popping by. They weren't even taking notes. I was almost disappointed. Because right at that moment, the bell rang and the door to our classroom opened. Thirty sets of eyes, including the cartoon bear's, peeked out, and it would have been somehow cooler if they'd been choking me with a nightstick. Mike Klingenberg, dangerous criminal. But unfortunately the two cops just wanted to say good-bye and be on their way.

"Shall I walk you to your car?" I asked.

Number two exploded immediately. "You trying to

show off in front of your schoolmates? You want us to cuff you too?"

That grown-up thing again. They see through you so quickly. I figured it was cooler not to try to deny it. But there was nothing more to do. I didn't want to be too pushy. After all, they'd already done plenty for me.

CHAPTER FORTY·NINE

One day, a while later, I had to go to the principal's office to pick up a letter. An actual letter. I think in my whole life I'd gotten maybe three letters. One I'd written to myself as part of an elementary school project — we were supposed to learn about the post office or whatever. And the other two were from my grandmother before she had an Internet connection. The principal had the letter in his hand, and I could see that there was a funny sketch of a car with two stick figures in it and beams surrounding the car as if it were the sun. Under that was written:

Mike Klingenburg
Student at Hagecius Junior High School
Ninth grade (approximately)
Berlin

It was a wonder it ever reached me. But since my name was actually spelled Klingenberg and there was a Mike Klinger in fifth grade, the principal wanted to know if I knew the sender of the letter.

"Andrej Tschichatschow," I said, because the only person who could have sent it was Tschick — he must have figured out a way to get it out of the detention center despite the no-contact rule. I was really excited.

"Anselm," said the principal.

"Anselm," I said. I didn't know anyone by that name. The principal dropped his head in dismay, but after a minute I said, "Anselm Wail?"

He handed me the letter.

Crazy. Anselm Wail, high up on the mountain. I ripped it open immediately to see who had sent it. But I was too excited to read it, so I put it back in the envelope and pulled it out again an hour later when I got home.

Because of course it was from Isa. I was so excited to read it. As excited as I was when I thought it was from Tschick. I lay on my bed the entire afternoon with it, thinking about whether I was more in love with Tatiana or Isa. I wasn't sure. Seriously, I didn't know.

Hi, idiot. Did you make it to Wallachia? I'm betting you didn't. I visited my half-sister and can give you the money back now. I punched a truck driver and lost my wooden box. I had fun with you guys. It's a shame that we didn't hook up. My favorite part was eating blackberries. Next week I'm coming to Berlin. If you don't want to wait fifty years, let's meet Sunday the 29th at 5 P.M. in front of the big clock on Alexanderplatz. Kisses, Isa

I heard noises downstairs. There was a scream, a crash, and a rumble. I didn't pay attention for a long time because I figured my parents were just fighting again. I rolled onto my back and stared at the letter. Then it occurred to me that my father wasn't around because he was out looking at an apartment with Mona.

I heard more crashing and looked out the window. Nobody was in the backyard, but there was a chair floating upside down in the pool. Something else — something smaller — splashed into the water next to the chair and sank. Looked like a cell phone. I went downstairs.

My mother was standing in the frame of the backdoor hiccupping. In one hand she had a potted plant — holding it like she was choking it — and in the other hand she had a glass of whiskey.

"It's been like this for an hour," she said with despair. "The fucking hiccups won't go away."

She stood on her tiptoes and threw the plant into the pool.

"What are you doing?" I asked.

"What does it look like?" she said. "I'm not attached to this crap. And besides, I must have been out of my mind — look at the pattern on this fabric."

She held up a red-and-green-checkered throw pillow and tossed it over her shoulder into the pool.

"Remember one thing in life! Have I ever talked to you about fundamental questions? And I'm not talking about the shit with the car. I mean really fundamental questions."

I shrugged.

She gestured around the room. "None of this matters. One thing that does matter: Are you happy? That. And that alone." She paused. "Are you in love?"

I thought about it for a second.

"That's a yes," said my mother. "Forget about all that other crap."

She had looked pissed off the whole time. And she still looked pissed off, but now she also looked a little surprised. "So you're in love? And does the girl — does she love you?"

I shook my head — for Tatiana. And shrugged — for Isa.

My mother got very serious, poured herself a fresh glass of whiskey, and threw the empty bottle into the pool. Then she hugged me. She pulled the cables out of the DVD player and tossed that into the pool. Then went the remote control and the big potted fuchsia. A huge splash went up when the fuchsia landed and dark clouds of dirt bubbled up as red flower petals floated on the choppy surface.

"Ah, isn't it lovely," said my mother, beginning to cry. Then she asked me if I wanted a drink. I said I'd rather throw something into the pool.

"Help me." She went over to the sofa. We carried it over to the side of the pool and threw it in. It flipped over and its feet bobbed just below water level. Then my mother pushed the round table onto its side and rolled it in a big half circle across the terrace. It finally fell into the back of the pool. Next she took apart a lamp, put the shade on her head, and tossed the base into the pool like a shot-putter. Then the TV, CD racks, and coffee tables.

My mother had just popped a bottle of champagne across the terrace and put the spraying bottle up to her lips when the first policeman came around the corner of the house into the backyard. He tensed, then relaxed when my mother removed the lampshade and greeted him with a bow, holding out the lampshade like a feather cap. She could barely stand upright. I stood by the side of the pool holding the comfy chair that matched the sofa.

"The neighbors called," said the police officer.

"Those snooping Stasi assholes," my mother said, putting the lampshade back on her head.

"Do you live here?" asked the policeman.

"Sure do," said my mother. "And you, sir, are on our property." She went into the living room and came back out with an oil painting.

While the cop was saying something about the neighbors, disturbing the peace, and suspicion of vandalism, my mother held the painting above her head with both hands like a hang glider and sailed into the pool. She did it well. And she looked cool doing it. She came across like somebody whose favorite thing in the world was hang gliding into pools using paintings. I'm pretty sure the cops would happily have hang glided in after her if they hadn't been on duty. I let myself fall into the pool with the comfy chair. The water was lukewarm. I felt my mother reaching for my hand as I sank. Together with the chair, we sank to the bottom and then looked up from there at the iridescent, glittering surface of the water, with furniture and other dark shapes floating in it. I know exactly what went through my mind right then, as I held my breath and looked up. I thought that everybody at school was probably going to start calling me Psycho again. And that I didn't care if they did. I thought that there were worse things than having an alcoholic mother. I thought that it wouldn't be long now until I was allowed to visit Tschick at the detention center. And I thought of Isa's letter. And of Horst Fricke and his carpe diem.

I thought of the storm over the wheat field, of nurse Hanna, and the smell of gray linoleum. I thought that I would never have experienced any of it without Tschick, and thought about what a cool summer it had been — the best summer ever. All of that went through my mind as we held our breath and looked through the bubbles and shimmering surface at the two perplexed policemen who were now bending over the pool and talking to each other in a muted, distant language, in another world. And I was insanely happy. Because you can't hold your breath forever, but you can hold it for a pretty long time.

Wolfgang Herrndorf (1965–2013) was born in Hamburg, Germany, and studied painting before turning to writing later in his career. He wrote several award-winning novels for adults, and *Why We Took the Car* received the German Youth Literature Award, Germany's top literary prize.

Tim Mohr is an award-winning translator of such authors as Alina Bronsky, Dorothea Dieckmann, and Charlotte Roche. He has also collaborated on memoirs by musicians Duff McKagan, Gil Scott-Heron, and Paul Stanley. Mohr's own writing has appeared in the *New York Times*, the *Daily Beast*, and the *eXile*, among other publications. Prior to starting his writing career, he made his living as a club DJ in Berlin. He now lives in Brooklyn, New York.

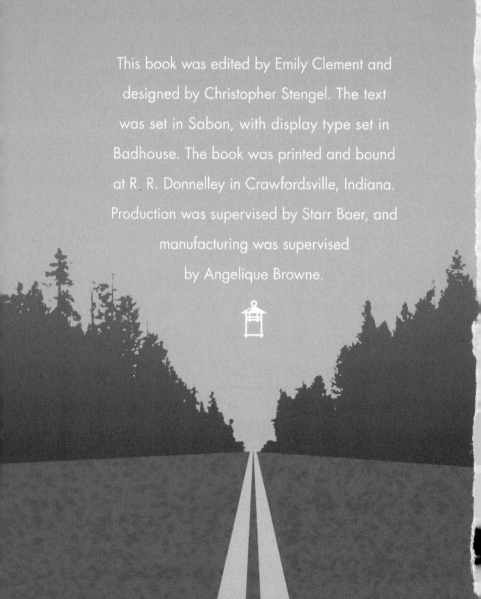

This book was edited by Emily Clement and designed by Christopher Stengel. The text was set in Sabon, with display type set in Badhouse. The book was printed and bound at R. R. Donnelley in Crawfordsville, Indiana. Production was supervised by Starr Baer, and manufacturing was supervised by Angelique Browne.

BLUE NOON

scott westerfeld

MIDNIGHTERS

vol. **3**

BLUE NOON

An Imprint of HarperCollinsPublishers

Acknowledgments

Like all books everywhere, this series has been
shaped and supported by a host of readers,
editors, and friends. Most especially: Liesa Abrams,
Holly Black, Gwenda Bond, Eloise Flood, Claudia
Gabel, Justine Larbalestier, Ursula K. Le Guin, Garth
Nix, Christopher Rowe, John Scalzi, Jonathan
Strahan, Tui Sutherland, Kathleen Thomas, and
Sean Williams, among others.

Eos is an imprint of HarperCollins Publishers.

Blue Noon
Copyright © 2005 by 17th Street Productions, an Alloy company, and
Scott David Westerfeld
Midnighters symbols by Scott David Westerfield

 Produced by Alloy Entertainment
151 West 26th Street, New York, NY 10001

Library of Congress Cataloging-in-Publication Data

Westerfeld, Scott.
  Blue noon / Scott Westerfeld.— 1st ed.
    p.   cm.— (Midnighters ; v. 3)
  Summary: The five midnighters from Bixby discover that the secret hour is start-
ing to invade the daylight world, and if they cannot stop it, the darklings will soon
be free to hunt again.
    ISBN-10: 0-06-051957-6 (trade bdg.) — ISBN-13: 978-0-06-051957-5 (trade bdg.)
    ISBN-10: 0-06-051958-4 (lib. bdg.) — ISBN-13: 978-0-06-051958-2 (lib. bdg.)
  [1. Science fiction.] I. Title.
  PZ7.W5197Blu 2006   2005017597
  [Fic]—dc22

1 2 3 4 5 6 7 8 9 10

First Edition

To John and Jan, and
Niki, for making me
part of the family

1 | 8:20 A.M.

PREDATOR

Bixby High's late bell shrieked in the distance, like something wounded and ready to be cut from the herd.

Rex Greene was always late these days, stumbling in confusion from one class to another, late with his father's pills or forgetting them altogether. But the worst was getting up for school. It didn't help that he'd unplugged his clock a few nights ago, unable to sleep with the soft buzzing sound it made all night, like a mosquito hovering just out of arm's reach. His newly acute hearing had turned every electronic contraption into something whiny and annoying.

But it was more than just the clock's noise; it was what it *meant*, with its false day of twenty-four hours. Since what had happened to him in the desert, Rex had started to feel time as something marked out in the sky—the rise and fall of the sun, the spinning stars, the interlocking ratios of the light moon and the dark.

The rest of the world still had their clocks, though, so Melissa had banged on his window again this morning, dragging him rudely out of his strange new dreams.

"Smells like . . . assembly," she said as they pulled into the school parking lot, her head tipping back a bit, nostrils flaring.

All Rex could smell was crumbling vinyl—the upholstery of Melissa's crappy Ford broken down by thirty-odd Oklahoma summers—and gasoline fumes leaking up through the floorboard from the car's rumbling engine. Humans loved their oil, a flash of darkling memory informed him. They scoured the desert for it, used it to make clever things like plastic and gasoline. . . .

Rex shook his head to clear it. On mornings like these, when he'd dreamed of Stone Age hunts all night, he had more trouble concentrating than usual. The old knowledge inside him seemed more real than his sixteen years of human memories. Sometimes Rex wondered if he would ever recover from what the darklings had done, the half change they'd effected before Jessica had rescued him.

Was he gradually healing from the experience? Or was the darkness they'd left inside him like a virus, slowly growing stronger?

As Melissa maneuvered the Ford into a parking place, Rex spotted a few stragglers making their way into the gymnasium entrance. The sound of an amplified voice echoed out from the propped-open double doors.

"Crap, that's right," Melissa said, gripping the steering wheel tighter. "Pep rally today."

Rex groaned and closed his eyes. He hadn't faced anything like this since the change, and he wasn't looking forward to it. The thought of all those bodies pressed in close around him, chanting together, brought a trickle of nerves into his stomach.

"Don't worry," Melissa said, reaching across to take his hand. "I'll be there."

At her touch, with no more insistence than a cool breeze, a calmness fell across Rex. His stomach stopped roiling, his mind growing still as Melissa's serenity poured into him.

A shudder passed through Rex; her strength became his.

Funny. A month ago it had been Rex who'd had to talk Melissa through the beginning-of-football-season pep rally. Now she was the sane one, and he was . . .

What, exactly?

He didn't know yet, and Rex hated not knowing. There were no halflings in the lore, much less recovering halflings.

Bad dreams last night?

Rex smiled and turned to face Melissa. The words had come through as clear as speech. They could have whole conversations now without her uttering a sound.

Her control was almost perfect, not a leaked thought anywhere, so different from the vomited rush of fear and pain that had struck him when they had first begun to touch each other. Although sometimes Rex missed those early experiments, the terrifying moments when he saw all of Melissa at once.

When his mind was focused, he hardly had to speak himself; Melissa simply pulled the words from him. But this morning he was too much of a wreck.

"Yeah, some bad dreams," Rex said aloud. "But not all of them."

The hunting dreams had been sweet—the cold, patient hunger as he tracked prey for days across the plain, anticipation building as the weakest were cut from the group, and then the burning rush of the kill.

But of course, there'd been those *other* dreams as well, memories of when the clever little monkeys had started hunting back. The beginning of the end.

"Jeez, lighten up," Melissa said, pulling her hand away and rubbing it, as if to wring out the ancient horror she'd felt in his mind. "I think someone forgot to drink his coffee this morning."

"Sorry, Cowgirl. Yeah, I guess I could use a cup. Or six." Rex shook his head again. His brain felt stuffed full, his own thoughts almost crowded out by the memories that the darklings had implanted to make him one of them. "Sometimes I wonder if I'll ever get back to normal."

Melissa snorted. "When were you ever normal, Rex? When were any of us?"

"Well, maybe not normal," Rex admitted. "But I'd settle for human."

She laughed and touched his shoulder, and he felt a spark of her pleasure even through the fabric of his long black coat. "You're totally human, Rex. Trust me on that one."

"Glad you think so," he said, smiling.

Melissa's fingers stayed on his shoulder, drumming out a nervous rhythm, and her glance strayed to the open gymnasium door. Rex realized that however much her control had improved, the thought of enduring a pep rally still made Melissa anxious.

"You'll be okay," he said softly, pulling her closer.

She turned to him, and their lips met.

At first Rex felt serenity in the warmth of their kiss, her new calmness and self-control flowing into him. But then Melissa allowed her composure to slip, and it was like their first time. Everything inside her crashed out in a torrent: the enduring wounds of all those years alone, memories of the constant hammering of other minds, the old fear of being touched. She let it well up and spill over, pouring into him. Rex was overwhelmed for a moment, but then he felt his damaged surety rallying, responding to her need. He twisted in the car seat to take her shoulders, and the kiss built, his strength becoming hers, until he felt Melissa's mastery of herself return.

She sighed as they separated. "I say again, Rex: fully human."

Rex leaned back into his seat, smiling. The heavy dread that he had felt since waking and realizing that it was a school day—and a Monday at that—had lifted from him at last.

Melissa's fingers played across his cheek, and she grinned. "You taste electric now, like you do after a jolt of coffee."

"Hmm. Maybe kissing is sort of like nature's coffee."

"Actually, Rex, *coffee* is nature's coffee. It is a plant, you know."

"Ah, right. Good point, Cowgirl."

He looked at the gymnasium door. A pep rally couldn't be *that* bad, could it? Better than the hated first-period math class it would replace, and he could use the time to cram for his upcoming English test. One thing about carrying ancient memories of an elder species around in your head, it could royally screw up your interpretation of *Catcher in the Rye*.

Rex checked his backpack. No English book. "Listen, I have to go by my locker. Save me a seat?"

"Back row?"

"Of course." He snorted. "I haven't changed that much."

She nodded slowly, then her eyes narrowed. "Should I come with you?"

"Don't worry about me." Rex ran his tongue across his teeth. They never felt as sharp as he expected them to, the canines never as long as they should be. Phantom limbs itched sometimes at night, as if parts of his body were missing.

But Rex took a deep breath and forced those thoughts from his mind. He couldn't complain about every discomfort. He'd been granted something that any seer would die for: a chance to learn more about the darklings than the lore could ever teach, to understand them from the *inside*. Maybe his kidnapping and transformation had been a gift in disguise.

As long as his human half stayed in control . . .

"It's okay, Cowgirl," he said. "I can take care of myself."

The hallway was as unpleasantly bright as always, sunlight spilling through the doors, the fluorescents buzzing over-head in a constant drone.

Rex squinted in the light, reminding himself to buy sun-glasses. That was one advantage since the change: his vision was much sharper. Rex didn't even need his eyeglasses at school anymore. A strange kind of Focus clung to every-thing here: the marks of human passage and invention, a million prey trails piled on top of one another, making everything crystal clear and somehow . . . appetizing.

It was almost too much. Sometimes he wished that school could be blurry and soft again, distanced behind the thick glasses he'd worn since third grade. Everything was so sharp now. It wasn't just the buzzing fluorescents that annoyed him; Rex could feel the fire alarms and public address system behind the walls, those razor-fine wires that clever humans always laced their buildings with. It felt like being in a metal cage with electrified bars.

And human places were so *ugly*. Rex noticed for the first time in his two years at Bixby High that the tiled floors were the exact same yellow hue as his father's nicotine-stained fingers. Whose idea of interior decorating was that?

At least the halls had been emptied by the pep rally.

As he headed for his locker, Rex ran a hand across his scalp, feeling it prickle his palm. When Jessica's white flame had freed him from the darkling body, big patches of his hair had burned away, his gothy haircut totaled. So Rex had cropped it to a half inch all over with the electric clippers that his father had once used to shorten the thick coat of their dog, Magnetosphere, for summer.

Rex's own reflection still brought him to a halt when he passed shop windows, and he found himself touching his scalp all the time, fascinated by the hairs standing up so straight, as hard and even as Astroturf under his palm. Maybe this meant that Melissa was right, that he was still human: even after all the other changes that had racked his body and mind, a new haircut still took some getting used to.

Rex reached his locker, letting his fingers open it by feel. The tricky part was not thinking of the numbers, that cleverest and most dangerous of human inventions. Fortunately, there weren't any multiples of the Aversion in his combination. It was hard enough already when his fingers faltered, and Rex had to start over, forcing his way through the sequence number by number, like some freshman on his first day of school.

When he looked at the locker's dial, he hardly even saw the Aversion anymore—it appeared as a wavering blurry spot between twelve and fourteen, edited out by his mind, like an FBI informant's face on the news.

He was thinking of taking Dess up on her offer to pull apart the lock and hack it, changing the combination to a smooth string of twelves and twenty-fours. She was already doing his math homework these days. Too many combinations awaited on every page that could paralyze the darkling half of his mind, leaving him with a snapped pencil and a pounding headache.

Math was deadly now.

Success on the first try. He heard the tiny click of the last cylinder lining up and pulled the locker open happily. But distracted by his thoughts of numbers, Rex realized too late that someone had crept up behind him. A familiar scent swept through him, setting off old alarm bells, fearful and violent memories suddenly rising up.

A fist struck the locker, slamming it shut again. The sound echoed through the empty hallway as he spun around.

"Hey, Rex. Lost your specs?"

Timmy Hudson. That explained the trickle of fear in Rex's stomach—the boy had beaten him up almost every day back in fifth grade. As strong as any flash of darkling memory, Rex recalled being trapped behind the school one day by Timmy and three friends, punched in the gut so hard that for a week it had hurt to piss. Though it had been years since Timmy had done anything worse to Rex than slam him against the wall, the tightening in Rex's stomach remained as knife-edged as it had ever been.

"Didn't lose them," Rex answered, his own voice weak and plaintive in his ears. "Don't wear glasses anymore."

Timmy grinned and stood closer, the smell of sour milk sharp on his breath. "Contact lenses? Huh. The funny thing is, makes you look like even more of a retard."

Rex didn't answer, struck with the sudden realization that Timmy Hudson was looking *up* at him. At some point he had grown taller than his old nemesis. When had *that* happened?

"You must think you're getting pretty cool these days, huh?" Timmy punctuated the last grunted word with a hard shove, and a combination lock rammed into the small of Rex's back, hard as the barrel of a gun. The feel of it focused his mind, and he felt his lips begin to twitch, pulling away from his teeth. His mouth felt suddenly dry.

Something was moving through Rex, something stronger than him.

He shook his head *no*. He was Rex Greene, a seer, not an animal.

"What's the matter? Too cool to talk to me these days?" Timmy laughed, then squinted up at Rex's scalp. He reached out and ran one hand across its bristly surface.

"And a new 'do?" Timmy shook his head sadly. "You trying to look tough? Like everyone doesn't remember what a little pussy you are?"

Rex found himself staring at Timmy's throat, where the blood pulsed close to the surface. One shallow rip through the frail skin and life would spill out, warm and nourishing.

"Think your little extreme makeover makes you Mr. Cool, don't you?"

Rex found himself smiling at the words. What had happened to him was so much more extreme than anything Timmy could imagine.

"What's so funny?"

"Your weakness." Rex blinked. The words had just popped out of his mouth.

Timmy took half a step back, blank-faced with shock for a moment. He looked one way down the empty hall, then the other, as if checking the reaction of some invisible audience.

"My *what*?" he finally spat.

Rex nodded slowly. He could *smell* it now, he realized, and the scent of weakness had triggered something inside him, something that threatened to spin out of control.

His mind grasped for some way to master himself. He tried to think of the lore symbols, but they had all flown out of his brain. All he had left were words. Maybe if he could keep talking . . .

"You're the kind we cut from the herd."

Timmy's eyebrows went up. "Say what, retard?"

"You're weak and afraid."

"You think I'm afraid, Rex?" The boy tried to put on an amused smile, but only half his face obeyed. The left side seemed frozen, taut and wide-eyed, his fear leaking out into his expression. "Of *you*?"

Rex saw that Timmy's pulse was quickening, his hands shaking.

Weakness.

"I can smell it on you. . . ." The words faded as Rex finally lost control. He watched the rest of what happened like a passenger in his own body. He took a step forward until his face was as close as Timmy had dared come a moment before.

The fear in Rex's stomach had changed into something else, something hot and cruel that surged through his chest and up into his jaw. His teeth parted, lips pulling back so far that he felt them split, baring his teeth and half an inch of gums. His whole body grew as taut as one long trembling muscle, swaying for balance like a snake ready to strike, arms out and fingers locked in rigid claws.

He made a noise then, right in Timmy's face, a horrific sound that Rex had never heard before, much less produced himself. His mouth still open wide, the back of his throat cinched tightly closed, a breath forcing its way out with a long and shuddering *hissssss*—a mix of fingernails on a chalkboard, the shriek of a hawk, and the last rattle of a punctured lung. The noise seemed to coil in the air for a moment, wrapping around Timmy's shuddering frame, squeezing the breath from him.

The hiss lingered in the empty hallway like the echoes of a shout, disappearing into the buzzing of the fluorescent lights.

Timmy didn't move. The twisted half smile stayed on his face, muscles frozen, as if some careless surgeon had snipped a nerve and he was stuck with the half-formed expression for the rest of his life.

"Weakness," Rex said softly, the hiss still ringing in his voice.

His body softened then, whatever demon had slipped

into him departing as swiftly as it had come. His jaw relaxed, and Rex's muscles lost their inhuman rigidity—but Timmy still didn't move. He looked thoroughly frozen, like a rat that had just lost a staring contest with a python.

He didn't make another sound as Rex walked away.

Halfway to the gym, Rex's heart was still pounding with the weirdness of what had just happened. He felt elated, confident, and powerful, finally cleansed of the fear that had stalked him through the halls of Bixby High School every day for the last two years.

But he was also afraid. He'd tried to fend off the darkling part of him, but it had taken control nonetheless.

Still, the experience had left him feeling so *good*—purposeful and somehow more complete. And he hadn't really lost it, had he? The predator had drawn its claws, but it hadn't used them. He hadn't struck for the pulse in Timmy's throat, the easy kill of the straggler.

Maybe the darkling side of him maintained a balance with his human half. Perhaps Rex Greene was still sane.

For now.

2

PEP RALLY

She watched the pep rally with awestruck fascination.

Melissa had been forced to attend dozens of these things before, of course, but she'd never really *seen* one. Battered by the mind noise, huddled in the back with eyes closed and fists clenched, the old Melissa had understood pep rallies about as well as a bird sucked through a jet engine comprehended aircraft design.

But the crowd no longer terrorized her, the horde of other minds no longer threatened to erase her own. Using the memories Madeleine had given her, the generations of technique passed on among mindcasters, she could rise above the tempest, ride its swells like a buoy in a storm.

Finally she could *taste* it all. . . .

The football team strutting in Lycra before the crowd, their testosterone and bluster mixed with a bitter backwash flavor—the growing realization that once again, they were going to lose every game this year. The clique of pretty girls clustered together a few rows down, surrounded by a force field of disdain for all the nobodies around them—unaware of how much the nobodies hated them right back. The bored minds of teachers stationed around the edges of the gym, jonesing for cigarettes and more coffee, quietly relieved that first period had been superseded. The group of freshman boys camped on the first row of bleachers, watching the cheerleaders' skirts fly up, their horny thoughts as sharp as sweat licked off an upper lip.

Melissa found it all hysterically funny. Why hadn't she ever understood this simple fact before? Why hadn't anyone told her? High school wasn't a trial by fire or some ordeal that had to be survived.

It was all a big joke. You just had to provide the laugh track.

Through the crowd noise the minds of the other midnighters reached her, their various flavors coming through loud and clear. The three of them sat together—about as far away from Melissa as they could. In particular, she tasted every cold glance from Dess, who was glowering behind dark glasses, her mind still full of acid hatred for what had happened ten days ago.

Melissa did feel bad about that—no one knew better than she how vile it was having your mind wrenched open against your will. But there hadn't been any choice. If she hadn't gone in and dredged up Dess's secrets, Rex would be a full-fledged darkling now instead of . . .

Well, instead of whatever he had become.

Jonathan and Jessica sat close to each other, their fingers

intertwined, separated from everyone around them by their coupleness. Of course, they would turn and talk to Dess every once in a while, throwing her a bone. Jessica had witnessed what Melissa had done to Dess and felt almost as bad as if she'd done it herself. Her thoughts were often layered with a sickly survivor's guilt: *If only I had stopped Melissa, blah, blah, blah* . . .

Of course, Jessica's indignation wasn't nearly as bad as what lurked in Jonathan's mind. Ever since he'd touched Melissa and felt what it was like to be her, a rancid pity polluted him from head to toe.

Of course, the joke was on him. Because being Melissa *didn't* feel like that anymore.

It felt sweet.

"Sucker," she whispered, and let herself be buoyed again by the chanting crowd.

Loverboy made his way in about fifteen minutes late, slipping easily past the teacher monitoring the door.

Melissa tasted his mind through the chaotic energies of the pep rally. Despite all the confusion he carried now, Rex's thoughts still reached her on their own special channel, even clearer than those of the other midnighters'. She knew instantly that something unexpected had happened to him in the empty hallways of the school. His mind was bright and buzzing, like just after they'd kissed.

But whatever had happened had also unnerved him. Melissa felt him scan the crowd anxiously, relaxing only when he spotted her atop the closest bleachers to the door. He made his way up with soft, effortless steps, as fluid as a cat across a rooftop.

Melissa smiled. Watching Rex show off his new feline grace was one of her great pleasures.

"Get what you wanted?" she asked as he settled beside her.

"Oh, my English book." He shook his head. "Forgot all about it, actually. Had some trouble on the way."

"Yeah, I figured that." She could taste it more clearly now: Underneath his excitement Rex was bubbling with the darkling flavor he sometimes had now—the sour lemon of a young hunter's mind jazzed by the smell of prey. "Hmm. Didn't eat anybody, did you?"

"Not quite. But it was a pretty close thing." He held out his hand, palm up. "Want to see?" His eyes flashed.

"Of course, Loverboy." She smiled and placed her hand over his.

The darkling taste redoubled, shuddering through her acid and electric, like kissing an old car battery that still carried some juice. The surging taste of it blotted out the insipid flavors of the pep rally.

She felt Rex's new predatory confidence, his worries about losing control, the fading buzz of his wild transformation. Someone had threatened him, she realized, had actually dared to get into his face. Sucker.

And there was something else . . . an unexpected cluster of memories carried on top of Rex's spinning thoughts.

Not a darkling flavor, but something fearful and human.

Melissa pulled her hand away, staring into the whorls of her palm to puzzle over the strange images: a rattler cut in two by someone's dad in a backyard, its fangs snapping together in its death throes. The two snake halves squirming for thirty minutes on either side of the shovel that had bisected them, as if trying to rejoin each other and wreak revenge.

Melissa blinked. "Someone's afraid of snakes?"

"Timmy Hudson is." Rex smiled, showing too many teeth. "Very."

She shook her head. "What the hell?"

Rex stared down at the cheerleaders, who were piling themselves into a shaky pyramid. His glassy eyes gazed straight through them, into some new mix of midnighter lore and implanted ancient memories.

"Well, you know how darklings take our nightmares and use them against us?"

"Of course I do, Rex." Every night Melissa tasted the old minds out across the desert. And she had personally witnessed their shape-shifting into all creatures vile and hideous—worms, spiders, slugs. "That's why they always pull the tarantula trip on you."

"Yeah, tarantulas." He nodded thoughtfully. "Well, Timmy Hudson was bugging me. And he's afraid of snakes, it turns out. Ever since he was little, when his dad killed a rattler in the backyard and then brought Timmy out to take a look at the results. So I sort of got . . . snaky."

He glanced at her, his tongue darting out for a split second. Then he smiled.

Melissa noticed that Rex's chapped lower lip was split, his chin a little reddened with wiped-off blood. She reached up and touched it, felt the fading tension in his jaw muscle. "Okay, Loverboy. But how did you know that? About Timmy? You and he were never exactly friends."

Rex shook his head. "I just knew."

"But *how*, Rex? I'm the mindcaster here, remember? How did *you* get into someone's nightmares?"

He turned away again, staring at the pep festivities without seeing them. His mind radiated a quiet confidence, an intensity Melissa had never felt from him before, not during daylight hours. His strength was flavored, though, with tremors of uncertainty, bitter as the dregs of Madeleine's tea. Rex felt a lot like a young trucker Melissa had once tasted on the highway, driving an eighteen-wheeler for the first time with no one else in the cab—heady with an overdose of power, but nervous that the rig was about to hurtle off the road.

Finally he answered. "That's what darklings do."

The pep rally dragged on for ages. Announcements were made about bake sales and car washes and school plays. Team banners were raised. The members of last year's district-winning chess club got a few seconds of applause— a token suggestion that being smart might actually be a *good* thing. And gradually the rally began to lose its pep. Even the cheerleaders started to look bored, pom-poms wilting in their hands.

Then came the part when everyone chanted together.

"Beat North Tulsa. Beat North Tulsa," the gnomelike principal began. He stepped back from the microphone, raising his tiny fist in rhythm with the words. Gradually the chant built, louder and louder, until the gymnasium thundered with the sound.

This ritual was supposed to channel the whole school's "spirit" into the football team, transforming them from a bunch of seventeen-year-old boys into the champions of Bixby High.

The funny thing was, the concept wasn't total nonsense. You could see it on the team's faces as they listened: it did affect them, as if a gathered mass of humans really could lend its strength to a few zit-faced boys. Melissa often wondered if the daylighter who had invented pep rallies actually knew something about how mindcasting worked.

This part of pep rallies had always terrified Melissa in the past—the assembled minds uniting their energy in the chant, every strand of individual thought swamped by the animal imperatives of the pack: *Stay with the herd. Safety in numbers. Kill the enemy. Beat North Tulsa.*

She looked down across the fists rising and falling in rhythm, felt the beat of stomping feet resonating through the bleachers. The clique of pretty girls had lost the force field around them, dissolving into the crowd. The freshman boys in the first row were taking it seriously, no longer ogling the cheerleaders. Even Jessica Day and Flyboy had joined in, trying to act halfhearted but overtaken by the power of the mob.

Melissa nervously took a few deep breaths. This pep

rally was a joke, she reminded herself. The crowd didn't know what they were doing, and not one of the minds in this gymnasium matched hers for sheer power. Just because they'd found a meaningless football game to channel themselves into didn't make them stronger than her.

She steadily gained control again.

Then Melissa noticed Rex sniffing the air, eyes twitching as his nostrils flared.

The chant was making him anxious as well.

"It's like a hunt," he hissed. "This is how they got themselves ready in the old days."

Melissa touched Rex's hand and for an awful moment felt the crowd as he did. Little humans, weak and frail—but *so many of them*. It had been rituals like this one that had helped them conquer their fear of the darklings. And one day they had begun to hunt their own predators, packs of humans armed with fire and their sharp, clever stones.

Finally a band of them had gotten lucky, taking down a young darkling that had thought itself invulnerable. And some of the dread that the master species had always depended on was lost forever. The oldest minds still remembered that moment, when the balance had begun to shift. Humans had slowly become more confident, scratching pictures of their kills onto rocks and into mud, the first hated symbols of their mastery.

Melissa pulled her hand away, burned by the memory.

Maybe this pep rally wasn't such a joke. After all, high school was all about the oldest human bonds—the tribe, the pack, the hunting party.

Rex's hands twitched. He was struggling with the part of him that wanted to flee.

"You need to leave?" she whispered.

He shook his head grimly. "No. This is important. Have to learn to keep control."

Melissa sighed. Rex could be a moron sometimes.

She often remembered a line she'd read once on a bathroom wall: *That which does not kill us makes us stronger.* As Melissa watched the sweat building on Rex's upper lip, she knew that he was making the same mistake as the bathroom wall guy.

Not everything made you stronger. It was possible to survive, yet still be crippled for your trouble. Sometimes it was okay to run away, to skip the test, to chicken out. Or at least to get some help.

She firmly took his hand, not letting him pull away, and reached inside herself for a place that Madeleine had shown her, an old mindcaster trick for chilling out. Melissa closed her eyes and entered Rex, gently pushing the crowd's chant out of his mind.

She felt him relax, his fear of the crowd—and of the beast inside him—slipping away.

"Whoa," he said softly. "Thanks, Cowgirl."

"Any time, Loverboy."

"Okay. How about tonight?"

She opened her eyes. "Hmm?"

"Maybe later we can—" Rex's voice choked off, his grip

suddenly tightening. "Something's coming."

"What do you—?" she started, but then she felt it too and slammed her eyes shut again.

A taste was thundering toward them across the desert, vast and ancient and bitter, tumbling over itself in a rushing wave. It grew stronger as it advanced, like an avalanche pulling down more snow from the mountainside, burying everything in its wake.

Then it struck, washing through the gymnasium, sweeping away the puny energies of the pep rally, obliterating the surrounding mind noise of Bixby leaking in through the walls. It consumed everything. Only Melissa's connection with Rex remained, his shock and alarm reverberating through her like the echoes of a gunshot.

She opened her eyes and saw what had happened. The blue light, the frozen bodies, a leaping cheerleader hovering suspended in the air. The whole world struck by . . .

Silence.

Melissa looked at her watch in amazement. It was just after 9 A.M.

But the blue time was here.

3

9:03 A.M.

BLUE MONDAY

Midnight gravity flowed into Jessica.

She clenched Jonathan's hand harder. "What the . . . ?" Her voice trailed off into the sudden and overwhelming silence, her heart pounding as her eyes scanned the frozen pep rally.

Everything was blue.

The shiny Lycra uniforms of the football team, the Bixby town seal in the center of the basketball court, the motionless tendrils of a pom-pom thrust into the air—it had all turned the color of midnight. And everything was perfectly still.

"Jonathan?" Jessica looked into his face, hoping to catch some glimmer of comprehension. Maybe this had happened before here in Bixby, a weird hiccup of the blue time, and Rex had simply forgotten to tell her about it.

Jonathan didn't answer. His eyes were wide with shock.

"This is messed up," Dess confirmed in a quiet voice.

Jessica gripped the edge of the bleacher she sat on, felt the grainy reality of the wood. This was not a dream—this was the blue time.

Her eye caught movement across the gym. Rex and Melissa were slowly rising, looking strangely isolated among the frozen human forms.

His paralysis suddenly broken, Jonathan let out a cry and sprang out of his seat. Jessica instinctively clung to his hand, and as he left his feet, he pulled her softly into the air after him—they were both light as feathers.

"Jonathan!"

"What the hell?" His voice faded as midnight gravity carried them helplessly up and over the crowd, spinning around each other like two balls on a string. "Is this really . . . ?"

"Yeah, really happening," Jessica managed, gripping his hand still harder. The floor looked miles below, and she flashed back to Climbing Day in gym class—peering down from the top of the thick, knotted rope, terrified of falling.

As their flight peaked and they began to descend, reflexes honed by countless hours of flying together kicked in. Jonathan twisted to bring their spin to a halt, and as they settled back onto the gym floor—right on the Bixby seal, as if they'd been aiming for it—Jessica's knees bent for a soft landing.

She looked back up at the bleachers and swallowed. The frozen crowd were all staring right at her and Jonathan. It reminded Jessica of her least-favorite recurring nightmare: being in a play she hadn't rehearsed, the motionless audience waiting for her first line. It was stunning to see so many people captured by midnight. Their faces were waxy and pale, their eyes lifeless, like an army of plastic dummies.

"Never seen this many stiffs before." Melissa's soft words carried across the gym, echoing Jessica's thoughts.

"Outside, quick!" Rex called. He was running down the bleachers, jumping over the frozen bodies like hurdles. Dess and Melissa followed him toward the door to the parking lot.

Jessica looked at Jonathan, who shrugged. "Might as well see what's in the sky," he said.

"Oh, right." If this were midnight, the dark moon would be up there, bathing the world in its cold blue light.

But this *wasn't* midnight. This was a Monday morning pep rally, which was just about as far away from the magic of the blue time as you could get.

"Come on," Jonathan said, his knees bending.

They jumped together, covering the distance to the door in one easy leap, landing just as Rex got there. The three of them burst out into the parking lot together, staring up at the sky.

Behind a few frozen and wispy clouds, the dark moon was huge and fully risen. Its vast bulk seemed perfectly centered, blotting out the whole sky except for a thin sliver around the horizon, hiding the sun. A few white stars glittered at its edges, their light dulled, as if they were being squashed down against the earth by the huge moon's weight.

Suddenly Jessica needed the feel of solid ground under her feet. She slipped her fingers from Jonathan's hand, letting normal gravity fall back across her. Dizzied by the weird, absent light of the moon, she dropped her eyes down to the asphalt.

Its cracked surface shone uncanny blue.

Dess and Melissa charged through the door, staggering to a halt as they stared upward.

"This can't be happening," Rex murmured.

"Yeah," Dess said, gazing at her own blue hand. "But it kind of . . . *is*."

For a long moment they all stood there in silence. Jonathan pushed off from the ground nervously, rising a few feet into the air.

Jessica checked her watch. The numbers were still pulsing: 9:05 A.M. Just like during a normal midnight hour, her flame-bringer's magic kept its electronic numbers flashing.

How many minutes had it lasted so far? Two?

"The moon isn't moving," Rex said.

"Isn't what?" Dess asked.

His skyward gaze stayed steady, his eyes flashing violet. "It's just stuck up there, halfway across."

"How can you tell?" Jessica asked, glancing up at the huge, baleful eye above them. The dark moon crossed the sky much faster than the sun, taking only an hour to rise and fall, but it was still like watching a minute hand move on a clock. "Isn't it sort of too slow to see?"

"For you, maybe." He smiled. "But I *am* a seer, you know."

"Oh, right." Jessica glanced at Jonathan, who shrugged back at her. These days it was easy to forget that Rex was gifted with special sight and deep knowledge of the lore. The transformation out in the desert had left him . . .

different. Lately his gaze was so freaked out and wild-eyed that he seemed more like a stoner than a seer.

"So the moon didn't rise?" Dess asked. "It just appeared out of nowhere?"

"Or it rose really quick." Rex glanced at his own watch; on a midnighter's wrist, windups worked in the blue hour. "We got out here in less than three minutes."

"Why is it such a big deal what the moon's doing?" Jessica asked quietly. "I mean, isn't this all completely screwed up anyway?"

"The moon makes the secret hour, as far as we know." Rex looked up again as he answered her, staring at the sky with a frown. "If it's not moving, there's no way to tell how long this will last."

"Oh." Jessica glanced at Jonathan, who had jumped to the top of a school bus to look around. "Um, then maybe . . ."

"Spot the problem, Rex," Dess said. "Let's do some math: zero velocity multiplied by *any* amount of time equals zero movement. What if the moon's just *stuck* up there?"

"Stuck?" Jessica said softly. "Like, forever?"

"I didn't say forever." Rex dropped his eyes from the sky. "That would be . . . crazy."

"This whole thing is crazy, Rex!" Dess cried. "It's not midnight, except in Australia or somewhere, but it's *blue*."

"Yeah, what's happening, Rex?" Jonathan said as he bounded softly back to the group.

Rex raised his hands. "Look, there's nothing like this in

the lore." His voice stayed calm. "So I don't know why you're asking *me*."

For a moment no one said anything, stunned by his words. Jessica realized that her jaw had dropped open. After all, that's what you did when things got weird: you asked Rex what was going on.

With a cool seer's gaze, he stared silently back at them for a moment, then smiled, his point made. "Okay, everyone, calm down and give Melissa some head space." He turned to the mindcaster. "Can you feel Madeleine?"

"No, she's staying hidden. But I bet you she's just as freaked out as we are."

"What about the darklings? Are they awake?"

Melissa stood in silence for a moment, eyes closed and head tilted back, casting her mind across the desert.

Jessica looked around at the others. It had been a while since the five of them had all been together. Probably since that night on the salt flats when everything had gone haywire—Rex kidnapped, Melissa thrown through the windshield of her car, and Dess . . .

Dess seemed the worst for it. She ate lunch with Jessica and Jonathan or alone these days—never with Rex and Melissa. She hadn't forgiven the mindcaster for pillaging her memories that night.

Not that Jessica could blame her. Or blame Rex for being freaked out by his transformation into a halfling. And the scars on Melissa's face from her accident still carried pink stitches.

But everyone seemed to have forgotten that Anathea, the young seer who'd been turned into a halfling back in the old days, had *died* that night. Which was a lot worse than anything that had happened to the rest of them.

Sometimes when Jessica watched the other midnighters interact, she felt like wearing a T-shirt with big letters on the front: GET OVER IT.

"They're awake, all right," Melissa said slowly. "I'm surprised you guys can't hear them."

"Hear them?" Rex glanced over his shoulder toward the badlands. "You mean they're coming this way?"

Jessica reached for Disintegrator in her pocket, but it wasn't there; she'd never expected to need the flashlight during the day. She had only Acariciandote, the bracelet Jonathan had given her. She reached to touch it, feeling the thirteen tiny charms dangling from her wrist.

Melissa shook her head. "Not coming, not moving much at all. Just so *loud*." She winced, her face twisting into the pained expression she wore whenever too many people were around.

"Melissa," Rex asked, "what do you mean by 'loud'?"

"I mean screaming, howling, raising a ruckus."

"As in afraid?"

Melissa shook her head. "No. As in celebrating."

Jessica's watch said 9:17 A.M., but it seemed like hours since the blue time had begun. The minutes seemed to drag along, as if time itself had become a formless, limping thing.

How could she even be sure if her watch was working right or not? It felt like they'd all been standing out there in the parking lot for hours.

"Get down from there!" Rex yelled again.

Jessica looked up and sighed. Jonathan was still on the roof of the school.

"I thought you said this could go on forever," he shouted down.

"Yeah, or it could end any second!"

"Nah, midnight only comes in one-hour slices, Rex. You know that." Jonathan laughed and took an arcing hop up to the top of the gym. From there he scanned the horizon, as if the Bixby skyline might hold some clue as to what was going on.

Jessica saw how high he was and swallowed. But she knew yelling at Jonathan was pointless. He always flew until the last moment of midnight, squeezing out every second of weightlessness; it hadn't taken him long to convince himself that this unexpected blue time would last a solid hour. For Jonathan this wasn't a terrifying mystery to be solved—it was a double helping of dessert, an extra recess, a free period spicing up an otherwise crappy Monday.

Jessica wanted to scream at him to quit being stupid, but if she sided with Rex in front of everyone else, Jonathan would probably stay up there until the world ended.

Unless, of course, it already had.

"Come on, Jonathan," Melissa called up to him. "There's nothing to see, and you really could get hurt."

Jonathan frowned at her, but a moment later he stepped from the roof's edge and floated down.

Jessica glanced sidelong at Melissa. The mindcaster had sounded so concerned, *and* Jonathan was listening to her. This was definitely too much weirdness for one Monday morning.

But at least Jonathan was safely on the ground again. She crossed the parking lot to grab hold of his jacket.

"Sorry," he said when he saw her expression. "But it seems like a waste, just standing around."

"You could get killed."

"But what if this really does last a long time?" He frowned. "Or forever."

She took his hand, but the feeling of his midnight gravity flowing into Jessica didn't help her mood. It would be just like the world to end on a Monday, especially *this* Monday, the day she was theoretically going to become ungrounded.

Only theoretically, of course. There had been a fierce debate this morning about what day was exactly one month from the night Jessica had been brought home by the police, tonight or tomorrow. Finally she'd given up arguing about it. Tuesday's promised freedom wouldn't take forever to come, after all.

Except now it might.

Standing here with the dark moon overhead, it made perfect sense that time had been halted, the darklings decreeing that Jessica Day would remain grounded forever. That's what she got for being born the flame-bringer.

"Hey, look! It's Sanchez," Dess cried suddenly. She was pointing at a stiff just outside the gym entrance. The frozen Mr. Sanchez was huddled close to the wall, out of sight from anyone coming through the door, a motionless geyser of smoke spewing from his mouth.

Jonathan pulled his hand away from Jessica and bounded across the lot. "Oh my God—he's sneaking a cigarette. I didn't know he smoked!"

"Well, well, Mr. Sanchez," Dess said. "Your secrets are revealed at last." She stepped into the smoke and laughed, waving it away. Released from the dark moon's spell by her touch, it drifted slowly upward in the still air.

"Get away from him, you two," Rex shouted. "Don't stand where he can see you. What if time starts up again?"

Jonathan got out of Sanchez's face, but Dess just stood there giggling. Rex sighed.

The sight of the frozen teacher caused a trickle of nerves to crawl up Jessica's spine. If time did start again, there was a good chance they could be caught out here, busted for skipping the pep rally. Then, like the seasons, the mighty grounding cycle would begin again. . . .

"Maybe we should wait inside?" she said quietly.

"Were you talking to someone in there?" Rex asked. "Or in front of anyone who'll notice if you suddenly disappear?"

"No," Jessica answered. "We were in the back row, like you guys."

"So what's the problem?"

"Well, you know," Jessica said. "Just in case time starts again, we don't want to get busted for cutting."

Rex looked at her like she was crazy. "Time is frozen during broad daylight for the first time in recorded history, and you're worried about skipping a *pep rally*?"

"Um, well . . ."

"Hey, maybe this is like an eclipse!" Dess called across the parking lot.

"How do you mean?" Jonathan said.

Dess stared at Mr. Sanchez as she spoke, as if drawing inspiration from the trig teacher's harried expression. "You know, an eclipse looks like a little bit of night that happens in the middle of the day. But it's not really night, it's just the moon blocking out the sun."

"And a long time ago," Rex added, "people used to freak out about eclipses, like it was the end of the world."

"Exactly. But it's not a big deal, just a totally random thing—two objects lining up. Doesn't even last that long." Dess crossed the lot as she spoke, Jonathan bounding along beside her. "The trick is not to have a heart attack about it."

"Can't you go blind from eclipses?" Jonathan said.

"Yeah, true." Dess glanced up at the dark moon. "If you're stupid enough to stare at the sun for too long."

Rex thought about this for a second, then shook his head. "But you can predict eclipses years in advance, right?"

"Centuries, Rex," Dess said, rolling her eyes, as if eclipse prediction was something she did for fun in study hall. (Of course, Jessica realized, it probably was.) "Thousands of years, even. You just do the math, and they happen right on schedule."

"So where's the schedule, then?" Rex said. "I repeat:

nothing like this has ever been recorded in the lore."

"The lore's not perfect, Rex," Jonathan said, bouncing a few feet into the air. "You can't look up everything. I thought by this point you'd have figured that out."

Jessica waited for an outburst. Those were fighting words as far as Rex was concerned. And a big fight was *just* what they needed right now.

But Rex only nodded and scratched his chin. "Yeah, you could be right. Maybe it is just an eclipse or something like that. Totally random." He looked up into the sky, squinting as his eyes flashed purple.

Jessica dared a quick glance at the dark moon, which was giving her a headache as usual. As far as she could tell, it hadn't moved an inch, or a degree, or whatever. When an eclipse happened, didn't the regular moon keep going across the sky?

"Well, the darklings must have known this was coming." Melissa spoke up. "Or at least, they must know something. They're still rocking out, like it's darkling Fourth of July."

"I guess maybe they've got the schedule, then," Dess said quietly.

Jonathan pushed himself softly up into the air ten feet or so, staring out across the desert. "Hey, Rex, could they have *made* this happen?"

"The darklings? Maybe."

"But it was daylight when it happened, Rex," Jessica said. "How could the darklings do anything? Aren't they, like, frozen during regular time?"

Rex nodded slowly. "Yeah, frozen. And buried deep in

the desert to escape the sun. But still . . . maybe." He shrugged.

Jessica sighed. She didn't know which was freakier, the complete rupture of time itself or Rex acting like he didn't know everything.

The way he'd changed was hard to pin down. On the one hand, he moved with much more confidence, like he was stronger, no longer afraid of the daylight world. But at the same time he could seem sort of dislocated, as if Earth was a new planet to him and every passing car something astonishing to behold.

At times like this she missed the old Rex, who could be depended on to at least *pretend* like he knew what was happening.

What if they were stuck here? What if this really was the end of regular time, at least for the five of them? What were they supposed to do? Spend the rest of their lives scavenging for canned food and being hunted nonstop by the darklings?

The secret hour was magical, but it could also be a trap; Jessica had already experienced enough since moving to Bixby to understand that. If they really were stuck here, she would never see her parents or sister again, except as pale, waxen statues—stiffs. She would never talk to anyone again except the other four midnighters or feel the sun on her face.

And she would never . . .

"Oh, jeez, would you knock it off, Jessica!" Melissa cried. "You're bumming me out, and I think something's happening."

Jessica felt a hot flush rising in her face. "Were you reading my mind?"

Melissa sighed. "It's not like I have a choice. Just chill out for a second. The darklings are doing something. . . ." Her eyes closed, her expression changing from concentration to puzzlement, then suddenly to alarm. "Flyboy! Get down!" she shouted.

Jessica spun around and saw Jonathan hovering eight feet or so in the air. He had been bouncing up and down with nervous energy, still thinking of this extra blue time as an invitation to fly to his heart's content.

He waved his arms uselessly, still drifting softly upward, powerless to change his course. Falling that far wouldn't be fatal, but the parking lot's asphalt surface was hard enough to twist an ankle or break a leg.

Above him the dark moon was dropping, sweeping across the sky faster than a second hand. The sun peeked out from behind it, a cold and lifeless eye against darkness.

As she ran toward him, Jessica remembered her lessons from flying and from physics class. Jonathan's midnight touch made things almost weightless, but the rest of the laws of motion still applied. If she could throw something heavy up to him, and he caught it while it was headed downward, its momentum would carry him quickly back toward earth.

But Jessica's backpack was still in the gym, and she didn't have anything heavier than loose change in her pockets.

All she could use was her own body.

She ran three steps and leapt up onto the hood of the

car nearest him, then jumped from it toward Jonathan's dangling feet. Her fingers grasped his ankle, giving it a yank earthward.

She expected lightness to flow into her, Jonathan's midnight gravity to take the sting out of her fall. But Jessica still felt heavy, tumbling like a brick toward the asphalt.

Then she realized that she wasn't touching Jonathan's skin, only the leg of his jeans. With only seconds before they hit the earth, there was no way to reach up to his bare hands, to share his acrobat's weightlessness. She was dragging him down too fast.

Jessica let go . . . and the ground rushed up.

The blue time ended just as she hit, the Oklahoma sun suddenly blinding as she stumbled across hot, black asphalt. One ankle twisted under her, and she crashed shoulder-first against the side of a car. The collision knocked the breath out of her.

Jessica fell to her knees, clutching her ankle and wondering why an earsplitting shriek had filled the air.

Suddenly Jonathan was crouching beside her.

"Are you okay?" he shouted above the noise.

"Ow. I don't know. What's that . . . ?" Jessica's voice trailed off as she realized that the wailing sound was coming from the car next to her. Crashing into it just as the blue time had ended, she'd set off its burglar alarm. "I did that, didn't I?"

"Don't worry about it. And thanks for saving me." Jonathan raised up a little from his crouch, peering over the hood of the car. "Dess is talking to Sanchez. It looks like he's more embarrassed than anything else. I think she's lecturing him about the evils of smoking." He ducked. "He's looking over here, though, wondering about the car alarm. Just stay down."

Jessica tested her sore ankle, wincing as pain shot up her leg. "No problem with that. So you're okay?"

He nodded. "You pulled just hard enough; perfect timing. I wound up with only a few inches of regular-gravity acceleration. And I was falling straight down, so I didn't stumble like you did." He smiled. "Plus I do have a couple more years' practice at landing than you."

"Oh." She sighed. "Guess I was stupid, trying to save you."

He took her hand. "Not stupid at all, Jess. I would have been at least ten feet up if you hadn't given me a yank. That's a long way to fall onto concrete, believe me." He leaned over and kissed her, then pulled away, smiling. "That was really fast thinking and excellent use of the laws of motion."

"Really?"

"Yeah. Like I said, thanks for saving me."

"From a sprained ankle. Brave me."

"Could have been worse than a sprain." He rose slightly and peered over the car again. "They're all sneaking back into the gym now, Mr. Sanchez too. Looks like no big deal."

"What about this stupid car alarm? Someone's going to check it out."

He shook his head. "I doubt anybody inside can hear it over that chanting. Can you walk?"

Jessica tested her weight on the ankle. "*Ow.*"

"Okay, let's just stay here a few more minutes. The rally's almost over anyhow. We'll blend in when it breaks up, get our stuff, and go to physics."

"Sure, great." She winced. "Only I think I've already had my physics lesson for today."

"Guess you have," Jonathan said. He knelt and began to rub her ankle tenderly. At first she flinched at his touch, but then the wrenched muscles began to loosen. "Guess I have too."

"How do you mean?"

He sighed. "Well, it was kind of stupid, flying around when we didn't know what the hell was going on." Jonathan looked up at the gym roof. "I could've taken a *real* fall."

Jessica reached out and brushed his hand with her fingertips. "That would have sucked."

"Yeah, well, the next time that happens, I'll listen to Rex."

She smiled, amazed to hear words "listen to" and "Rex" coming out of Jonathan's mouth in the same sentence. But then her mind played back the first half of what he'd said, and she frowned.

"Hang on. The *next* time it happens?"

Jonathan looked at her blankly, then laughed as he worked on her ankle. "Do you really think that whole thing was just an eclipse or whatever? That it means nothing and will never happen again?"

"Yeah, well." She swallowed. "I mean, it *could* be like Dess said. A totally random event . . ."

He chuckled.

"*What*, Jonathan?"

He stopped his massage and looked up at her with a wry smile. "Yeah, sure, could be totally random. Just like all the other totally random stuff that's happened since you arrived in Bixby." He started counting on his fingers. "The darklings go crazy and try to kill you, the Broken Arrows kidnap Rex, Madeleine reappears after fifty years in hiding. . . . How much more random could things get?"

The car alarm next to them switched off with a two-syllable *dweeping* sound, finally running out of steam.

"Great," Jessica said softly into the sudden, ringing silence. "The flame-bringer rides again."

4

MAJORETTE

"Don't worry, I'll take you over to Madeleine's at midnight."

"Yeah, sure," Jessica answered. "After you guys have already talked about all the important stuff this afternoon."

Both Dess and Jonathan sighed and looked away, apparently tired of her whining.

Jessica rubbed her ankle, which wasn't helping her mood. It had been getting gradually better all day, but it still twinged with pain. The three of them were sitting on the school's front steps. Around them students were spilling out of Bixby High, slowly sorting themselves among the line of idling school buses. The lawn was dotted with clusters of people saying goodbye or arranging rides home. The sound of a tuba warming up for band practice drifted across the football field.

Jessica, of course, was waiting for her father to pick her up for a final night of being grounded.

"You won't be missing anything, Jess," Dess said.

"Madeleine probably doesn't know any more about what happened this morning than we do. I doubt this is a mindcaster issue."

"But she's all old and stuff," Jessica said.

"Yeah, but if anything like this ever happened before, it wasn't fifty years ago. More like five thousand, if Rex doesn't know about it." Dess nodded slowly, rubbing her hands together. "My guess is, this is a job for a polymath."

"But doesn't she have all those memories in her head?" Jessica said. "All that stuff passed on from mindcasters in the olden days?"

Dess seemed to shiver a bit, and Jessica cursed herself for bringing up the subject of mindcasters and memories. Madeleine had also messed with Dess's brain, trying to keep her existence a secret from the darklings.

After an uncomfortable silence, Dess answered. "Anything this big would be in the lore. They wouldn't just use memory, would they?" She shrugged. "But maybe she did scoop some info from the darklings this morning. I can't wait to ask her if that blue time was shaped funny."

"Shaped funny?"

Dess's eyes lit up. "Yeah, like, did it go all the way to the edge of Bixby County? Or was it smaller than a normal midnight? Like . . . focused in some particular places."

"Why would it be?"

Dess shrugged. "That's just the way the blue time is: it has a shape."

Not for the first time, Jessica tried to wrap her head

around that concept. These days Dess talked about the midnight hour more like it was a place than a time. She was always playing with maps, and even as they sat there, she was fiddling—as usual—with her electronic gadget that spat out coordinates.

To Jessica it seemed weird that the blue time only went so far, then just stopped, like the edge of the world the way people imagined it before they realized it was round.

"So, Dess," she said. "What would happen if you went all the way to the edge of Bixby at midnight and then went just a *little* farther?"

"You mean go past the midnight boundary? You wouldn't . . . or couldn't. Time's frozen out there. So from your perspective, midnight would end as you took that step. But if another midnighter was watching you, they'd see you freeze up for the rest of the hour, just out of reach."

Jessica's head spun with that image for a moment. "So midnight's, like, a bubble around us?"

"You mean a sphere? Well, it's lumpy and uneven, but yeah."

"But say you were right on the border when midnight fell. Would, like, half of you keep moving and half of you freeze up?"

"And then you'd slide into two pieces," Jonathan added. "Like those guys in samurai movies?"

"Um, I guess I don't know." Dess laughed. "Why don't you try it and tell me?"

"Here they come," Jonathan said.

Rex and Melissa were making their unhurried way through the throng, their fingertips touching lightly, their expressions tranquil. As usual these days, the crowd seemed to have no effect on Melissa. She ignored the stares of the few freshmen who were freaked out by her scarred face, gliding past them as serene as a movie star on a red carpet.

Dess sighed. "I can see why you're bummed, Jess. You don't get to spend the afternoon drinking skanky tea and putting up with *two* mindcasters." She rose to her feet, her long skirt rustling. "See you."

"Yeah, really," Jonathan said. "You're lucky to miss this." He gave Jessica's hand a squeeze and stood.

"Yeah, *so* lucky," Jessica said. "If only I could be grounded all the time."

She watched the four of them walk away, chewing her lip and cursing her parents' calendar logic. Didn't they know she had more important things to do than be grounded these days?

For the first time ever, her dad was late.

He had faithfully picked up Jessica every day of her grounding, on the theory that left to ride the school bus, she would fall back into her criminal ways. But Don Day's car wasn't anywhere to be seen among the crawling traffic of parents picking up their kids.

Maybe after all the debate about exactly how long her

grounding should last, he had gotten confused about whether it ended today or not.

For this morning's argument Jessica herself had gone with the werewolf model: a month was twenty-eight days, which meant that she should have been ungrounded *last* night. But her parents had cruelly opted for the calendar month, and as her father liked to repeat: "Thirty days hath September (April, June, and November)."

Of course, it *still* wasn't fair that she was grounded tonight. Jessica had been detained and returned to parental custody (technically not arrested) on a Saturday night. So thirty days later should be a Monday night, to any sane person. But both her parents had raised the technical point that she'd been brought home Sunday morning, and so her grounding really hadn't begun until Sunday night, which meant that it was Tuesday before her sentence would be served.

Jessica had kept arguing until her dad had gotten angry and threatened to invoke the fact that most months were thirty-one days, which meant he could in good conscience extend her grounding until Wednesday. Even Mom had rolled her eyes at that one, but Jessica had finally realized she was beaten.

She looked at her watch, which she'd reset to regular Bixby time—it had gained twenty minutes during the eclipse. Her bus would be leaving soon. If she got on it and her father showed up looking for her later, he would go ballistic and ground her again. Of course, maybe this was all a trick to make her miss the bus, forcing her to walk home so then she could be re-grounded for showing up late.

Unless she'd forgotten something. Jessica searched her memory for any change in plans. Since the weird events of this morning, her mind had been a little vague. All day she'd kept expecting time to freeze again and blue amber to capture everyone around her. Every lull in the noise of lunchtime had made her jump as she'd wondered if the world of motion and sunlight and other human beings was fading out for good.

Finally Jessica spotted the familiar car, Beth's head visible in the front seat next to her father's, and suddenly she remembered why he was late. Beth had demanded to be picked up at the junior high school on the other side of town so she wouldn't have to walk home in her humiliating new marching band uniform.

"Oh, right," Jess said, smiling. Her little sister was a majorette again.

She ran through the horde of cars, opened the door, and slid herself into the backseat.

Beth whirled around. "Not *one* word."

Jessica smiled at her. "I was just going to say that you look ravishing in purple and gold."

"Dad! She's making fun of me!" She turned to him. "You said she wasn't supposed to make fun of me!"

"Jess . . ."

"I just said *ravishing*. Ravishing is not a bad thing. Dad, explain to Beth how poor kids in Bangladesh would love to wear such a ravishing costume."

"Stop talking about it, Jess!" Beth cried.

"*Girls* . . ." Don Day's tone was still only vaguely threatening as he concentrated on guiding the car out of the traffic jam.

"Could you just ground her again and get it over with!" Beth shouted.

"Beth! That is *so* not cool!"

"Will both of you please be quiet!" their father pleaded. In an attempt to be scary he fixed Jessica with a stern look as he backed the car up into the clear, then put it into forward gear, and stared at Beth for a meaningful second before accelerating out onto the road.

Jessica settled back into her seat, unbeaten. "Anyway, I'm not even really grounded right now."

"Yes, you are," Beth said.

"Okay, I am." Jessica waited for a moment, then played her final trump card. "So, Dad, you know my one night a week off from my grounding? Could I have it, say . . . tonight?" She sat back and smiled. Her parents had granted her this limited reprieve a few days after she'd been brought home by the police. One day a week—a solemn promise. It had been a little suspicious, Mom agreeing to change a punishment once it had been meted out, especially now that Jessica knew what Rex and Melissa could get up to with people's minds.

But at the moment Jessica was willing to use the exception for all it was worth.

"That is so lame," Beth said. "Dad, tell her that's lame."

"That is pretty lame, Jess."

"But you said one day a week."

"And you've taken four free days. And you were grounded a month, which is four weeks."

Jessica's jaw dropped open at this unjust change of definition. "But you said, and I quote, 'Thirty days hath—'"

"That's *enough*, Jessica." His voice had suddenly moved to fully threatening mode. "Or September will have *sixty* days this year."

Jessica swallowed. For once, he sounded like he really meant it.

Beth turned from the front seat and gave Jessica a worried look, hostilities briefly suspended by their father's outburst. Since coming to Bixby, Don Day had been jobless, a condition that had gradually turned into shiftless, then shirtless, and finally spineless. It had been a while since he'd gotten up the energy to raise his voice.

In fact, Jessica realized, it had been exactly thirty days—he'd yelled a lot when the police had brought her home for breaking Bixby's curfew with Jonathan. Maybe the end of the grounding was freaking him out and the concept of her being free to wander the streets of Bixby between the hours of three and 10 P.M. was too much for him. He wasn't like Mom, too tired out from having to impress her new bosses to obsess over anything but work.

Maybe it was time to change the subject.

"So, Beth, how was band practice?" she asked.

"It was lame."

"You used to like it."

Beth turned toward the front of the car again and didn't answer.

Jessica frowned, wishing she hadn't made fun of Beth's uniform. It was an old habit, from the days when Beth could take being teased without exploding.

Two years ago, back in Chicago, Beth had been a champion majorette. She could stick a three-turn every time and do a hundred thumb flips per minute, and she came home from camp every summer with tons of ribbons. But halfway through being eleven years old, she'd declared majorettes totally lame and exchanged marching band for being Ms. Social. Since the move down to Bixby, she hadn't even unpacked her baton-twirling trophies. Jessica had found herself missing the little silvery majorettes lined up on their marble pedestals, just like she missed the younger, happier Beth of the old days.

But having made zero friends in Bixby had apparently changed Beth's mind about majorettes. Maybe being in the marching band was a big deal at Bixby Junior High. Or maybe at this point she simply didn't know what else to do.

Seeing Beth in a gaudy costume after two years was so strange, as if time had broken down completely this morning and was heading backward now.

"Listen, you want to practice together later?" Jessica said. "I mean, I *think* I'm allowed to go in the backyard."

"Sure," her father piped up.

"Yes, Jess, that would be great." Beth turned around to

face her again. "Because it's *so* important to have an assistant while baton twirling."

"All right. Fine. Just trying to be helpful."

"And mature. Don't forget mature."

"I said fine."

Beth kept looking at her, the gold piping around her collar flashing in the sun.

"What's your problem?" Jessica finally asked.

"Why do you think I had Dad pick me up today?"

Jessica sighed. "Because you look so ravishing?"

"No, retard. I could have changed at school." She dropped her voice. "It was because of you."

Jessica shot a puzzled look toward the back of her father's head. Was Beth talking about Jonathan? Since Jess had introduced the two of them, she'd figured Beth was on her side on the secret boyfriend front. At least Beth hadn't told Mom and Dad about his late-night visits or how Jessica skipped out at night sometimes.

"What do you mean, Beth?"

"Just to make sure you know."

"Know *what*?"

"That even though you're not grounded anymore, I've still got my eye on you."

Jessica sighed again. "Beth, quit being weird. Dad, tell Beth to quit being weird."

Don Day was silent for a moment. Finally he said, "Well, Jessica, I kind of know what she means. After all, I've got my eye on you too."

5

3:27 P.M.

DREGS

"Milk, no sugar, correct?"

"Yes, please." Dess smiled politely, but the bitter taste of Madeleine's tea was already trickling through her imagination, the acid flavor of betrayal on her tongue.

By rights, this secret place should have been *her* playground. Dess was the one who had found Madeleine, after all. She'd struggled through sleepless nights to decode the weird dreams the old mindcaster had sent her; she was the one who'd *done the math*.

But it had all been in the service of Melissa and Rex. They were the ones really enjoying themselves here in Madeleine's crepuscular contortion, her little secret hideaway. Rex finally had all the lore he could possibly want. Years of reading awaited him in this house, every document the surviving midnighters of the last generation had managed to salvage when they'd been forced into hiding.

And Melissa . . . she had *totally* scored.

Dess noticed that as Melissa took her cup and saucer from Madeleine's hand, the two mindcasters' fingers brushed for a moment. Then they both smirked at some shared, silent joke.

The sight made her flesh crawl. The two of them communicated mostly by mindcasting, rarely uttering a word to each other. Dess wondered what they were saying to each other right now.

On the other side of the big dining table, Rex was also watching them. Besides Rex, Madeleine was the only person whom Melissa allowed to touch her—not that anyone else would *want* to—but he didn't seem jealous of little moments like this one. It was those long sessions, when the two mindcasters sat for hours at a stretch with eyes closed and fingers interlocked, that made Rex start to get all territorial.

Of course, Melissa did have some catching up to do. Growing up as a lone mindcaster, she'd never learned the old tricks that should have been taught to her by the previous generation. A trove had awaited her inside Madeleine's brain—the thousands of years of memories, techniques, and gossip accumulated since the first mindcasters had learned how to pass knowledge from hand to hand.

Dess wondered how *that* math worked. If every generation of mindcasters took all their memories and forwarded them onto the next bunch, who then passed theirs onto the next, who added *their* memories, and so on . . . wouldn't the pile get too big at some point? Wouldn't all that knowledge become less and less stable, like building blocks stacked higher and higher, until the whole thing collapsed at once?

Maybe the memories got fuzzier as you went back in

time, a blurry aggregate of thoughts and feelings, like the symbols that meteorologists used to represent weather. Dess imagined a big *H* hovering over Madeleine's house, warning of a high-pressure center of bitchiness.

"Don't rattle the cup when you stir, Jonathan!"

Speaking of which, Dess thought as Jonathan exchanged an eye roll with her. He kept stirring his tea, adopting a sarcastic little spoon twirl that Madeleine didn't seem to notice.

At least they didn't have to edit their thoughts here. Madeleine's house was built on a whopping big crepuscular contortion, a wrinkle in the blue time that made it almost impossible to plunder anyone's mind without physical contact. It was like living next to a power line that screwed up your TV reception.

This contortion was the only thing that had protected Madeleine for the last five decades. She was invisible to the darklings here, hidden along with her antiques and books, all the leftovers from the days when midnighters had ruled Bixby instead of skulking in the shadows.

Dess looked at the junk piled in the corners of the room, her mind automatically dissecting the angles of tridecagrams in rusted steel, all the patterns of thirteens and thirty-nines that had once guarded the town's key citizens. Some of the junk was pretty interesting, engraved with old-timey tridecalogisms like *accelerograph* and *paterfamilias.* She had to admit: Rex and Melissa weren't the only ones who'd found stuff to play with here.

Still, it bugged Dess that those two had gotten anything at all out of *her* discovery. Especially since the sweaty work of protecting Madeleine had been left to Dess, Jessica, and Jonathan. The three had spent hours making a big pile of the least-rusty darkling defenses. Then Dess had made sure every piece had its own brand-new thirteen-letter name and mounted them all around the house as a last line of protection should the darklings ever find Madeleine's hiding place.

And what thanks had they gotten? Mostly getting yelled at for making too much noise.

"So, now that we all have tea," Madeleine pronounced, "perhaps we should discuss the little incident this morning."

"About time," Dess muttered. Her fingers traced the deep scratches in the wood of the table. It had been completely covered by big, *heavy* iron tridecagrams before she'd cleared the room to make it habitable.

Madeleine arched an eyebrow. "Well, then, Desdemona. Since you're feeling feisty, perhaps you'd like to start."

"Me? What do I know about it? We were sort of hoping *you* could tell us something."

"But surely you have something numerate to contribute?"

Dess sighed. "Well, we checked Rex's fancy watch after the eclipse was over. He resets it every morning to the time on Geostationary, which is *always* perfect." She felt the comforting weight of the GPS device in her pocket. "Turns out it had gained twenty-one minutes and thirty-six seconds—that was the total length of time the dark moon was up. That's nine times 144 seconds, which is a very darkling number. Must mean something."

"But you don't know what?" Madeleine said.

"Not yet." Dess sipped at her tea. Maybe the bitter taste of it would focus her mind on the problem.

"There's nothing like this in the lore," Rex piped up. "Not that I've read. You don't have any old memories that would help, do you?"

Madeleine took a long while to respond, as if she was filtering out an answer from the centuries of thought echoes in her head. *Voices in her head . . .* That didn't sound particularly sane. Maybe the weight of all those piled-up memories had driven Madeleine madder and madder as she'd hidden in this house, alone. Maybe what mindcasters really passed on was a trick for acting serene and knowing when all of them, including Madeleine and Melissa, were actually as nutty as bat guano.

Dess smiled to herself. Maybe Madeleine could use a new mental nickname.

"No, Rex," Maddy finally said. "Like the lore, our memories reveal nothing of these events. I'm certain this is all quite unprecedented."

Dess allowed herself a smirk. Of course history wasn't going to be any help. This was a job for numbers, maps, and GPS precision.

"That's what I was afraid of," Rex said glumly.

"Afraid, Rex?" Madeleine snapped. "Chicken-fried baloney! In my day, seers didn't speak of being afraid. They spoke of action!"

It was Rex's turn to roll his eyes. He covered the expression by raising his own teacup and wincing at the acid taste.

Some mind reader, Dess thought. Maddy didn't even know that everyone hated her tea.

"Well," Jonathan said. "You must have sensed something while the eclipse was happening. Melissa said the darklings were celebrating. You think they were expecting this to happen?"

"Ah, now you're headed in the right direction," Maddy said.

Rex shot Jonathan an annoyed look for asking the obvious next question and scoring extra Maddy credit for it.

Very clever, Dess thought. The old mindcaster was good at playing the boys against each other. Dess had found a few old photographs of a youthful Madeleine around the house, and she'd been quite the 1940s cutie.

Of course, it was worth remembering that Maddy had been the one to spill the beans back then, coughing up the secrets of the blue time to a daylighter, Grandpa Grayfoot (probably one of her boyfriends). So in theory she could be blamed for the whole mess since: the creation of the halfling, the extermination of the previous generation of midnighters, and the fact that the five of them had been left orphaned and clueless.

"So what did you taste?" Rex asked.

Maddy paused dramatically, then looked across the table at her pupil.

Melissa stopped chewing her lip and said, "We aren't sure yet. We haven't had a chance to"—she glanced at Rex—"compare notes."

"But there were some ruptures," Maddy said. "Places where the false midnight felt very thin."

"Places?" Dess asked, her ears perking up. Places could be expressed as longitude and latitude—sweet numbers. "You mean like this crepuscular contortion?"

Maddy nodded. "Yes, but not hiding places. Spots where the barrier between the blue world and ours seemed almost to disappear."

"Oh." One hand inside her jacket pocket, Dess gripped Geostationary harder. "You mean like Sheriff Michaels?"

"Sheriff Michaels?" Jonathan asked. "That guy who disappeared?"

Everyone was quiet for a moment.

Some time ago—before Jessica, or even Jonathan, had moved to Bixby—the town sheriff had vanished out in the desert. Only his gun and badge had been found, along with his teeth and all their fillings—the darkling-proof, high-tech alloys of dentistry.

The rumor was he'd been killed by drug dealers, but between Rex's lore and her careful mapping of the blue time, Dess understood what had really happened.

She cleared her throat. "Well, you know that darklings have to eat, right? Even if they only live one hour in twenty-five, predators still need prey to stay alive. Normal animals can step through into the blue time if they're in the wrong spot at exactly midnight. So darklings mostly eat unlucky rabbits and cows, but every once in a while a human being slips through."

"Hmmph," Madeleine said. "In my day, people knew where not to be at midnight."

"Yeah, well, your day got canceled," Dess said.

"Wait a second," Jonathan said. "I thought darklings couldn't hurt normal people."

Dess shook her head. "Once you poke through into midnight, you're part of that world for that hour. And eligible to join the darkling food chain."

Madeleine nodded. "We sometimes brought daylighter allies through so that they could see the blue time for themselves. A special treat. The strange thing was, once that midnight ended, they became frozen, just like darklings during normal time. They stayed that way until the sun struck them."

"Like Anathea," Jonathan said softly. "Trapped in midnight."

"Great, so we could have civilians running around in the blue time," Rex muttered. "And you said the eclipse was focused around these contortions?"

Slowly Madeleine's wrinkled hand drew shapes on the scratched table. "Not exactly, Rex. What the eclipse seemed to do was make more of them."

"*Make* them?" Dess said. The wrinkles in midnight were baked into the map with numbers. "You can't just change longitude and latitude like they're property lines!"

"And the darklings moved toward the ruptures," Melissa added quietly. "They could feel them too."

Maddy stood, walking around the table to place a hand

on Melissa's shoulder. "But we haven't compared experiences yet. We'll tell you when we know more. I'm sure you can amuse yourselves."

The two headed up to the attic together.

Rex looked screamingly jealous for an ill-concealed moment, then got all official. "Okay. I'll check some of your older lore books," he said to Maddy's departing footsteps. "Just in case."

Dess sighed. "And while those two are having mindcaster time, I'm going to take a look at some maps."

Rex looked at Jonathan, raising one eyebrow. Without Jessica around, Flyboy was sort of hopeless—couldn't read lore, couldn't do math, and here in the afternoon couldn't even fly. Dess felt sorry for him. What was he supposed to do? Wash the curtains?

"Um, I was wondering," Jonathan sputtered. "Does she have a TV?"

The house was starting to smell less old and musty, as if having its first visitors in half a century had breathed some life into it. But whenever Dess moved anything, pulled a book or map from the shelves, dust rose into the air, threatening to make her sneeze. Going home from a long night's work here, her fingers always felt dry and brittle, as if the ancient, thirsty dust had sucked the moisture from them.

While cleaning out the dining room, Dess had discovered a cache of Maddy's maps, yellowing rolls of heavy paper that practically crumbled in your hands. The oldest were annotated in Spanish, which gave Flyboy some translating to do, though he found the spindly, old-time hand-writing hard going. Of course, what Dess was after wasn't really the words. The secret hour was centered at exactly 36 degrees north latitude and 96 west longitude, and all the weirdness of Bixby flowed from those coordinates. This was all about the numbers.

Dess's most interesting discovery was how the early midnighters' maps compared with more recent efforts. For one thing, in the old days they hadn't invented GPS or decent clocks yet and had to rely on star readings and guesswork to plug the numbers in. So as you went further back, everything looked more and more warped and dis-torted, as if they'd been looking at the world through a Coke bottle. And of course, as time had passed, the early midnighters had explored more of the secret hour. Every century the maps of midnight's domain grew to cover a greater part of southeastern Oklahoma, or Indian Territory, or Mexico—depending on who'd stolen what last.

She'd been happily sitting at the dining table for an hour, absorbed in the slow progress of midnighter cartog-raphy, when a voice, joined by a cool hand on her shoulder, almost made her jump out of her skin.

"Desdemona?"

"Jeez! Scare me, why don't you?" Dess stared at Maddy's hand accusingly. At least the mindcaster hadn't touched her bare flesh.

"Pardon me, then." The wrinkled hand withdrew. "I just thought you might want to see this."

Madeleine placed a roll of paper on the table. It was a

map from the 1930s, the first map Maddy had ever shared with Dess, back when it had just been the two of them. But it was covered now with a layer of colored swirls, as if some kid had stuck red and blue pencils to a Ouija board pointer and let it roam freely.

"You guys drew on this?" Dess said angrily, but after a few seconds of staring, the map's new eddies and whorls began to engage her brain. The mindcasters' marks seemed to flesh out the usual contortions of midnight, adding another dimension to the map. It was like seeing the latest version of a familiar video game, the same old characters suddenly rendered in high resolution. "Oh," Dess added.

"You were right, you know," Maddy said softly.

Dess didn't take her eyes from the map. "About what?"

"I don't think the lore or memories will help us much. As you suspected, this is a riddle best solved by a polymath."

Dess swallowed. Had the old woman sneaked a quick peek into her brain when she'd touched Dess's leather jacket? "Gee, Maddy, I don't remember saying anything about that."

Madeleine only smirked at the nickname. "Sometimes, Dessy, it doesn't require mind reading to know what someone is thinking."

Dessy? Jeez. Maddy's revenge hadn't taken very long.

"Well, thanks. I'll take a closer look at this when I get a chance." Like, the moment Madeleine was out of sight.

The old mindcaster smiled. "Let me know what you find, Desdemona."

"Hey, there's something wrong with your TV!" Jonathan called. He was hunched over the giant set in the living room, a wood-paneled monstrosity that he'd spent the last hour freeing from a pile of thirty-nine-patterned fire grates.

Dess looked over at the machine and smirked. She was glad to see that Maddy didn't harbor any grudges against television. Last Dess had heard, Madeleine blamed TV— and air-conditioning, of course—for the destruction of the midnighters fifty years before. Something about watching the tube instead of the kids.

Madeleine stared archly into the weirdly rounded screen. It looked more like a goldfish bowl filled with murky water than a TV.

"Chicken-fried baloney, Jonathan. It's working fine." She turned and strode from the room, adding over her shoulder, "Just takes a while to warm up. In my day, young people were more patient."

Jonathan looked dubious, but something was definitely happening in the television's depths: a flicker of light had appeared in the center of the screen. It grew slowly, like a fire spreading through a pile of damp leaves, until it filled the dark glass with a blurry image.

"Man," he said softly. "Black and white."

"Looks more like gray and gray," Dess said. The screen was mostly full of snow. You could barely make out the weather guy standing in front of a map, the sweeping Doppler radar circling behind him looking very out of place on the ancient TV.

Jonathan turned a big dial that went *ka-thunk*, and the screen filled with static. As he searched in vain for a channel with a better picture, or any picture at all, Dess watched the little gray pixels dance. She remembered some weird factoid about those little dots of static, how they were the remnants of the most perfectly random thing in all of nature. . . .

Finally Jonathan sighed and *ka-thunked* his way back to the local news.

Dess tuned out the anchor's voice and took the last sip of her lukewarm tea, a tiny glob of leaves catching in her teeth. The details of the factoid came back to her now: there'd been something on the Discovery Channel (the only television that Dess ever watched) about how the snow on old TVs actually showed leftover radiation from the big bang, the explosion that had made the universe. That's why the dots were perfectly random—they were the result of a perfect explosion.

Well, *almost* perfect. The big bang, after all, had left a few billion clumpy bits of matter that had turned into galaxies and clusters of galaxies. The universe was lumpy, sort of like . . . tea leaves.

Or the blue time.

Dess's eyes lit up. She looked down at the map Madeleine had given her. The new shapes scrawled across it were spirals and pinwheels—like galaxies, the dregs of the big bang.

Maybe the secret hour had been created by some sort of explosion, or at least something violent and big bangish, with a similar mix of chaos and order, randomness and patterns.

Dess looked down into her cup. Cosmology was like reading tea leaves, figuring out the future by looking at the remnants of the past. Except unlike tea leaves, telescopes actually *worked*. You could tell where the universe was headed based on the dregs of the big bang.

Maybe she could look at these old maps and figure out what the future of the blue time was.

"Oh, right," Dess said suddenly. Math happiness wavered in her mind as she remembered something else from that same Discovery Channel show.

The universe hadn't been created stable. It was still expanding from the bang, all its parts moving gradually away from the center. She looked at her old maps—and saw again how as the centuries passed, the secret hour always seemed to cover a larger area. Maybe it wasn't just that the old midnighters had explored more . . . maybe the blue time had actually grown *bigger*.

Dess swallowed, suddenly remembering one more thing about the universe. One day it would end, scientists said, either by spreading out into mush, a big whimper, or when gravity pulled it all together again into a big crunch.

Nobody knew which way it was going yet, but someday there would definitely come a big Game Over.

"Hey, Dess, check this out."

Jonathan's voice cut through her reverie, and Dess snapped from the end of the universe back into late-afternoon light and musty Maddy-house smells. Jonathan was standing beside her, pointing at the TV. A blurry older woman was talking about how her granddaughter had disappeared.

It cut back to the anchor, who started yammering about a police hotline, an ongoing search, state troopers bringing in dogs. Dess hardly listened, but that word kept being repeated in various forms . . . *disappearing girl, strange disappearance, she just disappeared.*

"Right in front of her grandma's eyes," Jonathan said. "As in, she was there one moment and gone the next."

"Crap," Dess said. "When?"

"This morning," Jonathan whispered. "Around 9 A.M."

"Where?"

He leaned over the map Maddy had brought down, outstretched hand sliding across to a cluster of whorls in the northwest corner. "They said it was near Jenks, on the railroad tracks." His fingers found the hatched path of the rail line, old enough to be included on an eighty-year-old map. The tiny town of Jenks was labeled there too.

Dess pushed his hand away, and her pencil moved to the spot, scribbling calculations. Rough and hand-drawn though they were, the new shapes that Maddy and Melissa had scrawled possessed their own logic, were ruled by their own patterns and laws. It *was* sort of like mapping the stars, seemingly random points of light that added up to show you the big picture—as long as you did the math right.

The whorls and eddies seemed to rise up from the paper and enter Dess, running like sugar-rushing hamsters on all the wheels of her brain. They made her dizzy, made her fingers tremble as they tried to record her intuitive leaps.

But finally they began to come into focus. . . .

After five long minutes she leaned back exhausted, pointing. "This is where it's broken."

"Where what's broken?"

"The blue time. It's starting to snap, Jonathan, probably to break down completely. But some coordinates will go quicker than others. And anyone who's standing around in the wrong place when they do . . ."

Jonathan sat down next to her, staring at the map with its chaos of scribbled numbers and mindcaster swirls. "So what happened to that girl?"

"*Midnight* happened to her, Jonathan. It opened up and swallowed her."

"So she's where now?"

"Well, she should have come out of it when time started again, when the sun hit her. Unless she was taken somewhere."

"Melissa said the darklings were headed that way."

Dess blinked. "They only had twenty-one minutes and thirty-six seconds."

"So she might still be okay?"

"Yeah, probably. Unless . . ."

Part of Dess's brain wanted to explain the whole thing to Jonathan: about snow on TV screens, the big bang, and the shapes of galaxies and tea leaves. About how you could know how something was going to happen in the future by looking into the dregs of the past, so maybe the darklings had predicted *exactly* where it would happen, exactly where their young prey would fall between the cracks of time. They could have lured her away to someplace dark and underground. . . .

She didn't have a chance to say a word before another set of images rushed into her mind—also straight from the Discovery Channel—and Dess found herself silent and shivering in her chair.

She wasn't thinking about the big bang anymore.

She was thinking about the food chain.

6

SPEED BUMP

Jonathan sat in his father's car, drumming on the steering wheel. Jessica was late. Halfway down the block, he could see her window still glowing. She hadn't even turned her lights off yet.

What was she waiting for? Tonight every second counted.

On the phone with Jessica this afternoon, the five of them had planned everything to the minute: Jonathan had driven here instead of flying during the secret hour. Jessica was supposed to sneak out at eleven-thirty, leaving time to get within a mile of the spot where Cassie Flinders had disappeared. Then when midnight fell, they'd be at most a few jumps away.

Dess, Rex, and Melissa were already there, which made it doubly important to stay on schedule. Jenks wasn't exactly the badlands, and the three were well armed with clean steel, but the spot was too far from the city's center for them to survive forever without the flame-bringer's protection.

He looked at his watch—11:38. "Where are you, Jessica?"

The words echoed in his mind, and Jonathan remembered what they'd kept saying on the evening news: *Where is Cassie Flinders?*

If Dess was right, the lost girl had slipped into the blue time.

Jonathan let out a breath through his teeth—a daylighter walking around in their private world. Just when he thought he understood the secret hour, it threw another curveball.

Of course, it was nothing like the curveball that reality had thrown Cassie Flinders.

Rex and Madeleine kept talking like she might be okay. Cassie could have wandered off during the eclipse and wound up somewhere out of the sun's reach, frozen in darkness, like the darklings were during daylight hours. And once midnight fell, she would awake again, and Melissa would find her, no problem. All they had to do was protect her until the secret hour ended, when a blast from Jessica's flashlight or—if that didn't work—the eventual arrival of sunrise would push her back into regular time.

Of course, there was also the possibility that Cassie hadn't wandered off—that she'd been taken. If the darklings had actually known in advance where the blue time was going to wrinkle, they could have flown straight to the spot and taken her away, deep into the desert where no one would ever find her again.

There was a third possibility as well: they could have simply eaten her on the spot, right in front of her grandmother's frozen, unseeing eyes.

"Come *on*, Jessica . . ." He tapped one fist against the hard, cold metal of the dashboard.

An endless, whispered count of sixty later, Jonathan swore, checked the rearview mirror for any sign of curfew-sniffing cop cars, and stepped out into the cold autumn air.

New flower beds edged Jessica's house, her father's latest project. He was getting into gardening in a big way, she'd said, trying to grow all the vegetables the family ate. Apparently he hadn't noticed that the season was changing into fall, the ground turning cold and hard at night.

Jonathan tried to step lightly on the overturned earth, wondering if Don Day's gardening efforts weren't just an excuse to look for footprints under Jessica's window. Jonathan cursed his Flatland heaviness; in the blue time he could have just floated over to the sill.

Voices. He ducked down.

He could hear Jessica speak, then someone answering. Muffled through the window, the voice's high-pitched insistence reminded Jonathan of a mosquito trapped under a glass.

His heartbeat settled a little. Probably only Beth. He eased his head up to peer inside.

They both sat on the bed, no parents in sight. Jessica was dressed, her little sister huddled in pajamas. Beth was still talking, waving her hands around frantically, as if warding off an attack of houseflies. Jonathan saw Jessica glance over at her bedside clock, where the approach of midnight was clearly displayed.

Why didn't Jessica just get rid of her? On a school night it had to be past Beth's bedtime by now.

Jonathan raised a fist to the glass, steeling himself to knock. Jessica wouldn't appreciate him announcing his presence in front of the little sister, especially on the very last night of her grounding. But Beth wouldn't tell her parents—Jessica's sister wasn't that uncool.

Besides, there were more important things at stake here.

According to the news, Cassie Flinders was thirteen, about the same age that Anathea had been when the dark-lings had taken her. Jonathan remembered how small she had been, almost disappearing into the darkling body they had grafted to her.

Of course, Cassie was no seer. She couldn't read the lore; the darklings wouldn't bother to make a halfling out of her. She wouldn't last very long in the blue time, except maybe for the fillings in her teeth.

He knocked.

Both sisters jumped at the noise, the sound of Beth's voice choking off mid-sentence. She stared at Jonathan's face in the window for a moment, then focused a cold gaze on Jessica.

As Jonathan pushed the sash up, he heard her whisper, "I *knew* it!"

Jessica just stared at him.

"Hey, guys," he said.

"Well, hey there, Jonathan," Beth said sweetly. "Just dropping by?"

"Jonathan!" Jessica groaned. "Couldn't you have . . ." Her voice trailed off.

He climbed in and looked from one sister to the other. Beth's eyes were narrowed, and Jess was staring at the floor and shaking her head. He sighed. "Look, I'm really sorry to interrupt, Beth. But something's come up. Something *important*." He looked at Jessica to emphasize that last word.

"You're sneaking out *tonight*?" Beth said, her whispering only making the words harsher. "You've only got one more day, Jess. Do you want to get grounded again?"

"Believe me," Jessica said. "I really don't."

"Listen, Beth, I only need to borrow your sister for . . ." Jonathan glanced at the clock. "Eighteen minutes. I promise she'll be back by then."

Jessica closed her eyes as Beth's stare swung across to the clock.

"Eighteen minutes?" Beth said.

Jonathan swallowed. Jessica's little sister didn't know anything about the blue time, of course, but she had an uncanny way of making you think she did. "Yeah. More or less."

Jessica stood, pulling her jacket from the bed. "Come on. Let's just go."

"*Jessica*," Beth whined.

"Look," Jessica said tiredly. "If you're going to tell Mom

and Dad, go ahead. I don't have time for this."

"Jess, I don't *want* you to be in trouble," Beth whispered, tears welling up in her eyes. "I just want to know what's going on with you."

"I'm sorry, okay?" Jessica paused, as if struggling for words. "But I need to get out of here *right now*, and I can't explain why."

"And you're going to sneak out right in front of me?" Beth crossed her arms. "So I'll be in trouble too when you get caught?"

"That's *your* fault, Beth. I told you to leave half an hour ago."

"Can you at least explain when you come back . . . in eighteen minutes?"

Jessica sighed. "Sorry, Beth, I'd love to. I just can't."

"Got your flashlight?" Jonathan said, one foot already out the window.

She thumped a bulge in her jacket. "Yeah, right here."

They slipped out, dropping to the soft earth of the garden. Jonathan heard one last complaint cut off by Jessica's sliding the window closed and thought again how he couldn't wait for midnight gravity to arrive. Finally he would be unstuck from Flatland, able to fly again, and all little sisters would be mutely frozen.

And the darklings will come to life, he realized, checking his watch as they jogged toward the car.

Midnight was coming, all right. Way too soon.

"Why did you have to say that?"

"Say what?"

"That thing about eighteen minutes exactly," Jessica said. "It was kind of obvious, don't you think?"

Jonathan shrugged. The clock had said 11:42, and he could fly Jess back here by the end of the secret hour, midnight on the dot. He did see her point, though. Maybe he had been a little too precise about exactly when Jessica would return.

He sighed, watching a flattened armadillo flash past on the road. Listening to Dess talk math all afternoon had crowded his brain with numbers. "What's the difference, anyway?"

"Beth's starting to figure out that midnight's important." Jessica was staring out the passenger window. "She's noticed that I'm always getting ready to leave around twelve, and she's started showing up just before the secret hour starts. If I kick her out, she'll probably just go get Mom and Dad. It's like she *knows*. Ever since that night I shoved her in the closet—right at the stroke of midnight."

Jonathan chuckled. "Well, maybe you shouldn't shove her in closets."

"You're lucky—nobody but your father, and no hassle from him."

He winced a little at that and took one hand off the wheel, reaching out to her. She was nervously playing with Acariciandote, the bracelet he'd given her, and he stilled her hand. "That was my mom's, remember?"

"Oh. Sorry, Jonathan."

"It's okay. She ran off all the time, so it wasn't a huge

surprise when she didn't come back. But you're lucky to have family."

She was quiet for a moment. "Yeah."

Jonathan wished he hadn't brought it up. Talking about this kind of stuff never helped. "Anyway, Beth probably isn't going to guess that time freezes at the stroke of twelve and a secret blue world full of monsters appears." Jonathan laughed. "She might be smart, but she's not that smart."

Jessica turned toward him. "You don't really mind her that much, do you? You *like* her."

"Sure. Don't you?"

"Yeah. But she's my sister. I sort of have to."

Jonathan chuckled again. "Listen. You guys used to get along before you moved here, right? You will again, once Beth gets used to the weird ways of Bixby. And yeah, I *do* like her. Since you introduced us, I feel like less of a stalker when I'm sneaking around."

Jessica drew closer, leaning her weight against him. "Yeah, it's been better since she got to know you. I think she trusts you. At least, she doesn't think you're a serial killer anymore."

Jonathan smiled, but the expression faded as he glanced at his watch: only ten more minutes before the blue time fell, and they were about that many miles from Jenks. He stepped on the gas, the old car shuddering as it accelerated. They had more important things to worry about tonight than little sisters.

They zoomed passed an old Chevy that was lumbering

down Creek Turnpike. This far out of town the roads were almost empty, which meant that his father's car would be easy for his old friends in the sheriff's department to spot. He was sure that by now, they'd recognize it from halfway across the county.

Jonathan didn't know what he'd do then. Get stopped for breaking curfew, maybe go to jail again, and risk Cassie Flinders disappearing forever? Or do a grand theft auto, get the cops into hot pursuit mode, and get Jessica and himself into more trouble than Beth could ever have imagined?

Not a great choice.

Jessica cleared her throat. "Um, I hope you're not planning on going this fast when time freezes. Don't want to fly through the windshield, personally."

"Midnight's not for ten more minutes. Unless there's another eclipse."

She pulled away, sitting straighter in her seat and checking her seat belt. "Oh, right. Thanks for reminding me. Midnight can come at any time now."

"Yeah. Cool, huh?"

"Uh, no, Jonathan. *Not* cool. What if it keeps happening?"

He shrugged. "Then we get to fly around more."

She sighed. "You'd love that, wouldn't you?"

"What? *More* midnight? The whole world belonging to just us five? Less time in Flatland? Sure, I would."

"But we don't understand what's happening, Jonathan. On the phone Dess said something about the blue time changing completely. And today we didn't know if the eclipse was ever going to stop. It felt like the world had ended."

"Yeah, right. Like that's going to happen." He snorted. "And anyhow, look at it this way: if the world ends, you won't have to worry about Beth anymore."

Jessica just turned away, staring out the passenger window and not saying another word.

Jonathan frowned, wondering what he'd said wrong now.

7

PREY

Melissa's eyes rolled back in her head, her nose wrinkling. Rex saw a shudder pass through her body from toes to fingertips.

"What, did they stop already?" Rex asked.

She shook her head. "No, Flyboy's still got his pedal all the way down. They'll get here in time, more or less. But the flame-bringer's not in a very good mood."

Dess glanced up from her GPS device and snorted. Rex shook his head. Great time for a lovers' quarrel.

He swept his eyes across the railroad tracks again. This place was wrapped in Focus, inhuman marks corrupting every piece of gravel in the rail bed, every blade of grass shooting up through the wooden cross-ties. Darklings and slithers had danced here. Even the steel spikes in the iron rails bore the traces of their claws and snouts and slithering bellies.

All this Focus couldn't have been laid down in twenty-one minutes. They must have come here before the eclipse.

Of course, Rex thought, there were always a few midnight places on the outskirts of town. Perhaps it was only a coincidence that this weak spot had been visited before.

He knelt to take a closer look at a slitherprint, a sinuous line that wound down the railroad tracks as far as he could see. It didn't look especially fresh, not like a trail left only fifteen hours ago.

But Rex frowned; his new hunter's nerves were twitching with all the metal around him. Why would a slither travel down a railroad line that reeked of iron rails, steel bolts, and buried telegraph lines? Most darkling places on the city's edges were open fields and empty back lots, places where little patches of the wild still clung—stands of native plants, snake holes, or small creeks not yet erased by buildings and concrete. But this iron path was an artery of the rail system, an old and powerful symbol of human cleverness and dominance. Only a hundred years ago it had represented the highest technology that humanity possessed, yet the darklings had embraced this spot. They must have come here with a purpose.

Rex saw how far the Focus stretched up and down the track, how it trailed off into the brush and extended even to the ramshackle houses backed up against the right-of-way. He wondered how far into the mesquite trees it went. The small town of Jenks was close to the Arkansas River, and the scrub in these parts was impenetrably dense, hiding much of the landscape from his new predator's eyes.

But old darklings had been here, of that Rex was sure. He could see deep, clawed footprints in the soil and a broad tree branch that had almost cracked under the weight of something huge and winged. There were slither burrows scattered throughout the underbrush; darklings young and old hid from the sun out in the deep desert caves, but some of their little minions nested closer to town, buried under the earth.

It took time to layer a place with this much Focus, this many signs. They must have begun months ago, maybe a lot longer than that. Melissa and Madeleine had felt their celebrations out in the desert: the darklings had somehow known that the eclipse was coming and exactly where it would happen. Which meant they'd probably also known what Dess had discovered today, that this first tear in the blue time would spread like a rip along the seam of an old T-shirt.

Maybe it had always been their plan that the blue time would one day come apart. But what would happen then?

Suddenly something caught Rex's eye. One of the railroad track cross-ties stood out, a halo of red surrounding it. He looked closer and smelled the inherent strangeness of the spot. The blue time was paper-thin here.

The old wood of the cross-tie was marked with a sliver of Focus, looking out of place here among the stains of darklings. He drew closer and saw in the half-moon shape the distinctive tread of a sneaker.

That was why it looked different—that *other* kind of Focus clung to it, the kind Rex had only learned to see over the last couple of weeks.

"Prey," he said softly.

"Five minutes," announced Dess, nervously rocking the long piece of steel pipe that rested on her shoulder. "How's the flame-bringer doing?"

"Close," Melissa said. "But they're slowing down. Wimps."

"Not everyone appreciates the subtle pleasures of flying through a windshield, Melissa," Dess said.

"They've got five whole minutes before midnight, and Flyboy's already parking it!"

"How far are they?" Rex interrupted.

"A few miles."

"Not good." He followed the trail of human Focus with his gaze. The glimmering footprints left the rail bed and headed down into the dense undergrowth. "She went this way. On foot, not being dragged."

"Who? Cassie?" Dess asked.

Rex nodded.

"You can *see* that?"

"I can see the traces of humans now," he said, pointing at the trail. "And these footprints look like they were made in the blue time. Cassie must have left them during the eclipse."

Dess's face twisted into a skeptical expression. Other than Melissa and Madeleine, none of them yet understood how different he had become.

Rex knelt on the tracks and sniffed. He could smell the uncertainty of the lost girl, could see her fear in the tentative distance between the steps. It made his mouth water, his palms sweat. This was a young one, weak and ready to be cut from the herd.

"Get a grip, Rex," Melissa said softly.

He shook the hunting thoughts from his head. "Okay, I'm going to track her. She might still be close by. You guys stay here. But yell out a countdown for the last thirty seconds, Dess." He slid down the loose gravel bank of the rail bed and plunged into the thick bushes.

"Rex!" Dess shouted. "There's only four minutes left! Get back here."

"Quit showing off, Rex," Melissa called. "Once midnight falls and her brain starts up again, I'll find her right away."

Rex glanced back. The two of them were standing inside Polychronious, a large and complex tridecagram that Dess had laid down on a patch of clearing, using a spool of fiber-optic cable stolen from Oklahoma Telecom a few midnights ago. The cable smelled bright and buzzy to Rex, like cleaning detergent fumes going up his nose, and the thirteen-pointed star Dess had woven with it made his head spin. They would be safe from darklings inside it, even if the flame-bringer was a few minutes late.

"Just give me that countdown," he called back.

"Rex!" Dess wailed.

He noticed that she and Melissa were standing as far apart as they could inside the tridecagram, like two rival cats locked in a small room together.

Whatever. They'd live.

Rex pushed his way deeper into the underbrush, fighting the bare, brittle branches of mesquite. He could see in the dark better than ever now, and the spaces between leafless

trees and scrub seemed to open up before him. He soon
realized that his prey's slender marks of Focus followed a
narrow path, probably an old animal trail.

As Cassie's footsteps went deeper into the brush, they
began to grow more sure and purposeful, as if after the first
few minutes of confusion in the blue time, she'd headed for
someplace where she felt safe.

A branch caught Rex, bending taut, then whipping
backward, leaving a long rip in his shirt. The girl must
have grown up around here to move so easily through this
overgrowth. He could tell she was much shorter than
him—from her footprints, she had walked almost upright
underneath branches that he was forced to crouch
beneath.

Her footsteps grew farther apart; moving more swiftly
now, as if coaxed forward by some goal. Rex swore—he
wasn't going to find the girl before midnight fell. She'd had
twenty-one minutes to get wherever she'd disappeared to,
and he had only . . .

"Thirty seconds, Rex!" Dess's voice called through
the trees.

He paused. To make it back to safety, he should turn
around now and start running. Inside Dess's ring of protection, they could wait for the flame-bringer. In the blue
time Melissa would be able to taste the lost girl's thoughts
even if she were miles away.

Of course, Cassie couldn't have actually gotten that far
in twenty minutes unless the darklings had swooped down

and carried her off. And if that had happened, she probably wasn't alive and certainly wouldn't survive the long minutes it would take Jonathan and Jessica to reach her.

Rex sniffed the trail before him. An electric trickle of fear still lingered in the human scent, mixed with excitement and wonder. It made something within him grow hungry. This was the smell of those young, adventurous humans who tended to stray too far from their villages—the call of easy meat.

Part of Rex knew that he should do the sensible thing. He should head back to safety and get everyone organized: keep Dess and Melissa from fighting with each other, tell Jonathan and Jessica what to do when they arrived, maybe fly along with them to the rescue. No one but he could be the leader that the group needed.

But the smell of the lone girl drew him forward, calling his entire body down the narrow path. Cassie Flinders felt *so close*. His hands tingled with how near she was, and a raw imperative filled him . . .

Reach her before the others do. She's yours.

Rex took an unsteady step forward. He had to get there first.

"Fifteen!" Dess's distant cry reached him. "Where the hell are you, Rex? *Ten.* You're-an-idiot-*nine*, get-back-here-*eight*, you-dimwit-*seven*. . . ."

Rex plunged deeper into the undergrowth.

Seconds later the earth shuddered under his feet. Blue light swept through the brush and across the sky, dulling the stars and bringing every branch and blade of grass into sharp relief, his vision suddenly seer-perfect.

He breathed in the hungry essence of the blue time, the mental clarity of midnight.

Ahead of him in the distance Rex's sharp ears caught a small cry of surprise and fear . . . Cassie waking up in the blue time.

It made him hungrier.

Only a minute after midnight's fall, things were beginning to stir in every direction. Slithers were worming their way up out of the deep burrows that protected them from the sun, signaling one another with their strange, chirping calls. It was like first light on some weird spring morning, the birds waking up and making a ruckus.

There were *lots* of slithers out here. Suddenly the steel hoops around his boots didn't feel like enough protection. He swept his eyes back and forth nervously across the dense brush, searching for the sharp Focus of their burrows, imagining the icy sting of a slither strike catching him on the leg. Rex had once worked on his grandfather's farm in Texas during harvest season; every step through these burrows reminded him of the anxious moment of lifting a hay bale and not knowing if an angry rattler lay underneath.

Another cry reached his ears, and Rex tore his eyes from the forest floor. Through the trees he saw a wedge of stone jutting up from the earth, cut in two by a narrow fissure. It was a tight fit even for a little kid but enough cover to hide Cassie from the sun.

Why had she gone in there? It seemed like incredibly bad luck to have wandered into a cave hidden from the sun's rays.

Unless she had somehow been coaxed into coming here . . .

Rex pulled his gloves on. These days the touch of stainless steel made his bare flesh itch during the secret hour, but leather gloves allowed him a solid grip on his new weapon. Dess had decorated the hunting knife's blade with a superfine guitar string wound in patterns that made his eyes burn and water. The knife had the clever human smell of a finely tooled bicycle part—all modern alloys and precise proportions—buzzing with a thousand ingenious angles.

It make his head hurt to look at it, even to think its name, which meant that the weapon could fend off any darkling, at least for the short time it would take for Jessica and Jonathan to get here. The secret hour had begun almost three minutes ago—they had to be on their way.

From just outside the mouth of the fissure, he stared into the gloom. A blue glow emanated from the rocks, revealing layers of slither Focus in the cave, plus one slender trail of human footsteps. The crevice went deeper than he'd thought, the Oklahoma shale crumpled into zigzags by some ancient earthquake.

He paused to listen. The short, raspy breaths of a panicking thirteen-year-old reached his ears.

"Cassie?" he called.

The breathing caught, then a voice answered softly, "Help me."

The girl sounded much younger than thirteen; probably she was frightened out of her wits. "Are you okay?"

"My grandma froze."

"She's better now, Cassie," he said calmly. "But she's worried about you. Are you all right?"

"It hurts."

"What hurts, Cassie?"

"My foot. Where the kitty bit me."

A cat. Rex remembered the slither that Jessica had followed on the first night the darklings had tried to kill her. It had disguised itself as a black cat and scratched on her window, then led her out onto Bixby's empty streets to where a darkling awaited. They must have used the same trick on Cassie Flinders. With the whole world transformed into a frozen, empty place around her, she had innocently followed the only other living creature she could see.

"It's okay, Cassie. My name's Rex. I'm here to take you home."

She didn't answer.

"Cassie, you have to tell me: is there anything else in there? Anything besides the kitty?"

"It went away."

"That's good." The slither must have struck as the eclipse had ended, just before heading back to its burrow. It had hobbled Cassie to make sure she didn't wander out of the cave, out to where the sunlight would free her from the blue time. Cassie had been frozen for the fifteen hours since the eclipse—to her the cat had only run off a few minutes ago.

"But there are snakes in here, Rex," Cassie said. "They're *looking* at me."

He tried to ignore the fear in her voice, the way it made him react. He could tell from her breathing that she was sick and remembered from the news that she'd been home from school with a head cold. Easy prey.

It was going to be tricky coaxing her out of the cave. In his darkling dreams Rex had seen humans paralyzed by their own fear when cornered.

Standing sideways, he tried to push deeper into the fissure, but after only a few feet, teeth of sharp stone closed on his spine and ribs. "Cassie? Try to come toward me."

"I can't."

"I know your foot hurts, Cassie. But you can still walk."

"No. They won't let me."

Crap, Rex thought. The slithers had her trapped in there. He wondered whether even the beam of Jessica's flashlight could reach back to where Cassie was. He reached out with his hunting knife and struck the stone a glancing blow. A single blue spark flared blindingly, illuminating the jagged walls of the fissure for an instant.

"Did you see that, Cassie?"

"That flash?"

"Yeah. Good girl. I'm not far from you." Rex leaned his weight against the stone and stood on one leg, pulling the metal hoops from his boot. Then he reversed his stance and yanked them off the other. "I'm going to throw some things, Cassie. They're going to scare the snakes. You have to run this way when you see sparks."

"I can't. They're looking at me." Her voice had gone flat, as if hypnotized by the lifeless stare of the slithers.

"They won't bite you if you're fast, okay? I'm going to count to three, then scare them."

"Rex. I can't. My foot."

"Just get ready. One . . ." He held the hoops almost to his lips and whispered their names—Woolgathering, Inexhaustible, Unquestioning, and Vulnerability—the Aversions sending a shooting migraine through the darkling half of his brain. "Two . . . three . . . *run!*"

He threw the handful of hoops as hard as he could, and they careened deep into the cave, raising up a shower of sparks as they clanged off the walls. The bright, ringing sound of metal striking stone cut painfully into Rex's ears.

"You scared them!" Cassie announced.

"Well, *run* then, dammit!"

As the echoes of his shout died, Rex heard her sneakers' squeaky footfalls carrying her through the sharp angles of the cave. She came into view a few seconds later, limping and white-faced as she pulled herself down the narrow channel of stone. Rex reached out a gloved hand and pulled her from the crevice after him, out under the rising bulk of the dark moon.

Outside he stumbled to a halt. An army of slithers surrounded them. A host of the creatures covered the ground, and their winged forms filled every tree branch.

"Snakes . . ." Cassie said softly.

Melissa, Rex thought as hard as he could.

In the depths of his mind he heard the faintest word—*Coming*—and wondered if that meant Melissa and Dess were coming, or Jessica . . . or if something else was on its way.

"It's all right," he said, drawing Cassie closer and thrusting the knife out before them.

Then he saw the darkling.

It seemed to uncoil from the ground, its eight legs spreading out from its bulbous center like the blooming of some horrific flower. A tarantula, the desert spider of his nightmares.

Rex wondered where it had come from, whether it had flown here swiftly from the desert or crouched in some rocky warren out of the sun, waiting since the eclipse for this ancient delicacy—a rare meal of human flesh.

"Rex . . . ?" Cassie said softly.

That had been the plan, of course: the slither-cat leading her to this spot, trapping her in the cave until its master arrived at midnight. Next the slithers inside would have driven her into its jaws . . . if Rex hadn't already coaxed her out himself.

"Go back inside," he whispered.

She only clung to him tighter.

"Go back in the cave, Cassie!" he shouted. "That thing can't fit in there!"

"But the snakes!"

Rex turned to look. The blue-lit depths of the cave were dotted with the eyes of slithers staring back at them.

"Here, take this," he said, pressing the hunting knife into her hand. "They're scared of it, and help is coming."

She held the knife loosely, looking down at it with wide eyes.

"It's name is Animalization," he said. His fists clenched in pain as Dess's pointed little tridecalogism passed his lips. "Keep saying that, and they'll be really scared. *Animalization.*"

"But—"

"Go!" He shoved her into the fissure, hoping she would find the courage to go deep into the cave, far enough to escape the thin, reaching arms of the darkling.

He whirled back around to face the creature, crouching down into a fighting stance. Its eight legs had extended to full length, pressing against the ground to lift the central body mass up into the air. The legs were covered not with hair, but with glistening spurs, like thorns on some vast and hideous rosebush. The entire beast was dripping with a viscous black substance, as if it had been dipped in crude oil.

Rex flexed his empty hands, realizing that he was completely unarmed. He had no knife, no metal on his boots, and yelling thirteen-letter words would hurt him more than it would any darkling.

"Where *are* you, Jessica?" he whispered, daring a glance at his watch.

His heart sank. Only six minutes of the secret hour had passed.

She wasn't going to make it here in time.

The darkling's two forward legs raised and its body rested on its rear, the posture of a tarantula facing an enemy. Rex could see the fangs in its oily maw, shivering with the creature's hunger.

He remembered being forced to stand still at ten years old as his father's pet tarantulas crawled across his bare flesh. The weird slowness with which they moved, the interlocking motions of their eight legs, the sickening fascination that they compelled.

His father's voice came back to him: *Relax, boy! They're not poisonous. They can't hurt you. Be a man!*

Hairy spiders had crawled through every one of his childhood nightmares.

Rex waited for the darkling to strike. Its two forward legs made slow circles in the air, like the arms of a dog paddling in water. The sinuous motion threatened to hypnotize him, and he tore his gaze away.

He stared at the ground, his heart pounding, every muscle tensed, ready to fight a hopeless battle. But somehow, Rex realized, something in his reaction was missing. The gnawing fear in his stomach hadn't come yet; the spider didn't terrify him as it should have.

In fact, he couldn't remember having a single dream since the darklings had changed him that had included his father's tarantulas. He and Melissa had killed them after the accident had left the old man helpless, but Rex had always known their ghosts were lurking beneath his house, waiting to wreak revenge.

He looked up at the giant spider again and realized that the cold sweat of those childhood traumas had disappeared. His arachnophobia (his brain twinged at the word's thirteen letters) was gone.

Another moment passed, and still the creature didn't strike.

Rex bared his teeth at the beast, and a sound gurgled up from his throat—the same hiss that had turned Timmy Hudson into a puddle of melted bully.

Of course, the darkling before him wasn't so easily scared. It stood firm on its six hind legs, the dance of its spurs still mesmerizing, its bulk glistening in the dark moon's light. But as the long seconds stretched out, it didn't strike.

Slowly the reason dawned on him. The beast hadn't taken a hunting stance at all—Rex wasn't prey. This wasn't the kill at the end of a chase; it was a ritual between two predators, like a standoff over some carcass. The spider's dance was posturing and bluster, a challenge made, hoping that another hunter would back down. But Rex had gotten here first to claim the kill.

He stood his ground.

Wolves didn't eat other wolves, after all.

For a long minute he faced the creature, letting the motions of the contest move through him. His fingers clenched into rigid claws, slowly cutting the air like a familiar ceremony unfolding. Neither he nor the darkling advanced, held apart by mutual respect and fear.

Then Rex felt a flavor in his mind, not Melissa's familiar taste—but something ancient and arid, like dust on his tongue, hardly words at all.

Join us.

He swallowed, his throat parched, staring back at the darkling.

We will hunt again soon.

Rex tried to hiss again, to ward off the murmurings inside his head.

Then he felt a rush of fear from the beast, its cold heart suddenly pounding, driving its bloated body like a lash. The darkling turned away and twisted quickly into a new shape, growing thin and long and sprouting wings. Then with one last hiss of its own, it leapt into the air, a host of slithers whirling around it. A great dark cloud of them gathered as the darkling disappeared into the sky, the local burrows emptying, running for fear of the flame-bringer.

As the creature left his sight, a last thought trailed from it . . .

Winter is coming, halfling. Join.

Rex fell onto one knee, exhausted and shaking. His head was throbbing, one half of his mind warring against the other. The world around him seemed to flex and bend, his seer's Focus overwhelmed by the warped vision of a darkling.

He'd actually heard the thing in his mind—not just caught fleeting tastes and emotions like Melissa casting across the desert. He could *talk* to them now.

"You scared it."

The small voice sucked him back into reality and the cool light of the blue time, and Rex whirled around to face its source. Cassie clutched the hunting knife with both hands, staring back at him, her eyes wide with amazement. The patterns woven onto the knife stung his eyes.

"How did you do that?" she asked. "It was so big."

Speechless, Rex found himself watching Cassie's heartbeat pulsing in her throat, the blood close to the surface. The awe on her face was like the hopeless gaze of paralyzed prey, caught and cornered by its pursuers. Helplessly he felt the hunger rising inside him.

The other darkling had left this prey for him, small and alone.

Join us, Rex heard the beast's words echo in his mind, and realized that he could end the awful struggle within himself now, with just one easy kill.

8

NIGHTMARE INTERRUPTED

"There they go," Jessica said.

A cloud of slithers was swirling up from the dense trees in the distance, like a flock of birds sent into flight by a gunshot. She and Jonathan were at the top of their arc, the straight line of the railroad track below them leading off toward the deep desert.

"Never seen that many before," Jonathan said. "Not since . . ." His voice trailed off.

Jessica saw that the swarm had split, half of them wheeling around, heading toward her and Jonathan.

"What are they up to?" she said. The darklings had mostly steered clear of Jessica since she'd discovered her talent. But this flock of slithers almost looked intent on attacking. The creatures were spreading out, flying low, rushing toward them like oil spreading across the treetops.

"Not sure." Jonathan squeezed her hand. "And I think we're lost. Hold up a second."

They were descending into a small clearing near the railroad tracks. She bent her knees on landing, the soft grass absorbing their momentum.

"Which way?" she asked. From the ground the trees looked the same in every direction.

Jonathan shook his head. "Don't know. And we're taking way too long."

The trip from the car had eaten up precious minutes, but at least they'd been moving fast, bounding straight down a dirt road, then through a neighborhood of shabby houses set on large, junk-strewn lots. At the rendezvous point Melissa had pointed in the direction Rex had wandered off, saying he was only half a mile away. But the dense brush had forced them to take small jumps from clearing to clearing, weaving their way toward him. This was the worst kind of terrain to fly across; mesquite trees were dangerous, with their razor-sharp thorns.

After all this aimless bouncing around, Jessica figured that the other two were probably there already, charging straight through the trees under Melissa's guidance. She just hoped they had enough Dess-made weapons to protect Rex and the lost girl—and themselves—until she and Jonathan finally managed to discover a flight path.

"I *think* it's that way," Jonathan said. "But what were those—?"

Suddenly a wave of silent shapes surged through the trees. The slithers' wings were furled into their snakelike bodies, like black arrows launched by invisible archers. Jessica's arms shot up just in time to ward off one flying toward her face. Acariciandote exploded with blue sparks, its charms glowing white-hot, but the icy needles of a slither bite shot all the way up into her shoulder.

"Jess!" Jonathan pulled her to himself, shielding her with his body. She heard the *thunk* of a slither plowing into his back, and he let out a grunt of pain.

With her good hand Jessica pulled Disintegrator from her pocket and turned it on, the beam of white light cutting through the blue time, turning a few of the darting shapes into flaming streaks of red fire.

She played her flashlight through the trees in all directions, the familiar glow of power moving through her. But the beam connected with nothing. The swarm had passed through the clearing in seconds flat.

Jonathan pulled away, groaning and stretching to reach the middle of his back. "Ow! Right on my spine! Little creeps."

"What was that all about?" Jessica cried, flicking off the flashlight.

Jonathan opened his eyes, blinking away the white light. "Who knows? Maybe they didn't realize it was you. . . . *Down!*" He wrapped his arms around her, pulling her to the ground.

Jessica heard the whistle of more slithers passing just overhead; they'd shot from the trees again, coming from a new direction, fearless of her flame-bringer's power. She turned Disintegrator on and waved it randomly, missing completely as the last slithers disappeared into the trees.

"We need to jump!" Jonathan cried, his eyes shut tight against the white light. "They're using the trees for cover!"

He pulled her up from the ground by her numbed hand, jumping straight up into the sky. They spun slowly around each other, their flight unbalanced from the uncoordinated jump.

Nothing was in the air with them, but Jessica saw another flight of slithers slicing from the trees and through the spot where they had stood a moment before. She angled Disintegrator's beam downward, and soon the clearing floor was dotted with screaming, burning bodies.

"What are they doing? Don't they know I'll just kill them?"

"I think they're trying to delay us."

As they reached the peak of the jump, Jessica whipped the flashlight around, but nothing flew nearby. In the distance, though, the rest of the slither cloud had gathered itself around a rising black nucleus, a single darkling on the wing.

"That's not good," she said. The rescue plan had assumed it would take a while for anything big to reach Jenks from the deep desert. But apparently a darkling had come early, while she, the flame-bringer, had been late.

"Can I open my eyes?" Jonathan said as they began to descend.

She swept the flashlight across the trees below them one more time, but nothing sparked to life, and she flicked it off. "Sure."

As they began to descend, Jonathan swept his gaze across the horizon swiftly, then pointed with his free hand. "That's it over there."

Among the low, gnarly mesquite trees a spike of rock

thrust into the air like a rude finger. It was in the general direction Melissa had indicated, and she'd said that Rex had found the lost girl in some sort of cave.

"Come on. Let's try to make it in one jump," Jonathan said. "If they're risking white light to slow us down, we should probably get there fast."

Instinct took over as they dropped, Jessica twisting in midair to reorient herself for a last jump toward the stone spire. They landed in the high grass and rebounded without any pause.

They rose above the trees again, and Jessica spotted two tiny figures standing close together by a fissure in the stone. "That's them!"

"They look like they're in one piece," Jonathan said softly. "Any slithers down there?"

"Close your eyes."

She switched the flashlight on again, playing it across the small clearing, the rocks, and the treetops. Nothing burst into flame; no slithers hurtled screaming from the undergrowth. Jessica did catch, however, the dark purple flash of Rex's eyes as he glanced up, then turned away, his expression of pain visible even from the air.

"Oops." Jessica turned the flashlight off. "Okay. You can look now, Jonathan. Landing in five, four . . ."

They came down softly in the thick grass, about ten feet from Rex and the small, thin girl who stood next to him, clinging to his arm. She was about Beth's age, wearing a ragged sweatshirt and pajama bottoms. Her eyes bulged as she stared at Jonathan and Jessica. She'd probably seen some pretty astonishing stuff tonight, but two people flying hand in hand was still pretty jaw-dropping.

"Are you okay?" Jonathan asked.

"Sorry about blinding you, Rex," Jessica said.

His eyes still covered, his hands shaking, Rex answered, "No, that's fine. It cleared my head. You got here just in time."

Jessica raised an eyebrow, wondering what that meant. There weren't any slithers here. Why had they been frying themselves just to delay her another minute?

Jonathan dropped Jessica's hand and crossed to the girl. "Cassie, right?"

She nodded dumbly.

"I'm Jonathan. Hey, your elbow looks ouchy."

Cassie looked at the red mark, then pointed into the cave. "Banged it in there. But you should see my ankle." She pulled up one pant leg, revealing the dark bruise of a slither bite. Jessica winced, shaking out her own hand, which was still tingling with icy needles.

"Ow!" Jonathan said. "I hate snakes."

"No. It was this stupid cat."

Jonathan glanced back at Jessica.

She remembered that night, only her second time in the secret hour, when the black slither-cat had transformed horribly into a snake before her eyes. Then another dozen slithers had shown up, along with a darkling in the shape of a giant panther. And then the biggest surprise of all: finding out that the whole thing hadn't been a dream, but an entire new reality opening up.

Jessica frowned. On the phone this afternoon no one

had mentioned what was supposed to happen *after* they rescued Cassie from the blue time. How would they keep her from spilling the beans to everyone in town?

Of course, maybe the answer was obvious. Melissa would reach into the young girl's mind and erase what had happened here. She had done it more than once before—to Jessica's own parents, probably. And back when her talent was young and unformed, Melissa had forced herself into Rex's father's mind, leaving the old guy half crazy. The thought of his milky, empty eyes made Jessica shiver again.

But maybe it didn't have to be that way.

"This is a pretty crappy dream, huh?" she said to the girl, rubbing her slither-bitten hand.

Jonathan raised an eyebrow, and even Rex, who still looked pretty shaky, snorted out a short laugh.

"What?" Jessica shrugged. "I'm just saying, as nightmares go, this one's on the weird side. Right, Cassie?"

The look of dazed confusion gradually faded from the girl's face, her expression turning more thoughtful. "Well, I was kind of wondering: what's going *on* here?" She looked up at the dark moon. "What happened to everything? And who are you guys?"

"You've got a fever, right?" Jessica asked.

"Not a fever. My grandma said it's just a cold."

"Oh. Right. Okay," Jessica said slowly and deliberately. "But sometimes when we're sick, we have funny dreams."

Cassie crossed her arms. "Yeah, maybe. But people in those funny dreams don't usually bring it up that I'm dreaming."

Jonathan laughed. "Nice try, Jess."

"Yeah, this kid's smarter than that," Rex said. "And tougher than she looks too."

"Smarter?" Jessica cried. "What's that supposed to mean? *I* thought the blue time was all a dream, remember?"

"Oh, yeah." Rex chuckled. "Well, feel free to tell her whatever you want until Melissa gets here."

Jessica frowned and glanced at Jonathan, who shrugged, a helpless look on his face. He didn't much like the idea either, but he clearly couldn't see any other way of keeping the secret hour secret.

A crashing sound reached them through the trees.

"Speaking of which," Rex said.

Dess emerged first, a long metal pipe balanced over one shoulder, like a spear ready to be thrown. She stumbled into the clearing and came to a halt, looking at them one by one. Then she lowered the spear with a disgusted noise. "No monsters left, are there?"

"All under control," Rex said.

"Rats," Dess said. "Jessica, I haven't slain jack squat since you became the flame-bringer."

Jessica sighed. "Yeah. My bad."

Melissa came into view, yanking on her long black dress, the hem of which was tangled with twigs and trailing branches.

"Jeez, Rex. That was freaky," she announced.

"You tasted it?" he asked quietly.

"It was pretty hard to miss," Melissa said, running a finger along one of her scars. "I mean, I already knew you were having an identity crisis. But I didn't think a darkling would *agree* with you!"

Jessica glanced from one of them to the other. Rex had a funny look on his face, and she noticed that his hands were still shaking, his fingers bent stiffly into claws. Melissa was staring at him like he'd grown antlers.

"Are we missing something here?" Dess asked aloud.

"Yeah, what happened?" Jessica said. "I saw a darkling running away."

Melissa took a step closer to Rex and the girl. "The darkling was here, but it seemed to think Rex was a—"

"Don't!" Rex interrupted.

There was a long silence, the two of them staring at each other.

"Not now," he hissed.

"Wow," Cassie Flinders said. "Maybe I am dreaming because you guys are really weird."

Everyone looked at the girl. She stood there, staring defiantly back at them. Jessica decided that she had a point.

"Okay, kiddo," Melissa said after another awkward moment of silence. "I think it's past your bedtime."

"But it's morning," Cassie answered, then looked up at the sky and frowned. "Or it *was* . . ."

"Either way, I can't believe your grandma let you out of bed," Rex said. "You being sick and all."

"She always lets me play in the backyard," Cassie said huffily. "Says it's good for a cold to get out in the cold."

"Well, I'm putting you back under the covers," Melissa said, reaching out a hand. "Come with me."

"Said the spider to the fly," Dess muttered.

Jessica looked across the clearing at Jonathan. There had to be some other way to keep the secret than messing with people's brains. She was just a kid, after all. Who would believe her?

As Melissa's hand closed around Cassie's, the girl seemed to relax. Then she yawned, her eyes growing sleepy.

Melissa turned to the others. "Chill, guys. I'm a lot better at this than I used to be." She shrugged. "Besides, I'm only going to calm her down and put her to sleep and maybe *suggest* that this all was a nightmare. When it comes to radical memory overhaul, I only work on stiffs. Which, you may have noticed, Cassie isn't. Anything else will have to wait."

"What are you guys talking about?" Cassie asked sleepily.

Melissa smiled, leading Cassie back toward the railroad tracks. "We're discussing how you're going to remember this crazy dream tomorrow." She winked at Rex. "But probably not the next day."

"So she'll tell people about it?" Jonathan asked. "And then just forget the next day? Won't that seem funny to everyone else? I mean, she'll probably be on the news tomorrow."

Rex shrugged. "She's a kid, she's sick, she wandered off. So what if she talks crazy for a day? And after we pay her a visit tomorrow at midnight—" He raised his fingers and snapped.

The sound sent a shiver through Jessica. Maybe they were right, and mindcasting was the only way to keep the secret. In the old days, when Bixby had practically been ruled by midnighters, they'd probably done it all the time. But still, the idea didn't make her very happy.

"So, Rex, should I leave her out in the sun?" Melissa asked from the edge of the clearing.

"No reason to," he said. "Jessica already gave us both a blinding dose of white light. It worked for me when I was half-darkling; it should work for her. Meet you at the car?"

"Sure thing, Spider-Man," Melissa called, waving good-bye.

Jessica watched the two of them disappear into the trees, wondering at how pliant and sleepy Cassie had become after Melissa had taken her hand. Maybe it was only shock, the poor girl overwhelmed after everything that happened. But Madeleine had suppressed Dess's memories with only a touch too.

Melissa was growing in power every day. Jessica wondered what she could do if she got really pissed off at someone.

"So, Jessica, you ready to fly home?" Jonathan asked.

She looked at Rex. He still seemed shaky, as if it had been a close thing tonight.

"Will you guys be safe, Rex?"

He nodded. "Sure. I'll stick around and see if there's any lore sites around here. Or any other clues about this place. I think you ruined the darklings' party, for the rest of the hour at least. And Dess here has . . ."

"Magisterially Supernumerary Mathematician," she said, hefting the spear proudly.

"But what about your car, Jonathan?" Jessica said.

He shrugged. "I'll get it tomorrow."

"I can drive it into town!" Dess offered.

"I don't think so," Jonathan said.

Dess snorted and prodded his ribs with the point of Supernumerary.

Jessica stood there, rubbing her wounded hand and thinking glum thoughts. They had saved a young girl tonight, but in payment for the rescue the memory of the most amazing experience in Cassie's life would be erased forever. And Cassie Flinders was only the beginning. If the blue time was tearing, more unlucky people were likely to step into the secret hour, where hungry monsters waited for them. And possibly normal time itself was coming to an end.

Worst of all, Beth was probably waiting in Jessica's room right now, ready to unleash holy fury when she got home.

"You know what?" Jessica said. "You can drive me back after the secret hour's over."

Jonathan frowned at her, rubbing at the middle of his back. "What about curfew?"

"I'll risk it. You guys do all the time."

"What about Beth? I told her eighteen minutes."

"I'll risk her too."

"But what—?"

"Jonathan, you *don't* have to take me home yet, okay?" She took his hands, felt weightlessness flow into her. "This whole night has sucked so far. Maybe we could just do some flying? *Real* flying, out in the open. We can take our time getting me home."

His frown faded, and a smile spread slowly across his face.

"Take our time getting home?" Dess said with a smirk. "Is *that* what they're calling it these days?"

Rex chuckled softly.

Jessica ignored them. The heart-pounding panic of the slither attack had erased the mutual irritation between them on the subject of little sisters. And although what he'd said about liking Beth had been maddening at the time, right now it seemed kind of sweet.

"Come on. Let's fly somewhere together," she said. She massaged her shoulder. "Now that we're not getting pelted with slithers."

"Well," he said after a moment's thought, "have you ever seen the river?"

"The Arkansas?" Jessica shrugged. "Just from the bridge on the way over here."

"You haven't seen the Arkansas River till you've seen it in the secret hour," Jonathan said. "Motionless water, excellent for skipping rocks."

"Oh, cool." For a moment she tried to figure out how the laws of motion would apply, but her new physics lobe quickly gave up. "So how does that work?"

Jonathan smiled again, his brown eyes flashing in the light of the dark moon. "It's kind of tricky to explain. But you get a lot more skips than on regular water. Swimming's fun too."

"Okay," Jessica said. "I could use some fun."

"Come on, then. I'll show you."

Jonathan offered her his hand, and she took it.

"You kids have fun now," Dess called.

"Okay," Jessica said. "See you, Rex."

The seer only nodded, his hands still shaking. Even in the blue light she could tell his face was ashen. What had happened to him before they'd arrived? And why had the darkling run away while she was still finding her way here, if its minions were sacrificing themselves to hold her up?

She shook her head. Evidently Rex and Melissa were still keeping secrets from the rest of them.

They leapt up and over the trees, finding their way back to the railroad bed and then across Jenks, until Jessica could see the glimmer of the river in the distance. From the air it looked like a giant slither winding its way down from the black hills, glowing with the cold light of the dark moon.

"You know," Jonathan said as they flew. "Maybe it's better for Cassie. Forgetting about all this."

"Maybe. Doesn't seem fair, though."

"Sure, but think about how much it would scare a kid like that. Knowing about all these weird creatures crawling across her while she's frozen for an hour every night?"

"Yeah, I guess so," Jessica said. "I mean, it scares me, and I'm the all-powerful flashlight-bringer."

"And on top of the fear factor, everyone would think she was totally crazy. Eventually, since she'll never see the blue time again after all, she'd probably decide they were right."

They landed on a stretch of not-quite beach, a narrow strip of dry earth dotted with patches of scrubby grass. The river stretched out before them, motionless wavelets glitter-ing like scales made of diamond, reflecting a shattered image of the dark moon.

It was beautiful, but Jessica shivered.

"Not cold, are you?"

"No. It's always warm here." She shook her head. "I was just wondering if Cassie might see the blue time again. I mean, what if Dess is right? What if the secret hour swal-lows all of Bixby—or even the whole world—forever? And *everyone* gets sucked through, like Cassie was? Suddenly cars and electricity don't work, and people can't even make *fires* anymore. Only five of us on the whole planet know anything about using thirteen-letter words and stainless steel to protect ourselves. What happens then?"

He squeezed her hand. "Then I'll come get you, wherever you are when it happens. We'll be okay."

"But what about everybody else?"

He stared out across the river, nodding slowly. "My guess is, everybody else is in big trouble."

9

MISS TRUST

At the kitchen door the next morning Jessica breathed a sigh of relief. She was safe for a few more minutes—Beth wasn't up yet.

"Morning, Jess. Toast?"

Jessica checked for signs of imminent re-grounding in her mother's expression but saw only sleepiness and the usual lines of stress. Apparently Beth hadn't raised any alarms last night.

"Sure, Mom. Thanks." Jessica sat down at the table. Maybe Jonathan was right, and the trick to dealing with Beth was to call her bluff.

Somehow, though, Jessica didn't think it was going to be that easy.

Her mother popped two slices of bread into the toaster, then turned her attention back to the coffeemaker gurgling happily on the counter. "Any plans tonight?"

"Um, no." Jessica frowned. "Hang on, was that question a subtle recognition of the fact that I'm not grounded anymore?"

"Not exactly subtle," her mother said. "I don't do subtlety before coffee." She splashed milk into an empty mug, her eyes remaining fixed on the black brew now dribbling into the pot.

"Well, you're tons more subtle than Dad. Yesterday afternoon he said he was keeping an eye on me."

"He is." Mom looked at Jessica. "But I'm just going to say that I trust you. How's that for good parenting?"

"It's great. But didn't you used to be the bad cop?"

"Yeah, I think so." Her mother gave the coffeepot a look of intense concentration. "Takes too much energy, though. At least your father's taking up the slack somewhere."

"Well, thanks anyway. I won't let you down." The words came out automatically, but Jessica felt a twinge of guilt as they left her lips. She had crossed a new line just the night before. It was one thing sneaking out during the secret hour, which hardly counted as breaking curfew; when every clock in the world was frozen, surely time was a meaningless concept. Plus there were darklings to slay and lost kids to rescue.

But last night she hadn't gotten home till about 2 A.M., cutting solidly into school-night real time. Crusty sleep still caked her eyes, and red Oklahoma dust had spun around the drain for a solid minute while she'd showered.

Not that she regretted it. Their visit to the motionless river had been worth any amount of lost sleep. Just like air during the blue time, the water had been as warm as a summer day. Jonathan said that you could go swimming in the middle of winter. With the current arrested, the broad river was like one big heated swimming pool. The water had seemed to wash away the pain in her slither-bitten hand, not to mention all the tension between her and Jonathan.

"That's Jessica, all right: Miss Trustworthy," Beth said from the kitchen door.

Jess wondered how long she'd been standing there. Maybe she had been waiting for the sounds of Jessica getting up and had followed her down the hall.

Not much fun, having a spy in your own house.

Jessica cleared her throat. "That's me."

Beth came in and flopped down on a chair, smiling sweetly at her sister. "Get it?" she asked. "Miss Trust?"

At the exact same moment Jessica's toast popped up and the coffeemaker's gurgling ended with a final sigh.

"I got it, Mom." Jessica jumped up and pulled a knife and fork from the drawer, wielding them like chopsticks to remove the toast.

"Put some in for me?" Beth asked.

Jessica glanced at her mother, who was giving Beth a puzzled look with her sleepy eyes, the pot in one hand, mug in the other. The coffeemaker let a last few drops fall onto its hot metal plate, which hissed like angry slithers as they boiled away.

"Be polite, Beth," Mom finally said. "Say 'please.'"

"I'm very polite. Aren't I, Jessica?"

"Amazingly polite." Jessica depressed the toaster's handle and stared down into its double maw, watching as the elements glowed red. "For example, you'd never hang around when you're *not wanted*."

"Yeah, and always *on time*. That's me."

"*What* are you two talking about?" their mother said.

Jessica glared at her little sister, daring her to go ahead and blab to their mother about everything: her sneaking out the night before, Jonathan, whatever she wanted. It gave Jessica pleasure to think that no matter how much Beth snitched about, she didn't know half of what was really going on.

And for that matter, what difference did being in trouble make? Yesterday Jessica had discovered that everything she knew could disappear at any time—maybe in a week, maybe this morning—her whole reality swallowed by the darklings. She definitely wasn't going to let a little twerp like Beth push her around in the meantime.

Besides, her boyfriend could fly. Grounded was a relative state of affairs.

She stared at Beth and thought, *Go right ahead.*

"Nothing," Beth finally said. "We're just fooling around. No big deal."

Their mother raised an eyebrow but then just sighed and looked at her watch. "Okay, whatever. I'm late. You guys try to have a good day." She looked at Jessica and held up her cell phone. "Call me *and* Dad if you do anything after school, okay?"

"Sure, both of you. No problem."

Beth's toast popped up, and Jessica carried it to her little sister on a plate. "Here you go."

"Thank you, Jess. See, Mom? Totally polite."

"That's nice, Beth. 'Bye, you two."

The sisters said goodbye, then waited silently as their mother hoisted her heavy bag onto her shoulder and walked, footsteps fading, to the end of the hall. The door opened and closed.

Jessica turned to her sister, who was chewing toast thoughtfully. "Thanks, I guess."

"For what?"

Jessica swallowed. "Not telling Mom about . . . everything."

Beth shrugged.

"Like I said, Jess, I don't want you in trouble. I just want to find out what's going on here in Bixby." She gave her older sister a sweet smile. "And I will too . . . one way or another."

10

MEMORY FIX

The mind noise of Jenks rumbled softly at this time of night. A fair percentage of the locals seemed to be awake—most watching the late-night dreck of unemployment TV—but this area was sparsely populated compared to Bixby. The thinly sprinkled minds dotted the mental landscape like lazy fireflies.

"Anybody near the tracks?"

She opened her eyes, licked her lips, and shook her head. "No, Rex. Nothing bigger than a squirrel."

Her old Ford was parked in the same field as the night before, facing the long hump of the railroad line. Melissa couldn't taste any human minds among the trees, which was one less thing to worry about.

Rex was almost being his old self, getting anxious over everything. He'd been worried that Cassie Flinders had told her friends everything she'd seen last night—or worse, spilled the beans to the local news channel.

Of course, Melissa had to admit, a bunch of thrill seekers showing up to dare "haunted" railroad tracks would be a pain. It was bad enough out at the snake pit, having to crawl over frozen teenagers playing games with so-called magic rocks. But this rip in the blue time was actually dangerous—they didn't need any more Cassies crossing over and causing all kinds of inconvenience.

As Melissa cast her mind across the contortion, she realized that she could faintly taste the rip. There was something unnatural and vaguely *wrong* about this place, like the smell of chlorine on your own skin after swimming. She wrinkled her nose, wondering if the rip had grown since last night or if it only got bigger during eclipses.

"Maybe it's too soon," he said. "Any rumors Cassie started haven't had much time to spread."

"Well, we can come out here again tomorrow night if you want." She flexed her fingers. "Scare the hell out of them. Of course, it does seem like a waste of effort."

"What do you mean?"

"Saving every little kid who wanders into darkling land when all of Bixby's fixing to get turned into one big buffet." She saw his fists tighten, felt the tension course through him, and sighed. "*Kidding*, Rex. You know me, always happy to rescue people."

He relaxed, took a breath. "Well, you rescued me."

She smiled. The great thing about Rex was, he'd never forgotten the night she'd walked across Bixby to find him, back when they were kids. Even after all these years, all the mistakes they'd made, he was still that eight-year-old, forever grateful to her for showing him that the blue time was real, not just some recurring nightmare.

But what was he so nervous about tonight? Even with her new and improved skills, Melissa still couldn't tease out the details sometimes. Not without physical contact, anyway, and Rex had been very edgy about touching today.

"Maybe Cassie hasn't told anyone," he said. "Maybe she really does think it was a dream."

"I don't know. She tasted really . . . clever." Melissa paused, unsure if *clever* was what she meant. The kid was tough, and Melissa had detected a crafty streak in her that was a mile wide. Cassie Flinders might not have said much last night, acting very much like a kid in shock, but she'd listened to everything the midnighters had said in front of her, recording it all. The sooner Melissa rejiggered her memories, the better.

"Just don't push too hard, Cowgirl."

Rex's guilt washed over her, sour milk mixed with battery acid, and she groaned. "That's all behind us, Rex. No more screwups. I'll be light as a feather in there. Just trust me, all right?"

"Okay." He looked at his watch. "So what do we do for eight minutes?"

"Jeez, Loverboy, if you have to ask . . ."

He smiled and turned to her, leaning across the car seat. But his movements were tentative.

What are you hiding, Loverboy? she wondered.

As they kissed, she felt Rex's nervous energy buzzing across his lips. She ran her tongue lightly across them, transforming their flavor from anxiety into desire, drawing him closer. Melissa's own excitement—her anticipation of midnight, of using her new skills to manipulate Cassie's frozen mind—began to build. It overwhelmed Rex's tension, mixing with his arousal like two sharp tastes colliding in her mouth.

He reached to grasp her shoulders, his hands gloved against the accidental touch of steel, and pulled her closer. She ran a hand inside his jacket, feeling her mind begin to spin. She could taste the ferment of Rex's ongoing transformation and wondered at its sweet electric taste, like Pop Rocks under her tongue, fizzing as it trickled down her throat.

Usually when they touched, her generations of mindcaster technique ensured that Melissa kept herself under control. But tonight Rex's newfound confidence, the strength in him that grew every day, threatened to overpower her. She caught glimpses of what had happened the night before, saw through his eyes the darkling in its dance, acknowledging him as another predator. *Talking* to him, almost.

And then the real cause of his guilt and anxiety came through: how close he had come to letting his darkling side boil over. She wondered what would be left of Cassie Flinders if *that* had happened. . . .

Her ancient memories cautioned Melissa that Rex was becoming something no mindcaster had ever kissed before. There were shadows in him, ancient and terrifying.

But she ignored the warnings—this was *Rex*, after all. He was the only reason she had survived this long. All through those years while her mind had been untutored and undefended, *this* was all she'd wanted: to be able to touch him. Melissa felt herself let go of everything Madeleine had given her, all mastery and control, and allowed herself to sink into the darkness inside him.

Like the old minds across the desert, the things down there didn't have words, just images she could barely grasp—lore signs, a pile of bones, the smell of burning . . . the glorious rush of taking prey.

There was a moment of sharp pain, and then he pulled away, his body shuddering.

Melissa sat for a moment, watching his eyes flash violet in the moonlight, the echoes of what she'd felt in him subsiding slowly. She tasted salt and wondered for a moment what sort of mind noise it was, then realized that the taste was real—blood in her mouth.

"Crap," she said, putting a hand to her lips. "I bit my lip. How lame is that?"

"It wasn't you." He turned away. "Sorry . . . if that was weird."

"It's okay, Rex." Melissa touched her wounded lip tenderly. "I had some spooky stuff in me too the first few times we touched. Remember?"

He turned back to her and pulled off one glove. He reached out, his fingertips lightly touching her mouth.

A shudder traveled through the car at that moment, all the random mind noise around them extinguished at once. Blue light swept across the world, and against the suddenly quiet mental landscape, the visions she'd taken from Rex's mind grew clearer.

She saw a piece of paper covered with the spindly symbols of the lore and knew that those unreadable signs were what had made him so edgy tonight.

Melissa squinted in the dark moon's light. "What the hell?"

"I found it this morning." Rex's voice was rough.

He reached into his jacket, pulling out a folded piece of paper. He opened it, revealing the same scrawled symbols she'd seen in his mind.

"So this is what's got you spooked?" She settled back onto the driver's side, sighing. "Ancient seer wisdom about the end of the world?"

He shook his head. "Not exactly ancient. Look."

She peered closer. The symbols were written on lined paper, three-hole punched, with a confettied edge from being torn out of a spiral notebook.

"I don't understand. These are your notes?"

"I didn't write that. I found it on my kitchen table this morning."

"Wait a second." Melissa's mind spun. "But it's written in lore signs, Rex."

He nodded. "That's right, Cowgirl. A slightly odd dialect, but readable."

"And it just showed up on your kitchen table? But no one knows how to write the lore besides you. And . . . oh, crap." Melissa placed the nail of her ring finger between her front teeth and bit down on it furiously. Her teeth slipped from the fingernail with a jarring *snap*. "Those dominoes that the Grayfoots used to communicate with the darklings—they had lore symbols on them."

"That's right. With the same slight differences as this one. It's even signed." He pointed to the bottom right-hand corner of the page, where a cell phone number was written next to three spindly symbols grouped by a circle. "*Ah-nu-gee.*"

"What the hell is *ah-nu-gee?*"

"Each lore sign usually stands for a word, but when you put a circle around them, they turn into sounds, like using the alphabet. It's a way to spell out names and write about objects that didn't exist a few thousand years ago."

She raised her eyebrows. "And people back then didn't have *ah-nu-gee?* I repeat: what the hell?"

He laughed softly. "What they didn't have back then were certain sounds. It was a Stone Age language, after all. '*Ah-nu-gee*' is as close as they could get to '*Angie.*'"

"*Angie.*" Melissa's blood ran cold at the name. Angie, last name unknown, was one of the Grayfoots' agents. She'd translated the darklings' messages, had been in the desert that night Anathea had died, and it was her—Melissa was certain—leading the party that had kidnapped Rex. "She *wrote* to you?"

He nodded. "She wants to meet me."

"*Meet* you? What the—?" Melissa pressed herself back against the car seat and growled, fists tightly clenched. "Is she crazy?"

Rex gave that question a shrug. "More scared than crazy, sounds like. The Grayfoots are up to something, and she doesn't know what. She says that after Anathea died, they cut her out of the loop because she's not family."

"Oh, poor Angie," Melissa hissed, her fingernails cutting into her palms. "This is such crap. They just want to kidnap you again!"

He shook his head. "Why? The darklings can't turn me into anything. Jessica burned away their special halfling-making spot."

"So they just want to kill you, then. Spiteful little creeps. Finish what they started fifty years ago."

"Melissa," he said with maddening calm. "They left it on my kitchen table, while I was *sleeping*. If they wanted to kill me, I'd be dead, right? What she wants is to exchange information. Like I said, she's scared."

Melissa got herself under control, concentrating on her heartbeat until it slowed. "Okay, then, Rex, an exchange of information sounds like fun. Why don't you offer to meet her at your house, say, around eleven fifty-five at night?" She felt her lips curl back from her teeth. "I'll show her what *scared* really means."

"I thought you were all featherlight these days."

She snorted. "Come on, Rex. It's a win-win situation. We'll know everything about the Grayfoots that she does, and she'll be left a drooling vegetable."

He just stared at her, the old guilt of what they'd done to his father spreading through the car like a gas leak.

Melissa held his gaze for a moment but then let out a sigh. "Sorry." She turned away. "Why did you keep this a secret from me, anyway?"

"Because it gave me an idea. Something you won't like."

"You are *not* going to meet with her, Rex," she hissed. "Not unless it's in the middle of Bixby right before midnight and I'm there to rip that bitch's mind inside out. I don't care if the darklings can't make you a halfling anymore—Angie's a psycho. What's to stop her from trussing you up and giving you to the Grayfoots just to get back on their good side!"

"Don't worry. Meeting with her wasn't the idea I'm talking about." He scratched his chin. "I'm not even tempted to call. But something big is happening. And the information we need isn't in the lore. I may have to go directly to the source."

"You're going to talk to Grandpa Grayfoot *himself*? He's an even bigger psycho than Angie. This is a guy who had a hundred people killed in one night!"

"Not him. When Anathea died, he was cut off from the darklings. He's probably panicking too."

"So who else is left, Rex?"

He reached out and let his fingers stray across her lips again. She felt them glide across the sticky trickle of blood, tugging at the wounded skin beneath. Then an appalling thought drifted into her mind from his. She saw the desert, the light cool and flat and blue. . . .

"No," she said.

"They know what's going on. You said so yourself."

"They'll eat you, Rex."

He shook his head slowly. "Wolves don't eat other wolves."

"Um, Rex?" She cleared her throat. "Maybe you're right. But I'm pretty sure that wolves do *kill* other wolves."

"Hmm, good point." He took a breath. "But you felt what happened last night. It *talked* to me."

She shuddered, recalling the images that had come from Rex's mind during their kiss—that huge spider practically doing the two-step with him, like they were old friends. The taste of its forelegs in their sinuous salute was still in her mouth. "That was *one* darkling, Rex. You're talking about the deep desert. Dozens of them, maybe hundreds. We don't even know how many."

"I haven't decided yet, okay?"

She looked out at the sliver of dark moon on the horizon, checking for winged shapes against it. When Rex had first suggested coming out here tonight without Jessica, she'd wondered if it was a good idea. They'd faced darklings on their own together, but this place had drawn huge clouds of slithers, and the taste of old minds lingered here.

But during their kiss Melissa had realized that she was safe here with Rex. Safe from darklings, anyway. He had become as much one of them as he was human.

Suddenly something odd caught her eye—a few leaves were falling near the tracks, giving off a soft red glow that looked completely strange here in the blue time. It was the rip, the sliver of unfrozen time. It must have been there that Cassie Flinders had been standing the morning before.

Melissa sighed. They had to deal with that girl tonight, not sit around talking. "Okay, Rex, maybe you really can talk to darklings. But tell me before you do anything."

He laughed. "Think you can change my mind?"

"I'd never do that to you, Rex."

"Do you swear, Cowgirl? No more of that, on me or anyone else, unless I'm there."

"Absolutely."

He took her hand, and Melissa let the surety of her promise flow into him. Whatever Rex was turning into, whatever crazy risks he decided to take, she would never twist or change a single thought in his brain . . .

Not even to save your life.

They crossed the tracks, pausing to look at the rip in the blue time. A red glimmer ran along its boundaries. It was about the size of an eighteen-wheeler now, much bigger than when Cassie had stepped through while her grandmother, only a few yards away, had remained frozen. The leaves from two trees caught within it were drifting down.

Rex stepped into the rip and caught a leaf. He dropped it, and it fell again.

"Feels different in here somehow."

"Is it spreading all the time? Like, right now?"

He shook his head. "Only during the eclipse, Dess says. It's like a fault line shifting during an earthquake."

She pulled him away. This whole rip business gave her the creeps. The last thing Melissa needed was a bunch of annoying human minds invading midnight. "Come on."

Cassie Flinders's house was an old double-wide trailer, its concrete teeth sunk deep into the hard soil, gripping tenaciously against the Oklahoma wind. Halloween decorations were already up on the door—a grinning paper skeleton with swinging joints, orange and black bunting that glowed blue.

Rex stared at the skeleton for a moment.

"Friend of yours?" Melissa asked.

"Don't think so." He pushed open the screen door, and its rusty hinges rang out in the blue time. The wooden door inside was unlocked. Rex smiled. "Good country folk."

They pushed into the blue-lit home, the floorboards creaking as they walked. Melissa wondered if the old wood stayed pressed down until the end of the secret hour, then popped up with a final complaint—letting out a sudden chorus of creaking just after the stroke of midnight. Flyboy was always wondering about stuff like that. If she was ever on normal speaking terms with the rest of them again, she'd have to ask him.

An old woman sat at a kitchen table, a bowl of something glowing an unappetizing blue in front of her. Her eyes were locked on a blank-screened TV. Melissa avoided her and the motionless cloud of smoke that rose from the cigarette clutched in her fingers.

Cassie's room was in one corner, the door plastered with drawings and more Halloween decorations. Rex pointed at the black cat. "Funny, even after last night she didn't take that down."

"Cats." Melissa snorted. "Smug, self-centered little beasts." Then she remembered to add, "Except yours, of course."

"Daguerreotype's smugness is part of his charm." He pushed the door open.

The room didn't reek of thirteen-year-old. No boy band posters, no dolls. The walls were covered with more drawings, crayon landscapes of Jenks, the Bixby skyline, and oil derricks, all drained of their color.

"Not bad," Rex said. He pointed to a music stand, a clarinet leaning against it. "Creative kid."

"Good. Nobody believes the artistic ones."

Cassie was lying on her bed, eyes closed and sheets tangled around her—a bad night of sleep in the making. Melissa wondered if being frozen for fifteen hours had given the girl some sort of jet lag and cracked her knuckles. She could fix that.

Even Rex's crazy plan to visit the darklings hadn't taken the edge off her excitement. This was her first serious mindcasting since Madeleine had started tutoring her.

"Featherlight," she murmured softly.

She rested her fingers lightly on Cassie's waxy skin, her hands like a pair of pale blue spiders splayed across the girl's face. Melissa closed her eyes, entering the cool domain of a mind frozen in time.

Low-level nerves were scattered throughout Cassie, lingering shock from her trip into the secret hour. The taste of dread stung Melissa's lips, anxiety that the black cat would return, terror that the spider thing was still out there in the woods.

The girl had an artist's eye, Melissa had to admit. The slithers, the old darkling, the midnighters' faces were all in there, as crisp as if she'd snapped photographs. As she soothed the fears away, Melissa blurred the memories into shadowy figments.

This was so *easy* now, she thought. Not like the clumsy attempts she'd once called mindcasting. Thoughts and memories stood before her like chess pieces awaiting her command.

She remolded the images trapped in Cassie's mind, erasing the words they'd said in front of her, turning everything into the sort of nonsense mush remembered from a dream. Melissa softened the sense of danger, made it all vague and formless, divorced it from the reality outside the double-wide's doors.

But she left intact one perfectly shaped bit of terror, a phobia a few yards across and a thousand miles deep . . .

Stay away from the railroad tracks at midnight. Something nasty *lives under them.*

"Done." Melissa smiled as she withdrew her hands from Cassie's face. "Now, *that* was some awesome, featherlight mindcasting."

"That's it?" Rex asked. "You were so fast. Like thirty seconds."

Melissa smiled. It had seemed like long minutes. "Bada-bing, bada-boom."

"Has she talked to anyone? Told anyone what she saw?"

Melissa took a breath, stretching her muscles. "She's been right here since I put her down, sleeping it off and doodling. Grandma didn't even let her talk on the phone. Her whole day was bedsores and boredom."

"But what if she told—"

"Relax, Rex. Even if Cassie made a full report to the

National Guard, when she wakes up tomorrow morning, she won't remember what she was babbling about. This is a done deal."

"Maybe you should check her grandmother."

"Rex, it's not a problem. Trust me. We've been doing this for thousands of years."

His breath caught, and Melissa felt a twinge of jealousy from him; she had reminded him of all the knowledge she'd received from Madeleine. He'd finally gotten over that time when she'd touched Jonathan, and he understood about Dess, but when Melissa and the older mindcaster went up to the attic, he lost all rationality.

Funny, he was the one who knew the history. How mindcasters used to pass on information with a handshake, silently spreading midnighter news and gossip throughout Bixby. Compared to those days, Melissa was hardly some sort of mind slut.

She took a step closer to him. "Come on. Let's go back to the car. I'll show you everything."

"She saw what I almost became last night. Are you sure she—"

"Everything." She drew him closer, silencing his lips with hers.

11

GOODBYE, BIXBY

"So the *weirdest* thing happened yesterday."

Jessica nodded. She'd been expecting Constanza Grayfoot to tell her all about it. "Yeah, I heard."

Constanza came to a sudden halt in the hall, letting lesser mortals flow around them. "You did? From who?"

Jessica shrugged. For once she'd known what everyone would be talking about way ahead of time. "I don't remember who told me. Wasn't it on TV last night or something? How that lost kid just turned up in her bed yesterday morning, totally okay?"

"Oh, that. *Ancient* news, Jess. Pay attention here, please. I'm talking about something much weirder and much more likely to affect our lives. Especially my life."

Jessica blinked. "Okay. What are you talking about?"

"My grandfather called me last night."

Cold, dry fingers walked down Jessica's spine. "He did what?"

"Called me, with the most incredible news. Come on,

let's get to study hall. And I hope you don't have any stupid trig homework today because I'm going to need everyone's full attention."

"You've got it."

As they made their way up to the library, Jessica's heart pounded. Any mention of Constanza's grandfather definitely got her attention.

Grandpa Grayfoot was like anyone else not born at midnight—frozen during the secret hour. But as a kid he'd been a sort of super-evil version of Beth, spying on everyone and uncovering Bixby's secrets. He'd figured that the darklings were ghosts, or ancient spirits, or something equally creepy and had tried to communicate with them in secret midnight rituals. Eventually the darklings had answered, exchanging messages with him through a half-human, half-darkling creature—a translator between the two worlds.

Years of doing the darklings' bidding made his family rich and powerful, but the things that the midnight creatures asked him to do got more and more hideous. Fifty years ago the Grayfoots and their allies had been ordered to wipe out an entire generation of midnighters. They had all but succeeded; only Madeleine remained.

Just two weeks ago the translator who had made the whole thing possible had been close to death. The Grayfoots had tried to kidnap Rex so the darklings could turn him into a replacement, another halfling.

But the other midnighters had rescued Rex, and Anathea—the halfling—had died, destroying the old man's link to his masters. If he and his pals were still trying to contact the darklings, they were leaving messages that would never be returned.

Jessica followed Constanza into the library, wondering what on earth the old guy was up to now.

"Okay, this is absolutely top secret. I'm not even supposed to be telling you guys, so everyone here must swear never to tell a soul. Well, at least not until this is all final."

"Until what's all final?" Liz asked.

"Whatever she's going to tell us," Maria said. *"Duh."*

"So, do you all swear?"

They went around the library table one by one, promising to keep the secret: Jen, Liz, Maria, and finally Jessica. By the time it got to her, Jess managed to get away with just a nod. She was pretty sure that she was going to have to tell the other midnighters about this in a big way, promise or no promise.

"Okay," Constanza began once the ritual was complete. "Remember when my house got trashed by those weirdos?"

Everyone nodded, eyes wide. Jessica tried to put on her not-guilty face. She'd witnessed the aftermath of Rex and Melissa burgling Constanza's house, back when they'd first been looking for evidence about the Grayfoot-darkling conspiracy. Not that the damage had all been their fault; there was nothing like a horde of midnight monsters showing up to leave a mess.

"Well, you probably remember how that totally freaked out my grandfather. He's always had this thing about not living in Bixby."

"You guys stayed with him in Broken Arrow after that happened, right?" Liz asked.

"We did. And let me tell you, I was totally sick of commuting to school. So . . ." Constanza leaned closer, indicating that the top secret part was coming up, and Jessica dared a glance at Dess, sitting in her usual corner. Dess held her trig book up to cover her face, which meant she was listening to every word. She needed to study trigonometry about as hard as a darkling needed to study scary.

"Well, Grandpa must have had a slow leak about me coming back to Bixby," Constanza continued. "You know, he cut my dad out of the family oil business when he and Mom moved here, ages ago. He still hardly talks to them, even when we were staying out there. So anyway, he called me last night, trying to convince me to leave town."

"What's his problem with Bixby, anyway?" Maria asked.

Constanza shrugged. "He never tells anyone what happened. He grew up here, but something weird went down when he was a teenager. I think the Anglos chased the family out of town during the oil boom because we're Native American and everything. He hasn't set foot in Bixby in, like, fifty-something years."

Except for slipping across the edge of the midnight border to leave his little messages, Jessica thought. Then a horrible notion occurred to her.

"He wants you to go live in Broken Arrow?" Jessica asked. She'd always wondered if the old man knew that Constanza and she were friends. Maybe he planned to finally bring his granddaughter into the real family business—working for the darklings.

"Excuse me, Jess? Me, living in puny little Broken Arrow?" Constanza shook her head and snorted. "No way."

"So where, then?" Liz asked. "Tulsa?"

"No." Constanza lowered her voice still further, and Jessica saw Ms. Thomas, the librarian, straining to hear. "You know how I'm going to be an actress?"

Everyone nodded, a few of them exchanging glances. You only had to know Constanza for about ten minutes to hear about that aspiration.

"Well, my grandfather said that if I wanted to start right now, I could come stay with him. Because in a couple of weeks he and a whole bunch of my cousins are moving to . . . now get this . . . *LA!*"

"Los Angeles?" Maria cried.

"No, Maria," Liz said with a sneer. "Lower Argentina. That's the new LA. Haven't you heard?" She turned to Constanza. "Los *Angeles*? I hate you. You are *so* lucky."

"You've got to be kidding," Jessica said. Her mouth had gone dry.

"Grandpa's got it all worked out," Constanza said. "He's already found a school for me there, and this movie agent who's a business friend of his wants to meet me. And he says I can have an awesome allowance to pay for acting lessons and stuff."

"I can't *believe* you!" Liz said. "I'm going to *kill* you. After I come visit, of course. I can come visit, right?"

"So why exactly is he going to LA?" Jessica asked.

Constanza shrugged. "I don't know. There must be oil wells there. Right?"

"In Los Angeles?" That didn't seem likely. Nor did it seem very likely that the old man was concentrating on his oil business anymore. He seemed more focused on getting himself and his family as far away from Bixby as possible.

"Who cares *why* he's going there, Jess? As long as the result is"—Constanza pointed both her index fingers toward herself—"movie star!"

"Girls!" Ms. Thomas called from her desk. "Could you *please* keep it down to a dull roar?"

Jen turned to the librarian. "But Constanza's going to—"

"Shhh!" Constanza hissed. "Could we please all remember about the top secret thing?" Then she turned and called out in a normal voice, "Sorry, Ms. Thomas. We'll try to be more quiet." She glared at Jen. "Especially you."

"Wait a second," Jessica said. "Why is this all a big secret?"

"Well, believe it or not," Constanza said. "I haven't mentioned the weirdest part of this yet." She paused, waiting until all eyes were on her again. "It's like this whole moving-to-LA thing just appeared out of nowhere. Grandpa hasn't even talked to my parents about it yet. But in the meantime he says that there's this agent who needs somebody like me right away, for some new TV show or something. So first I'm going to go 'visit' Grandpa out there, supposedly just for a week or so. I can audition then, and if I get the part, I'm not coming back!"

Everyone was quiet for a moment as Constanza's words gradually sank in. Jessica felt her own pulse pounding in her fingertips and saw Dess lower her book slowly so that she could see the other girls. Even Ms. Thomas shot them a glance, intrigued by their sudden silence.

Liz spoke first. "Right away?"

"Like . . . when?" Maria asked.

Constanza shook her head, her mouth slightly open, as if she still couldn't believe it herself. "Well, they're holding auditions in a couple of weeks, right about when Grandpa and my cousins are all moving out there. So he said I have to be there before the end of this month or the whole thing's off. So in a couple of weeks or so, it's goodbye, Bixby!"

"You're kidding!" said Jen.

"You are so psychotically *lucky!*" said Maria.

"I repeat: I *hate* you!" said Liz. "And you've *got* to have a going-away party!"

Jessica didn't say anything. Suddenly the library's fluorescent lights were buzzing too loud for her to think clearly. The old man and his family moving, this agent for Constanza—all of it was happening way too fast for any innocent explanation to be believed.

Constanza's last words rang in her ears: *Goodbye, Bixby . . .*

Jessica glanced over at Dess and saw the polymath drop her trig book onto her lap and pull out a few pieces of paper. She hunched over them, scribbling furiously, filling page after page with grids drawn in blue ink. One of the pages fell to the floor. . . .

Jessica squinted and saw that it was divided into seven squares across and five down, like a wall calendar. Each of the squares was filled with cryptic formulas in tiny, manic handwriting.

She closed her eyes and did a few simple calculations herself.

It was the eighth of October today and she knew from her father's annoying little rhyme that October had thirty-one days.

The end of the month was just over three weeks away.

12

LUNCH MEAT

"Okay, guys," Dess said. "There's some good news and some bad news."

The others looked at her tiredly, already shell-shocked from the weirdness of the last fifty-three hours. Dess was glad she'd waited until all five of them were here; no sense explaining this twice.

Dess found it oddly comforting to be sitting here at the old corner table, the one farthest from the windows, where she and Rex and the Vile One had always eaten together, back before Melissa had revealed her totally evil side. The lunchroom rumbled along around them in its familiar state of chaos, daylighters jockeying for prime table space, unaware of the major trouble that was on its way.

Rex, of course, spoke up first. "Okay. What's the bad news?"

Dess shook her head. "Sorry, Rex. But it's one of those things where the good news has to come first. Otherwise there's no punch line."

"Come on, Dess," Jessica said. "This is serious. Don't you think this is serious?"

"Good question." Dess stared down at her pile of extremely rough calculations. On the one hand, all their information had come from Constanza Grayfoot, which made it inherently suspect. Her instant TV-star status had sounded more like a psycho-cheerleader wet dream than a prophecy of the end times. Dess often wondered how the same family that had managed to undo thousands of years of midnighter rule in Bixby had also produced Constanza.

But as the girl's revelations in study hall had gotten weirder and weirder, Dess had stopped smirking and done her own calculations. The numbers were grim.

The four of them stared at her expectantly, but she just waited. That was the good thing about being the one who actually did the math. Other people had to play by your rules.

Finally Jessica sighed. "Okay, Dess. What's the *good* news?"

Dess allowed herself a victorious smile. "Well, it doesn't look like the *whole* world is going to end."

That got a reaction. Rex raised both eyebrows, and Jonathan managed to stop eating for five whole seconds. Jessica was already freaking out, of course, but her expression angsted up a notch. And Melissa . . . Well, the bitch goddess looked like she always did at lunch: a bit pained by all the mind chaos of the cafeteria, even though she was supposedly in control these days.

"Of course, the math isn't 100 percent sure at this point," Dess admitted.

"So wait," Rex said. "What's the *bad* news, then?"

"The bad news is that Bixby County, including the whole area of the blue time as we know it, plus definitely a big chunk of Broken Arrow and probably Tulsa, and possibly the top half of Oklahoma City—and hell, let's just throw in everything from Wichita to Dallas to Little Rock while we're at it—might very well get sucked into the blue time. In about three weeks."

Dess took a deep breath, feeling a rush of relief now that the proclamation had been made. It was sort of like being the first astronomer to spot one of those big dinosaur-extermination-sized asteroids on its way toward Earth. Sure, this was majorly unpleasant news for everyone, including Dess personally, but at least *she* got to announce it. Doing the calculations always gave Dess a feeling of control. After all, it was better to be one of the astronomers headed for the hills than, say, one of the dinosaurs.

"And you just found this out," Rex said slowly, "in *study hall*?"

"The library is a wonderful place to learn new things, Rex."

"It was Constanza," Jessica said.

"You got this from that cheerleader?" Jonathan snorted. "Well, that makes me feel a *lot* better."

Jessica gave him a nasty look. "This isn't about Constanza. Her grandfather—who's definitely *not* a cheerleader—knows something. He's evacuating his whole family."

"Evacuating?" Rex said. "But they don't even live in Bixby."

"That's the point, Rex." Dess spread her hands. "Remember when I said the blue time might be expanding? Well, it looks like Broken Arrow isn't far enough away from the darklings anymore. So the Grayfoots are bailing out, running away, heading for the hills. Got it?"

Rex paused for a moment before saying, "That's . . . interesting."

"And how far away is the old guy going?" Dess continued. "Tulsa? Nope. Oklahoma City? Sorry, too close. What about Houston, oilman's paradise? Five hundred miles away but still not far enough, apparently. Because he's taking himself and his whole extended family, including his annoying granddaughter, all the way *to California*."

"Yeah," Jessica added. "And there's not much oil business in LA."

Dess leaned back and crossed her arms, waiting for their tiny little brains to catch up. She wished she had a map to show them. When astronomers in movies had to explain that the world was getting clobbered, they always had those fancy computer simulations to make the disaster come to life, or at least a whiteboard.

"But how does he know anything?" Flyboy asked, his jaws still working on a peanut butter sandwich. "Anathea's dead. There's no other halfling to translate for them. So the Grayfoots are cut off from the darklings, aren't they?"

"Exactly," Rex said. "And probably *that's* why Grandpa's freaking out. Maybe since the darklings have stopped answering his messages, he believes those words we left for him: YOU'RE NEXT."

Jessica shot Dess a puzzled look. Apparently she hadn't thought of that one.

Dess had, though. "I admit he's afraid of the darklings, Rex. You made sure of that. But he's not just nervous; he's working on a schedule."

"A schedule?" Rex leaned forward. "How do you mean?"

"Okay: history lesson." She leaned forward, addressing Rex directly. "Grandpa Grayfoot kicked Constanza's parents out of the clan when they moved to Bixby, right?"

"Because he knew about mindcasters," Melissa said. "He didn't want anyone in the family business here, where we could rip their memories."

A shudder went through Dess. "Lovely choice of words, Melissa. But basically, yeah. So maybe he doesn't care what happens to her parents because they disobeyed the no-Bixby rule."

"But Constanza's still his favorite granddaughter," Jessica said.

"Mystifyingly," Dess muttered.

"She's really nice," Jessica said defensively. "And it's true, he really likes her. He buys her tons of clothes."

Melissa nodded. "We've seen the closets."

"Lucky you," Dess said. "But closets full of tacky clothes are nothing compared to what the old guy's bribing her with now. He's invited her to come live in Los Angeles and *promised* that she's going to be a TV star. But there are two catches. One: she can't tell her parents about it."

A guilty look crossed Jessica's face. "Actually, she wasn't supposed to tell anyone at all."

"Yeah." Dess chuckled. "Good move, telling Constanza to keep a secret. It would've been smarter to just come by in a van and grab her. Worked on Rex, after all."

"Like I said, he thinks the darklings are coming after his family," Rex said. "But that doesn't prove the world's ending."

Dess shook her head. "No, it doesn't. Which brings us to catch number two: Constanza has to get her butt out to Hollywood by the end of the month or, and I quote, 'the whole thing's off.' And Grandpa's moving the rest of his clan out there in two weeks—from *Broken Arrow*, Rex, where the darklings can't reach. Not yet anyway."

She let that sink in for a moment. The noise of the lunchroom seemed to grow around them, like the rumble of a coming storm.

"But how would he know the blue time's expanding?" Rex said. "There's no halfling to tell him."

"Maybe he already knew," Melissa said suddenly. She squinted, chewing her lip. "The oldest darklings did."

Rex shook his head, still unconvinced. Dess realized what the problem was: he refused to believe that the Grayfoots knew something he didn't.

Jessica spoke up. "It's so sad. Constanza thinks that she's going to an audition and that she'll get an agent and acting lessons and stuff. But she's leaving her parents behind forever."

"She's one of the lucky ones," Dess said. "At least she'll be out of town before October 31."

"Hey," Flyboy said. "That's Halloween!"

"Um, yeah." Dess raised an eyebrow. "I hadn't thought of

that. It's kind of . . . interesting, but it's not numbers." She frowned at Rex. "Anything about Halloween in the lore?"

"Of course not." He shrugged. "There was no Halloween in Oklahoma until about a hundred years ago."

Dess nodded. "Fine, enough with history. Here's the math: when you boil it into numbers, October 31 seems like no big deal at first. I mean, the sum is forty-one, and you get three hundred-ten when you multiply. No relevant numbers there. But in the old days October wasn't the tenth month, it was the eighth. You know, *Oct*ober, like an *oct*agon, with eight sides?" They all looked at her blank-faced, and Dess suppressed a groan. Next time she was definitely bringing visual aids. "Come on, guys. Eighth month? Thirty-first day? And eight plus thirty-one is . . . ?"

"Thirty-nine?" Jessica said.

"Give the girl a prize."

"Wait a second, Dess," Flyboy said. "I thought thirty-nine was a major *anti*darkling number. Like all those thirty-nine-letter names."

"Magisterially Supernumerary Mathematician," Dess supplied. "An instant classic. And yes, the number thirty-nine is totally antidarkling. The real problem is the *next* day."

"Isn't that All Saints' Day or something?" Jonathan said.

Dess let out an exasperated breath. This wasn't about spooks or ghosts or saints; it was about *numbers*. "Don't know. Don't care."

Melissa brought her fingers up to her temples. "Hang on, guys."

Dess ignored her. "But November 1, here in the modern era, is the *first* day of—"

"Guys!" Melissa cried out.

They were all silent for a moment, and Dess thought she heard the hubbub of the cafeteria fade for a few seconds, as if a chill had spread through the room. Her fingertips were tingling, and a trickle of nerves filtered their way down to the pit of her stomach.

"Something's *coming*," Melissa whispered.

As the words passed the mindcaster's lips, a tremor rolled across the room, the shudder of the spinning earth halting in its tracks. The roar of the cafeteria was sucked away all at once, leaving the five of them surrounded by almost two hundred stiffs, faces blue and cold and waxen, caught throwing food and picking their noses and chewing with their mouths open.

"What time is it, Rex?" Dess's own voice sounded small in the awesome, sudden silence.

Rex looked at his watch. "Twelve twenty-one and fifteen seconds."

Dess wrote the number down and stared at it, wondering how long this one was going to last.

Jonathan bobbed weightlessly up from his chair. "Cool, this again."

"What are we supposed to do?" Jessica said softly.

"We just sit here," Rex said. "We wait it out. And get *down*, Jonathan!"

"Why?" Jonathan said. "I can fall from here, no problem."

"There are people all around, Jonathan. If you fly off

someplace and the blue time ends, they'll see you disappear."

"Come on, Jonathan." Jessica reached up and took his hand. "Plenty of time to fly when the world ends."

"All right, whatever." Jonathan sighed, settling back onto his chair like a deflating balloon.

No one said anything for a moment. Dess's eyes were drawn to the tray in front of Rex, whose cafeteria lunch had already been left to congeal during the discussion. Its waxy layer of interrupted time made it look even more unappetizing, his Jell-O glowing blue, its wobble arrested.

Melissa held her head tipped back, tasting the air to her heart's content, and for once Dess was glad that the mind-caster was around. At least they'd know if an army of dark-lings was on its way.

Of course, this wasn't the end of the world, not yet. You could tell just by looking. If the secret hour had snapped completely, all the stiffs around them would still be moving, having been sucked into the blue time along with everything else within a few hundred miles.

Dess didn't have to do any math to know what the result of that would be. All those predators suddenly escaping from their midnight prison, unleashed on their prey—maybe millions of people, if the blue time really expanded across the whole state. No phones, no cars, not even fire, and only the five midnighters knew how to defend themselves.

Dess fixed her gaze on a constellation of french fries hovering over a motionless food fight across the lunch-room. She wondered if what she'd told Jessica yesterday after school was really true. Could you make it to the border of the blue time, freezing yourself at the edge until the long midnight ended?

Not too many people would be lucky enough to make it that far. Not with all those hungry darklings pouring in from the desert. And what if the blue time *never* ended? What if everyone on the outside was permanently frozen and everyone in the inside was lunch meat—most of humanity gone with a whimper, the rest with a bang?

"So, Dess?" Jessica said, finally breaking the silence.

She pulled her gaze from the hovering french fries. "Yeah?"

"In study hall, what were you scribbling on those papers? You said Halloween was safe. What's wrong with the next day?"

"Oh, yeah." Dess looked down at the papers before her, tinged blue by the eclipse. "Well, the weird thing is what happens at midnight, Halloween, if you switch from the old system to the new. October 31 was an antidarkling fiesta back when October was the eighth month. But now November's the eleventh month. Right?" Dess spread her hands. "Man, you guys are hopeless. So it's November 1. And eleven plus one is *twelve*, as in midnight. As in darklings."

They were all silent for a moment.

Finally Jonathan asked, "How long is that from now?"

"Twenty-three days, eleven hours, and thirty-nine minutes," Dess said. "Minus fifteen seconds."

"Three weeks." Jessica looked at Rex. "So what should we do?"

Dess was glad to see him scratch his brow, at least pretending like he was coming up with a plan. However messed up Rex's head was, the coming end of the world might screw it on a little bit tighter.

"I'm not convinced yet, Dess," he said after a minute. "But I guess we have to find out more about what the Grayfoots are up to."

"How are we supposed to do that?" Jonathan said. "Just drive over to Broken Arrow and ask them?"

He smiled. "Maybe it's better if we get them over to Bixby."

Everyone stared at him, but Rex didn't blink.

Dess leaned back into her chair, wondering what Rex was smoking. When the last bunch of midnighters had gotten in Grandpa Grayfoot's way, he'd made a hundred prominent citizens disappear overnight. Less than two weeks ago the Grayfoots had kidnapped Rex right out of his own house, then left him in the desert to have his humanity stripped away.

But for some reason he wasn't scared of them. Dess might not be a mindcaster, but she could see that. What the hell was happening to him?

It was funny, but ever since the bitch goddess had gotten under control, Rex had gone six kinds of crazy. It was like the five of them only had so much sanity to go around.

"Rex, be serious," Jessica said softly.

"I am serious." He reached into his jacket and threw a piece of paper on the table. It was covered with scrawled lore signs. "This is a message from Angie."

"That psycho who kidnapped you?" Jonathan asked.

"That's the one."

"Um, Rex." Dess shook her head. "Why didn't you mention this earlier?"

"Sorry. It only showed up yesterday morning, and I wasn't sure what to do about it—until now."

"Burn it, maybe?" suggested Dess.

Rex ignored her. "From what Angie says, the family is closing ranks, leaving outsiders like her in the dark. She's just as freaked out as we are." His fingers drummed the table. "Which means that Dess might be right."

"About burning it?" Dess said.

"No, about what's going to happen in three weeks and that the Grayfoots know more about it than we do. So I guess I should meet with her."

Jonathan stared at the piece of paper with a horrified expression, like a live rattlesnake had flopped onto the table. "What the hell, Rex? You're actually going to trust her?"

"I don't trust her at all. But I've been wondering about this message and figuring out a way to get Angie over to Bixby, whether she wants to come or not. We'll all have to work together, though." He looked around at them, a seer-knows-best expression on his face.

Dess sighed, wondering if anyone else had noticed how every time all five of them did anything together, things went totally haywire.

"Hang on, guys!" Melissa said suddenly. "It's ending."

Rex snatched the scrawled paper from the table. "Get ready."

Jonathan pulled himself firmly down onto his seat. Melissa put her fingers back on her temples, the way she'd been when the eclipse had hit. Dess tried to remember what she'd been doing—probably looking at Melissa and wondering what the hell she was yelling about.

She turned toward the mindcaster and gave her a suitable look of contempt.

A few seconds later the world shuddered again. The cold blue light was swept from the cafeteria, which exploded around them into a mass of motion and sound and sunlight. The seventeen french fries sailed on their various trajectories, two hundred mouths resumed their chewing, and Rex's Jell-O began to wobble once more.

Dess pulled at Rex's arm and looked at his watch, comparing it with the time on her GPS device. This eclipse had been shorter than the first one, lasting only seven minutes and twelve seconds. But it had followed a similar pattern: three times 144 seconds.

Now that it was over, Dess allowed herself a long sigh. However certain she'd been that the big event was three weeks away, it was a relief to know the end hadn't come.

Not this time, anyway.

13

BRILLIANT PLAN

Broken Arrow hadn't changed much, as far as Rex could see.

The town was still Bixby's little sister, with no buildings over a few stories marking its skyline. Clanking oil derricks and mesquite trees went right up to the city's edge, and instead of green lawns most people had dirt front yards. The native desert scrub they planted to keep the soil from eroding needed a lot less water than grass—and looked better, Rex thought—but in Bixby not having a real lawn meant that you were poor or lazy, which most people figured was pretty much the same thing.

He drove carefully, checking the street signs, following the exact route that Dess had used for her calculations. She'd complained about that part of the plan because too many things could mess with the math—how fast Rex drove, the air pressure in the tires, even the temperature outside. She spent a lot of time complaining about something called "fumes."

Rex couldn't think about all that. It was all he could do to drive this rumbling, smelly, *human* machine. His reflexes were much faster now, but the plastics and metal in the car put him on edge.

Besides, there were lots of ways this plan could go wrong. The precisely measured gas in the Ford's tank was only one.

It was strange being in Melissa's car without her along, but Angie had demanded three things: that they meet no later than 11:00 P.M., that they didn't go *anywhere* near Bixby, and that Rex come alone.

He remembered how nervous Angie's voice had sounded on the phone. But Rex didn't want her too anxious. He wouldn't get any information from the woman if things got violent.

He found the corner Angie had named, two narrow back alleys that intersected among dark and looming warehouses, the prey marks of humans scant—the perfect place for Rex to disappear, if that's what Angie had in mind. Of course, if Rex were still relevant to the family's plans, they probably wouldn't have gone to this much trouble.

Still, he was glad it was just him here in the car and not all five of them. The Grayfoots were old hands at making people vanish.

Angie was already there, smoking a cigarette and wearing a leather coat that reached her knees. She gave him an angry glare, checked her watch, then cast a wary glance around. As she walked toward the Ford, Rex realized that he'd never seen her in normal time before. In motion and without the waxy pallor of the secret hour laid across her skin, she didn't look that much older than a college student.

He remembered to turn off the Ford's engine; Dess's calculations didn't include any idling time.

"You're late," she said.

"Sorry. My mom came over. Had to sneak out—school night."

Her eyes narrowed with suspicion, but then she let out a smoke-tinged sigh. Nothing like being reminded that the latest person you'd kidnapped was still in high school. Rex hoped that seeing Anathea dead out in the desert had made Angie think twice about her employers. Hopefully she was fed up with the kid-snatching business.

"Fine, let's talk," she said. "But in exactly twenty minutes I'm out of here. You're not going to pull any of that spook crap on me."

Rex laughed. "What sort of 'spook crap' are you expecting? We're miles from Bixby."

"Yeah, I know where the edges are," she said. "But before the Grayfoots stopped talking to me, Ernesto said that things were changing."

Rex nodded. Ernesto was Constanza's cousin—the family definitely knew something.

"They are," he said. "Get in and I'll tell you what we know."

"What? Get in that car with you?"

He gave her a bored look. "Don't be so paranoid, Angie.

Midnight still comes at midnight, not . . ." He checked his watch, as if he hadn't planned this all out to the minute. "Eleven-fifteen. And I'm not standing around in the cold." He tugged on the front of his T-shirt; not wearing a jacket had been Jessica's idea. "So get in."

Her nervous eyes scanned the buildings around them again. "Okay, but *my* car."

"Forget that," he said. "My wheels or no deal."

Rex held her suspicious gaze, wondering if that last line had been too much. He'd rehearsed it on the way over here, trying out various inflections, settling on a dramatic pause between "no" and "deal." But maybe he'd blown it. The rest of the plan wouldn't work unless Angie got into Melissa's car.

But as he watched her think about it, Rex felt something else replace his jitters—the same calm he'd experienced just before he'd turned Timmy Hudson into jelly. He could smell Angie's fear now, could see it in the play of lines on her face, and he realized that she'd been telling the truth about the Grayfoots cutting her off. She carried the anxious scent of a human rejected by its tribe, left to its own devices on the harsh desert.

A trickle of anticipation went through Rex, the same excitement he'd felt tracking Cassie Flinders across the blue time. He was the hunter here, not this human.

"Take it or leave it, Angie. But don't make me sit here." He drew his lips back from his teeth. "Like I said: it's a school night."

A long moment later she said, "Okay. But if you start that engine, I'm sticking this between your ribs." Steel flashed in the darkness.

At the sight of the knife Rex felt some of his predatory confidence slip away. He could smell that the blade was tungsten stainless; its very touch would burn him. Rex couldn't imagine what the weapon would feel like thrust into his side.

Angie walked the long way around the car, checking the backseat for any surprises. Finally she opened the passenger door and slipped inside, bringing in the scents of anxiety and cigarette smoke.

"You know," he said. "Seeing as how you kidnapped me, you've got a lot of nerve acting like I'm the bad guy."

She snorted, running nervous fingers through her blond hair. "Spare me. I know what you midnighters are."

"What? High school students?"

She turned away to stare through the front windshield, watching the empty alley. "It doesn't matter how old you are. A monster is still a monster."

"*Me?* A monster?" For a second the word made him shudder. Did she know about the way he was changing?

Angie turned to him, her words spilling out with furious speed. "Listen, Rex, the family may have shut me out after what happened two weeks ago, but I know a lot about the history of Bixby. Probably more than you do."

Rex's jaw dropped open. "I doubt that."

"Right, I'm sure you think you know everything." She smiled. "You may know a few tricks, like how to read fifty-year-old propaganda, but you don't know what things were really like in Bixby back then. You weren't there. The old guy I work for was."

"What? He's a . . ." Rex started, but he was too indignant to finish. This traitor to humanity, this Grayfoot lackey, this *daylighter* was lecturing *him* about the lore? Rex's amazement sputtered out of him like an old car engine giving up the ghost.

He'd made Melissa swear to take it easy on Angie's brain, but Rex doubted it would be tough to make her break that promise.

"After they freed Bixby," Angie continued, "the Grayfoots discovered a lot of what you midnighters call 'the lore.' That's how I learned to read the symbols, practicing on all that old rubbish about how the great midnighters kept everyone happy and safe."

"The Grayfoots *freed* Bixby?" was all Rex could manage. "From what?"

"Come on, Rex. What do you think it was really like back then? A small, unelected group of people running a tiny town in the middle of nowhere. People who could play God with time, who could ruin the brain of anyone who disagreed with them. Doesn't that sound great, Rex, growing up in a place like that?" She paused, giving him a disgusted look. "Of course, you would have been one of the people in charge."

"But midnighters aren't about controlling people's minds."

"Are you kidding?"

"Well, they only did it to keep the secret hour hidden, to keep the town safe."

Angie barked out a single-syllable laugh. "Sometime, Rex, you should read some *real* history. Everyone who abuses power says exactly the same thing: 'We only do nasty, secret things to keep everyone safe. Without us in charge, you're all doomed.'"

"What are . . . ?" He growled, unable to organize his thoughts. "You *kidnapped* me!"

She looked away, letting out a slow breath, and Rex thought for a moment that he had finally quieted her madness. But after a moment she turned back and said, "It was the only way to stay in contact with the darklings. Without them we couldn't keep you from re-creating the old Bixby." She shrugged, the thick leather coat creaking. "Besides, do you know how many hundreds of children the old midnighters kidnapped over the years?"

"What?" Rex cried. But then he remembered the ancient tales: when mindcasters detected newly born midnighters nearby, war parties had been dispatched to steal them. More recently, offers of jobs and money had been sent to their parents. Rex found himself wondering, though—if those inducements hadn't worked, had the old midnighters resorted to stronger tactics? There wasn't anything like that in the lore, but what if they had just pretended it hadn't happened?

"Well," he said, "maybe a long time ago they did some

things that seem weird now, sort of like . . . George Washington having slaves or whatever." Rex shook his head firmly. "But *we're* not like that!"

"I've seen your father, Rex," she said calmly. "Did a stroke leave him that way?"

"That was . . ." His voice broke. "We were just kids."

She rolled her eyes. "Yeah. Born monsters, like I said."

They were silent for a moment, Rex's head spinning from everything Angie had said. When he'd seen her name in lore symbols at the bottom of the note, there had been a moment of curiosity; even if she wasn't a seer, here was someone else who could read the lore, who knew the signs of midnight. But after just a few minutes of talking to her, he felt his oldest sureties in danger of crumbling.

Was she making all this up? Could there really be a secret history *behind* the secret history?

He took a deep breath, checking his watch. The only way to find out was to stick to the plan; Melissa could get to the bottom of this.

"In any case," Angie said. "I didn't come here to debate midnighter ethics. Just don't sit there pretending like I'm some kind of demon, all right?"

"Fine." Rex forced himself to calm down. This was nuts, sitting here questioning what was what. It was probably the new predator part of his mind, willing to believe anything said against the humans who had dared to challenge the darkling kind.

He just had to let the plan unfold. Keep stalling and

make sure that Angie stayed nervous.

"Just one quick question," he said. "Your employers? The nice people who 'freed' Bixby. What would they do if they knew you were here talking to me?"

She let out a short, dry laugh. "Probably cut me into small pieces. Maybe you too."

Rex allowed a grim smile to show on his face. He'd been hoping she would say something like that. "Talk about monsters."

"I never said they were perfect. Far from it." She crossed her arms. "All right, since it's a school night and everything, shall we move on from the mutual recriminations? I told you some of what I know in my note. Maybe I'll have more to tell you later. But you go first."

"Okay." Rex glanced at his watch. He still had fifteen minutes to kill. "There have been signs of change in the blue time."

"Blue time?"

"You know, the secret hour." Rex blinked. He'd forgotten that "blue time" had originally been Dess's term—not part of the lore. "Everything turns kind of blue when time freezes."

Angie just looked at him.

"What?" he said. "You didn't know that?"

"Yeah, I've read the accounts. But I never got used to the idea of you midnighters," she said. "It's one thing that spooks live in the secret hour, but *human beings* walking around while the rest of us are frozen?" She shivered. "It's so creepy."

He snorted a laugh. "Trust me. They're the creepy ones, not us. Whatever you've read about the darklings, I've *seen* them."

"But you haven't read their words," she said. "And I have."

Rex was silent for a moment. It was true—Grandpa Grayfoot had managed to do something that no seer had ever done before. He'd communicated with the enemy.

But now Rex had gone one better—he'd actually communicated with a darkling face-to-face. He thought again about heading out to the desert, meeting with the old minds there, hearing what *their* perspective was about all this history.

Now, that would be a brain bender . . . if they didn't kill him first.

As Rex stared out the window, he saw a car flash past at the end of the alley. He swallowed, glancing at his watch again. They were early.

Angie hadn't seen it, though.

"Well, whatever," he said. "When time freezes, it's blue. But this last week something really strange happened. Something that's not in any lore I've ever read."

"A timequake."

He looked at her. "A what?"

"A spontaneous fluctuation of the prime contortion. Releasing the energies built up over the centuries."

"Um, yeah." He drummed his fingers on the seat. *Prime contortion?* Maybe Angie really had read a few things that

Rex hadn't. "We've been calling it an eclipse. But it might be more like a tremor, a warning of bigger things to come."

"And that's why the Grayfoots' houses all sprouted For Sale signs last week?"

He nodded. "We think that the blue time is going to expand, suddenly and without much warning, getting big enough to swallow Broken Arrow."

She stared at him for a moment, then said, "Jesus. No wonder they're running. When?"

He shook his head and smiled. "I think I'll save that piece of information until you tell me more. Such as, when are the Grayfoots leaving Broken Arrow?"

"Well, I'm not a hundred percent sure," she said. "But there is something they've all been talking about for a while."

"What is it?"

Suddenly lights swept through the interior of the car.

"What the . . . ?" Angie said, turning to look back.

Rex winced as he glanced in the mirror. A pair of headlights loomed at the other end of the alley. *Jonathan and Dess, you morons,* he thought. *Can't you read a clock?*

They'd come way too soon.

But there was only one thing to do: stick with the plan. He started the engine.

"What the hell are you doing?" Angie shouted.

"They're coming for us," he said. The headlights were closing fast. "They must have followed you!" He put the car in gear and rolled down the alley.

"Oh, Christ! Let me out!" She started to open her door.

Rex accelerated, and the door crushed a trash can with a sickening sound, swinging closed with a thunk. *Sorry, Melissa,* he thought.

"You'll never make it to your car!" he shouted. "Just hang on. I'll get us out of here."

He accelerated down the alley and out onto the first street on Dess's route map. As he turned right, the Ford's freshly filled tires screeched across the asphalt.

The headlights swept out of the alley behind them, clinging to his tail.

Very convincing, Flyboy.

"I don't know if I can outrun them," he said. "This car's pretty old."

"Oh, great! You know, *my* car goes plenty fast!"

"I didn't know you were going to bring company!" he shouted. "I'll head for the highway."

He hit Highway 75 and turned west, bringing the Ford up to eighty miles per hour. This was the diciest part of the plan. Going over the speed limit was bad enough, given that it was curfew time back in Bixby, but if another eclipse—or timequake, or fluctuation of the prime contortion—suddenly struck, Rex would plow through the windshield like a bullet.

"Hey! You're headed to Bixby!" The knife flashed in the corner of Rex's eye—he smelled steel inches from his face.

"Oh, crap." He swallowed, finding it easy to sound scared. "Just headed home by reflex. Sorry."

He heard a growl rise in her throat, but no burning

blade of steel pierced his ribs just yet.

"Listen," he said. "There aren't any exits before Bixby except the access road. We can follow it through Saddleback."

"Don't try to mess with me, Rex. That's inside the contortion!"

"Yeah, but we can go straight through to the other side of the county. You'll be in and out of the blue time inside ten minutes."

"Dammit, Rex . . ." She looked at her watch.

"Maybe the Grayfoots will be afraid to follow us in!"

Angie's voice suddenly grew very calm. "Okay, keep driving. It's before eleven-thirty, so you can get me out by midnight. But if you stop *anywhere* in this county, Rex, I swear I'll kill you."

"Hey, don't threaten the driver. I won't stop, okay?"

Unless of course, I happen to run out of gas.

There was movement in his peripheral vision, and the glimmer of the knife disappeared. "All right, then," she said.

Rex breathed a sigh of relief. Things were going more or less according to plan. Jonathan and Dess might have shown up a bit too early, but at least Angie hadn't stabbed him yet.

"They're catching up," she announced.

He looked in the rearview. *Idiots.* They weren't supposed to overtake them or force Rex to drive over seventy-five, which would draw cops like flies.

Couldn't Jonathan and Dess do *anything* right?

"Like I said, the Grayfoots probably won't follow us into Bixby. Right?"

"If they know I'm meeting with one of you midnighters, they might make an exception."

"But maybe not." Rex pushed the accelerator a bit farther down, trying to make it look convincing. The old Ford's engine began to make a grinding sound, and Rex hoped he wasn't screwing up Dess's calculations too much.

Of course, the most worrying question was whether Angie would go crazy when his car ran out of gas right smack in the center of the emptiest, least traveled part of the county.

Rex swore under his breath. It would have been better if Dess and Jonathan had shown up ten minutes later. As it was, Angie would have too much time before midnight to wonder if this had all been arranged. Or she might get lucky and have a passing car pick her up.

Still looking backward, she swore. "There's two of them now."

"Huh? Two of *what*?"

"Two cars following us, you pinhead."

"How could there . . . ? Oh, crap!" he shouted. It had to be the police. "Does one of them have a flashing light on top?"

"No, they're both black Mercedes. Standard Grayfoot issue."

"Mercedes . . . ?"

A few seconds later Rex let out a strangled little laugh of pure amazement. On the other side of the highway, headed into Broken Arrow right on schedule, was Jonathan's father's car, complete with him and Dess in the front seat, their expressions of surprise briefly visible as they flashed by.

"Oops," Rex said softly.

"What?"

"You actually let the Grayfoots *follow you!*"

"I thought we already covered that," Angie said. "They're closing in! Doesn't this thing go any faster?"

"I guess it does," said Rex, and pushed the pedal to the floor.

He looked down at the gas gauge, which hovered just above *E.*

But not for much longer.

14

CHANGE OF PLAN

"So, Flyboy—clue me in here. Was that *Rex* we just saw speeding down the other lane?"

Jonathan's eyes swept the highway frantically. Now that the shock was wearing off, he'd realized they needed to turn around. Fast. "Yep."

"And that was Angie sitting next to him?"

"I don't think it was his mom."

"And—now this was the confusing part—there was this big black car chasing them, right? Like we were supposed to be doing? I mean, this isn't one of those time travel things where we just saw ourselves in the future, is it?"

"Not unless ten minutes in the future we've got a pair of Mercedes between us."

"There were *two* of them?"

"That's what I saw." Although at this point Jonathan wasn't completely sure what he'd seen.

Then he spotted a familiar exit, a mile up. He could pull off here and head back west without getting completely tangled in downtown Broken Arrow's web of warehouses and alleys.

Dess tapped her fingers on her window for a few seconds. "So that means Rex's plan isn't going very well, is it?"

"Nope. Hold on." Without slowing at all, Jonathan brought the car off the highway. Dess crushed against his shoulder as she leaned into the turn.

"Seat belt?" he suggested. He heard the slithering sound of vinyl as Dess scrambled to secure herself, then the click of a metal clasp.

He found himself glad that Melissa and Jess were still back in Bixby. Rex hadn't wanted them all inside Broken Arrow together in case this whole thing was some kind of Grayfoot trap.

Frankly, Jonathan had never thought much of the plan. It was pretty complicated, which always meant there were lots of things that could go wrong. Being involved in Rex's schemes had taught Jonathan that someone was always late (usually Jessica) or didn't pass along the message (usually Beth) or simply didn't do what they were supposed to do because they didn't feel like it (typically Melissa). And even if all the midnighters decided to play their parts, there were always cops, or parents, or teachers to screw things up.

Of course, even with all his doubts, Jonathan hadn't actually thought of this particular possibility.

"So wait," Dess said as they zoomed through the dark underbelly of a cluster of overpasses, huge concrete columns flashing past on either side. "The Grayfoots really *did* know that Angie was meeting with Rex?"

"Yeah. They must have been following her or something."

"Stupid cow."

"That's usually the problem with brilliant plans: not-so-brilliant people."

Dess shook her head as they climbed onto an entrance ramp and shot back up onto Highway 75. "Wow. So this afternoon, when Rex made us siphon most of the gas out of Melissa's tank? That was kind of a waste of two hours."

"My guess is that Rex feels the same way," Jonathan said. "When's he supposed to run out?"

"At exactly eleven forty-seven and . . . oh, wait. We're ahead of schedule here, aren't we?"

"About ten minutes."

She looked at Geostationary. "Well, they were supposed to come to a stop right when they got to the middle of Saddleback. Of course, Rex looked like he was driving a little faster than we figured, which is less fuel efficient, especially in an old beater like Melissa's car. So . . ."

"Pretty soon, right?"

"Yeah. About eleven-forty. Unless those guys in the Mercs have guns and shoot out their tires or something."

"Oh, right. Good point." Jonathan realized that he had been going a bit slower than maximum, not wanting to send Dess through the windshield if an eclipse sneaked up on them. But the more he thought about it, the worse trouble he figured Rex was in. He pressed the accelerator down harder.

"So, Dess, if you see any blue sweeping across the sky, you know what to do, right?"

"Grab your hand. No problem."

Jonathan nodded. If he was sharing his midnight gravity with someone, they probably wouldn't carry their momentum into the blue time. Two weeks before in the desert, Jessica and Dess had been whacked against their seat belts when his car had frozen and Melissa almost killed when she'd been, but nothing had happened to Jonathan.

Of course, no one had been crazy enough to test this hand-holding theory yet.

This zooming along at seventy-five miles an hour was another reason he was glad Melissa and Jess weren't here. He only had two hands.

They shot along the highway, the lights of central Bixby glowing before them, a great mass of darkness all around.

"Can you see anything?"

She leaned forward, squinting through the windshield at the dark road ahead. "Barely. I think that little cluster of taillights is them."

"So what are we supposed to do now?" Jonathan said. "Try to catch up and help Rex? Or stick to the plan when we hit the county line and head out to pick up Melissa and Jess?"

"Crap, I don't know. I hate all this plan stuff."

"Me too," Jonathan said.

"Maybe we should keep following Rex. We can swoop in and pick him up after he runs out of gas."

Jonathan swallowed. "You do realize that'll be trickier than it sounds, right, Dess? Remember what you said about them maybe having guns?"

"Absolutely. But we can't just leave him out here with

real Grayfoots chasing him. Who knows what they'll do to him?"

Jonathan couldn't argue with that. Melissa's car couldn't outrun those two Mercedes even if it wasn't about to conk out. "I guess I could fly over and get Jessica after midnight falls."

"What about Melissa?" Dess said. "We'll need her if we're going to get into Angie's mind. You actually going to hold *her* hand?"

Cold fingers stroked Jonathan's spine at the thought. He'd touched Melissa exactly once before, for an emergency jump across a hundred yards of angry tarantulas. In those few seconds her tortured mind had flooded into him like a wave of nausea; it was something he never wanted to repeat.

He sighed. "I guess I'll have to. But what about you and Rex being alone in Saddleback? It'll take me ten minutes to get Jessica there, and that's the deep desert—darkling country."

"Don't worry about me." Dess kicked the duffel bag on the floor in front of her, which let out a clank. "I think our big problem right now is Rex staying alive *until* midnight."

"Yeah, you got that right. Those guys in the Mercs looked pretty pissed." Jonathan took a deep breath. "Okay, we go after Rex and save his sorry ass from the Grayfoots."

He accelerated still more, squeezing every drop of speed out of his father's car.

Dess scrunched down into her seat. "Sounds like a plan to me."

15

OUT OF GAS

As they crossed the county line, Rex kept his eyes locked on the road ahead. "Are they giving up?"

Angie turned to stare through the back window, then let out a string of curses. "No, still with us. And if they're risking Bixby at this hour to catch us, that means they're in a really bad mood."

Rex gripped the steering wheel, trying not to scream with frustration. In all his detailed planning, it had never once occurred to him that the *real* Grayfoots would show up. "How did they know we were meeting?"

"No one followed me, Rex, I'm positive."

"What about your phone?"

"They couldn't have tapped it. That number I gave you was a disposable cell phone I bought last week at the Tulsa Mall. Never used it before you called, so they couldn't have . . ." Her voice turned cold. "You didn't call me from *your* house, did you?"

Rex didn't answer for a few critical seconds, and by the time he found the right words, it was too late to lie.

"Was I not supposed to?" he finally managed.

She let out a groan.

"You mean, my phone is tapped?" he cried.

"Only for the last two years. Pinhead."

Rex drove on, waiting for the burning sensation of a knife slipping between his ribs, but all he heard was Angie muttering beneath her breath. "Jesus. Maybe you really are just a bunch of kids."

The pursuers drew closer, filling the old Ford with their headlights. They were easing up on either side now, like wolves shepherding wounded prey away from the herd, out to a nice, private killing ground. This abandoned stretch of the access road was probably just the sort of place they'd been waiting for. Rex's plan had brought them to a perfect spot.

Angie pulled out a phone. "All right. I'm calling the police."

"It won't work out here," Rex said softly. He and Dess had picked this route to make sure Angie couldn't escape the blue time after the car ran out of gas. Since the new highway had been built, hardly anyone ever drove through Saddleback. There were no cell phone towers, no houses, no cops—just rattlesnakes, slither burrows, and plenty of places to bury a couple of bodies.

Rex checked his watch. If Dess's calculations were on target, they'd be sputtering to a halt in about three minutes. He had to think of something soon or they were both dead.

But what could he do, trapped on a road with no turnoffs, no choices but to keep driving straight?

Suddenly Rex felt something deep inside himself laughing

at his own paralysis. Why was he thinking like prey? Why was he letting his pursuers dictate the terms?

Why not make *them* take some risks?

He gritted his teeth and pulled the wheel sharply to the left. The Ford slid from the road and onto the sandy shoulder, where it swerved like a sidewinder for a few seconds. Then the tires gripped the hard-packed desert floor, and the car straightened, rattling like an old washing machine as it crashed through mounds of scrub grass and rumbled over prairie dog holes.

For a moment the pursuing headlights angled off into the distance behind them. But then the two Mercedes swerved from the road, turning onto the desert in pursuit.

"What are you *doing*?" Angie cried, her teeth snapping as the car shook.

"Out here there's a chance one of them will get a flat."

"Isn't there also a chance of *us* getting a flat?"

Rex only nodded, deciding not to explain that one way or another, the Ford was about to stop moving. "Have you got a better idea?"

"My better idea was not using *a tapped phone!*"

"You could have mentioned that in your note!"

"It was so obvious we were watching you! Jesus. How did you people ever take control of a whole town?"

"That wasn't *us* who . . ." Rex's words trailed off. Up ahead was a cluster of glistening humps, like a field of spiky basketballs glowing in the moonlight. He smiled at the sight. If all three cars were disabled, he and Angie might stand a chance of escaping on foot.

He aimed toward the humps, ignoring the Ford's rattling complaints and building up as much speed as he could. Gas or no gas, tires or no tires—once Melissa's car got going, it took a while to come to a stop.

"Rex? What is that ahead?"

"Big patch of rainbow cactus."

"What the hell? Are you *trying* to get us killed?"

"No. But we're about to run out of gas."

"What?"

"Long story. This way at least we've got a chance."

"Of *what*? A quick death?"

His answer was cut off by a sudden *bang* beneath the car, a sound like a watermelon hitting concrete at eighty miles an hour. More collisions rocked the Ford, Angie crying out as each cactus struck. The shock of the impacts shot up through the car seat, jolting Rex like a series of kicks in the butt.

Behind them a pair of headlights dropped back. One of the Mercedes had ground to a halt, with either a tire burst or an axle busted. As Rex watched in the shuddering rearview mirror, the car was overwhelmed by its own cloud of dust.

Only one to go.

Then, with a parting *bang*, the cactus patch fell behind them. Melissa's Ford was wobbling, its right-front tire making a sound like a rubber flag in a strong wind. But the engine kept rumbling underneath Rex, and the desert still flashed past in front of their headlights.

"They'll be getting nervous now," Angie said, looking back.

"Nervous?"

"If they lose the other car, they'll have no way to get out of the county in time. They're Grayfoots, brought up so they'd rather die than be in Bixby at midnight."

Rex blinked. After all his careful planning for tonight, would his insane, wildly improvised idea of barreling through a cactus patch be the one thing that actually worked? Inside him, the darkling half of his mind was quietly pleased.

"Rex, did you say something about running out of gas?"

"Well—" he started, but suddenly another explosion shook the car. The steering wheel jerked out of his hands, and the car began to swerve out of control across the desert floor, swinging into a bootlegger's reverse, tipping so far to the right that Rex thought it was going to roll over. The horrible screeching of bare metal skimming across rocks and hard-packed sand filled his ears, and a cloud of dust rose up to swallow the world around them.

Somehow the Ford didn't roll over, but when they finally skidded to a halt, it was listing to one side like a sinking ship. Rex was pretty sure that both right tires had been reduced to rubber confetti.

The engine died then with a cough, finally realizing that it had run out of gas.

Rex waited for a pair of headlights to lance through the dust swirling around them. The other Mercedes couldn't be far behind.

The view gradually cleared, revealing a starry sky, the dark mountains in the distance—and a pair of red taillights receding into the desert.

"What the hell?" he said. "They totally *had* us."

Angie took a while to catch her breath, her hands slowly releasing their grip on the upholstery. "It's too close to midnight."

Rex looked at his watch. "But they still had fifteen minutes. Plenty of time to kill us and get to the county line."

"Yeah, but first they had to drive back around the cactus to pick up whoever was in the other car."

"What? They're too nice to just leave them out here?"

"Those were all Grayfoots." She let out a snort. "And they'd never leave family behind."

He looked at her. "Just you."

Angie nodded slowly. "Just me." Her dazed eyes took in the slowly clearing dust, the empty desert, and finally dropped to stare at her watch. "I guess I'm screwed. Your little mindcaster friend will be here soon, won't she?"

The smell of terror from Angie had become almost overwhelming. Her hands were shaking now, as if she were even more afraid of a mindcaster entering her brain than of the Grayfoots catching her.

Rex let out a slow breath, willing his thudding heart to calm down. With Angie's fear scent filling the car, a hunting frenzy threatened to take over his mind. But he needed to keep control, to keep talking to her.

"Let me be honest, all right?" he said through gritted teeth. "It was always my plan to trap you in Bixby for midnight. That's why I only had so much gas."

"So you *knew* the Grayfoots were going to show up? And you came anyway?" She whistled. "You've got guts."

"Well, not exactly. Things didn't quite go the way I planned." He sighed. "But listen, Angie, have you really been telling me the truth about the past? The way the old midnighters—" Rex's voice choked off as his nose suddenly caught the sharp smell of stainless steel. Angie's knife flashed in her hand. "Hey, what the hell?"

"Listen, Rex, I know that in fifteen minutes you can do anything you want to me, make me drooling and stupid like your father, maybe turn me into your slave. But that doesn't mean I can't even the score."

"Hold *up*, Angie! No one's going to turn you into a vegetable!"

"Yeah, right." She snorted. "So you lured me out here to steal my bank card password?"

"No, to make sure you were telling the truth!" The knife came closer, and his darkling mind writhed at the smell of steel. "We had to do this! If the world's ending, we had to know for sure!"

Angie paused, her eyes narrowing. "What did you just say? If the *what's* ending?"

"The world . . . or at least a great big chunk of it." Rex spoke quickly, his eyes never leaving the knife. "We think the blue time is expanding far enough to swallow millions of people. They'll be defenseless against your darkling pen pals."

She shook her head. "That's crap, Rex. Darklings can't hurt normal humans."

"Not usually. But the barrier between normal time and the secret hour is weakening. In certain spots daylighters can slip through. You know that girl on the news this week, the one who disappeared in Jenks? She walked into the blue time."

"Come on, Rex," Angie said. "Didn't she turn up the next day?"

"Yes, because we saved her . . . from a huge, hungry darkling, I might add."

Her eyebrows raised. "I don't remember that part being on the news."

"Well . . . no." Rex swallowed. "We may have asked her not to say anything about the, uh, incident."

"You erased her memories," she said coolly.

He narrowed his eyes. "We *had* to."

The knife drew closer, the tip barely touching his cheek, where it burned like a spent match tip. Rex's eyes focused on the pulse in Angie's throat, the darkling part of his mind set on edge by the steel against his flesh, thinking killing thoughts. He knew that if he lost control, the short, brutal fight between them would be more evenly matched than Angie would expect, knife or no knife. But that wouldn't accomplish anything. They had to communicate, not kill each other.

"And what will you do to my memories?" Angie said softly.

Rex tore his eyes from her throat. Would she believe that he'd wanted to change as little as possible inside her mind? Just find out what she knew about the Grayfoots leaving town and maybe introduce a strong phobia about kidnapping people in the future. Unless, of course, Melissa lost her temper in the middle of the whole thing and forgot her promises . . .

If that happened, Rex wouldn't want to be in Angie's shoes.

Maybe there was another way to do this—one that didn't involve any mindcasting.

Rex tried to ignore the knife in his face. "Do you really believe all that stuff? About how the old midnighters were totally evil?"

"I don't believe it, Rex, I *know* it. I'm a real historian, not some amateur. Before I found out about the secret hour, I was researching a book on Oklahoma's early statehood. I've documented everything the old man told me about his childhood. I've found the court records in Tulsa, from when they got his parents."

Rex's eyebrows rose. He'd collected old newspapers and handbills from Bixby's past but not court records, and nothing from as far away as Tulsa.

"What are you talking about?" he asked.

"It was a big case in the nineteen-forties. Old Man Grayfoot's parents contested an oil claim made on Indian land by some of the town fathers—seers like you, pillars of the community. Normally the trial would have been rigged so the midnighters would win, no problem. But the case wound up in a court in Tulsa, a judge that they couldn't control."

Rex frowned. "So what happened?"

"One day all the Native American parties involved decided to back down. They gave up the case, then sold their houses to pay the town fathers' court costs. They lost everything they had."

He swallowed. "That sounds . . . unfair."

"Doesn't it? And you know what's worse, Rex?" she said. "After that day, Grayfoot's parents never showed another ounce of backbone, except to agree with whatever the town fathers said. Just like a whole lot of other people always did. So the old guy got to thinking that things weren't right in Bixby."

Rex blinked. He'd spent his whole life learning this history; how could there turn out to be a completely different side?

The odd thing was, whenever Rex read normal day-lighter history, he never took the word of just one historian. You had to check with several sources—everybody knew that. But until Angie had gotten into his car tonight, he'd never had another viewpoint to compare against the lore.

But after all she'd done, how could he trust her to tell the truth?

"Okay," he said. "I want you to pull that knife back a few inches."

"Why should I?"

"Because now you're going to tell me what happened between you and the Grayfoots," he said. "Are they really blowing you off just because you're not related?"

The knife wavered. "Well, that night in the desert, the night we gave you to the darklings, none of us expected that little kid to appear. She was the first halfling, wasn't she?"

"Her name was Anathea," Rex said.

"I mean, I know she was a midnighter, and she would have become a monster like all the others. But Jesus, she didn't look any older than twelve."

"She wasn't, much," Rex said. "She spent those fifty years mostly in frozen time. Afraid and alone, surrounded by *real* monsters."

Angie sat silently for a moment. "So I started wondering out loud if it was worth it, making another halfling. I thought the old man would listen to me. But the darklings weren't even talking to us. So the Grayfoots started getting cagey around me and nervous about the future."

"How do they know what's going to happen?"

She shook her head and lowered the knife still further. "The last thing Ernesto told me is that there was something coming up, something that had been planned for a long time. The Grayfoots had been looking forward to it, but now that the darklings weren't talking, it might be dangerous for them."

"Not just for them," Rex said. "You should leave town too."

"I'd love to. Except in about . . . five minutes I'm going to get my brain turned to mush."

Rex shook his head. "No, you're not. I'm not going to let Melissa touch you."

Angie snorted. "You're just saying that so I won't slit your throat." She let out a deflated sigh and put the knife back into her coat pocket. "Well, you can relax. I think maybe my child-sacrificing days are over."

As the knife disappeared, a cool sensation went through Rex. Not just a feeling of relief, but a decision. "No, I mean it. We're not like that. Melissa doesn't need to touch you at all. It's quiet out here, mind-noise quiet, and she can tell if you're lying to us, even in normal time. After midnight—when you unfreeze—just tell us everything Ernesto said."

"And you're going to trust me?"

Rex shrugged. "Like I said, Melissa will know if you're lying . . . *without* having to touch you. But once midnight passes, you can just walk away if you want. So yeah, I'm trusting you."

She narrowed her eyes, glancing at her watch. "And after midnight I'm not going to find myself suddenly mush-brained or wanting to give you my bank account?"

"Bank account?" He shook his head. "Did you get a look at this piece of crap? It's not exactly a Mercedes, like your buddies' cars back there."

"I guess not." She took a slow breath. "All right, I supposed I don't have much choice about . . . Uh-oh. Speaking of cars."

Rex followed her gaze through the front windshield. Headlights had reappeared on the horizon, making their slow way through the ravaged cactus patch.

"Crap!" he cried, reaching for the Ford's dashboard and killing the headlights. "I hope that's not the cops."

She squinted. "No, it's not a police car. Or a Mercedes, either. Looks like . . . I don't know. Looks about as crappy as this piece of junk."

Rex breathed a sigh of relief—it was Jonathan and the others.

"Okay. It's just friends."

A shudder went through Angie. "Including the mind-caster?"

"Yeah, but I promise she won't touch you." He leaned forward and turned the headlights back on, then blinked in disbelief as the car rolled to a stop a few yards away.

Jonathan and Dess were visible through the front wind-shield, but there was no one in the backseat. They'd followed him and Angie here without picking up Melissa and Jessica, expecting to be heroes.

He let out a frustrated sigh. Had they actually thought they were going to *save* him from the Grayfoots? Didn't they know how full of darklings this part of the desert would be in two minutes?

"What's the matter?" Angie asked. "You said they were friends, right?"

"Don't worry. It's not a problem . . . for you." He shook his head. "Just the rest of us. If we all disappear after midnight, don't bother leaving any more notes. We'll all be dead."

"Dead? Why?"

"Because your darkling pen pals are very nasty, Angie, much worse than you'll find in any court records. And because my brilliant schemes don't seem to be working very well tonight."

Rex leaned back in the driver's seat, waiting for the last few seconds of normal time to tick away. He'd been following his darkling instincts when he'd turned the car onto the flats, and they'd led him out here—miles into the deep desert, farther than he had ever been before at midnight.

Maybe part of him had wanted this.

It looked like his meeting with the old ones had come sooner than he'd planned.

16

FLYING LESSON

"Well, as of now this plan officially sucks," Melissa said. "No way is Jonathan getting here before midnight."

"We should have gone along with them." Jessica groaned, huddling in her coat against the chill wind. "I told Rex I wasn't afraid to."

"It's not your fault, Jess," Melissa said. "Rex didn't want all five of us in Broken Arrow. You heard him."

Jessica nodded sullenly. He'd said something about a Grayfoot trap catching them all at once—the end of the midnighters. It seemed unlikely to her.

"He probably just figured I was worried about getting busted for curfew violation," she said. "And was trying not to make me feel like a weenie."

She sighed. So now they were stuck here at a cold, windy roadside picnic stop just outside the county line, sitting on their butts. Next time she was going to announce to Rex that she was the new, non-weenie Jessica, unafraid of official, parental, or even sisterly punishment.

"No, Jess. I happen to know it wasn't you he was trying to protect."

"What do you mean?"

"It was me." Melissa held out her hand, palm down. It was quivering in the cold. "The thought of driving fast gives me the shakes."

Jessica looked at the mindcaster, wondering if she was kidding. Of course, flying through a windshield at eighty miles an hour might make you not want to repeat the experience.

"And they might not be here yet because they really did get busted by the cops," Melissa continued. "In which case, we're both lucky we didn't go along."

Jessica sighed. "That's a lovely thought." Jonathan wasn't a big fan of spending the secret hour trapped in a jail cell, bouncing off the walls.

"Just trying to make you feel better. There are worse things than being arrested."

"I suppose so."

"I mean, you've got kidnappers and high-speed car chases involved," Melissa continued.

"Jeez, Melissa. Who elected you Miss Sunshine?"

"I'm just saying is all." The mindcaster looked at her watch. "Anyway, we'll know for sure in five, four, three . . ."

The secret hour struck, spilling toward them across the desert floor like a sudden tide of blue ink. The picnic table shuddered beneath them, the air grew warm and still, and the stars turned ghostly pale above.

"Yeah, that's the stuff." Melissa sighed, tipping her head back to sniff the air. A few moments passed, then a faint smile broke across her face. "You can relax. Every-one's okay."

Jessica breathed a sigh of relief, glad that Melissa was here. When Rex had put the final touches on his plan, she'd been nervous about spending a whole hour in the middle of nowhere with Melissa. But actually, it hadn't turned out so bad. Melissa wasn't the bitchy snob she used to be.

The mindcaster fixed her with a cool glare. "Gee, thanks, Jess."

"Oops. Sorry." Jessica reminded herself to censor her thoughts, especially now that midnight had fallen. "But I mean . . . it's true, though," she sputtered. "You are much nicer these days."

"Whatever." Melissa looked skyward again, closing her eyes. "Okay. They're all together, way out in the desert for some reason, miles off the access road. Something got screwed up—tastes like Rex and Flyboy have been arguing."

"Funny, but I could have guessed that last part."

Melissa smirked. "Now Jonathan's on his way here. In a big hurry . . ." She frowned. "Things are waking up out there."

Jessica drew her flashlight, whose new name was Enlightenment, from her pocket. "Are they going to be all right?"

"If we get out there before anything big jumps on them."

"We?"

One of Melissa's eyes opened a slit. "As in me, Flyboy, and you."

Jessica realized it was pointless to hide her dismay. "That's right, you'll have to fly along with us."

"You got it, Jess. I don't *want* to, but the whole point of this plan is for me and Angie to have a little face time. And it's not like I'm going to walk." Melissa spread her hands. "Look, don't worry about it, Jessica. I'm not going to spew my crippled mind into your boyfriend's, all right?"

"I didn't say you were."

"You thought about it. Don't tell me that little twinge was you worrying about a dentist appointment."

Jessica shook her head. "It's just that Jonathan told me—"

"I *know* what he told you, Jessica. I can taste the way he pities me. I pretty much know how you guys feel about me, got that? And the more you worry about offending me, the *more* I know it. And frankly, I really don't *want* to know about it anymore, so just give . . . it . . . *a rest!*"

Melissa's voice broke on the last words, the awful sound disappearing into the flat, echoless desert. She sighed then, shaking her head.

"I'm sorry—" Jess began.

"Yeah, well." Melissa waved her silent. "I'm sorry too. Didn't mean to rant, but I thought maybe you might want to know what *I* was thinking for a change."

Jessica swallowed, a dozen apologies tumbling through her brain. But of course, Melissa wouldn't want to hear any of them. So Jessica concentrated hard, trying to banish all excuses and regrets and pity from her mind.

She cleared her head with thoughts of flying—imagining

weightlessness rushing into her at Jonathan's touch, the rolling quilt of Bixby's streets from midair, the pleasure of a perfectly timed jump taking them directly to a target, the desert floor passing below. . . .

The images crystallized, erasing the bitter aftertaste of the argument, and on an impulse Jessica reached out and touched Melissa's wrist lightly.

Melissa didn't respond at first, but she didn't pull away. Jessica could feel the struggle in her not to flinch from human contact, fighting reflexes trained by years of isolation. And then the connection took hold.

Images and emotions spilled from Jessica's mind—the sheer exhilaration of soaring at top speed across the badlands, scrub and sand and salt all reduced to a blur—and Melissa drew in a breath, amazed by the visions shared between them.

Jessica realized she was the only midnighter who had never touched the mindcaster before. It wasn't like Jonathan had said; there was nothing twisted and pitiable about Melissa's mind now. Through her eyes the blue world was suffused with a stately calm. And under that an old sadness, and worry about Rex.

After a long moment Melissa pulled her hand away.

"Flying . . ." she said softly.

Jessica smiled. "It'll be fun."

Melissa turned away, looking down at her hand as if Jessica had somehow marked it. Finally she said, "Just as long as we get there fast. Rex needs us."

"Is he scared?"

Melissa's head tilted, like that of a dog listening to a far-off sound. "Not really. He's not afraid of darklings anymore."

Jessica frowned. "Shouldn't he be?"

The mindcaster shrugged. "I guess we'll find that out soon enough."

Jonathan came skimming over the desert like a rock flung across frozen water. His flying shield flashed, warding off a pair of fast slithers who were buzzing around him like gigantic flies.

Jessica stood and aimed Enlightenment.

"Don't. You'll blind him," Melissa warned.

Jessica lowered the flashlight, sighing. Jonathan would probably rather deal with the slithers himself anyway. Why ruin his fun?

"I know what you mean, Jess," Melissa added. "He's enjoying all this way too much."

Jessica looked at her, suddenly wondering if their brief physical connection had made her thoughts permanently easier to read.

But Melissa shook her head. "It's pretty obvious, Jess. I used to hate daylight too, you know? But I never loved midnight as much as that boy does."

An explosion pulled Jessica's gaze back out to the horizon. One of the slithers had glanced off Jonathan's shield, blue sparks arcing across the sky as it fell, and the other turned and fled. Jonathan bounded to a halt a few yards away, raising a cloud of pale blue dust that froze in midair—his acrobat gravity working its strange magic.

"Come on!" he cried, holding out both hands.

Jessica was glad to see that he didn't flinch as Melissa grasped his hand, just looked at her, and said, "Do you know how this works?"

"Yeah, Jessica just taught me."

A look of surprise crossed Jonathan's face, and he shot a glance at Jessica. She could only shrug. She hadn't thought about it that way, but all the techniques of flying were recorded in well-used grooves in her mind, honed by long hours at Jonathan's side. Even those nights they didn't fly together, she dreamed about it or puzzled over the mechanics of midnight gravity when she was supposed to be doing physics homework.

Had Melissa really taken all that in so quickly?

"Let's go," Melissa said, bending her knees.

The three of them jumped together, a small tentative leap at first. Melissa didn't send them spinning or stumbling when they landed thirty feet away. They pushed harder on the second jump, launching into a low, fast trajectory across the desert. They built up speed, growing in confidence, dodging scrub and cactus bulbs without any exchange of words, as if Melissa had been flying with them a dozen times before.

Jessica wondered what was going on in Jonathan's mind, if he was thinking about Melissa reading his thoughts as they flew. Or remembering his horror at their first contact, before Melissa had gotten herself under control. Or perhaps the emergency was too great, his mind too focused on flying . . .

Maybe that was the trick when dealing with mindcasters; maybe you just had to give your head a rest.

"Halfway there," Melissa said, breathing hard.

Jessica asked, "Are they okay?"

"Dess is fine. Rex . . . he's with the others."

"With *what* others?"

Melissa stumbled on the next landing, and the three of them twisted in the air, spinning once all the way around before they set down again. Jonathan dragged them to a halt as they landed.

On the horizon ahead, a flicker of blue sparks rose up from the desert.

"What's happening out there?" he asked her.

"Dess is holding them off. And they'll scatter once they taste the flame-bringer on her way."

Jessica frowned. "What about Rex?"

"Don't worry about him. Moron—he said he'd warn me before he tried anything like this."

"Anything like what?"

Melissa shook her head. "We should keep moving if we're going to get there before Dess blows a fuse." She looked at them both, pleading with them not to ask any more questions. "Let's just keep going, okay?"

Jonathan glanced at Jessica, then bent his knees again. "Okay."

They jumped again, eating up the landscape in long, bounding leaps. Melissa flew as if she'd practiced for months.

Half a mile from Dess they passed over a patch of small, stubby cacti. Jessica spotted a big black car with blown-out tires at its edge.

"That's not Melissa's, is it?" she asked.

"No. Grayfoots'," Jonathan said. "Real ones."

"Oh." No wonder things had gotten messed up.

At the height of their next jump Jessica saw a huge black cat rising onto its haunches among blue sparks, surrounded by a whirling cloud of slithers. A thirteen-pointed star was traced out on the desert floor in glowing wires, Dess inside it, the darkling just outside. Melissa's car sat nearby, looking battered and broken.

"That cat smells blood, Jess," Melissa said. "It's too young to be afraid of you."

"Blood?" Jessica said as they landed, but the mindcaster didn't answer.

They jumped again, hurtling toward the struggle. Jessica saw Dess's long spear swing through the air, the panther batting at it with its claws, catching the spear point with a flash. The weapon spun out of Dess's grip as the creature screamed, leaping backward from the contact through its entourage of winged slithers. It rolled across the desert, salt and sand flying into the air.

But like a cat, it sprang to its feet in an instant and bared its fangs.

Dess stood glaring back at it.

"Close your eyes," Jessica warned through clenched teeth.

Enlightenment's beam shot across the blue desert, reaching the darkling at the limit of its power. White fire played across its fur, bringing another howl of anger. All around it slithers burst into flame, wheeling to escape the scorching light.

But the darkling didn't flee. Its purple eyes flashed as it glared at Dess, directing all its wounded fury toward her.

It readied itself to spring.

Jessica kept the flashlight steady as they flew, squeezing it with all her strength, sending every ounce of her will through it. The white fire grew stronger as the darkling leapt, enveloping it in a hissing ball of flame. Jessica felt the blue world shudder around them, the mountains in the distance seeming to warp as her power surged through Enlightenment.

The beast screamed one last time, disintegrating in midair like an exploding meteor, scattering glowing white coals across the desert floor.

"Eyes open," Jessica said hoarsely. Another jump took the three of them into a skidding landing near the circle of singed earth and metal stakes. Dess stood inside, dusty and scared-looking, blood running from her forehead.

"Are you okay?" Jessica cried, dropping Jonathan's hand and running toward her, leaping over the strewn and blazing remains of the darkling.

"I'll live. But Rex went out there!" Dess cried, pointing into the desert. "I couldn't stop him!"

"I know," Melissa said.

"Jessica, Jonathan, go get him!"

"No, don't."

The other three looked at the mindcaster in disbelief. Her eyes were half open, rolled back in her head, nothing visible of them but two pale slits of glowing purple.

"He wants us to stay here," she said softly.

"But you should see the thing that came for him!" Dess cried, wiping the blood from her forehead.

"I *can* see it, Dess." Melissa slowly moved her head from side to side, like a drunk piano player grooving to her own music. "He's okay. And he'll be back soon."

"He'll be dead!" Dess said.

Melissa opened her eyes, which flashed as she stared straight at Jessica. "Trust me—don't go out there. Rex is in the middle of a big crowd of wicked-old darklings. If you spook them, you'll only get him killed."

Jessica noticed that the other three were all looking at her too, waiting for her answer. She was the flame-bringer, after all; only she could save Rex.

She looked at Melissa again. The mindcaster wore an expression of absolute certainty. Jessica remembered the calm she'd felt when they'd touched, as well as how she sensed Melissa's love for Rex, and found herself suddenly certain about what she had to do.

Nothing.

No matter how screwed up Melissa was now or ever had been, whatever she had done to Dess or anyone else, she would never, ever hurt Rex. Not in a million years.

Jessica nodded. "Okay. We'll trust Melissa."

"Jessica!" Dess cried. "She's a psycho!"

"No, she's not. We wait here."

Melissa smiled, her eyes drifting closed again. "It won't be much longer. They know the flame-bringer's nearby, so they won't be in the mood for a long conversation."

"Conversation?" Jonathan said. "Are we talking about darklings here?"

"Old ones. Smarter than this turkey," Melissa said, kicking at the sputtering embers near her feet. "By the way, Jess, you were right."

"About what? You not being psycho?"

"No. About flying. That *was* fun." She opened her eyes and turned toward her old Ford, inside of which Angie's frozen form could be glimpsed, and cracked her knuckles. "But not as much fun as getting a shot at that bitch's brain."

Dess shook her head. "Before he walked off, Rex said for you to wait. He said it's totally important you don't touch Angie until he comes back. And he said that if you were a pain about it, I get to hit you with that." She pointed to where the darkling had flung Flabbergasted Supernumerary Mathematician, its tip blackened by ichor and fire. "So, go ahead."

Melissa gave Dess a sneer but stayed where she was. "That bastard. He made me promise." She clenched both fists as she looked across the desert, swearing. Finally she spat out, "Fine. Seer knows best, even if he is nuts. Maybe I can stand to wait for a few more . . . *whoa*. What the *hell* happened to my car?"

17

THE OLD ONES

They hovered overhead, like spiderwebs suspended from the air itself. Their tendrils snaked out into the sky, silhouetted against the midnight moon as if sucking energy from its dark light. Other strands anchored them to the desert floor or were wrapped around the necks of darklings, like leashes on giant panthers. The beings seemed to have no head or body, just a matted center where the grasping arms converged.

Rex wondered if this was the darklings' original form before they had taken the shapes of humanity's nightmares. These were certainly the old ones Melissa had always felt across the desert; just as she described, he tasted musty chalk, as if his mouth were full of the remains of something long dead and crumbled to dust.

One of them had come for him across the desert, its arms like glistening threads, resplendent in his seer's vision even from miles away. He'd known he had no choice but to follow—the thing could reach its long arms through Dess's defenses, and it called to the darkling part of him irresistibly.

For that matter, he'd *wanted* to come, even his human half. After everything Angie had told him, Rex realized how imperfect and incomplete the lore really was. If there was a way to stop what was happening, these old minds would know.

There were three of them, each twenty yards across, and an entourage of another dozen creatures in nightmare shapes: pale snakes and bloated spiders, slugs that dripped black oil, all of them unmoving, as if in thrall to the old ones hovering overhead. Wingless slithers pulsed in the ground beneath his feet, like an eruption of earthworms turning the threadbare soil.

Rex had never felt so small.

How wrong he'd been, thinking he was *half* darkling. Only a tiny fraction of him had changed, a sliver of strength gained, enough courage to express his paltry human anger. These creatures were so much more powerful than he would ever be. Rex found himself unable to move or speak, his humanity shrunk into a terrified corner of his mind, their darkness lying across him like a blanket of lead.

And what was he supposed to do, anyway? Say *hi*?

A liquid motion caught his eye. One of the creatures' long tendrils was approaching, sliding across the desert floor like a snake. As Rex watched in horror, it stretched toward his boot, wound around his leg as soft as feathers. Every muscle in his body strained against it, but he couldn't move.

Cold swept through him then, and an arid voice . . .

Winter is coming.

Rex tried to open his mouth to speak, but his teeth were

clenched so hard it felt like they would shatter. He let out a growl, pulling his lips apart, forcing his tongue to form words in his captive mouth.

"What will happen?"

We will hunt again. Join us.

"No," he said.

We are hungry.

Images exploded in Rex's mind, every bully who had ever taunted him, all his father's beatings, the spiders making their way across his pale, bare flesh. Every old fear came surging out of his memories, tearing at the foundations of his human side. Suddenly he knew he was a failure. The lore he had taught himself to read was nothing but lies. All along he had been a blind seer, a fraud.

Laughing, the old ones showed him the coming change, how the blue time was tearing open, unleashing the darklings' ancient hungers.

"No," he said, already exhausted. "I'll stop you."

There was a shudder from the beasts.

You are not the one who threatens us.

Rex's body suddenly went rigid, as if something was stretching him, prying his mind wide open. All his senses grew a thousand times. The world was suddenly crystal clear all the way to the dim stars on the horizon, even more perfect than in his seer's vision. He could hear the sound of his own blood rushing through his body, like freight trains pouring past. And he tasted the blue time itself, ash and corruption on his tongue.

More images poured into him—the world moving at

darkling speed, the seasons flashing past, only one hour in twenty-five visible, every day almost a month. He saw the prime contortion that the old ones had made, the secret hour itself, groaning under the weight of all that missing time. It was beginning to fray, a steady drumbeat of eclipses until it shattered, and then the hunt would begin.

Unless . . . Rex saw a bolt of lightning, the ancient pressures released and spreading across the earth, the rip diminishing.

"We can stop this," he whispered.

She can. You must take her.

"No."

More images, like his hunting dreams but a thousand times more vivid. He saw a pile of burning bones, human forms wearing horned masks. He felt the rush of galloping pursuit, smelled the fear of the prey, tasted the warm vitals of the kill. Rex felt himself gorging on flesh.

His stomach clenched against the vision, but what horrified him most was how complete it made him feel, how sated. And how powerful. As Rex Greene, he was trapped in a body that was weak and small, that would sicken as it grew old and certainly die in a laughably short time. But the old ones were offering him millennia.

All he had to do was let his humanity slip away. He could join in the feast.

Just take her. You alone can bring her down.

He shook his head, fighting back with his shredded humanity. Then a long-buried Aversion rose up in his memory, one Dess had taught him long ago.

Join us, they coaxed him.

"Unconquerable," Rex spat at them hoarsely. His mind almost split from the effort, but the grip of the old ones shuddered again, disgusted with him.

Then away with you.

With astonishing suddenness his mind was released from the creatures' awful grip. Rex felt his muscles unlock, and he was falling like a dropped rag doll, every ounce of will expended in the struggle. They had given up, he realized. Somehow he had beaten them.

Rex opened his eyes and found himself lying facedown on the desert floor, dirt in his mouth, his jaw muscles aching. But he managed a smile. The darklings had shown him something about the coming hunt . . . something important.

But as the cluster of nightmare shapes moved away, leaving him there exhausted and spent, Rex felt his mind contracting, his senses turning back to merely human. Like a great maw closing around him, darkness consumed the new knowledge, leaving only disjointed images and scents and the taste of dust in his mouth.

By the time the old ones had disappeared on the horizon, he hardly remembered what had happened at all.

18

MONSTER

Rex shambled back across the desert like a zombie.

His face was pale, his hands shaking as they had immediately after his transformation weeks before. He looked strangely like his father—eyes glazed and milky, his gait barely a shuffle.

He wasn't bruised or bleeding, and his clothes weren't torn, but the empty expression on his face made Jessica's skin crawl.

"Are you okay, Rex?" she said.

He didn't answer, just turned to Melissa. "Did you touch her?"

"No, I waited. I promised, didn't I?" Melissa reached toward him. "Loverboy, you look like crap."

"Feel like it too." Rex took her offered hand and shuddered, then straightened, as if taking strength from her. "Thanks."

"What the hell, Rex?" Jonathan said. "Are you *trying* to get yourself killed?"

Rex thought about the question for a few seconds, like it was a tricky one, but finally he shook his head. "I'm just trying to get all points of view. I think I've been a pretty crappy historian."

"Pretty crappy *driver*, more like!" Melissa cried. She pointed at the old Ford, which was listing to one side; both tires on the right were reduced almost to bare metal rims. "The first time I let you take my car somewhere without me, and you totally kill it?"

"Yeah. Looks that way."

"I can't believe you, Rex! Mr. Responsible, who always gets his library books back on time, but when it comes to *my car*, you don't even bother to use the *road*? The front axle's busted!"

As Jessica watched Melissa continue her tirade—holding Rex tighter with every insult, their fingers intertwining, their bodies leaning against each other for support—she realized how well the mindcaster had concealed her fear that he might never return. Even when they'd touched, Jessica had only caught a glimpse.

Finally Melissa's diatribe sputtered to a halt. Rex held her in silence for a moment, then said, "I'll always remember the old beast fondly. It died saving me and Angie."

Melissa pulled away and turned to stare at the frozen figure in the wrecked car, her voice lowering to a growl. "Well, she's my consolation prize, then. She *really* owes me now."

"Wait a second," Rex said.

"No way. I've already waited too long for this."

He drew Melissa back to him, placing one palm against her cheek.

After a moment her eyes widened. "What? Why *not*?"

"I made a deal."

"Well, *I* didn't make any deal!"

"You did. With me." He shook his head. "We have to wait for midnight to end."

Jessica wondered if anyone else was having trouble following this. "What are you talking about?"

"Yeah," Dess added, still holding a bloody rag to the cut above her left eye. "Could those of us who aren't psychic at least get some subtitles?"

Melissa yanked herself out of Rex's arms, stumbling back a few feet and glaring at him. "He doesn't want me to mindcast Angie."

"Excuse me?" Dess said.

"Angie's told me some things about the past," Rex said. "About midnighters and Grayfoots. And we made a deal. We're going to wait till midnight ends, then we'll talk to her. Just talk."

"Hang on," Jonathan said. "Are you saying we all risked our lives tonight to have a *chat*?"

"No way!" Dess cried.

Rex looked at Jessica, his exhausted eyes asking for her help. "We don't have to use mindcasting," he said. "We can trust her."

"To what?" Melissa spat. "Kidnap us less often?"

"I'm not saying Angie's our friend or anything," he said,

his gaze not wavering from Jessica. "Far from it. But she is like us in one way: she wants to learn the truth about midnight. We don't have to take her thoughts against her will."

Jessica drew in a slow breath. The night they'd rescued Cassie Flinders, she'd tried to talk them out of erasing the girl's memories, and they'd basically ignored her. But if Rex himself was actually having second thoughts, maybe this time it wouldn't have to work out that way.

"I agree with Rex," she said. "I think."

The other three stared at her, and Jessica half expected one of them to shout, *Who cares what you think?* But as the silence stretched out, she felt something shift within the group. Even Melissa's manic energy seemed to fade a little, like a child's tantrum left unanswered.

Jessica crossed her arms. Apparently they did care what she thought.

After a long moment Dess said quietly, "So let me get this straight. I'm bleeding here. An inch lower and psycho-kitty would have taken out my eye. And we're just going to talk to her, which would imply that we could have done this with a *phone call*?"

"Possibly resulting in less damage to my car?" Melissa said.

"Not really," Rex said. "Here in person you can make sure Angie isn't lying. I believe her, but the rest of you also have to be certain." He let out a short laugh. "And frankly, I don't think it would have worked this way on the phone. Sometimes a little shared danger helps."

"Well, no problem then, you two wrecking my car," Melissa said, "as long as you *bonded*."

"No, no." Rex shook his head tiredly. "My bonding tonight happened out there. Angie's just confused."

"Confused!" Melissa groaned. "She's a kidnapper, Rex. She should be in jail forever! And *nothing* happens to her?"

He smiled, his eyes flashing with the dark moon's light.

"I didn't say that."

As the dark moon set, real time swept across the desert, followed by the sudden return of the cold autumn wind. Next to Jessica, Rex jumped a little, like dishes left behind by a yanked tablecloth—as if he didn't belong in normal time anymore.

He had refused to answer their questions about what had happened to him out in the desert, saying he couldn't remember. Not yet, anyway.

In that same instant Angie's face sprang to life, emotions fluttering across it like a TV flipping through channels: confusion, fear, suspicion, and finally *lots* more confusion. She touched her own head gingerly with her fingertips, as if checking to make sure her ears hadn't fallen off at the stroke of midnight.

The five of them were standing in a row in front of the car, arms crossed—sort of like a band posing for an album cover, Jessica thought. Even the still-seething Melissa had decided to join them, once she realized that this little moment of surprise was the only revenge she would get to wreak on Angie.

The woman's eyes widened as she saw them through the front windshield.

"Come on out," Rex called. "Let's talk."

Angie slowly pulled herself out from the battered Ford and stood facing them, staying behind the protection of the open car door.

"Wow," she said softly.

Jessica guessed that people appearing out of nowhere might be a lot more impressive than a few dominoes jumping around.

"How's your mind doing?" Rex asked. "Still feel like yourself?"

Angie puzzled over that one for a moment, then shrugged. "I guess so."

"Like I would dirty my hands with your rank little brain," Melissa said.

Jessica gave her a sidelong glance. *So* not true.

"Then let's talk about the history of Bixby," Rex said.

"I thought we already covered that."

"Maybe I want to hear it all again." He patted Melissa's shoulder. "And this time I can be sure you're telling the truth. Or at least, if you *think* you're telling the truth."

"It's all true," Angie said. "I can show you the documents."

"Just talk," Rex said.

Angie nodded and began telling them all about the early midnighters, the Grayfoots' revolution, and the rest of the *other* secret history of Bixby. She started slowly and softly, her baffled expression at their sudden appearance taking a while to fade. But gradually her voice gained in strength, and soon she was declaiming with the utmost confidence.

Rex had already explained most of it to them while they'd waited for the blue time to end, but as Jessica heard the revelations repeated in Angie's methodical tones, the story began to settle in her bones alongside the desert chill of the Oklahoma autumn night.

If this was all true, then how much had Madeleine known about everything that had gone on back in her day? She'd only been seventeen when the Grayfoots had swept the midnighters from power, but she carried the memories of generations of mindcasters. Wouldn't she know about it if midnighters had been doing creepy things for thousands of years?

And would any of them have the guts to ask her what she thought about all this? Of course, Melissa wouldn't have much choice in the matter the next time the two of them touched. Jessica was just glad it would be Melissa, and not her, doing the asking.

By the time Angie drew her lecture to a close, she didn't seem scared of them anymore. She was smoking now, looking at them like they were just kids.

"So now that I've explained reality to you," Angie finished, "what are you going to tell me in return?"

Jessica narrowed her eyes at the woman. She was glad Melissa hadn't turned her into a drooling idiot, but that didn't mean she *liked* Angie. Not at all.

"Here's the main thing you need to know," Rex said.

"As far as we can tell, all hell's going to break loose on November first."

"The midnight before, actually," Dess added. "When October 31 rolls over into November."

Angie smirked. "Midnight on Halloween, huh?"

"It may sound cheesy," Dess said coolly. "But numbers don't lie."

"I don't know if I believe all that numerology stuff."

"Numerology?" Dess's jaw dropped open. "This is *math*, you dimwit."

The woman stared at Dess skeptically for a long moment, but then a troubled look crossed her face. "You know, before they cut me off, Ernesto Grayfoot kept saying that something was arriving soon. And after the darklings stopped answering, everyone started getting anxious about it. He said it had to do with the flame-bringer." She looked at Jessica. "That's you, right?"

Jessica nodded.

"But the Grayfoots never got all their instructions before the halfling died."

"What exactly did Ernesto say?" Rex asked.

"All he told me was a name—the old man was nervous because 'Samhain' was coming." She shrugged. "He never told me who that was."

Melissa shook her head. "Not 'who,' dimwit, *when*. Samhain is the ancient name for Halloween."

"Spot the goth," Dess muttered.

"Like *you* should talk," Melissa answered.

"Halloween again." Rex sighed tiredly. "Can't seem to get away from it."

"Come on, you guys. Don't be stupid," Angie said. "Halloween's just pop culture nonsense. It didn't exist here in Oklahoma until a hundred years ago, and as I've explained to you, the monsters got here a lot earlier than that." Her gaze drifted across the five of them. "They're still here."

"Monsters?" Rex said. He took a step toward Angie, then another, and Jessica felt a nervous tingling in the bottom of her stomach. Something was changing in Rex, exhaustion leaving his frame. He seemed suddenly taller, his expression harder, a threat implicit in every line of his face. Then the most astonishing thing—Jessica saw his eyes flash violet, though the dark moon had long set.

He was arm's length from Angie, but the woman stumbled backward, shrinking against the broken car. The cigarette dropped from her fingers.

"Maybe you're right, Angie," he said. "Maybe monsters have lived in Bixby for a long, long time. But you should just remember one thing."

His voice changed then, turning dry and cold, as if something ancient was speaking through him. "Monster or not, I'm what *you* made me when you left me out in the desert. I'm *your* nightmare now."

A hissing sound came from him then, and his neck stretched forward, as if his head were straining to leave his shoulders. His fingers seemed to grow longer and thinner, cutting the air in mesmerizing patterns. The hiss sliced through Jessica's nervous system like a piece of broken glass traveling down her spine.

Angie's smug confidence melted, and she slumped down, only her back against the Ford holding her from sinking to the dirt.

The hissing faded until it was lost in the wind, and then Rex's body seemed to fold into itself again, back to its normal human size and shape. Jessica wasn't sure if she'd really seen him change so completely or if the whole thing had been a massive psych-out.

He turned away from Angie. "Come on, guys."

"But she knows more," Melissa said.

"Not anything important. *They* told me what I really need to know."

His voice was normal again, and as Rex strode toward Jonathan's car, he looked tired, the energy that had coursed through his body during the sudden transformation now gone.

Jessica and Jonathan cast a wary glance at each other, then followed Melissa, who was trailing worriedly after Rex.

"What about her?" Dess called. Jessica paused and glanced over her shoulder; Dess was looking down at Angie as if she were a particularly interesting bug found smashed against the ground.

Rex didn't turn back, just spoke to the empty desert in front of him.

"She's walking. She knows the way out of town."

19

SPAGHETTI SITUATION

"The rule is in force tonight," Beth announced.

Jessica glanced up from her physics textbook. "Um, Beth? I'd like to point out that I am in my own bedroom, not in the kitchen. Therefore there is no *possible* way that I can be found in violation of the rule."

"I'm just warning you," Beth answered.

"Warning me?" Jessica said with a look of annoyance.

It was Beth Spaghetti Night, which meant that her little sister was cooking dinner. Over the last four years, since Beth had turned nine, the ritual had been held every Wednesday night, interrupted only in the first few tumultuous weeks after the family had arrived in Bixby.

The one rule of Beth Spaghetti Night was simple: Beth cooked, and everyone else had to stay away from the food.

Even now, the scent of reducing onions was already drifting through Jessica's open door. The familiar smell had been making her happy until this interruption.

"Warning me about what exactly?"

"That I am enforcing the rule in its maximum form tonight," Beth said.

"What does that mean? That we all have to leave the house while you cook?"

"No, but just . . ." Beth wrinkled her nose and checked over her shoulder, as if the smell of something burning had reached her. "Just stay in here. Okay, Jess?"

"Why?"

Beth smiled. "It's a surprise."

Jessica considered getting Mom to pass judgment on this new and irksome interpretation of the rule, but it probably wasn't worth the effort. Jessica had been planning on studying until dinner anyway, and maybe the threat of Beth's irritation would keep her from winding up in front of the TV.

Physics was Jessica's only test scheduled before Halloween, and it seemed a shame for the world to end on a D+.

"Please?"

"Sure. Whatever," Jessica said, making sure to roll her eyes.

"Good. You'll like my little surprise."

"Okay." Beth's smug expression didn't reassure Jessica. "Can't wait for it."

"Can I close your door?"

Jessica groaned. "Don't I smell something *burning*, Beth?"

Her little sister spun on one heel, an expression of alarm crossing her face. Something really *was* burning. But she still managed to slam the door closed behind her as she fled.

Jessica listened to her footsteps thundering back toward the kitchen, wondering what this "surprise" was. Beth had been much easier to get along with in the last week, snooping a lot less, talking about her new friends at marching band, and practicing her twirls. Maybe she really did want to surprise them all with something special.

And even if she wanted to make trouble, Beth could hardly have anything up her sleeve that would really make things worse.

There hadn't been any more eclipses—or timequakes, or whatevers of the prime whatever—since lunchtime a week ago. But as far as Melissa could tell, the darklings were expecting another one soon. After the last eclipse the rip in Jenks had grown to roughly the size of an oval-shaped tennis court. One of them checked it every midnight now, just to make sure that no more normal people had fallen through. Along with the usual blue glow everything inside it was tinged with red and nothing was frozen—autumn leaves fell, earthworms crawled, mosquitoes buzzed and bit. Too weird for words.

According to Dess, every eclipse would make the rip larger, like a tear traveling down a set of old stockings. Finally on Halloween the fabric of the secret hour would fall apart, and everyone for miles in all directions would find themselves engulfed in a world of red-blue.

As Jessica scanned her physics textbook, trying to focus on a chapter called "Waves and You," images of last Wednesday night kept popping into her mind—the way Rex had looked as he stumbled back across the desert, as pale as a prisoner released after years in a tiny, lightless cell. The way he had transformed into something inhuman in his anger.

Rex said he still couldn't remember what had happened to him out in the desert, and even Melissa hadn't gotten far enough down into his mind to dredge up anything. He said he was having weird dreams, though, like ancient darkling memories running through his head in high definition. All from one conversation with the old ones in the desert.

It had been more of a brainwashing session than a conversation, as far as Jessica could tell. Or maybe a whole *body*washing—his freaky transformation seemed to make Angie's accusations come true, as if Rex really was a monster now.

Jessica shivered at the image and gave up trying to concentrate on toroidal and sinusoidal waves. Instead she closed her eyes and drew in the smell of tomato sauce filtering under her door. If everything was about to change, Jessica wanted to relish these few last slices of normality.

Only two more Wednesdays before Samhain. She might as well enjoy Beth Spaghetti Night while it lasted.

"Dinnertime!" Beth shouted from right outside the door.

Jessica jerked out of her reverie, blinking. "Thanks for scaring me."

"No problem." Footsteps scampered down the hall.

Jessica smiled. Spastically enthusiastic Beth she could deal with. Rolling off the bed and to her feet, she paused to stretch away the muscle kinks of too much studying, then opened her door.

The mouthwatering scent of Beth's tomato sauce rolled toward her from the kitchen, and the house echoed with the sounds of her whole family in animated conversation. Just for tonight, she could pretend that everything was normal here in Bixby.

But as Jessica made her way down the hall, a stranger's voice spoke up, gentle but certain of itself—and somehow vaguely familiar.

"No way," she said softly. Beth was talking again now; she must have misheard.

But dread grew in Jessica as she reached the kitchen doorway and looked down at the empty table—for the first time since they'd arrived in Bixby, the dining table had been set.

Which meant that company was here.

She went through the kitchen and into the dining room until she found herself facing the four of them: Beth, Mom, Dad . . .

And Cassie Flinders.

"Hey, Jess!" Mom said. "Beth brought a friend home from school today."

Jessica managed only a zombified, "Oh, yeah?"

"Cassie's in marching band with me," Beth said, an amused smile playing on her lips. She turned to the girl. "I told you about my sister, Jessica."

Cassie Flinders looked her up and down, as if comparing her with some mental checklist.

"Hi," Jessica squeaked, her voice gone all tinny and her mind racing.

Hadn't Rex and Melissa gone back out to Jenks and

dealt with Cassie's memories? Wasn't this kid supposed to have only the vaguest recollections of her moments in the blue time?

"I think we've met," Cassie finally said.

"Really?" Mom said, all smiles. "Where was that?"

"Yeah, where?" Jessica said, taking her seat in front of the empty plate, trying to keep her voice normal and her expression only mildly puzzled instead of totally flabbergasted. "I don't think I remember."

"I don't remember either, exactly." Cassie's eyes were still scanning Jessica's face, as if recording her features in great detail. "But I drew a picture of you."

"You did what?"

Cassie shrugged. "Drew a picture, with a pencil. The other day when I was sick."

"Yeah," Beth said. "And it's a really good one. She brought it in to show around. You can really tell it's you, Jess. Cassie draws all the time."

"But you two don't remember meeting?" Mom asked.

"No, not at all," Jessica said. "I mean, I've never even been to Jenks."

"Jenks?" Beth said, smiling radiantly. "How did you know Cassie lived out there?"

"I don't know . . . how I knew that," Jessica said slowly. Now even Mom and Dad were looking at her funny. She realized that it would be better if the conversation moved along. "So, um, are you a majorette too?"

"No. I play clarinet."

"And she's a really good artist," Beth repeated.

"Yes," Jessica said. "I got that."

"She also has this other drawing of this guy," Beth said. "What was the name you wrote on it? Jonath—"

"Oh, hang on!" Jessica said, playing the only card she could be certain would change the subject. "Aren't you, like, Cassie *Flinders*?"

No one answered for a second, then Cassie nodded slowly.

"Now, Jess," her mother said. "I'm sure Cassie doesn't want to talk about that stuff last week, okay?"

"Sorry." She shrugged. "But I mean, it *was* on the news and everything."

"*Jessica.*"

She didn't say anything more, just let Beth serve the pasta, slithering spaghetti onto their plates and glopping sauce on top of it as the awkwardness stretched out.

Uncomfortable silences were fine with Jessica, definitely better than the uncomfortable noises coming out of Beth's mouth. The pause in the conversation gave her a few minutes to figure out what had happened.

According to Rex, Melissa had checked Cassie's brain to make sure she hadn't spilled the beans. But maybe instead of blabbing about what she'd seen, she'd *drawn* it.

Jessica wondered what other pictures Cassie had made before her memory had been erased. One of Jonathan, apparently, and probably she'd sketched the other midnighters as well. And she might have written their names down too.

Had she drawn the black cat slither or the darkling she'd seen?

Everyone started eating, and soon Beth and Cassie were telling stories about how geeky the rest of the marching band was, acting like nothing weird or unexplained had been mentioned at the table.

Jessica wondered if the drawings would jog Cassie's memories, pulling them out of whatever corner of her mind Melissa had stuffed them into. Or if seeing Jessica in person would make her recall more of what had happened that night.

Still, Cassie didn't have much to go on—just a few names and half-remembered faces and maybe a black cat or monstrous spider straight out of a nightmare. She had no way to connect Jessica and Jonathan to the other midnighters, no more clues about what had really happened that day.

Cassie Flinders wasn't really the problem.

As usual, Beth was.

She had already recognized Jonathan's face and probably remembered from taking phone messages that Jessica had friends named Rex and Dess and Melissa. Worst of all, Beth knew that Jessica liked to sneak out at midnight—the time when the growing rip in Jenks was at its most dangerous.

And—as Jessica knew from long experience—if anyone could turn a small amount of information into a big pain in the ass, Beth could.

Jessica wondered about Rex's new policy against mind-casting. He hadn't let Melissa mess with Angie's brain, but Angie had known all about the secret hour for years. This was a different matter entirely. If rumors started to spread around Bixby Junior High that weird things happened near the Jenks railroad line at midnight, Rex might make an exception for little sisters.

Jessica decided not to mention any of this to him or even *think* about it too hard around Melissa. A quick look into Beth's brain would reveal that she knew more about midnight than was safe.

Way more, now that she was friends with Cassie Flinders.

Jessica kept eating, trying to enjoy the mingled tastes of long-simmered tomatoes, number 18 spaghetti, and almost-too-many reduced onions. But as dinner continued—Beth glancing at Jessica knowingly whenever she got a chance—the familiar flavors turned bitter in her mouth.

"Mom?" Beth said as the meal drew to a close.

"Yeah?"

"Can I go spend the night with Cassie sometime?"

Jessica watched as her parents' faces broke into smiles. Marching band had paid off, big time. Beth had finally made a friend here in the new town. Everything would be much easier from now on.

"Of course you can," Mom said.

Beth smiled, and her gaze turned to her older sister, making sure to show that she knew there were more clues to find, more trouble to make, out there in Jenks.

Jessica tried to put on an innocent expression, as if nothing tonight had disturbed her, but she felt the smile wither on her face.

It was just too depressing. Even Beth Spaghetti Night had been touched by the blue time.

20

MINDCASTERS

"Give it one more chance, Loverboy. Please."

Rex didn't answer, didn't even stop climbing the stairs toward the attic. His expression didn't change, as if he hadn't heard her plea at all. Not that she'd expected him to sit down for a chat about it. Since that night in the desert, Rex put up a normal front for the others, but around Melissa he often let his not-so-human side show.

Even here in Madeleine's house Melissa could taste the darklings inside him, as dry as a mouthful of chalk dust leeching the moisture from her tongue. Might as well talk to the desert sand as try to reach that part of him.

But this was Rex, after all. She wasn't letting go that easy.

Melissa dashed after him, far enough up the stairs to grab his left ankle from below. She sank her nails into the leg of his jeans, bringing him to a halt with all her strength.

"Wait a damn second, Rex!"

He turned, looking down at her, emotionless. His eyes

flashed in that creepy new way they did, somehow catching the dark moon's light even in normal time.

His lips curled away from his teeth, and for a horrible moment Melissa thought she'd gone too far. He would turn into a beast once and for all and devour her right there, leaving Madeleine's staircase littered with her bones.

But then the expression on his face turned into a wry smile.

"What's the matter, Cowgirl?" he said. "Jealous?"

"Just wait a minute, Rex. Please?"

He looked down at his captive boot and raised one eyebrow.

Melissa turned his ankle loose, realizing that she was half kneeling on the stairs, like some drunk trying to crawl up to bed. She took a deep breath to calm herself and turned away from Rex, sitting down on the steps. Then she pointed one black fingernail at the spot next to her.

After an infuriating pause, as if his oldest friend in the world was *so* hard to deal with, the staircase began to creak and shift under his weight as he descended. He sat down beside her.

"I'm not jealous of Madeleine," she said. "But *you* used to be, remember?"

"Vividly."

Melissa snorted. "Glad to hear that. I'd hate it if you gave up jealousy. It's probably the only thing in the world everyone's good at. Everyone besides me, of course."

"Of course."

"This isn't about me, though. It's about us." Melissa

winced at her own words and glanced up at him. His eyes had gone back to normal, at least. She had the foul feeling in her stomach that she'd tasted so many times in Bixby High girls, that sour paranoia that their boyfriends' interest in them was evaporating. Melissa had always written them off as dorky and contemptible; she'd never realized that rejection was so *painful*.

Of course, things were bound to be awkward when your boyfriend was changing into a different species.

She took his hand, and his taste filled her. She focused on the surface of his mind—the steady, calming thought patterns of Rex Greene. Even during all those years she'd been unable to touch him, his surety and seer's focus had always been something Melissa could cling to. The old Rex was still in there.

Of course, that familiarity only made the other part of him more disturbing. How could something so comforting and reassuring be wrapped around such darkness?

"Let me try again."

"We already tried. It's useless." He shrugged. "And who knows? Maybe Madeleine can't get inside me either. But it's been a week; I don't want what I got from the darklings to fade before she has a chance to look for it."

"Believe me, Rex. It isn't fading." The blackness at his core was as solid as tar.

"Well, it isn't any clearer either, Cowgirl, no matter how many times we've done this. We need Madeleine's help. Samhain is only sixteen days away."

Instead of answering, Melissa pushed herself farther

into him, letting her thoughts flow across the human surface of his mind.

This time she didn't try to crack the darkness at his center. Rex was probably right: whatever the darklings had left behind was too inhuman for her to reach. Melissa instead offered her own store of implanted memories, the accumulated legacy passed from hand to hand across the generations.

Before he went up to the attic, Rex had to know what mindcasters were capable of.

Melissa took Rex to a place in the core of those memories, an event that mindcasters had shared since the old days. A long time ago, back even before the earliest Spanish settlers had come to Oklahoma, long before the Anglos and the eastern tribes, there had been a gathering. Mindcasters from several tribes had met before a large fire to exchange images of far-off places they'd seen—east to the still waters of the Gulf of Mexico, north to where the Rockies reared up; one had traveled as far as the Grand Canyon. Since that first meeting the memory had been added to, layered with more images as it had been passed from generation to generation. It was as if the gathering had grown to a thousand mindcasters, all of those who had ever come to Bixby and discovered their power, until finally it had made its way to Melissa.

"Wow," he said after a moment of marveling at it all.

"And not a hint of guilt," Melissa said softly.

"What do you mean?"

"None of them thought that mindcasting was a bad

thing, Rex. Of those hundreds of minds, not one thought it came with any cost."

Rex pulled his hand away, shaking his head to clear it. "So you're saying Angie's wrong? That the Grayfoots fooled her somehow?"

"No." Melissa glanced over her shoulder toward the top of the stairs, reassuring herself that Madeleine wasn't within listening range. "Since Angie gave us her little lecture, I've been sifting through the memories for the kind of thing she was talking about—destroying people, altering minds for profit, mass manipulation. But I haven't found them." She drummed her fingers on her knees. "For some reason, though, I still think she's telling the truth. Does that make any sense?"

Rex nodded. "Maybe they passed down an edited version."

"What they passed down was unbelievable smugness, Rex. They never questioned what they were doing. I don't think they *could* question it."

"How do you mean?"

She reached for his hand again and showed him an unpleasant memory from only a few weeks before—the moment when she had touched Dess against her will and pried the secret of Madeleine's existence from her. Melissa forced herself to linger over how Dess's mind had been locked by the old mindcaster, effortlessly twisted to hide what she knew. And how Melissa had torn it open.

When she felt a chill run through Rex, she released his hand.

"Why did you show me that?" he asked.

"Because you have to remember what we're capable of," she said. "Mindcasting doesn't just affect normal people. It can be used against other midnighters too."

"I know." His eyes narrowed. "But what does that have to do with Bixby's history?"

She looked up at him. "Before us five orphans came along, every midnighter grew up surrounded by mindcasters, all of them sharing thoughts every time they shook hands. But what if it wasn't just news and memories they were passing on? What if they were passing on *beliefs*? And what if at some point they all decided to believe that midnighters never did anything bad?"

"*Decided* to believe?"

Melissa leaned closer, speaking softer now, imagining the old woman upstairs listening from just around the corner. Melissa had chosen Madeleine's house to have this conversation with Rex for one simple reason: inside its crepuscular contortion, their minds couldn't be overheard.

"Over the centuries," she said, "midnighters started to believe whatever they did was okay, just like people who owned slaves used to think they were being 'good masters' or whatever. Except unlike slavery, nobody from the outside ever questioned what the midnighters were up to in Bixby. It was all secret, and anytime doubts cropped up, there were mindcasters around to squash them. It was like some clique of cheerleaders going through high school together, all thinking the same way, talking the same way, believing they're at the center of the universe . . . but for *thousands of years*."

She looked into his eyes, hoping that he would get it.

"Until we came along," Rex said.

"Exactly. We're more different from our predecessors than we thought, Rex. Maybe they really did all that evil stuff, but they didn't *know* they were being evil. They *couldn't* know."

"You haven't asked Madeleine about this yet?"

Melissa shook her head. "No way. I haven't let her touch me since Angie gave her little speech."

Rex smiled softly. "So you're an Angie fan now, are you?"

"Not really, but she has the same good point that most scumbags have: she makes me feel a lot better about myself."

"Because you never kidnapped anyone?"

"Oh, much better than that." She placed her palms together, hoping that the realization would still make sense once she'd said it aloud. "Madeleine always says I'll never be a *real* mindcaster—I started too late. Those memories are just figments to me; to her they're like real people." Melissa shook her head. "But what if it's a *good* thing that I never got indoctrinated? What if I'm not the first crazy mindcaster in history, Rex? What if I'm the first *sane* one?"

"Sane . . ." he said, not quite understanding yet.

Melissa pressed on. "Because no matter how screwed up I happen to be, no matter what I did to your dad, at least I can see that ripping the minds of a whole town for a hundred generations is *not* cool."

He took her hand, and all of Melissa's thoughts, which had tumbled out in clumsy words, seemed to order themselves at his touch. They flowed into him, along with the thing she hadn't said aloud.

I'm sorry about your father, Rex.

"You saved me from him, the best you knew how," he answered.

Melissa looked away, her emotions churning. Her shame at her own past, her worries that she'd already lost Rex to the darklings, her fear of what Madeleine might do to his mind—all of it squeezed into a single tear. It traveled down her cheek like a drop of acid.

Rex sat there thinking, then finally said, "I think you're right. Madeleine's going to find my new view of history . . . challenging."

"Then let me go up there with you, Rex. I don't care what a badass darkling you are these days. You need my protection."

He smiled again, and she saw a violet spark in the depths of his eyes. "You have no idea what I am."

She let out a short, choked laugh. "Whatever, Rex. Even if you are a monster, I don't want to lose you to *her*. And don't think all those creepy old midnighters in her brain won't give you a run for your money."

Unexpectedly he leaned forward and kissed her—the first time their lips had met since last Wednesday night. His taste hovered on the edge between bitter and sweet, like chocolate that was almost too dark.

But what scared her most was that she tasted no fear in him at all.

"We'll see about that," he said. "Come on, Cowgirl. She's waiting."

Madeleine sat in her usual spot in the corner of the attic, tea things arranged around her. "Both of you, is it?"

"Maybe I can help," Melissa said.

The old mindcaster gave a little snort but didn't send her away. Like Rex, Madeleine had no fear.

"Well, sit down then, both of you. Tea's getting cold. In my day, young people didn't keep their elders waiting."

The more I hear about your day, Melissa thought, *the more I'm glad the Grayfoots came along.*

She and Rex sat down in the corner, the three of them forming a triangle around the tea service. Melissa had never done this before—held two midnighters' hands at once—but she knew from her store of memories that mindcasting circles were an ancient practice.

No wonder they all thought the same way. All those minds tuned together and reinforcing one another's beliefs—add a few pom-poms and they'd be just like the pep rallies of Bixby High, except without anyone sneaking out the back to smoke.

Melissa took a sip of tea. It had indeed grown cold, bringing out its bitter taste even more than usual.

"What you did last week was very dangerous, Rex," Madeleine scolded. "I watched from this very spot. No one has ever survived anything like that before."

"We didn't have anywhere else to turn," he said.

"I've worked hard the last sixteen years to keep you alive, Rex. You could have thrown away all that effort in a matter of minutes."

Melissa took a slow breath. In their training sessions Madeleine never tired of reminding her why she and Dess had been made—to help Rex, the only natural midnighter in Bixby's recent history. The old mindcaster had subtly manipulated hundreds of mothers during their labor, trying to create babies born at the stroke of midnight. And all to make sure Rex had a posse to lead, like a proper seer should.

Melissa understood all too well now what the five of them really were: Madeleine's attempt to re-create the Bixby she had grown up with, a paradise for midnighters . . . at the expense of everyone else.

"I'm still alive," Rex said in a flat voice. The human softness he'd allowed himself to reveal on the stairs had disappeared again.

"They could have eaten you," Madeleine said.

"The things I was talking to don't eat meat," he said. "They eat nightmares."

She raised an eyebrow.

"But they wouldn't have eaten me anyway. I carry their smell." Rex gave the old mindcaster a cruel smile. He must know how much it offended her, Melissa thought, to have her little seer infected with the darkness.

Madeleine's face twitched. "You taste more like them every day. But do you really think they would tell you something useful? Why should they?"

"The darklings didn't *tell* me anything," he said. "They share their thoughts naturally, like animals crying out when they've spotted a kill. You know that, Madeleine. You hear them thinking all the time."

"If you can call it thinking." She made a face, as if fifty years of her own bitter tea was finally hitting her taste buds. "Well, let's see if your little experiment accomplished anything other than almost giving me a heart attack."

She held out both her hands, palms up.

Melissa caught Rex's eye, and they joined hands first with each other, waiting for a moment until their connection was complete. Her heart was pounding, and even though she was certain that the memory was all part of a big lie—propaganda, like Angie had said—Melissa recalled that long-ago mindcaster gathering, letting her wonder at those ancient images shared around the fire calm her.

As her mind stilled, she felt herself drawing strength from Rex's dark confidence. Whatever the horde of old mindcasters inside Madeleine had in store for the two of them, at least they were facing it together.

"Come now. Don't lollygag," Madeleine snapped.

As one, they raised their other hands and let her grasp them, completing the circle.

As Madeleine stilled herself, she changed, becoming a congress of minds.

Melissa was always awestruck at the vastness of it: memories stretching back to shadowy recollections of the ice age, when glaciers could be reached in a month's walk to the north. Ten thousand years of history, hundreds of generations, thousands of mindcasters.

She squeezed Rex's hand. Facing that accumulated mass of minds, she was glad for his dark presence beside her.

"What have they done to you?" Madeleine murmured. She was probing the black sphere of Rex's darkling half, searching its smooth surface for purchase. As the fingers of her mind settled in and began to pry, Rex's hand flinched in Melissa's.

"It's for your own good," the old woman muttered. Her concentration deepened, her raspy breathing slowing in Melissa's ears.

After a long moment the darkness inside Rex began to swell, like something viscous and heavy coming slowly to a boil. The muscles in his fingers twitched again in her hand, a dry taste stirring among the patterns of his mind.

Eyes closed, Melissa watched the changes shifting through him and wondered if Madeleine really knew what she was doing. Melissa could taste arrogance in the mass of memories, their certainty that they could control anything and anyone. But they'd never faced something like Rex.

Then bitter metal filled her mouth, like old pennies on her tongue.

A seam had begun to open in Rex's mind, his darkling inner core shivering, its surface cracking. Melissa tasted Madeleine's satisfaction.

Rex made a pained sound.

Melissa sent calming thoughts toward him, but Madeleine

pushed her back. *You don't know what you're doing, girl. Stay clear.*

The old mindcaster turned her attention back to Rex, pressing harder, and the darkness inside him began to split—a black and radiant shaft spilled across the mental landscape, bleeding color from it like the dark moon's light. Images of an ancient Samhain flowed from his mind: masked humans piling up the bones of cattle and setting them alight, fires dotting the landscape for miles, raising up a slaughterhouse smell. Melissa felt a twitch of hunger at the scent and realized that the reaction was a darkling's. Soon she was ravenous, feeling the call to hunt, to kill.

Abomination, whispered the mass of memories.

They meant Rex—seer and darkling mixed; he horrified them.

Madeleine grew bolder, her mind prizing into the cracks of Rex's darkling half. He let out a short cry, and his fingernails dug into Melissa's hand.

"Stop!" Melissa whispered hoarsely. "You're hurting him."

Abomination, a thousand voices hissed. The mindcasters' memories had known nothing like him before; he had to be constrained, controlled.

But the darkness inside Rex only grew, swelling into a huge black storm cloud in Melissa's mind, spilling more visions: Bixby as the old ones had seen it fifty years ago, a psychic spiderweb of midnight glittering across the desert. In the darklings' eyes the town was an infected organism, the tendrils of a parasite extended into every fiber of its host—mindcasters quietly toiling, spreading obedience across the city, certain that it was only natural for them to rule.

Even the darklings knew what you were, Melissa thought.

Madeleine made a choking noise, the mass of memories inside her roiling as it beheld its own reflection in Rex's mind. He was an abomination, and his thoughts were an insult to ten thousand years of history.

He had to be destroyed.

A shudder of horror passed through Madeleine at the thought, but she couldn't pull her mind back. She couldn't go against the mass.

"No," Melissa whispered. *Egotistical morons!*

They ignored her. She tried to wrench her eyes open, to reach over and separate Madeleine's hand from Rex's, but her muscles were locked rigid.

Melissa felt hatred rising up in her, disgust at the conceited, clueless pride of her predecessors. She focused all of her loathing—everything Angie had said about the reign of the midnighters, their greed and child-stealing and brain-ripping—and hurled it at Madeleine as hard as she could.

The mass of memories reared at the insult and turned on her in a flood of contempt and arrogance. They had borne the secrets of midnight for thousands of years; Melissa was an upstart, an orphan, a nothing.

That which sticks up must be pounded down.

But before the mass could do any pounding, Melissa's mouth filled again with the taste of darkling. She'd distracted them just long enough.

The thing in Rex was *really* boiling now. . . .

Like a predatory cat, it sliced straight through the mass, down into Madeleine's own memories, her deepest secrets. With a hunter's instinct it found her fears . . . and ransacked them.

"No, Rex!" Madeleine gasped, but he was a wounded animal now, pitiless and rabid. Melissa watched aghast as fifty years of terror erupted from the depths of the old woman's mind, every nervous minute of hiding since the Grayfoots' revolution.

You gave them Anathea, he hissed, and decades of guilt surged up in Madeleine. The mass of memories spun in a tempest, unable to order themselves in her churning mind, like rats in a house on fire.

Melissa tried to focus her mind. *Rex . . . that's enough!*

"We're knocking at your door!" he said aloud, his voice inhuman. "We've found you at last. We've come for you!"

A single choked scream of terror came from Madeleine's lips, darklings from a thousand nightmares shredding her mind; her hand jerked once, then slipped from Melissa's.

Suddenly the mass of mindcasters was silenced, Madeleine's mind gone; Melissa found herself alone with Rex in the blackness behind closed eyes. The darkling thoughts moved through him, still powerful, still hungry. Melissa watched in horror as her oldest friend transformed, the darkness consuming still more of his humanity.

She wondered if she was next.

Rex, she pleaded. *Come back to me.*

"Unconquerable," he said softly, his voice dry.

The storm began to subside, and what remained of Rex's humanity settled over the boiling darkness. She felt his sanity return.

With a *snap* her muscles were her own again. Melissa pulled her hand from his and opened her eyes.

Madeleine lay on the attic floor unmoving, shards of her shattered teacup strewn about her. Her face was locked in an expression of horror.

"It worked," Rex said, his voice calm.

Melissa stared at the stricken woman on the floor. She was still breathing, but her eyes were glazed over, her fingers twitching.

Melissa looked up at Rex, and his eyes flashed violet. "You call that *working*?"

"I remember now." His lips curled into a smile. "I know what Samhain really was."

Melissa tried to gather her wits and tore her eyes from Madeleine's twisted face. The darklings were coming, and thousands of lives were at stake. "Can we stop it?"

Rex shuddered for a second, as if one last memory remained fugitive in his mind. But then he nodded slowly.

"We can try."

21

SAMHAIN

Every night it seemed like the secret hour took longer to come.

Jonathan drummed his fingers on his windowsill, waiting for the cold wind to be silenced, for colors to blur together into blue, for weightlessness to pour into him. He didn't look at the clock, which never worked. Knowing how many minutes of Flatland were left only made the torture worse.

These stretches right before midnight were always the hardest. Jonathan wanted to be out there *now*, soaring over the still cars and softly glowing houses, feeling his muscles propel him across town.

To pass the time—to force the time to get *moving*—he counted off the coming days on his fingers. It was Thursday night, tomorrow was Friday, exactly two weeks until Halloween. If Dess was right, he would only have to endure this wait fifteen more times, including tonight.

And then he would be free of gravity altogether.

His eyes closed. Jonathan realized, of course, that the weakening of the blue time was a disaster; it would give the darklings free rein to hunt down thousands of people, maybe a lot more than that. His father, his classmates, everyone he knew was in terrible danger.

But he couldn't keep his mind off one fact: for however long the frozen midnight lasted, Flatland would be erased, and the world would have three dimensions. For a guilty moment Jonathan let himself feel the pleasure the thought gave him—being able to fly for days on end, however far the blue time expanded.

Maybe it would swallow the whole world.

At last midnight came, almost surprising him in his reverie. The earth shuddered, dropping its claims on his body, the chains of gravity finally falling away. He drifted upward, sucking in a deep, rib-cracking breath. Only at midnight did his lungs feel like they filled completely, no longer constrained by the suffocating weight of his own body. The weight of Flatland.

It was crazy to feel guilty about the joy this gave him. It wasn't his fault the world was ending.

Jonathan launched himself out the window, passing over his father's car and up onto the neighbor's roof with one well-practiced bound. There his right foot landed on its usual spot, a circle of cracked shingles marking where so many nightly flights began.

Then he pushed off toward Jessica's and—as he watched for flying slithers and power lines, calculating the best course down empty roads and across newly harvested fields—his mind kept returning to one thought . . .

Only two more weeks of gravity, and then I'm free.

"Okay, everyone," Rex said. "Madeleine went into my mind last night."

Jonathan frowned. The five of them were meeting in Madeleine's house, seated around her scuffed dining table surrounded by the clutter of tridecagrams and other tangled shapes. But the old woman hadn't appeared tonight, and Rex had started talking as if she wasn't coming down. Wasn't she home?

Where else could she be at midnight?

"You actually let her *touch* you?" Dess asked.

"Melissa was there to protect me," Rex said.

Jonathan glanced at Jessica, and they both flinched, waiting for the nasty response they knew was coming, but Dess just coughed into her fist and rolled her eyes. Eerily, the scar the darkling had left over her eye was shaped just like one of Melissa's.

Jonathan was glad she kept quiet. Tonight Rex was scary enough without anyone provoking him. His expression seemed vacant somehow, as if there were some other creature inside him, showing off the Rex mask it was going to wear while trick-or-treating.

He looked weird enough in daylight, but in the secret hour the new Rex was almost too much to face.

"The darklings remember Samhain," Rex said.

"So that goth holiday is the real thing, huh?" Dess asked, shaking her head.

"It isn't a Gothic holiday," Rex answered. "The Goths were from Asia. Samhain was Celtic."

"From Asia?" Dess said, then groaned. "No, Rex, not the guys who conquered Rome. I mean the kids in black."

"Um, Dess?" Melissa said. "Mirror check."

"This dress is *charcoal*," Dess said.

"Probably the Goths had something like Samhain too," Rex kept going. "A lot of cultures have festivals at the end of October. The Feast of Souls. Something called Shadowfest. The Death of the Sun."

Jessica raised an eyebrow. "Shadowfest? That sounds . . . festive."

Dess let out a long sigh. "Why are we even talking about this? All that pagan stuff is from the Old World, but here in Oklahoma, Halloween is just an excuse to sell a bunch of candy and costumes to little kids. Like Angie said, the darklings hid themselves way before any Europeans got here."

Jonathan cleared his throat. "Actually, Dess, it's not just a European thing. You know the Day of the Dead down in Mexico? Even though it's the same day as All Hallows' Eve, the natives already had a holiday around then."

Rex nodded. "And some Native Americans had festivals celebrating the Old Crone around this time."

Dess laughed. "Excuse me, Rex. The *Old Crone*?" She looked around at the others. "And what were those other ones? Shadowfest? Death of the Sun? Dawn of the Dead?

Is it just me, or do all these holidays have a trying-too-hard-to-be-creepy ring to them?"

"Of course they do," Rex said, his scary mask unruffled by her teasing. "Look at the bare trees outside, the gray sky, the dead grass everywhere. The word *Samhain* is Celtic for 'summer's end.' The beginning of winter." Suddenly Rex's voice sounded dry, like he'd been out in the desert without water for a few days. "The dying of the light, when warmth turns to cold."

Everyone was silent for a moment, even Melissa looking a little spooked by Rex. Jonathan heard a creaking noise above his head. So Madeleine *was* here. But why was she hiding upstairs?

He glanced at Melissa, wondering what exactly had happened between the three of them the night before.

Dess broke the mood, letting out an exasperated breath. "This isn't about spooks and ghosts, Rex, it's about *numbers*. The eleventh month plus one is twelve. That's all it is."

Jonathan frowned. Back in Philadelphia, his mother had always taken him to church on All Hallows' Eve. Even the Catholic version of Samhain had given him the willies.

"So tell us, Rex," he said. "Way back when, before Halloween got all cutesy, what was the point of Samhain?"

"Well, believe it or not, people did wear costumes," Rex said. "But the most important ritual was building bonfires. They burned everything they could, even the bones of their slaughtered cattle, hoping to drive away the night for a little while longer. Of course, they knew winter was going to win sooner or later. Samhain recognizes the coming of darkness."

"Hey," Dess said. "Now there's a snappy greeting card: 'Hope that you and yours have a lovely coming of darkness.'"

"I agree," Rex said. "It doesn't seem like the best time of year for a holiday. But for some reason, the coming of darkness wasn't a bad thing."

"Like I said, it's a *goth* holiday," Dess muttered.

"Yet during all of recorded history, it was a time of celebration," Rex continued. "But what were they celebrating? Think about it. Back then winter must have been a pretty scary time of year."

"Because everyone starved?" Jonathan said.

Rex's face curled into something resembling a smile. "Everyone but the darklings. Remember, even before the secret hour was created, darklings hunted at night. In winter, nights get longer and longer. So originally those bonfires weren't symbolic; they were designed to keep the predators away for as long as possible."

The rapturous expression on Rex's face made Jonathan shiver; his eyelids were fluttering, as if he was mainlining darkling memories. Jessica reached over and squeezed Jonathan's hand beneath the table.

He coughed. "Sure, Rex. That's not something a normal person would celebrate."

"No. But one Samhain a long time ago, everything changed. The darklings never showed up again, even after the bonfires burned down. They had retreated into midnight. So those bonfires changed in meaning. Instead of a last-ditch survival maneuver, they were now an act of celebration. Halloween is the anniversary of the beginning of the secret hour, the day humanity finally reached the top of the food chain."

Dess sat up straighter. "Huh. So maybe this whole history thing does actually make sense. I mean, if the darklings really did disappear on October 31, that's why it was such a good day in the old system. It was the day when everyone was finally safe from them forever."

"Not forever," Rex said.

"Oh, right." Dess's voice softened. "November 1 is going to be a darkling holiday from now on, isn't it?"

He nodded. "They're going to turn the food chain around again. But the good news is this long midnight won't last forever—just for twenty-five hours, a single day by the old reckoning."

Jonathan knew he should be relieved, but somewhere deep inside him, he felt a little spark of disappointment.

"Okay, Rex," Dess said. "What's the bad news?"

"The long midnight will happen every Halloween, the rip getting bigger and bigger every time. From now on, humans are the candy."

Jonathan's disappointment lifted a little. *A whole day every year.*

"So what do we *do* about this?" Jessica said. "Wasn't that the point of you talking to the darklings? To find out some way to stop it?"

Rex didn't respond for a while, his face strangely unmoving. Jessica looked over at Jonathan, who only shrugged. He realized that some part of him was scared that the seer already had a plan, something that would shove the secret hour back into its bottle. Which would be a *good* thing, of course, saving thousands of lives at least.

But it would also mean Jonathan would never fly for more than one hour a day. . . .

Finally Rex spoke. "We'll try to stop it, to do whatever we can. When it comes, we'll gather people together and teach them how to fight for themselves."

"Um, Rex?" Jessica said. "What about keeping the secret hour a secret?"

"We don't anymore. After the long midnight we won't be able to." He looked down at the table. "And after what we saw in Madeleine's mind last night, I'm pretty sure I don't want us midnighters to stay in shadows anymore."

Everyone was silent for a moment as the idea that the blue time wouldn't be secret any longer slowly sank in.

Jonathan wondered again why the old mindcaster wasn't down here with them. But there were more important questions right now, he supposed. "So how do we organize a whole town in one night?"

Rex shook his head. "I don't know yet." He turned to Jessica. "But you remember how Angie said Samhain had something to do with the flame-bringer?"

"Yeah," she answered. "That was kind of hard to forget."

"Well, I've got a few ideas about how the rip works. And they have to do with you. But we need to do a few experiments. I want all of you to meet me in Jenks tomorrow morning. At six-thirty."

Dess let out a snort. "Hold on there, Rex. There's a six-thirty in the *morning* now? No one told me about that."

"Yeah, really," Jonathan said.

Rex rose from his seat, suddenly inhumanly tall, his bulk seeming to crowd against the ceiling. His features shifted on his face, the eyes growing as long and wide as a wolf's and burning violet. His hands slammed down onto the table, crooked like claws, then scraped across the wood in one slow, deliberate movement, his fingernails catching every imperfection.

Jonathan swallowed—the creature had come out from behind the mask.

"Do you think we have time to waste *sleeping*?" Rex said, his voice gone cold and dry and ancient. "Thousands will be killed, and for some it will be worse than dying. The old ones will suck them dry first, wringing out every drop of fear. They're coming for you, don't you see?"

He stood there, glaring at them all, while the old house filled with the echoes of his words, like whispers coming from every corner. Jonathan thought he saw the piles of junk around them glow brighter for a moment, their soft blue metal rimmed with cold fire.

A vague, choking noise came from Madeleine upstairs, as if she was crying out in a dream, but Jonathan didn't dare look up. The four of them just stared at Rex in stunned silence. Even Melissa looked bowled over by his sudden transformation.

A long moment later he sat back down, taking in a slow breath. "I know this is hard. But you can catch up on your sleep after Halloween."

His voice had gone back to normal, but they all still sat

there, dumbfounded. Jonathan wished he could think of something to say, anything at all to break the silence. But the whole concept of language—hellos, goodbyes, jokes, mindless banter—it all seemed to have fled from his brain.

Rex was suddenly so *alien*. It would be like making small talk with a snake.

Finally Dess cleared her throat. "Okay, then. Six-thirty A.M. it is."

Jessica looked up at Jonathan, mouthing the words, *Let's go.*

Jonathan didn't have any problem with that. Some serious flying was what he needed right now, stretching his limbs and soaring away from the earth, as far as he could get from Rex's weirdness.

But he remembered to ask, "So, Melissa, will you guys need a ride out there? I mean, since your car's all busted."

She looked at Rex, who shook his head no but didn't say anything more.

Great, Jonathan thought. *Maybe they'll fly out with one of his darkling pals.*

There was still time, so the two of them headed toward downtown.

"So what the hell is up with Rex?" Jonathan said softly, once Madeleine's house was safely behind them.

"Don't ask me," Jessica answered, squeezing his hand. "Did you notice what he said at the end, 'They're coming for *you*'?"

"As in *us*—not him. Makes sense, though. He's on

speaking terms with the darklings these days." Jonathan waited until they'd caromed from the long top of an eighteen-wheeler on Kerr Street, then added, "But I guess we're safe, you and me."

"Oh, *that* makes me feel a lot better."

He glanced at her. "I just mean, we're safe as long as we stick together."

She didn't say anything, just squeezed his hand again.

They climbed the buildings of downtown like stepping-stones, bounding to the summit of the old Mobil Building. This was where they had hidden in the days before Jessica had found her talent, back when the darklings were desperate to kill her—before she discovered who she was.

Jonathan looked out across Bixby, laid out before them in the even, deep blue glow of the secret hour. He looked in the direction of Jenks, trying to see the rip, but its red tinge didn't show on the horizon.

Not yet, anyway. It was growing every time an eclipse fell.

"We haven't been up here in a while," Jessica said.

"Yeah. I was kind of missing Pegasus." He looked up. The huge neon Mobil sign in the shape of a flying horse hovered over them protectively.

"That's not all I missed," Jessica said, a smile playing on her lips. "You remember what happened here, right?"

Jonathan nodded. "You mean, us hiding from the dark-lings?"

"Yeah. But not *just* that."

He thought for a moment. They hadn't really been up here since those early days. He shrugged.

Jessica let out a groan. "I can't *believe* you. This is where we first kissed!"

"Oh, *right*!" He swallowed. "But that was around the same time, yeah? I mean, I just said how we were hiding here, and that was when we . . ." Jonathan stumbled to a halt, realizing that explanations were only making things worse.

He took her hands, hoping that his midnight gravity would bring her smile back.

She just stared at him. "I can't believe you forgot."

"I didn't forget. I just didn't know what you were talking about."

"Ugh. That's even worse!"

"Why?"

"Because it's like you've totally forgotten." She pulled her hands away, looking out over the blue-lit city. "We haven't exactly . . . This last week we've hardly touched each other."

"No, I guess not." He sighed. "It seems like we're always in crisis mode."

"I guess it's not that big a deal, compared to the whole town getting sucked into oblivion. But shouldn't that make us closer or something?" She looked at him for an answer, like this was a particularly tricky problem from physics class.

"Look at it this way, Jessica," he said, putting his arm around her. "Once Samhain comes, we'll get to spend a whole day flying together."

"*Jonathan!*"

"What?" He held up his hands in surrender. "I'm just saying."

She groaned, turning away from him. "I *knew* you were thinking that way."

"What way?"

"You're *excited* that this is going to happen, aren't you?" she cried. "You'd probably be happy if it went on forever: blue time, all the time. No more Flatland. What could be better?"

He rolled his eyes but couldn't bring himself to contradict her aloud. After all, he'd been thinking that exact thing as midnight fell.

But that didn't make him a terrible person, did it?

Jonathan took a deep breath. Usually with Jessica, explaining things just seemed to make an argument go downhill. But for some reason, he always tried anyway. You had to keep talking to each other or nothing ever got resolved.

He began nervously. "Listen, Jess. Haven't you ever imagined the world ending? I mean, kind of *fantasized* about a nuclear war or a plague or something wiping out everybody—except you and a few friends? And of course it's all tragic and everything, but suddenly the whole world belongs to you?"

"Mmm . . . no, actually." She frowned. "In my fantasies I'm more of a rock star who can fly. And has no little sister."

He smiled, took her hand, and nudged them both a few feet into the air. "Well, one out of three isn't bad."

"Are you saying I'm not a rock star?"

"You don't even sing."

"I do in the shower." A smile finally crossed her face as

they settled back to the rooftop, but then she pulled away again. "Jonathan, the problem is that this *isn't* a fantasy. It's real. I feel bad even joking about it."

"But Jessica, *we* didn't make this happen. It's not our fault. All we can do is try to save as many people as we can."

"And enjoy the extra flying time?"

"No! If we can stop it, we will. But maybe we should leave the planning to Rex. It's what he's good at, even if he's been a weirdo lately."

"Even if it means keeping Flatland on its current schedule?"

"*Yes.*" He was silent for a moment, looking for words. "I don't hate the world the way it is, Jessica. I don't want my dad and your family and everyone else sucked into some nightmare. I know the difference between a stupid fantasy and the *real* end of the world. Okay?" He paused, not quite believing what he was about to say. "And whatever Rex comes up with, I'll follow his orders."

"You promise?"

"Sure. I promise. Even if he's acting totally crazy. Anything to stop this."

She looked at him, then finally nodded. "Okay."

He took her hand, felt his midnight gravity connect them. "Let's not worry about Bixby right now."

She smiled faintly and leaned toward him. His eyes closed as their lips met, and for a moment the rest of the world really did fall away. Jonathan pushed them up into the air until they seemed suspended in a dark blue void, with only each other to cling to.

When they parted, he said softly, "Whatever happens in the long midnight, we'll be okay—you and me. You know that, right?"

She shook her head, a sad look crossing her face, then silenced him with another kiss.

22

FIREWORKS

"If Rex doesn't show up on time, I'll kill him."

Jonathan looked tiredly at Dess, then at his watch. "He's got another minute."

"One minute to live, you mean."

"Not really," Jonathan said. "Either Rex gets here in one minute, in which case he's on time and you don't kill him. Or he's late, which means he won't be here, so you *can't* kill him. Either way he has more than one minute to live."

Dess cast a cold glance at Flyboy. He was making logical sense, which was *totally* unfair at this time on a Saturday morning.

"Jess," she said. "Tell Jonathan to stop making sense."

Jessica, her head leaning sleepily on Flyboy's shoulder, started to answer, but a yawn consumed her words. She wound up waving her hand noncommittally.

"Wait a second," Jonathan said. "Is that them?"

Jessica sat bolt upright. "What? In *that* thing?"

Dess felt her jaw dropping. "No way!"

A pink Cadillac was rumbling toward them through the field, its vast frame bobbing across the furrows.

"Rex said he had a new ride," Dess said with quiet awe. "But I didn't think he meant his *mom's* car." She felt a smile break across her face. Teasing him about this was going to be so much more fun than killing him.

Rex's mother worked selling Mary Kay cosmetics door to door, and in recognition of her millionth facial or whatever, she had received a pink Cadillac. But Dess had never actually seen the fabled machine before; Rex refused to ride to school in it, and she'd never imagined him actually *driving* it.

Yet there he was, cruising through Jenks at daybreak like he owned the whole town.

It rolled to a stop next to Jonathan's car, and Flyboy barked out a short laugh as the front window came down. "Wow, Rex. *Ding-dong!*"

"That's Avon, actually," Melissa said as she stepped out of the Cadillac's passenger side. "You're not even trying."

"Oh, right," Jonathan said. "Well, it's not like I have to try *that* hard. I mean . . ." He spread his arms to indicate the car. "It's so *pink*."

Flyboy's voice trailed off as Rex stepped out, looked down at the car, and said, "Hey, yeah, it is. I hadn't noticed."

Then he turned back to them and cracked a smile.

Dess breathed a sigh of relief; that was the first joke he'd made in days. His messed-up morning hair made him look more human than he usually did. Maybe the effects of

Maddy unleashing the darklings in his brain had worn off a little.

"How did you get your mom to lend it to you?" she asked. Since his father's accident, Rex's mother hardly ever showed her face in Bixby. Dess couldn't imagine her handing over the keys for an early morning joyride.

"She dropped by for a visit night before last," Rex said. "And I got the idea of pulling her starter cable out."

Dess's eyes widened. "Excuse me?"

"It was easy. I snuck out while she was in the bathroom and pulled out the starter cable." Rex gave his new evil smile. "She was in a hurry to get somewhere else, like always, so I called her a cab. She's already rented another Caddy, so this one's mine until I tell her it's fixed."

Dess and Jonathan exchanged a glance, and she saw that even Jessica had woken up enough to be impressed.

"Rex," Dess said. "That is so cold-blooded."

"True." He nodded. "But I needed a car. We have important things to take care of."

"Like getting us all out of bed at six-thirty on a Saturday morning?" Flyboy asked.

"Exactly." Rex looked at his watch. "Come with me."

He led them across the field toward the rip, and Dess found herself glad that she'd worn a skirt that didn't fall below her knees. At this time of morning the long grass was heavy with dew, and her sneakers got soaked as fast as if she'd been strolling through a car wash.

As they marched, the sun began to crest over the distant

tree line, its glaring eye finally putting a dent in the fierce pre-dawn chill.

"This better be good, Rex."

"Don't worry, Dess," he said. "I think you'll find it interesting."

"At six-thirty in the morning I was hoping for better than 'interesting,' Rex."

"I'm sure Jessica won't disappoint us."

Dess looked at Jessica, who just shrugged back at her.

Suddenly Dess noticed that Melissa hadn't walked with them. "Hey, where's the bitch goddess? She's not back at your Caddy *sleeping*, is she?"

Rex shook his head. "She'll be along in . . . two minutes."

"Great. More split-second timing." Dess sighed. "Hope this goes better than your last little scheme."

"There's just one thing, guys," Jessica said nervously. "Cassie Flinders lives right over there. What if she sees us?"

"She won't remember us."

"Are you sure about that?"

Rex raised an eyebrow. "Why would she?"

Jessica looked over at the Flinderses' double-wide with an unhappy expression on her face. "Well, I wasn't going to mention this, but she and my sister have been . . . hanging out. I was afraid to tell you guys in case . . ." She didn't finish.

In case the bitch goddess decided to rip your little sister's brain in half, Dess thought.

She looked at Rex, wondering if he was about to do one of his psycho transformations. But after a pause he only shrugged. "Everyone will know about the blue time soon enough, Jessica. It doesn't matter."

"Wow," Jessica said, looking stunned. "That's actually kind of a relief."

Flyboy put his arm around her, smiling, but the idea of Rex not caring about secrecy sent a minor shudder through Dess. As she turned away to study the rip, the realness of how Samhain would change everything sank in yet another notch.

The rip wasn't glowing red here in normal time, but Dess could see its current shape in the color of the grass, as if the contortion were a giant piece of lawn furniture. Maybe the dark moon was mutating the chlorophyll or something. She noted the rip's geometry: a long, thin oval pointing almost due east and west.

She took out Geostationary and noted the coordinates of its center. Almost exactly on the 36th parallel.

Maybe not worth getting up at six-thirty in the morning for, but interesting.

"Okay, good. No daylighters around," Rex said.

"That's because they're all *in bed*," Dess pointed out.

Rex ignored her. "I want to do a few experiments here today, and I want all of you to see them. When Samhain comes, all of Bixby—at least—is going to be swallowed by this contortion. And as we've noticed, the rip isn't exactly the same size as the blue time. You've all seen those leaves falling at midnight?"

"Yeah," Dess said. "But what's the point? It's not midnight now."

"Not yet," Rex said.

"No." Dess looked down at Geostationary. "And it won't be for another 62,615 seconds. So why are we here so—?"

"Whoa!" Jonathan interrupted. "What's up with Melissa?"

Dess turned to see the Cadillac galloping across the field. It climbed up the railway embankment and straddled the tracks, its tires spitting gravel and dust as it bore down on them like a maniacal pink freight train, headlights flicking on.

"Has she gone crazy?" Dess shouted.

"Nope," Rex said, glancing at his watch. "She's right on time. But we might want to get out of the way."

The four of them skidded down the slope of the embankment, and the Cadillac seemed to roar its approval, bolting forward with a burst of acceleration, the spinning tires churning up a giant cloud of dust.

Dess felt a tingling in her fingertips, stronger than she had in the lunchroom, and suddenly knew what was about to happen.

"It's back," she said softly.

"You got it," Rex answered.

Dess looked up at the charging Cadillac with alarm. "But won't she . . . ?"

The inky blue of an eclipse swept in from the east, across the cloudless sky and open fields, stilling the icy wind and blanketing the world in silence. The dark moon shot into the sky, like a huge flying saucer hovering just out of reach.

Yet the Cadillac kept rolling across the red-tinged oval of the rip.

Its engine died, the headlights going dark, but it didn't freeze like it should have. The car continued to coast until it finally skidded to a halt in a shower of dust and gravel.

Dess blinked as she took in the sight: instead of throwing Melissa through the windshield, the pink Cadillac had maintained its momentum.

"Is she okay in there?" Flyboy asked.

Rex nodded. "She's fine. As I suspected, the rip brings *everything* into the blue time, not just people. I figured if dead leaves could still fall, then dead metal would cross over too."

"It's awfully lucky you figured right." Dess didn't much care for Melissa anymore, but it wasn't like she wanted her back in the hospital. Her current scars were creepy enough.

"She was wearing a seat belt," Rex said calmly.

"Wait a minute, Rex," Dess said. "How did you know there was going to be an eclipse?"

He was silent for a moment, his violet eyes narrowing. "There's a pattern. I can see when they're coming, all of them between now and Samhain. This one should last for a while longer."

"You can see a pattern?" Dess cried. "Then write it down for me."

He shook his head. "I can't express it in numbers, not without my head exploding. But she can give it to you." He pointed toward the Cadillac.

The driver's side door opened, and Melissa got out shakily, grinning from ear to ear. "That was cool!"

Dess shook her head. No *way* was Melissa touching her again.

"I thought you were afraid of driving fast," Jessica said.

The bitch goddess shrugged. "You have to face your fears to conquer them, Jess. That's what Rex has been telling me lately."

"You two are both nuts," Dess said softly.

Rex raised an eyebrow. "This experiment wasn't just for kicks, Dess. We had to make sure that when midnight falls on Samhain, it won't kill everyone who happens to be in a car. Which is one less thing to worry about."

Everyone was quiet for a second, and Dess realized she hadn't even thought about that. If the rip really did expand to consume a million people, and only one percent of them were driving at midnight, that would have been *ten thousand* Melissas going through their windshields all at once.

She swallowed. This thing just got bigger and bigger the more she thought about it.

"So cars are okay," Flyboy said, pushing himself up into the air. "But what about planes?"

Rex thought for a moment. "Small aircraft can do dead-stick landings. But the big airliners will be a problem."

"We could phone in bomb threats to all the airports on Halloween," Jonathan suggested from above.

"*Bomb* threats?" Jessica cried. "Wait a second, Rex. Why are we even talking about all this? Didn't you say we were going to try to *prevent* Samhain? I thought the point was to make sure that half of Oklahoma *doesn't* get sucked into the blue time."

Rex took a slow breath, then shook his head. "We can try to stop some of what's going happen—the worst accidents, some of the panic. We can prevent most of the unnecessary deaths."

"The 'unnecessary' deaths, Rex?" Dess said. "Are you saying that some deaths are *necessary*?"

He fixed her with a cold stare. "The predators are coming back, Dess. We have to get used to the fact that we can't save everyone."

She stared back at him. This new darkling-infected Rex seemed perfectly happy thinking the unthinkable. The old Rex would have been appalled by the thought of *one* death, but here he was, talking about thousands like it was just the Bixby Tigers losing again.

"All we can do is follow the old traditions," Melissa said. She was leaning against Rex, her legs still unsteady after her maniacal ride.

"Like what?" Dess asked. "Dressing up in costumes?"

"Be my guest," Rex said. "But that's not the tradition I was thinking about. We have to organize people, bring them together and teach them how to protect themselves. In the meantime we have to keep the darklings away as long as we can." He looked at Jessica. "Maybe that's why you're here."

"Why I'm where?" said Jessica.

Rex's eyes narrowed. "Here in Bixby, Jessica. Here on earth. You're the flame-bringer, after all, and we're going to need a *really* big bonfire."

Rex had brought three experiments for the rip.

First he had Jessica light a candle and step away from it. Normally it would have sputtered out when she took her hand away—without the flame-bringer, fire couldn't exist in the blue time.

Yet as Jessica stepped back, first one yard, then a few more, then finally walking to the other side of the glowing red boundary, the candle stayed alight. Her eyes widened. The rip really did have different rules. Like the pink Cadillac, a fire would keep going once it was started.

"That's the price the darklings pay for making the blue time weaker," Rex said. "If normal people can move through the rip, so can flame."

"So anyone can start a fire?" Dess asked.

"I doubt that." Rex flicked his lighter a few times; it didn't even make a spark. But when he held down its button and placed its jet of gas to the candle, it came back alight. He smiled, lifting the tiny yet blinding flame. "But once Jessica's started it, a fire can spread on its own. People can pass it to each other."

"Whoa, Jess," Jonathan said. "See if your flashlight works the same way."

Jessica waited until all their eyes were covered, then whispered Enlightenment's name and switched it on. Squinting through her fingers, Dess saw its white beam cut through the blue time in a blinding wedge.

But when Jess put it on the tracks and stepped away from it, the light sputtered and died.

"I didn't think so," Rex said. "The chemical reaction in

a battery is too complicated to sustain itself—like a car engine. But if Jessica lights a bunch of torches, we can protect a lot of people at once."

"Yeah, eventually. But this happens at *midnight*, Rex," Jonathan said. "People will be scattered all over Bixby or however far the rip spreads. So how do we organize everyone without radio or phones?"

"We *don't* organize everyone, Jonathan. We save who we can."

They were all silent for a moment.

Dess realized that an awful feeling was growing in her stomach. For the first time she was starting to take this end-of-the-world thing seriously. This wasn't like saving one little kid. The lives of uncountable strangers depended on the five of them.

How many people could one darkling eat in a night? How many darklings were there altogether? The math almost made her head spin. Numbers were one thing when they were abstract: coordinates or computer bits or seconds between now and midnight. But when they represented human lives, the thought of all those numerals in a row suddenly became obscene.

Yet Rex stood there, calmly planning the long midnight.

"First we'll need a way to get the maximum number of people awake," he was saying. "Then we should create some sort of signal that's visible from all over town. Hopefully that will gather people together. And finally, we'll need a way to defend them all from the darklings."

Rex produced a bottle rocket. "I was thinking fireworks might do all three things at once."

Dess nodded. Rex might be cold-blooded about this, but at least he was making sense. When Jessica had first discovered her talent, she'd tried to shoot Roman candles in the blue time out of curiosity, but the flaming balls always sputtered out after flying a few feet. Inside the rip, though, they would keep burning—an instant antidarkling flamethrower.

Jessica was just standing there, looking stunned by what they were talking about. But when Rex stuck the rocket's stick into the gravel, she got herself together. Kneeling, she lit the fuse, then stepped back as the blinding sparkles made their way up into its tail. . . .

With a *whoosh* it shot into the sky, rising twenty feet or so before its flaming trail choked off suddenly.

"Was that a dud?" Jonathan asked.

"No." Dess shook her head. "The rip is three-dimensional. It extends only so far up." She could see the rocket frozen at the edge of the rip above them, waiting for the eclipse to end before resuming its flight.

Rex started talking about airliners again, how they would be too high to be caught by the rip on Samhain.

Dess had heard enough about airplane crashes. She turned away and walked to the edge of the rip, wondering if it was still growing.

What she really wanted Rex to do was get over his darkling number phobia and write down the exact dates and times of all the coming eclipses. If he could glimpse a pattern with his math-impaired brain, Dess knew she could analyze what was happening. Then maybe the five of them could do something more useful for Bixby than setting off bottle rockets.

Like finding a way to stop this thing.

Suddenly Dess heard the scrape of gravel behind her. She whirled around—it was Melissa.

"Don't touch me," she spat.

Melissa held up her hands. "Relax. I'm not going to force you."

"Force me? You're not going to *anything* me."

"Listen, Dess, I was there when Madeleine opened up Rex's mind. I saw what he knows. I can give it to you."

Dess shook her head.

"I'm sorry for what I did to you, all right, Dess? But we need you now. I know you see how serious this is."

Dess looked away. Of course, the mindcaster had tasted her nausea.

"There might be a way to stop this, Dess. But only you can find it."

The image of darklings rampaging through Bixby came into Dess's mind, and she wondered for a moment if Melissa had placed it there. Of course, even if the mindcaster was manipulating her, the awful picture would become a reality in thirteen days unless they found a solution.

"The answer might be waiting for you right here, all around us," Melissa said. "But this eclipse is ending soon."

Dess took a slow breath, realizing that she had the choice of facing the mindcaster's touch or of going along with Rex's dire calculations. She could either open her mind now or watch the slaughter.

It wasn't fair, having to save thousands of people. Not fair at all.

"Make it quick," she said through gritted teeth, and held out her hand.

Melissa closed her eyes.

At the first contact of their fingers something massive and dark came into Dess. Images swept through her, a wire frame of the earth, red fire spreading along its lines of longitude and latitude. She saw the days between now and Samhain midnight, a steady beat of eclipses until the blue time shattered, the rip streaking across the earth for thousands of miles. She saw how long it would last, twenty-five hours of frozen time—humans within struggling to survive while everyone outside stood frozen and unaware.

Then she saw the rip's true shape . . . and the beginnings of a solution.

Dess pulled her hand away from Melissa's touch, realizing that she was hearing a sound in the distance. It was a soft spattering noise, like a light rain on a steel roof.

She turned away without a word and walked down the tracks to where the Cadillac had roared up onto the embankment. At the glowing-red edge of the rip, a dark curtain of something was falling lightly through the air.

Dess held out an open palm. . . .

Dust gradually collected on her skin. Then a hard *ping* came from the metal rail next to her—the fallen piece of gravel skittered across the tracks.

She stepped back a few yards and looked up, her eyes making out a smudge against the dark moon. Like the arrested bottle rocket, the dirt and gravel churned up by the huge pink car still hung overhead, suspended in frozen time. But carved into the dust cloud was a long, oval shape. . . .

Dess nodded; suddenly it all made perfect sense. The Cadillac's tires had put a lot of debris into the air just as the eclipse had arrived, flash-freezing it up there until normal time started again. But the dust *inside* the rip had swirled down to the ground, falling in regular gravity. So now Dess could see the whole thing in three dimensions. Its blimplike shape had been cut into the cloud, like a long, oval space carved into a mountain.

But why was the dust still raining down?

Dess walked back to the edge, put her palm out again, and found that now the dirt was falling a bit farther along the tracks.

Of course . . . The rip was *growing*, tearing the blue time in half. And as its edges traveled outward, more of the suspended dust fell to earth.

Dess looked up, her heart beating harder. She was actually *watching* the rip expand. She peered into the vague blur of suspended dust, trying to see its exact dimensions and cursing the dim blue light. If Rex was going to perform dramatic experiments, why hadn't he released a cloud of

Ping-Pong balls right before the eclipse so they could see what was really going on? Then Dess could calculate how fast the tear in the blue time was spreading and in exactly what direction.

She scrambled down the embankment to the longer edge of the rip and put out her hand. Hardly any dust was falling here.

"Dess?" Rex called.

"Hang on." She climbed back up to the tracks. Yes, the rip was spreading much faster at the oval's narrow end.

She ran by the four of them, all the way past the Cadillac to the other end of the rip. Glancing up, she got an eyeful of dirt. The dust fall was harder here too. But why would it follow the direction of the railroad tracks?

She closed her eyes, letting the knowledge that Melissa had given her take shape.

"Of course," she said aloud.

"Of course *what*?" Rex called.

Dess waved him silent. She could see it now—so obvious that she wanted to thump herself on the head for not realizing it before. Until now she had imagined the rip expanding like the universe—a great big bubble, a sphere. But what if it were long and narrow instead?

The rip was heading in two directions, stretching along a single axis, just like a real tear in a piece of fabric. But what was at either end?

Dess visualized the map of the county she carried in her head and instantly knew exactly what was going on and why this godforsaken spot lay right in the middle of the rip. Jenks was halfway to nowhere, precisely poised between the center of town and the deepest desert.

The blue time was opening up long and straight, like some sort of darkling highway, a conduit between predators and prey. It was reaching west out into the mountains, where the oldest minds lived, the ones who hadn't had a decent meal in thousands of years. And at the same moment the rip was traveling east, directly toward the populated center of downtown Bixby.

"Dess?" Rex said, frustration creeping into his voice.

She still didn't answer. If he wanted to get all scary, let him.

Her eyes closed, Dess let her mind follow the direction of the tracks, recalling the images of wire frame globes that Melissa had given her.

What if the rip just kept growing year after year, shooting across the country like a lit fuse every Halloween?

It was tearing along Bixby's ill-fated latitude: 36 degrees. That line led east through Broken Arrow, which was why the Grayfoots were evacuating. Then it whipped through a lot of small and medium towns after that . . . until eventually reaching Nashville, which sat at exactly 36.10 degrees. From there, it would go on to swallow Charlotte, North Carolina, at 35.14. Westward, the rip would cruise straight through downtown Las Vegas, which was centered at exactly 36.11. And it would pass a hundred miles north of Grandpa Grayfoot's new digs in LA.

"Dess?" Rex called. "What *is* it?"

"We might be able to save more people than you think, Rex. Or at least delay the darklings long enough to get Bixby organized."

He walked over, his violet eyes flashing, a smile on his face. Suddenly Dess knew he'd planned the whole thing to work this way—Dess too tired from getting up so early to resist Melissa touching her.

Well, it had worked.

"How do we do it?" he said.

"We need to build two big bonfires—or better yet, fireworks displays. The one out here will bottle them up for as long as we can."

"Bottle them up?"

"Yeah. The rip will open up long and narrow, Rex, like a road. It leads right through here, straight from the mountains to downtown. If we stop them in Jenks for a while, make them go around us, we may have time to organize people back in Bixby."

As Rex's eyes followed the path of the tracks back toward the mountains, a thoughtful look crossed his face, as if he was accessing the numberless darkling math stored in his mind. "Yeah. You could be right."

The world shuddered then—the dark moon falling like a rock, the red-tinged blue time fading—and the cold wrapped itself around Dess, driving its way into her bones. She shivered with excitement.

They had a way to stop the darklings . . . for a while, at

least. Maybe they could give the people of Bixby time to understand what was going on and a fighting chance to survive their night in hell. Maybe thousands didn't have to die.

Above Dess's head the bottle rocket was suddenly released from frozen time. It shot farther into the sky, where it exploded with a tiny *bang*.

23

SLUMBER PARTY

Noises came from inside the hardware store, the clattering of falling metal and a million small things spilling.

"Jesus, Flyboy," Dess yelled in through the window. "It's good you're not a *real* burglar."

"Never said I was," he shouted back. Another crash erupted.

Even though it was the blue time, Jessica flinched a little at all the ruckus. It felt like they should at least *try* to be quiet, given that they were breaking and entering.

Again.

"Found them!" Jonathan's voice came.

She and Dess walked around the corner to the front of the store. Through the glass doors she saw Jonathan trying the keys from a big ring, one by one.

"Should have just climbed through the window," Dess muttered as the process stretched out.

"Some of the stuff on your list is too heavy," Jessica said, stifling a yawn and happy to be going in through the door. She could hardly keep her eyes open, and she still had to get back to Constanza's tonight.

Since Rex's demonstration out in Jenks, the five of them had spent every midnight gathering the materials they needed to bring the darkling invasion to a halt. Mostly that meant breaking into every store in town that sold fireworks and making off with the stock. The nightly burglaries in the blue time were getting tiring. And obvious too—the *Bixby Register* had run a story about the unknown vandals collecting a dangerous cache of fireworks. According to the article, the sheriff's office had actually figured out it was a bunch of kids planning something big for Halloween.

Of course, no one had a clue *how* big.

Tonight Rex and Melissa were knocking over the last fireworks stall in town while the other three picked up a few items from Bixby Hardware and Keys, after which, hopefully, Rex would let them get a few nights' rest. Halloween was only six days away.

Jessica scowled at the big paper skeleton taped to the glass door, swinging lightly from Jonathan's attempts with the keys. There were decorations up everywhere in school, orange and black bunting running down the hallways, pumpkin faces glowering at Jessica from the cafeteria walls. Every time she saw a witch or black cat on a classroom door, it reminded her of what was coming.

"Come on!" Dess said, just as the lock clicked.

"Ladies," Jonathan said, opening the door with a bow.

"Good, let's hurry," Jessica said, walking in among the

rows of tools and appliances and paint cans. "Constanza thinks I'm in the bathroom."

Jonathan snorted. "That would psych her out, wouldn't it? If you just disappeared in there?"

"Yeah, very funny," Jessica said tiredly as Jonathan began to gather up a big plastic tarp.

On Monday morning, the day after tomorrow, Constanza was flying to LA. Supposedly it was only for a week. But as she mentioned to Jessica at least once every day, she might never set foot in Bixby High again.

Tonight could be the last time Jessica would ever see her.

Jessica pulled her coat tighter, wondering how many more people she would lose in the next week.

"Hey, check this out," Dess said.

Jessica turned. "An empty paint can?"

"Formerly a lowly paint can." Dess swung it by its wire handle. "But in its new incarnation, it will be a major explosive device."

Jessica swallowed. Some of the stuff Rex was planning was on the edge of crazy. But there was no backing out now.

She pulled Dess's list from her pocket and started walking among the blue-lit shelves, searching for nails and wires and metal tools—sufficient fresh, clean steel to make a hundred weapons.

Jessica wondered if it would be enough.

A half hour later Jonathan tapped her on the back.

"Come on." He offered his hand. "We should leave soon if I'm going to get back here in time."

"Thought you said it would be funny if I just disappeared."

"Sorry." He touched her hand softly, midnight gravity shivering through her body for a moment. "You could have stayed there. Dess and I could have done this on our own."

"Glad to help." She shrugged. "Slumber parties aren't much fun when your host is a stiff." Jessica looked into his eyes. "Plus I hate midnights when I don't get to fly."

He held out his hand, smiling. "Let's fly, then."

"Okay." She took it, feeling the connection take hold, her body light as the air. "See you tomorrow, Dess."

Dess looked up from the open front door, where she was piling the stolen merchandise. "Sure, Jess. And Flyboy? If you don't get back before midnight, I'm leaving all this stuff in your car with a big note to the sheriff."

"Don't worry, I'll be back."

They flew toward Constanza's, shooting down an empty stretch of highway to the colony of large houses on a circular road. Jonathan jumped with Jessica up to the roof, just outside the open window of the second-floor bathroom.

Jessica glanced at her watch; Jonathan still had plenty of time to make it back to the store before midnight ended. "Thanks for the lift."

"Listen, I know you needed to see Constanza tonight." He stood. "Seeing as how she's your only normal friend and everything."

Jessica looked up at him, wondering if he was being sarcastic.

"I mean it, Jess. It's okay to need somebody who's not a

midnighter." He swallowed, looking uncomfortable. "And I'm sorry I never made friends with her."

"Thanks." Jessica sighed. "After what's coming, she won't be back, will she?"

"Yeah, I guess. But at least she'll be safe in Los Angeles."

"Sure." She sighed again. "I just hate goodbyes." Before she'd moved to Bixby, the last three months in Chicago had been nothing but farewells. And now she seemed to be losing everything again.

"Well, I'm not going anywhere," Jonathan said. "You can count on that."

Inside, Jessica changed back into her pajamas, waiting for midnight to end. When the blue light faded, the house shuddering to life around her, she flushed the toilet and stepped out into the upstairs hallway.

"So, *as* I was saying," Constanza began as Jessica opened her door. "This shirt can be retired, right?"

Jessica looked at the black pullover with red shoulder pads. "Yeah. Way too eighties."

"Eww." Constanza threw the shirt into the discard pile, then turned to the three giant suitcases that lay open on the floor. They were packed crushingly full of dresses, shirts, skirts, and what seemed like dozens of shoes.

"Won't your parents be suspicious? I mean, you're supposedly only going for a week."

Constanza snorted. "I always pack this much for a week. You wouldn't believe all the great stuff I'm leaving behind. But I think that's it."

"So . . . we're done?" Jessica said hopefully. They'd been packing pretty much all day.

"Done for tonight." Constanza stood up, surveying the wreckage of her room. "Thanks so much for helping me, Jess. I *hate* packing." She looked longingly into her huge closets. "All these clothes crying out to me. So many left behind."

Jessica felt herself smiling. The whole last week had been spent preparing for a battle that seemed unwinnable. It felt good to have accomplished something concrete, even as minor as packing Constanza's bags. And it was a relief to make a few choices that nobody's life depended on.

"Glad I could help you. It was fun, if exhausting."

"Ernesto *said* he was going to help, but he's long gone."

Jessica frowned. "None of your cousins are still around, are they?"

"No. And even if they were, Grandpa's being extra insane about anybody setting foot in Bixby before the move."

Jessica nodded. This close to Samhain, only Constanza's unlucky parents would still be here. Their house was on the opposite side of Bixby from Jenks but still in the path of the rip. If the darklings broke through, her folks would be in serious danger.

"Isn't it going to be weird?" she said. "Not seeing your parents . . . as much?"

Constanza shrugged. "I'm almost seventeen. I figure I'd be out of their house soon anyway. At least this way they'll be able to see me on TV."

Jessica had to smile.

"But you know, leaving them behind doesn't really make me sad," Constanza continued. "They'll always be around, one way or another. It's more my friends I'm going to miss. You especially."

"Me? *Especially?*"

"Of course, silly. I mean, sometimes I feel like I've hardly gotten a chance to know you. It's only been what? Two months since school started?"

"I suppose so," Jessica said quietly. It felt like years sometimes, but she'd only arrived in Bixby in late August. She sat next to one of the suitcases, staring at the profusion of clothes and shoes inside. "Two months can seem like a long time, I guess."

"That's *so* true." Constanza leaned closer. "In fact, my theory is that two months in friendship time is actually longer than a year, you know?"

"Um . . . not exactly."

Constanza bent and picked up a stack of shirts that hadn't made the cut. She took them to one of the room's huge, now half-empty closets. "Listen, Jess, I *know* you're all sad about me leaving. You've been moping around ever since I told you about LA. But sometimes these short friendships are totally the best."

Jessica raised an eyebrow. "They are?"

Constanza slid the shirts back onto hangers thoughtfully, one by one. "Sure! Didn't you ever have a best friend at summer camp or something? You make friends quick, and you know you're only together until the end of summer, so it's *super* intense?"

Jessica nodded. "Yeah, I guess I know what you mean."

Constanza reached over to brush a lock of Jessica's hair out of her face. "But those are always the people you remember for the rest of your life. At least I do. Even though I usually forget to write to them or whatever."

Jessica swallowed, a lump rising in her throat. She couldn't believe that tears had sneaked up on her and knew she'd feel like a total dork if she cried. She tried to focus her mind on Jonathan's words: Constanza was one of the lucky ones. She wouldn't be here for Bixby's big Halloween surprise.

Constanza sighed. "Maybe it's because when friendships end like this, instead of growing apart, you get ripped apart. So you never get to the phase where you don't like each other anymore."

Jessica blinked, and one tear traveled down her cheek.

Constanza reached out with an elegant finger and softly brushed it away.

"Come on, Jess. That's enough of being sad." She laughed. "I'll be back in Bixby whenever my shooting schedule allows. Still have to see the parentals, you know."

"Okay. Sorry."

"Don't be sorry." Constanza turned her smile up to its full wattage. "But now that we're all packed, we've got to have some fun so I can remember you happy."

Jessica nodded, letting Constanza's mood lift her out of the sadness that had haunted her all week. Dess kept saying that her plan should work, that maybe they could save everyone in Bixby, or almost everyone. And after twenty-five hours of midnight, the blue time would retreat again.

Maybe once the darklings realized they had a fight on their hands, they wouldn't keep coming back every Halloween.

Jessica decided that tonight, at least, she would have a good time.

"Okay, this is me being happy." She forced a smile.

"That's the spirit," Constanza said. "We can still talk on the telephone, after all. It's not like it's the end of the world.

24

TRICK OR TREAT

"Looks like Halloween might be canceled," Don Day said from the other end of the couch.

Jessica looked up from the book she'd been trying, and failing, to read. As usual the Weather Channel was on. A man in a bow tie was coaxing a swirling mass of white out of the Gulf of Mexico and onto the Texas plains.

It was headed straight for Oklahoma.

"Is that rain?" she said. "For *tonight*?"

"It was a hurricane, but by now it's just a tropical depression," her father said in his Weather-Channel-lecture voice. He leaned forward to peer out the back window. "By the time it gets here, it'll only be a thunderstorm."

"Only a thunderstorm . . ." Jessica watched in horror as the satellite image repeated its course across the TV again and again, stopping at the border of Oklahoma every time. "Um, when's it supposed to get here?"

"Sometime tonight. It might rain out all the fun." He gave her a puzzled look. "You're not going trick-or-treating, are you?"

"Duh. Of course not." She rolled her eyes dramatically. "I'm probably doing trig homework all night. But thunderstorms are kind of scary, you know, especially on Halloween."

Especially at midnight, and particularly when you were trying to keep two hundred pounds of fireworks dry because you were fighting off an invasion of monsters. In the last two weeks of planning, no one had brought up the possibility that it might *rain*.

"So, Dad," she said a minute later, trying not to sound *too* interested. "Are they saying the storm should be here by, like, midnight?"

He shrugged. "It's hard to tell what's going to happen once a hurricane, or even a tropical depression, hits land. Could take until tomorrow morning. Might break up into nothing. Or it could keep going strong and get here by nine or ten."

"Whatever!" Beth announced from the doorway. "I'm going trick-or-treating even if it's raining golf-ball-sized hail. Or even golf balls."

Jess looked up at her little sister and had to suppress a snort of laughter. Eight coat hangers stuck out from Beth's shoulders at all angles, covered with black paper and bobbing wildly. Her face was mostly blackened with makeup, exaggerating the whites of her eyes, and she was wearing plastic vampire fangs.

"What are *you* supposed to be?"

"I'm a tarantula, stupid." Beth took a step closer to the couch, angling one of the legs so that it menaced her father.

"Ow," he said as it struck his head, eyes still trained on the Weather Channel.

"You're calling *me* stupid. Look in a mirror." Then Jessica frowned. "Where'd you get that idea?"

"From Cassie. We're both going as tarantulas. She has this thing about spiders."

A chill ran down Jessica's spine. "She's coming over here tonight?"

"What? Don't you like Cassie, Jess?" Beth said sweetly.

"Yeah, she's wonderful." Jessica lowered her eyes to stare at her book. Cassie had been over a few times since that first awful Spaghetti Night. The two of them had left Jessica alone so far, but tonight she had a feeling they were going to show up at exactly eleven-thirty, when she had to slip out of her room.

At least in one way it was a good thing: it would be a lot safer for Cassie here than in Jenks. Once midnight fell, the rip was going to start expanding, zooming down the 36th parallel. Hopefully it wouldn't grow wide enough to swallow houses on the north side of Bixby. But even if it did, the darklings might not make it this far.

That's what Jessica had been telling herself all week, anyway.

"Well, you won't have to put up with us in any case." Beth swiveled her hips so that one of the tarantula legs banged against Jessica's head. "I'm going over to her house."

"What, in *Jenks*?"

Beth looked at Jessica with surprise, and even her father's eyes lurched away from the Weather Channel.

"Um, yes, Jess. Because that's where Cassie, like, *lives*."

"When are you getting home?"

"Jess, you're being weird. Dad, tell Jess she's being weird."

"Jessica?" her father said.

"Well, trick-or-treating in a strange part of town and everything."

They both looked at her in puzzlement a little bit longer, and then a knowing smile broke out slowly across Beth's face.

Their father turned back to the TV, which was filled with images of the storm roiling the Texas coast. "Lighten up, Jessica. It's Halloween. Cassie's grandmother promised they'd be in bed by eleven and that they wouldn't eat too much candy."

That last word seemed to remind him of the open bag of candy corn on the coffee table, and he leaned forward to grab a handful.

"Mom said not to eat that," Beth said.

"Mom's not home yet," he answered.

"But it's dangerous!" Jessica cried.

"What?" her father said. "Candy corn?"

"No. Being out there in the country. With a possible storm coming and . . . everything."

Beth was still smiling. "You don't want me in Jenks tonight, do you?"

Jessica ignored the words, staring at her book, trying not to chew at her lip. Her little sister was headed right into the path of the darkling invasion, but she couldn't think of a single way to stop it. Beth had that smug look on her face—this time she really was ready to spill everything she knew if Jessica got in her way.

And this was *not* the night to get grounded.

"Come on, Dad, let's get moving," Beth said. "The Weather Channel will still be here when you get back. Like it ever changes."

"The weather changes all the time, smarty-pants," he said, scooping his keys and another handful of candy corn from the coffee table and rising to his feet.

Jessica found herself wishing that she'd become all predatory, like Rex, so that she could slip outside right now and pull the starter cable out of her father's car. But she didn't actually know what starter cables looked like and wasn't a hundred percent sure she could even get the hood open.

What else could she do? Explain that the food chain was about to turn upside down? That Bixby was about to be invaded? They'd only think she was kidding or crazy.

She would have to deal with this at midnight. Along with everything else tonight, Jessica was going to have to make sure her little sister was okay.

"See you later, Jess," Beth taunted from the front door.

Jessica didn't answer, and the door slammed with a booming note of finality. She looked at her watch, her stomach slowly winding itself into knots.

Only five forty-five, and already Samhain was off to a brilliant start.

25

RAIN

"Can you still taste him?"

"Relax, Flyboy." Melissa shook her head. "He's headed off down Division."

Jonathan let the car speed up again but glanced in the rearview one more time. Relaxing didn't seem like such a good idea at the moment. Cops were crawling all over Bixby tonight, hoping to catch Halloween vandals and impose curfew on any kids who'd stayed out late after trick-or-treating. And of course, the sheriff's department were dying to find whoever had stolen all those fireworks before they were put to use.

The fact that Jonathan's trunk contained about half of the collection of firecrackers, smoke bombs, Roman candles, sparklers, and rockets of every description certainly didn't fill him with relaxing thoughts.

"Just let me know if he comes this way again."

"Don't worry about the cops. I can taste those rednecks a mile off."

He leaned forward to look up into the roiling sky, a

flicker of lightning illuminating the clouds from within. "What do you figure about that rain?"

"In general, Jonathan, storm fronts don't have minds. So I have no idea."

He let out a short laugh, only half sure that she was kidding. Melissa wasn't usually Jonathan's favorite traveling companion, but he was glad she was with him tonight. He was too nervous to ride around alone, especially with the police hunting for what was in his trunk.

"All excited about tonight?" she asked.

"Nervous."

It was Melissa's turn to laugh. "Jonathan, I know you're not completely dreading this."

He sighed. There was no point in bluffing a mindcaster. The night before had been one long flying dream, a half-anxious, half-thrilled rehearsal in his mind.

Jonathan shrugged. "It's something different."

"That's what I like about Bixby: always something different."

"What about you?" he asked. "A whole day without . . . what do you call it? Mind noise? Isn't that your dream?"

"You'd think so, wouldn't you?" Melissa said. "But as the rip grows, all those other minds will be sucked in, polluting our *midnight*. Frankly, Flyboy, I wish the secret hour would just stay between the five of us forever."

"Yeah," Jonathan said softly. He hadn't thought of it that way, but in addition to all the death and destruction, midnight was about to become something public, something less special. "Me too."

They pulled onto Jessica's street, five minutes early.

She was already outside and ran to the car, pulling open the door even before he'd rolled to a stop. She threw herself into the backseat and said, "Okay. Go."

"Relax, Jess," he said. "We're ahead of schedule."

"I need to get out there early, okay?"

For a moment Jonathan wondered what she meant, but then, slowly but surely, the only possible explanation crept into his mind.

"Beth?"

"Just . . . drive."

"She gave you trouble tonight?" Jonathan shook his head. "It doesn't matter, okay? By the time the sun comes up tomorrow, thousands of people will have seen the blue time for themselves. The secret's over!"

"I know all that." Her voice was tight, afraid. "But we have to get moving. Beth's in trouble."

He put the car back in gear, easing into the center of the street. "She's not still out trick-or-treating, is she?"

"Much worse. She's in Jenks."

"*What?*"

"She's spending the night with Cassie Flinders."

Melissa put a hand to her head. "Guys . . ."

Jonathan's eyes widened. "But that's right next to the rip!"

"I *know*!" Jessica cried.

"Guys!" Melissa said, her head tipping back, eyes closed. "Shush your minds!"

Jonathan brought the car to a stop at the next light, looking both ways and then into the rearview mirror, trying to think quiet, relaxed thoughts . . . and failing.

"Turn left," Melissa suddenly whispered. "Don't wait for the light."

Jonathan spun the wheel and accelerated, whipping the car onto Kerr Street.

"He saw us. He knows your car . . ." She twitched. "Crap. It's St. Claire."

Sheriff Clancy St. Claire—Jonathan's knuckles went white on the steering wheel as he imagined the lawman's grinning face. The sheriff could recognize Jonathan's car from a mile away.

"Which way?" he hissed.

Melissa shook her head. "Don't know yet. Can't feel any other cars, but he's calling it in."

Jonathan breathed through clenched teeth. They didn't have much time to get clear of St. Claire. Soon there would be another cop car involved in the pursuit and then another—Bixby police never did things in small numbers. By the time midnight rolled around, they'd all be in handcuffs and miles out of position. Totally unable to help Beth or anyone else, for that matter.

"Hang on," he said, and pushed the gas pedal to the floor, speeding down Kerr. A few seconds later lights spun in his rearview mirror, the whoop of a siren splitting the night.

"Oh, no," Jessica said softly. It occurred to Jonathan that she'd been taken home by the cops right after she arrived in Bixby—part of her introduction to the hazards of the midnight hour.

"Don't worry, Jess. We'll get there." He spun the wheel again, turning onto a small residential road called Mallard and hoping there weren't any trick-or-treaters still out. Fortunately he'd flown over Jessica's part of town dozens of times and could visualize it perfectly from a bird's-eye view. Mallard took a winding route toward downtown, then branched into two roads a mile before hitting the highway.

If he could just get to the fork before Clancy caught sight of them again, they'd have a fifty-fifty chance of getting away. Which was better than nothing.

They swerved along the winding street, shooting through the narrow straights between parked cars. Jonathan had to force himself to look ahead instead of checking the rearview mirror.

Then—with a sudden *whack!*—something struck the windshield, and Jonathan felt the steering wheel slip from his fingers. Tires squealed for a moment before he pulled the car straight again.

"What was that?" Jessica shouted.

"I don't . . ." Jonathan started, then saw a delta of yellowish goo oozing upward on his windshield, spreading wider as it was pushed by the wind of their passage. A tiny white fragment clung to the ooze, fluttering for a moment before it was ripped away.

"Just kids," Melissa said. "And I think they've got a few more eggs for St. Claire's car."

Lightning flickered in the distance, illuminating the goo as it crawled across the windshield.

They reached the fork, and Jonathan veered left. Another mile ahead was the highway that led toward Jenks.

"Wait! Stop!" Melissa suddenly shouted.

"Do *what*?"

"Pull over and park! Clancy's backup just turned onto this street. They're right in front of us!"

Jonathan squashed his foot down on the brakes, bringing a screech from the tires. He swerved the car in behind a camper van and switched off the lights and motor.

"What are you doing?" Jessica cried from the backseat. "We can't just sit here!"

"We're not just sitting, Jess!" Melissa hissed. "We're hiding!"

"It's okay, Jess. We'll get there." Jonathan hoped it wasn't an empty promise.

He slid himself under the wheel, one hand still clutching the dangling car keys. He wondered how fast he could get the engine started again if the other cop recognized his car.

Of course, if they pulled in behind them, they'd all be stuck here behind the camper van. . . .

"Here they come," Melissa whispered, huddled against the passenger door.

Jonathan heard the swoosh of tires whipping by and listened for the sound of them slowing. But no lights flashed, no siren sounded, and gradually the car faded into the distance.

"They're gone," Melissa said. "And Clancy's headed the other way. He thinks he's got us now."

Jonathan let out a slow sigh of relief, but as he pulled himself back up into his seat, his heart sank.

A few raindrops had already spattered on the windshield. As he watched, they began to fall more swiftly, diluting the egg goo and catching the flicker of lightning like a hundred glowing eyes.

Thunder rumbled again, this time right over their heads.

He looked at his watch. They still had time to get to Jenks, but by midnight it would be raining like crazy.

"Perfect night for fireworks," he said, turning the engine back on and putting the car in gear.

26

THE BOMB

Rex threw himself at the roof door again, ignoring the horror that trembled through his body at the sharp smell of its bright, unrusted steel. As his shoulder hit, the door pushed outward another few inches.

"Can you fit through there yet?" he asked.

Dess looked at the narrow gap between the door and its frame. "No way."

Rex stepped back and hissed through his teeth. He and Jonathan had been up here just the night before to dump off most of the fireworks, and this door had been unlocked. Now it was secured with a chain an inch wide and a padlock as big as his fist.

Rex hit the door again, his shoulder banging against steel with a dull thud, pulling the chain tauter and winning another inch of space.

"Still too small," Dess said.

Rex cursed. The fireworks show at Jenks wouldn't keep the darklings at bay for a whole twenty-five hours. They couldn't afford for this part of the plan to fail.

They'd chosen an empty building on the west side of town, tall enough that it could be seen from pretty much everywhere in Bixby. Once the rip reached downtown, anyone who was awake would notice that their TVs, radios, and phones weren't working. Hopefully when they stumbled out of their houses and into the blue time, they would spot the shower of rockets shooting up from this roof. Anyone who made it here could shelter under the protection of the flame-bringer until the long midnight ended.

But the first trick was to make sure as many people as possible were awake at midnight. And to do that, they had to get out to the roof, where Dess's makeshift bomb lay hidden.

Thunder rolled overhead, and Rex smelled a change in the air.

"Oh, crap." He thrust his hand out through the crack in the door, and a few drops struck his palm. "Perfect. It's raining."

"You guys covered the fireworks with plastic, didn't you?" Dess asked.

Rex just looked at her. There'd been so much preparing and planning this last week, rain was one thing that had slipped his mind. The fireworks were on the other side of the door, outside, hidden under some old cardboard boxes. They'd be reduced to a soggy, useless mass if they didn't get out there soon.

"Didn't you hear the weather report?" Dess cried. "They've been predicting rain all week!"

"I can't watch TV anymore." Since Madeleine had

unleashed the darkling part of his mind, the clever, human flickering box in his father's house gave him fits to look at.

Dess groaned.

Rex took a few steps back, as much of a running start as he could get in the small stairwell shed, and threw himself against the door again. It budged outward another inch against the chain. Still not enough gap between door and frame to squeeze out onto the roof.

The rain outside was falling harder now.

Rex noticed that the metal was bending outward from the center, where the chain held it. Maybe if he focused on pounding the bottom half of the door, he could open up enough room to crawl through.

He drew his foot back and kicked the metal, sending another booming sound echoing down the stairwell.

Dess looked down the stairs. "Jeez, Rex. Make some more noise, why don't you?"

"I didn't smell anyone on the way in."

"But if someone locked that door today, they might still be around."

"So?" he said. "At least they might have the key."

"They might have a gun too."

"Humans don't scare me anymore." He gave the metal another kick; it scraped outward a little farther. Inside his cowboy boot Rex's foot stung, but he ignored the pain, focusing on raising up the darkness inside himself.

Black spots appeared in the corners of his eyes, and he felt his body shifting within his skin. Pain turned to anger, and he began to thrash at the door harder and harder, ignoring the damage it was doing to his foot.

Wild thoughts eclipsed his human mind: the flat metal expanse was his enemy, the clever alloys inside it an abomination. He had to escape this human structure and get out under the open sky.

The door buckled and twisted under his assault, its bottom hinges tearing from the wall. Flakes of paint flew from the battered metal, which cried out dully with every kick. Finally the ring that held the chain snapped off, and the entire door tumbled outward onto the roof, like a drunk passing out cold.

"What the hell, Rex," Dess said softly. "Are you okay?"

Rex got himself under control, letting the darkness fade, taking deep breaths and feeling the pain swell in his right foot.

"Ow," he said softly, turning to the stair rail to peer down. If anyone was in the building, they must have heard that.

But no sound of approaching feet met his ears.

"Come on," she said. "We're behind schedule."

He followed Dess out onto the roof, every limping step pure agony. The cold rain fell on his face and hands, stronger now.

The fireworks were still there under the rain-spattered boxes, still dry. Ignoring his foot, Rex helped Dess drag the whole pile across the black tar and through the door into the shelter of the stairwell.

He checked his watch: four minutes to midnight.

Dess started throwing the boxes down the stairs, clearing some room in the tiny stairwell shed. The bomb sat atop the other fireworks, a paint can with a three-foot fuse protruding from its top.

"There's my baby," Dess said with a smile.

Rex had watched her make the bomb, the terrifying smell of its contents almost panicking him. The soldered-shut paint can was stuffed full of gunpowder emptied from a dozen packages of M-80s. Its purpose was simple: to create as loud a boom as possible. Dess had calculated that its shock wave would set off car alarms for miles in every direction, waking people up all over this side of town.

Of course, for that to work, they had to set it off in the next four minutes, before the long midnight fell.

"I'll take it from here," he said.

"No way. My toy."

She lifted it with both hands and carefully carried it out into the rain. Still limping, Rex followed her to one corner of the roof, where a cell phone repeater sat, a five-foot-tall antenna that faced out toward the suburbs. Dess balanced the bomb atop it. She'd explained to Rex that it had to go up high so the roof wouldn't muffle the shock wave before it could travel out across Bixby.

"Okay. Let me do this part," he said.

Dess looked at the bomb for a long moment, then nodded. "Fine by me. But if that fuse starts to burn too fast, run like hell." She paused. "You know what? Run like hell no matter what." She stepped back.

Rex took a deep breath and pulled out his lighter. His foot was throbbing dully now, keeping time with his quickening heartbeat.

He reached down and lit the long, dangling fuse. It sputtered to life and began crawling slowly upward toward the paint can.

"Okay, let's go," Dess said.

He watched the fire climb for a long moment to be sure the rain wouldn't put it out, finding himself fascinated by the shower of sparks that were carried off in a little trail by the wind.

"Rex!" she called from the other end of the roof. "Come on!"

Then thunder boomed overhead, and for a split second Rex thought the bomb had gone off. He stumbled backward onto his bad foot and, swearing at the pain, turned to limp after Dess. They huddled against the far side of the stairwell shed.

"Are you sure we'll be okay back here?" he asked.

"According to my research, Rex, bombs can kill you in two ways. Stray bits of flying stuff, which this shed is solid enough to protect us from, and the shock wave. My little baby isn't strong enough to crush our heads, but make sure you cover your ears unless you want to go deaf." To reinforce this point, she placed her own palms flat against her head.

Rex checked his watch. Only a little more than one minute left.

Then a terrible thought occurred to him. They'd used

the slowest-burning fuse they could find, three feet of it for the maximum amount of time. But kicking through the door had already put them behind schedule. . . .

"How long did you say that fuse would take?" he asked.

"About two and a half minutes."

"Good. There's just about a minute to go before midnight."

"Really?" She looked at Geostationary. "Sixty seconds? Crap, Rex, we took too long!"

"But the bomb will go off before midnight."

Dess shook her head. "Shock waves travel at the speed of sound, Rex, which is *slow*—almost eight seconds to go one mile. The shock waves have to get out to the suburbs, and then car alarms have to go off long enough to wake people up. That'll all take extra seconds we don't have!"

Rex took a breath, then peeked around the corner of the shed.

About a third of the fuse had burned. Dess was right; he'd lit it too late.

After a second of panicked deliberation Rex swore loudly, then hobbled back toward the bomb, pulling out his lighter.

"Rex, what the hell are you doing?"

"Dealing with it!"

He stumbled up to the bomb just as the fuse reached the halfway mark. Thrusting his lighter out, he aimed its flame at a point only a few inches from the top of the can. The lighter sputtered out once, a direct hit from a big raindrop extinguishing it.

"Come *on*," he muttered, flicking it back to life.

"Get back here!" Dess cried.

Finally the flame caught. A foot-long section of fuse dropped to the roof, lit at both ends now. The shorter piece attached to the can sparked and hissed in the rain, then steadied and began to crawl its last few inches.

Rex didn't stick around to watch. He spun on his left heel and ran back toward the stairwell shed, his hands already over his ears.

Just as he rounded the corner, his boot skidded on the rain-slick roof, sending him sprawling painfully to the tar. He crawled the last few feet and huddled beside Dess against the side of the shed, eyes closed and ears still covered.

"Rex, you moron!" Dess shouted. "You almost gave me a heart atta—"

The bomb exploded with a vast noise—a physical blow more than a sound, like a sack of potatoes hitting Rex in the chest. Even his closed eyelids felt the concussion, and a single, awesome flash of light shot through them.

For a moment all other noises disappeared, as if the bomb's roar had sucked sound itself from the rest of the world. But slowly the murmur of the rain returned, and Rex dared to open his eyes.

He glanced at his watch: twenty seconds to midnight.

Rising to their feet, he and Dess peered around the corner. Nothing was left of the paint can, of course, and the cell phone antenna was a blackened wreckage, bent and twisted metal sticking out in all directions.

"Whoa, cool!" Dess said.

Rex limped after her to the edge of the roof, training his darkling hearing on the city below. . . .

The sweet sound of car alarms rang out across Bixby, a hundred whoops and screams and buzzes all mingled in a great, untidy chorus. Rex imagined people turning over in their sleep, glaring accusingly at their alarm clocks and wondering what all the noise was about. Even the sleepiest would still be awake in ten seconds when midnight fell. Perfect timing.

Here in town they wouldn't feel the blue time strike right away, of course: the rip still had to travel to downtown from Jenks. But for those the bomb had awakened—and all the others already up watching late-night TV or reading in bed—that delay would only seem like an instant. Suddenly at midnight the world would turn blue, everything flickering with the red tinge of the rip, TVs, radios, and car alarms all silenced at once.

Those who went out to investigate would find the dark moon risen overhead, the last few seconds of rain settling to earth. And soon they would see the fireworks display downtown, the only movement visible on the frozen horizon.

Hopefully many of them would start to make their way downtown then, searching for some kind of explanation. By that time Jonathan would be flying among them, telling everyone to get to this building as fast as possible. And as long as the midnighters' defenses at Jenks had held off the main darkling force long enough, they'd have time to get here.

As he and Dess waited for the last few seconds of normal time to elapse, Rex took a deep breath. For the next twenty-five hours humanity would be a hunted species, dispossessed of all its clever toys and machines, toppled from the summit of the food chain. Those who understood that quickly enough would run and would live; those who refused to believe would perish.

In the darkling part of his mind, Rex thought for a moment that perhaps this wasn't such a bad thing. Without predators to cull the herd, humanity had spread across the earth unchecked, crowding the planet beyond its resources, prideful and arrogant.

Maybe one night a year of being hunted would do them good.

He shook his head then, shivering in the cold rain. Darkling notions had teased his mind all week, but he knew he couldn't let himself think that way—he had a job to do. The people of Bixby didn't deserve to be slaughtered just because the world was overpopulated. No one did.

He listened to the car alarms and forced himself to hope that everyone down there was listening too.

Just before midnight fell, a peal of thunder started to roll, sounding directly over their heads. And then the earth shuddered, the blue time descending over everything, freezing the rain into a million hovering diamonds around him, cutting off the thunder, the car alarms, everything.

"Can you see it from here?" Dess asked.

Rex looked toward Jenks, and his seer's vision picked out the slim red glimmer of the rip. It was starting to swell.

"Yep. The red time is on its way."

"Good going on that fuse." Dess breathed out a slow sigh. "Guess now we just sit back until the fireworks start."

As per the plan, the other three midnighters were out in Jenks. Soon they would light the first fireworks display to forestall the main force of darklings. Once that was going strong and before the darklings started to flow around them and into town, Jonathan would fly Jessica and Melissa back here, where the five of them would make their stand.

At least, that was the way it was supposed to work.

"Whoa, Rex! Look at that!"

Dess was pointing back toward downtown. Rex turned, following her gaze to the Mobil Building, the tallest in Bixby. The neon winged horse at its summit hunkered just under the low ceiling of heavy clouds, strangely illuminated against their dark bulk.

Rex's heart began to pound. "Oh my God."

"Have you ever seen anything like that?"

"No, but I've always wanted to. Melissa and I have been looking for one of those since . . . forever."

A frozen bolt of lightning reached down from the cloud, its motionless fire forking into a hundred tendrils that caressed the metal framework of the neon horse. In Rex's midnight vision the arrested lightning was mind-bogglingly complex, every inch of it divided into a million burning zigzags.

He remembered all the times he and Melissa had set off on their bicycles as kids, tunneling through the rain toward some frozen flicker of light on the horizon. They'd never made it before the secret hour finished, always having to plow back through the resumed storm empty-handed.

But they'd kept trying; one of the first fragments of lore Rex had discovered was all about frozen lightning, though it had never explained what you were supposed to do when you found it.

Still, there was something in his mind. . . .

He felt the fissures that Madeleine had made, the still-tender wounds of her attack, begin to throb. He saw it now, thrown whole into his mind by the sight of the frozen lightning. *This* was the last remnant of what the darklings had hidden from him.

Rex blinked. "Oh, no."

"What?"

He couldn't answer, a shudder passing through him. Suddenly he knew what tonight was really all about and what had to happen before the rip reached downtown and set the lightning free again. He knew the instructions that the Grayfoots had never received before their halfling had died.

And finally he understood the real reason why the darklings were so afraid of Jessica—why they had always wanted her dead.

He looked out at Jenks; the glowing red of the rip was still moving toward them. "We can stop this."

"What, Rex?"

"We need Jessica here."

"But they haven't even lit the—"

"Shhh." Rex dropped to his knees and let his head fall into his hands. In planning tonight he'd put Melissa on the front line for two reasons. She could guide Jessica and Jonathan safely there and back, through cops or darkling invasions as needed. And Rex had also known that if anything went wrong, she could taste his thoughts for miles across the secret hour, just as she had when they were eight years old, when she'd made her way across Bixby wearing only pajamas covered in pictures of cowgirls.

Now he needed her to hear him again.

"Rex?" Dess said softly.

He waved her silent and focused himself, setting all of his will to the task of summoning his oldest friend.

Cowgirl . . . he thought. *I need you now.*

27

IN THE RIP

Silence . . .

Midnight fell, extinguishing the mind noise of Jenks, turning the world blue and still and . . . *red.*

Here in the center of the rip everything began to glimmer purple—red and blue mixing together, time arrested, yet . . . not. The rain pattered down for a few more seconds, then petered out; the rip hadn't expanded enough to include the heavy clouds above their heads. Melissa wondered if when it reached them, the rain would start again.

Weather in the secret hour. Just when I thought I'd seen everything.

"Where is she?" Jessica asked.

Melissa closed her eyes, trying to ignore the flame-bringer's coppery, panicked taste. She sent her mind across the rip, feeling it growing, stretching in the opposite directions toward downtown and the mountains. It was moving slowly now, but she could already feel its speed increasing.

No little sisters in it, though.

"Sorry, Jess. I can't feel her."

"Why not?"

"Your sister's not inside the rip. Not yet, anyway. She must still be frozen, so I can't taste her mind."

"But Cassie's house is right there!" Jessica pointed down at the double-wide at the edge of the tracks. The red-tinged boundary had already swallowed it.

"Yep. And I can taste her grandma in there, still sleeping," Melissa said. "But nobody else is home."

Jessica's face twisted into an expression of fury, her mind all fiery peppers and burned toast.

"That little creep snuck out!" she cried.

Melissa raised an eyebrow, suddenly relieved she didn't have an older sister of her own. Madeleine's interfering had included making sure that none of her pet midnighters in Bixby had siblings—and this was why.

"Calm down, Jess," Jonathan said. "She can't be too far away. Once the rip reaches her, we'll deal with it."

Jessica looked at Melissa. "And you're sure you'll recognize her mind?"

"I know Cassie's taste. They'll be together, won't they?"

"What if they aren't?"

Melissa sighed. "I have an idea what your sister tastes like, okay? I've been to your house at midnight."

Jessica stared back, her fury twisting into new shapes as she realized what Melissa was admitting. "Damn you!" she said, and turned and stalked away.

"I never touched the shrimp," Melissa said to Flyboy. "Just the parents."

He offered a shrug, then went to calm the flame-bringer down.

Melissa let out another sigh, feeling weighed down by her long, rain-soaked dress. She and Rex should have admitted what they'd done to Jessica's parents a long time ago. They always figured that it would come up eventually and at a time like this, when everyone needed to stay calm.

They had the fireworks already in place, rockets stuck into the gravel, flares and sparklers divided into separate boxes, all of it covered with a tarp from Jonathan's trunk. Melissa decided to make herself useful while the other two were stressing. She flicked the tarp to knock the rainwater off, then pulled it from the fireworks.

The arsenal looked formidable: candles and hurricane lamps so that Jessica didn't have to light every fuse herself, Roman candles and rockets to bombard the main force of darklings when they arrived, and highway flares that would last for hours, giving the residents of Jenks a fighting chance after the three of them had retreated downtown.

How long now?

Melissa closed her eyes again and swept through the expanding space of the rip. More humans were inside it now, startled by the sudden silence of their TVs and the strange shimmery light that had come over everything.

It was really happening; the blue time was swallowing everyone.

Then she felt a far-off twinge, a familiar mind cutting through the confused babble of normal humans and the mutterings of awakening slithers.

Cowgirl . . .

Rex was calling.

She smiled at first, but as she focused on the distant beacon of thought, Melissa tasted the emotions animating his cry. He was anxious, begging for her to respond, needing something. . . .

"Oh, crap," she said.

"What?" Jessica called. "Is she okay?"

Melissa shook her head. "Still no Beth. It's Rex. He needs us to get downtown."

Jonathan frowned. "Sure, but not until we—"

"It feels like he needs us *now*. Something's gone wrong!"

"Forget it," Jessica hissed.

"Listen, just because your sister—"

"No way, Melissa," Flyboy said. "We can't leave Jenks undefended just because you've got a *feeling*. They're right in the path of the invasion here. We have to light these things before we head into Bixby."

"So let's light them," she said. "He needs us!"

"Not until I find Beth." Jessica grasped Jonathan's arm with a white-knuckled grip.

Melissa realized that arguing wouldn't get her anywhere. The taste of the flame-bringer's mind was set. "Okay," she said. "You and I can stay here until I taste your little sister. Then I'll go get her while you light up the fireworks."

Jessica crossed her arms. "We'll both go get her."

"Whatever. But Flyboy, you have to head downtown now. You can get there in five minutes if you go alone."

"But why?" Jonathan asked.

"Because Rex needs us!" Melissa shook her head. "I don't know exactly why; he's too far away for me to taste his mind that clearly. Just go and see what he needs."

Jonathan looked at Jessica, and Melissa tasted the sickly sweet coupleness passing between them. "I'm not leaving you," he said.

Jessica frowned, and Melissa tasted a twinge of her guilt that their plans were revolving around her as usual. "But maybe Rex—"

"We said we'd stick together tonight!" he cried.

Melissa groaned inwardly, wondering how long this discussion was going to last.

Jessica took his hand. "Listen, Jonathan. You promised me you'd do what Rex said, remember?"

"Yeah, but not—"

"Just go. I'll be fine. I'm the flame-bringer."

For a moment Melissa felt the alternatives evenly balanced within Jonathan, like a coin on its edge. But then Jessica squeezed his hand, her expression set and unblinking, and he nodded.

"Okay. I'll be back in ten minutes."

He kissed her, and the electric taste of their contact swept through Melissa's mind. And then he was gone, leaping out of the rip and over the trees, zooming toward downtown.

Jessica turned to her and said coldly, "Is Beth inside yet?"

"Listen, Jess, about your parents . . ."

"I don't care. Just look for my sister, *please*."

Melissa nodded, tipping back her head to taste the growing area within the rip. She tried to ignore the stirrings deep in the desert, the salty taste of anticipation, of ancient hungers ready to be sated at last.

So far, the oldest minds were still hiding in their mountain lairs. They had waited for thousands of years for this night; they could delay another few minutes until they were sure everything was working. Then they would charge toward Bixby, consuming every human in their way, a linear feast.

Melissa tasted something familiar at the edge of the rip— the quiet, self-assured thoughts of Cassie Flinders. She was surprised at how the world had suddenly changed but unafraid. She'd been inside the rip once before, after all.

A moment later Melissa tasted the other mind beside Cassie, a frightened, mewling, panic-stricken ball of little sister.

"Got her."

"Where?"

Melissa turned her head, sensing the direction. "*Of course.* The cave where Rex found Cassie. They snuck out to go back there, figuring it was a magic spot or something." Melissa shook her head. "Funny. I really thought we'd fixed her memories."

"She must have drawn a picture of it," Jessica said.

Melissa nodded slowly, remembering the drawings all

over Cassie's walls. She hadn't thought to check for that. "The little sneak. Okay, let's go."

"No. Just me. I remember the way."

Melissa frowned. "Listen, I know you don't like me, but I can—"

"It's not that." Jessica glanced at the row of houses by the railroad; more of them had been swallowed by the expanding rip. "They need you here."

"But what am I supposed to do without you?"

"Light the fireworks when the darklings come. There are other people in Jenks who need protection. Listen, Melissa, I know I'm being selfish. I shouldn't only be thinking about my sister. So you stay here."

"But I can't even . . . Oh, right."

Jessica had taken out a lighter and thrust it into one of the hurricane lamps. She adjusted the wick until it was burning bright, then handed Melissa a sparkler.

"Let's just make sure this really works," she said.

Melissa nodded and thrust the sparkler into the flame of the lamp. It burst to life, shooting out a blinding shower.

"Damn, that's bright!" Melissa said, dropping it to the wet gravel and stamping on it until it sputtered out. A swarm of spots remained brutally burned into her vision, but she founded herself smiling.

Maybe Samhain really *was* a holiday if Melissa was going to do some flame-bringing of her own. "Okay, get moving! I'll be fine here."

Jessica nodded, cramming highway flares into her jacket pocket. She skidded down the embankment and thrashed her way into the trees. Melissa closed her eyes, following in her mind as Jessica found the path that Cassie, and then Rex, had taken three weeks before.

She let her mind drift back to the cave. Cassie was getting nervous now, and Beth was a basket case. Their flashlights had extinguished when the blue time had fallen, and though most slithers had left this area permanently after the flame-bringer's last visit, Cassie still imagined she heard snakes in the darkness. They were making their way slowly out of the cave.

Which was a bad idea. There were young darklings not too far away, probing the edges of the rip, wondering if they could take a few quick prey before their elders arrived in force. Melissa just hoped that the scent of the flame-bringer would keep any midnight creatures away from Cassie and Beth.

She turned her focus back toward the city, where Rex's mind still tugged at her. He was growing more anxious as the rip built up speed, heading toward him down the Bixby-bound railroad line. It was moving at running speed now.

Then it became a little clearer: he needed help to get there before the rip arrived.

Don't worry, Loverboy, she called. *Jonathan's coming.*

Opening her eyes, Melissa looked down at the trailer houses along the railroad right-of-way. Someone had wandered out of the house next to Cassie's, an old man wearing only a T-shirt and undershorts. He was looking around wide-eyed at the blue-red world, tasting of fear and wonderment.

"You ain't seen nothing yet," she murmured.

Then she twitched, a taste reaching her from the deep desert again.

They were coming . . . daring to issue from the mountains now. They flew slower than their offspring, their muscles creaking with age, with millennia of disuse. But their ancient hunger drew them toward Bixby, with its hated spires of metal and glass.

Finally we hunt again.

Melissa shivered, then something reached her from in the middle distance—a human mind awakening in the desert, at the farthest end of the rip from Bixby. Someone was *camping* out there, she realized with horror, out with the spiders and the rattlesnakes. And tonight with much worse things . . .

They were already waiting for him, a trio of young darklings.

Melissa felt it all, the tastes surging into her mouth like stomach acid. They tore into his tent the moment the rip arrived, only seconds after the earth's shudder had pulled him out of his slumber. He fought back against them, swinging a flashlight whose stainless steel case brought a howl of pain from the youngest darkling. But it wouldn't light, and it had no thirteen-letter name, and soon their claws had cut across his face, then his chest, then finally found his throat.

And then the darklings were *eating*, slaking their thirst with the man's still-warm juices, reveling in his last gasps, fighting over scraps . . .

Melissa felt bile rising in her throat, and her brain spun with the darklings' killing frenzy. She struck her own head with her hands, trying to drive the images out, and stumbled half blind across the tracks, dizzy and close to vomiting, her mind caught in the whirlwind of hunger and death.

Then pain shot through her outstretched hand, a sharp sensation of burning, and she heard glass breaking.

She wrenched her eyes open, tried to tear her mind back into her own body.

Fire was everywhere, its white light blinding in the secret hour. She'd overturned the hurricane lamp, and it had shattered, spilling its oil across the fireworks. Through the dazzling flames Melissa saw fuses beginning to sparkle.

It was too soon; the darklings weren't here yet. She had to put the fire out before the rockets and flares and sparklers began to explode, wasting all their ammunition.

Melissa threw herself down on the gravel, rolling across the flaming oil, trying to stifle the flames. Her long black dress was still soaked, wet from trudging through the falling rain from Jonathan's car. Waterlogged enough to protect her body. But her hands burned, and she inhaled the bitter smell of her own hair igniting, its damp, sizzling strands shooting across the corners of her vision. A rocket shot into space beside her, climbing until the upward edge of the rip silenced it.

Melissa rolled back and forth, spreading out her dress as far as she could. She smelled its singed cotton, felt the muffled hiss of a bottle rocket trapped under her, its detonation like a quick jab to her ribs.

When she opened her eyes a moment later, they stung with smoke, but she saw that the fire was mostly smothered. The last flaming tendrils of oil spread across the wet gravel, sputtering out.

Melissa sighed with relief. Her hands and face were blistered, her hair felt like a total disaster, and she smelled like a wet dog that had been set on fire. But she'd saved the cache of fireworks. Jenks wouldn't die because of her mistake.

A second later she frowned, realizing her new problem.

The hurricane lamp was destroyed, her only fire extinguished, and Jessica was off chasing her little sister. Until the flame-bringer returned, Melissa was defenseless.

She sent out her mind and soon found a coppery taste on the midnight landscape—the familiar, metallic flavor of flame-bringer. Jessica was still moving, thrashing through the rain-heavy trees on her way to the cave. She hadn't reached her little sister yet.

Off to the east Jonathan was just now closing in on Rex, climbing toward the last-stand building in leaps and bounds.

And from the deep desert darklings were coming, old ones.

Lots of them.

"Come on, Jessica and Jonathan," Melissa said, rising to her feet. "Hurry the hell up!"

28

FLYBOY, FLY

"Where are they!" Rex shouted.

"Who?"

"Jessica! Melissa!"

Jonathan spread his hands. "They're still back in Jenks."

Rex let out a half-animal howl, his hands twisting into claws. Dess looked up from where she knelt inside her thirteen-sided arrangement of fireworks and shrugged. "He wanted you to bring Jessica," she said.

"Yeah, I'm getting that."

Jonathan was soaked. Barreling through the suspended rain at seventy miles an hour had been like swimming in his clothes. If the secret hour wasn't so warm, he probably would have died of exposure by now.

And some thanks I get.

"Why didn't you bring them?" Rex cried.

"Listen, Melissa didn't know exactly what you wanted, so she said I should come and see." He coughed into a fist;

he'd inhaled a lot of water on the way here. "Plus Jessica had to sort of look for her, um, sister."

"Look for her *what*?" Dess said.

"We need her here!" Rex hissed.

"Okay. Should I go back and get her?"

"*Yes*. But I'll come with you." Rex made his way across the roof toward Jonathan, limping, his teeth clenched with pain.

"Are you okay?" Rex didn't answer, and Jonathan held out his hand. "Are you sure you can fly?"

Rex shot him a look, and for a moment Jonathan thought he was going to get all scary-faced.

"Don't worry about me."

"Hey, Rex," Dess called. "Sorry to do the math, but if there's four of you out there, how are you all going to get back?"

Jonathan nodded. As far as he knew, he could only fly with two midnighters in tow—one holding each hand. With four of them out in Jenks, someone would have to stay behind.

"If we can get Jessica back here in time, it won't matter."

"What won't matter?" Jonathan asked.

Rex took his hand in a deathlike grip. "I'll explain on the way."

He looked into Rex's eyes; the exhaustion and madness had only gotten worse in the last week. What if the guy had snapped, and this was all a wild-goose chase? What if Rex decided he was a winged darkling in mid-flight and let go of Jonathan's hand?

What if he really *was* a darkling?

Jonathan paused, but then remembered his promise to Jessica and decided to follow the seer's orders, no matter how crazy he seemed.

"Fly," Rex said, his voice cold.

"Okay. But I have to warn you, you're going to get really wet."

They jumped from the building's edge, cutting two tunnels through the suspended rain, building speed as they fell. Water spattered against Jonathan's face, forcing his eyes closed to slits. Flying through frozen rain was like standing under a shower and staring straight up into the faucet.

Before the other buildings rose up around them, Jonathan caught a glimmer of red in the distance—the rip was moving faster now.

"Can we make it?" Rex shouted, covering his mouth with his free hand to keep the water out. "All the way to Jenks and back before the rip gets here?"

"I don't know. Normally it would only take ten minutes or so. But this damn rain—" He broke off, coughing up water from his lungs.

Rex grunted as they hit the next roof over, and as they pushed off again, his fingernails dug into Jonathan's flesh, his face twisting with pain.

"Ow, Rex!" The pressure eased. "Why do you need her back here anyway?"

"It's complicated."

Jonathan shot Rex a sidelong glance. He should have

known that the promised explanation wouldn't be forthcoming.

He sighed. No point in arguing now. How did Dess always put it? *Seer knows best.*

"Ten minutes? That's cutting it close." Rex winced as they hit the next roof, taking two long strides across its rain-slick surface, then leaping into the air again. "Dess says the rip will reach downtown in less than twenty."

"Yeah, and that's assuming we find Jessica right away," Jonathan said. "I mean, she might still be out looking for her sister."

"Don't worry, I can find her," Rex said.

"Huh?"

The seer didn't answer as the outskirts of downtown rose up around them. They had landed at street level finally and angled onto the highway. Jonathan imagined the cars around them springing to life again in twenty minutes, all weaving to a stop, people struggling to control them with brute strength, their power steering and brakes suddenly heavy as lead.

Rex made a strangled noise with every bound.

When they reached a light patch in the frozen storm, Jonathan spoke up again. "Listen, Rex. Why don't you let me go on alone? You could still make it back there in time. You're killing yourself on that sprained ankle."

"It's broken, actually."

"What the hell?" Jonathan looked down at Rex's right cowboy boot. It was turned wrong somehow. The next time they landed, he watched Rex hold the foot up off the ground, taking all his weight on his other side.

"You have to stop, Rex. I'll take you back to Dess first. You're going to tear your foot apart!"

"No. You need me to track Jessica."

"*Track* her?"

"She smells like prey to me now. You all do."

Their next bound took them over a frozen pickup truck piled high with sharp, deadly scrap metal, giving Jonathan a moment to think before he answered.

Rex had really lost it; he was certain now. For once his plan had actually made sense, yet the seer seemed determined to screw everything up.

Except for the parts that Beth has already *managed to screw up.*

He let out a sigh through clenched teeth, wishing he hadn't promised Jessica that he'd do what Rex said. Of course, following orders didn't mean he couldn't try to make sense of them. "So, wait. *Why* do you need Jess downtown?"

"Lightning," Rex said in a strangled voice, then cried out as the ground rose up and struck them again.

He refused to say another word the rest of the way.

29

BETH

"Beth!" Jessica shouted for the hundredth time. "Where *are* you?"

The cave had to be around here somewhere, she was positive. But three weeks ago Jessica and Jonathan had flown here, not walked. Somehow the path had disappeared right under her feet, fading out into scrub and tree roots. Everything looked weird and unfamiliar here in the rip, the edges of the leaves glinting with purple and crimson fire.

She checked her watch. It had been almost ten minutes since she'd left Melissa behind. Soon the younger darklings would be closing in.

She pulled out her flashlight and whispered its new name: *Foolhardiness.*

The beam surged through the forest, driving away the violet shimmer of the rip. Jessica heard movement ahead, a slither—or something larger—fleeing before the white light.

"Beth!" she cried. "Where are you?"

Finally an answer came. Not to her ears, but in words that sounded distantly in her mind.

To your right, fast. They need you.

Melissa. The mindcaster's taste washed across Jessica's tongue—a strange sensation, given that she'd never thought of Melissa as having a taste before. But there it was, bitter and caustic, like chewing some pill you were supposed to swallow.

Jessica began to run, veering right until a high-pitched scream reached her through the trees. She barreled toward the sound, ignoring the branches whipping at her face and clothes. The rip had cleared the suspended raindrops from the air, but the trees were still heavy with water—dumping gallons on her as she crashed through them.

Another scream came from dead ahead. Close.

She burst out into the familiar clearing, saw the finger of stone thrusting into the air, then stumbled to a halt, eyes wide. A *thing* was wrapped around the cave entrance, like a great jellyfish attached to its prey, its tendrils sinking into the rock itself. It had no head that Jessica could see, just a tangled knot of stringy appendages, all matted together like hair caught in a bathtub drain.

A small human figure stood just inside the mouth of the cave, pale and shaking, the creature's tendrils wound around her arms and legs.

Jessica ran toward it, playing Foolhardiness's white light across the creature.

But its tendrils didn't burst into flame; instead they sizzled angrily with blue fire, coiling tighter.

Rex had warned them that they might see new things tonight, things born well before midnight had been created, so old that mere white light wouldn't be enough to slay them.

In which case, he had said, there was always fire.

Jessica pulled a highway flare from her pocket and, in a move she'd practiced all week, flicked its top off, banging the two pieces against each other in a glancing blow.

"Ventriloquism," she said, and the flare burst to life, its radiance white-hot and blinding.

In its radiance she saw one of the thing's legs reaching for her, snaking across the ground. She knelt, thrusting the flare at it. The tendril sizzled, a low flame racing across it, bringing up a gagging smell of burned hair and dust.

It retreated, slithering away from her, but another reached through the air.

"Haven't had enough?" Jessica said, fending it off. The arm darted around her, just outside the reach of the hissing flame. In the corner of her eye she saw another arm stretching its way from the creature.

She swallowed. Since she'd become the flame-bringer, the darklings had been so afraid of her. But apparently these old ones didn't cut and run.

This was their night, after all.

Jessica lunged forward, swinging the flare into the closest tendril. A gout of flame exploded, bringing a low, mournful scream and another rush of the burned-hair smell.

She looked around for the other arm. . . .

At that moment something wrapped itself around her

leg, soft and feathery but bitter cold. The chill climbed through her, shooting up her spine, bringing with it a tidal wave of emotion: old fears and nightmares rose in her, forgotten terrors dredged up to the surface of her mind.

Suddenly Jessica felt lost, filled with the certainty that she was failing out of school, was leaving her old friends forever, going to a place where reality was warped and strange. The panic of finding a new classroom after the tardy bell had rung paralyzed her, cold as the stares of a thousand unfriendly strangers.

Everyone in Bixby hated her, she suddenly knew.

Open your hand, Jess, a distant voice implored.

She obeyed unthinkingly, hoping to please the voice in her head, her fingers releasing the flare. Her only weapon fell from her grasp.

Then, like a phone line going dead, the cold disappeared, all her terrors vanishing in the space of a heartbeat. And again the screaming sound filled the air, slow and piercing and mournful, like the Bixby firehouse's noon siren.

Jessica looked down; the flare's burning end had cut the tendril as it had fallen, releasing her from the creature's spell.

"Thanks, Melissa," she whispered, kneeling to retrieve the flare. She held it in front of herself, charging toward the thing wrapped around the mouth of the cave.

Tendrils began to writhe as she approached, slithering from the arms and legs of the small, pale figure in the cave's entrance, abandoning their grasp of the stone spire. A smaller set of extremities whirled around the thing's

matted center like the blades of a helicopter, hissing with
the sound of escaping steam. It rose slowly into the air.

Jessica hurled the flare directly at the creature and in
the same motion reached into her pocket for another. As
she worked to light it, the darkling thing burst into
flame above her, the smell of dead rat and rotten eggs
filling the air. It unleashed its mournful howl again, still
rising, then flying across the sky. The flame seemed to
be riding the creature, somehow unable to consume it. And
then the burning mass passed over the horizon of trees.

Jessica held the new flare out, lighting the mouth of the
cave. The small figure had fallen to the ground and lay
huddled and sobbing. Another pale face appeared out of
the darkness.

"Beth?" she said, squinting through the smoke of the
flare.

"It's me—Cassie." The girl took another step into the
light, then knelt next to the fallen figure, turning her face up.

It was Beth, so pale she was almost unrecognizable.

Jessica dropped the flare and fell to her knees. "Beth!"

For a moment the only answer was a wild fluttering of
eyelids. Then Beth sucked in a sudden, sharp breath, and
her eyes opened.

"Jess?" she answered.

"I'm here. Are you all right?"

"Yeah. Sure. What a nightmare. Was I screaming or
just . . . ?" Beth's eyes opened wider as she took in Cassie,
the burning flare, the red-tinged blue time all around them.
"What the hell, Jess?"

"What are you *doing* out here?" Jessica cried.

Cassie's expression was dazed, but she answered calmly. "We snuck out tonight. We figured something was going on out here at midnight."

"You guys were right about that."

"What was that thing?" Cassie asked.

"What thing . . . ?" Beth said weakly.

"I have no idea. I mean, it was a darkling, but not the usual kind."

"A darkling?"

Jessica shook her head. "I'll explain later. Beth, can you stand up?"

Beth rose slowly to her feet. The highway flare cast wildly jittering light into the cave behind them, and both the girls' faces looked ghostly in its harsh shadows.

"I remember the flashlight conking out," Beth said, then looked at Jessica. "Why are you here? What's going on?" Her voice had regained some strength.

"*Later*, Beth. Can't you see we have to go?"

"Go where? I mean, what is all this? Is *this* what you sneak out to do every night?"

"Beth!" Jessica reached back and grabbed her sister's hand. "I'll tell you later! Come on!"

"But you won't!" Beth planted her feet, not letting Jessica take another step. "You never tell me anything!"

Jessica groaned. Her little sister apparently didn't remember the creature that had taken hold of her; she didn't realize how close she'd come to being lunch meat. Even Cassie had folded her arms across her chest.

Part of her wanted to scream, but another part wanted nothing more than to stop in her tracks and tell Beth everything. Finally no secrets between them.

Jessica put her hands on her sister's shoulders. "Okay. *This* is what I couldn't tell you about. This is what's weird about Bixby. It changes at midnight, becomes . . . something terrible. And we have to deal with it, me and my friends."

Beth's eyes were still glazed. "It's like some kind of nightmare. . . ."

"Yeah, except that it's real." Jessica shook her head. "Especially right now. You picked the wrong night to spy on me."

"Spy on you? I was *worried* about you, Jess. You were keeping secrets and lying all the time. . . ."

"I'm sorry about that," Jessica cried. "I really am. But can't you see why now? You wouldn't have believed me anyway!"

Beth looked around at the purple light of the world, the silenced wind and rain, and nodded. "Yeah. You got that right."

"I never wanted to lie to you, Beth. But I just didn't have a way to tell you. And we have to go right now. Just come with me and I'll tell you everything. I promise I'll *never* lie to you again. Just trust me, please?"

Beth looked at her, and Jessica wondered if she was really listening or whether her suspicions were still whirring away, looking for something to doubt, to scorn or mock. Maybe everything was too broken between them.

But then, slowly, Beth nodded. "Okay. I trust you."

Jessica smiled, relief washing through her. "Truth later? But do what I say now? No matter how weird it is?"

"Sure. Truth later. But can we get out of here? This place smells funny."

"No problem."

Jessica led them out of the cave, Foolhardiness in one hand, the hissing flare in the other. As they crossed the clearing, her eyes searched for the path back to the railroad embankment.

"Hey, can I ask a question?" Cassie said.

Jessica turned. "Do you *have* to?"

"Kind of." Cassie pointed into the air. "What's that?"

Jessica spun around, Foolhardiness sweeping across the sky. Its beam found Jonathan and Rex hurtling down toward them, hands across their eyes against its light. She flicked it off.

Rex landed sloppily, skidding to a stop, but Jonathan bounded from the edge of the clearing, soaring to where they stood. He corkscrewed to a halt and wrapped Jessica in his arms, his midnight gravity flooding into her along with the sudden feeling that she might cry with relief.

He pulled back to look at her. "Are you okay?"

"Yeah."

He turned. "Hey, Beth. How's it going?"

"Uh, hi, Jonathan," Beth said, her voice small again.

Jessica took both his hands. "I think they're okay, but there are some weird-ass darklings out tonight."

"No kidding. But Jess, you and I have to go now. We have to get back downtown."

"Why? Melissa hasn't even set off the first round yet."

Rex hobbled up to them, wincing with every step. "We can stop all this, Jessica," he panted. "Right now, save everyone."

"What? How?"

"There's a bolt of lightning caught by midnight. It's striking the Pegasus sign over the old Mobil Building. You need to get there before the rip does."

"And do what?"

"Put your hand into the lightning."

"*Do what now?*"

Rex raised his hands in surrender. "I can't explain how I know this. It's something I got from the darklings, combined with an old piece of lore. But you can force the rip closed again, I'm certain of it. That's why the darklings were so afraid of you. All along *tonight* is what they feared."

Jessica blinked. "But what about my sister and Cassie?"

"I'll take care of them. Just give me that." He took the hissing flare. "Melissa needs it. The fire you left her got put out."

"But there's darklings everywhere!"

"I know." His voice broke. "They're closing in on her now."

Jessica grabbed Jonathan's hand. "We can fly there—"

He waved her silent. "You have to go downtown *now*. There's no time to waste."

She stared at Rex. He didn't look capable of walking another step, much less fighting off any darklings. But his pleading expression silenced any argument.

"*Now*, Jess!"

In the next split second Jessica realized that she was here again—not knowing what to do, having to believe what the others told her. From the moment she'd set foot in Bixby, the rules of reality seemed to shift every week, as if the blue time were one big practical joke the universe had decided to play on Jessica Day. As usual, there was never time for a full explanation, never time to think anything through.

She could only trust that Rex, whatever the darklings had done to him, was still human enough to want to do the right thing. She had to believe that even though Bixby had been deceived and manipulated for thousands of years, this orphaned generation of midnighters was different. Most of all, she had to remember that Rex Greene would never leave Melissa in danger for an extra second unless thousands of lives were at stake.

"All right." She turned to Beth. "Follow Rex, okay? Just do what he says. He'll keep you safe." Jessica smiled. "Trust me."

Beth sputtered wordlessly for a moment, then finally blurted, "Your boyfriend can *fly*?"

Jessica smiled. "Yeah, actually, he can."

She turned to Jonathan, extending her hand. "Okay, let's go."

30

BONFIRE

"Come *on*!" Rex shouted.

He took another painful step, one gloved hand clenched around a tree branch, pulling himself along to reduce the weight on his injured foot. Even so, a strangled cry escaped through his teeth—this was much worse than the flight here. Without Jonathan's midnight gravity moving through him, Rex felt every ounce of his tall frame. The hissing flare in his free hand brushed against a wet branch, scattering blinding white sparks across his vision.

"You're Rex, right?" Cassie said from behind him. He didn't answer, but she went on. "I'm starting to remember now."

"He looks just like you drew him," Beth whispered.

"You're the one who saved me, right?" Cassie asked. "A few weeks ago?"

"I'm the one who's saving you *now*! Can we focus on that?" The darkling hiss in his voice silenced her and brought a fresh burst of fear from Beth. He tried to concentrate on the painful task of walking, not the defenseless scent of the two girls behind him.

Melissa . . . he called.

Again there was no response. Rex forced despair from his mind, hoping she was simply too busy fighting to answer. The last message he'd received from her had shown the hurricane lamp breaking, its flames extinguished, and the acid taste of darklings on their way.

He moved faster through the trees, ignoring the pain. The narrow trail before them danced in the jittering white light, and he recognized a low, twisted mesquite tree. Another hundred yards and they would reach the railroad tracks, only a few minutes away from Melissa and the cache of fireworks.

A hunting cry cut through the trees, and the flutter of leathery wings came from all directions. Rex paused, lifting the flare and shielding his eyes from its glare. Slithers darted in the corners of his vision, and larger shapes shifted among the crooked lines of branches, wary of the white light sputtering in his hand.

Rex could smell their hunger, finally unleashed after millennia, and knew that tonight there would be no respect among predators, no safety for him. This was their night at last—Samhain.

"What *was* that?" Cassie said.

"Monsters." Rex pulled Animalization from his belt, thrusting its hilt into her hand. Of all the metal Dess had carefully prepared, it was the only weapon he'd brought on the frantic flight with Jonathan. Of course, there were plenty of weapons at the railroad tracks, if they could only get there.

"You remember this?"

She stared down at the knife, eyes wide, head nodding slowly.

"It's called Animalization." He winced as the tridec left his lips. "Say it."

As Cassie carefully sounded out the syllables, Rex heard something flying through the trees toward them. Something bigger than a slither.

"Duck!" he cried, raising the flare as he crouched.

A roar came through the forest like a sudden storm, bringing the overwhelming smell of predator. A huge winged creature burst into view, tearing at the treetops with four outstretched arms. It uttered a shriek at the spitting white light of the flare, then passed overhead, trailing the sound of breaking branches like snapping bones.

A sudden downpour descended in its wake, sheets of water dislodged from the rain-soaked trees by the creature. A vortex of wet leaves and branches swirled around the three of them, and the flare sputtered in Rex's gloved hand, its flame almost smothered by the deluge. Just in time he dropped to his knees and sheltered the burning weapon under himself, protecting its flame from the watery onslaught.

At that moment the air was full of slithers streaking past, their timing perfect to take advantage of the flare's concealment. One stung Rex in the middle of his back, sending a bolt of ice down his spine. A burst of blue sparks shot into the night from Animalization in Cassie's upraised hands, and he heard Beth cry out.

Rex lifted the flare again, exposing it to the dwindling tempest. A slither was caught among its white sparks and burst into flame in midair, disintegrating like a shovelful of embers flung through the trees. The others split into a panicked mass and whirled off into the forest trailing a chorus of screams.

But as the torrent of dislodged water subsided, the flare sputtered weakly, barely staying lit. It burned unevenly now, half extinguished by the remains of wet leaves wrapped around it.

Rex heard the many-armed darkling circling, ready to come at them again. He saw Beth staring dumbfounded at a purple welt on her hand. "You two okay?"

"It bit me!" Beth shouted angrily.

"They're afraid of fire?" Cassie asked.

He nodded, gesturing with the flare. "They're trying to put this out."

"Why didn't you say so?" She started scrabbling among the leaves. "We can start a fire."

"It's too wet!"

"Not under here." She pushed aside handfuls of glistening damp leaves. "My grandma says you can always find dry leaves at the bottom of a pile. And they're better for burning 'cause they're rotten."

Rex raised his eyebrows. In the jittering white light the exposed patch of leaves did look dry. The flare still sizzled wetly in his hand, as if it might not withstand another pass by the creature. He reached down to thrust its blinding tongue into the pile. Flames curled the leaves' edges, and a rich smell like an autumn burn-off struck his nose.

"Bonfires," he said, remembering his images of ancient Samhains.

"Not exactly a bonfire yet." Cassie cleared more leaves, adding to the smoking pile.

"It's coming back!" Beth said. The darkling was closing in again, the sound of snapping branches building as it neared them.

This time, Rex realized, its attack would be less effective. The beast had already shaken most of the water from the rain-soaked leaves. They could hold out here indefinitely, or as long as they could feed their little bonfire. If they moved from this spot, though, the creature could douse them with fresh tree-loads of water.

But they had to reach Melissa and the fireworks, not sit here huddled around a shred of safety.

Rex felt his teeth bare, smelling the arrogance of the young and clever darkling. It thought he could be frightened into immobility, like some cornered prey.

It was wrong.

"Take this!" he cried, handing the flare to Beth. "Keep it covered!"

He snatched the knife back from Cassie, readying himself to spring, feeling the hunting frenzy rising up in him. The darkling approached again, tree branches rocking and shaking free more water, and Rex leapt into the air toward its black silhouette with a scream in his throat, hardly feeling his injured ankle. He thrust the knife out before him, plunging the steel blade into the creature's flesh.

Blue sparks spat from the wound back into his face, and the creature's arms wrapped around him, flailing to claw at his back and legs. Rex felt himself carried along on a few powerful strokes of its wings—away from the two girls. He howled, twisting the knife as hard as he could. The beast let out a cry, its grasp loosening. Rex kicked at it with his good foot . . .

And then he was tumbling from its arms, crashing through branches and undergrowth, slashing blindly at the slithers shooting past. He landed heavily on a bare patch of ground, his breath knocked out of him as if the earth were a huge fist. He lay there for a moment, staring at the blue fire coursing through the knife. Somehow he'd held on to it.

But the forest was alive with sounds: big things pushing through the branches, slithers on the wing. Coming for him.

Rex rose painfully, his bruised ribs creaking, the slither bite shooting pain down his spine. A shape shot toward him out of the forest, and he brought the knife up to slice into a wing. The slither kept flapping, jerking away like a broken kite into the trees.

In the distance he saw a flicker of red. Cassie was getting her bonfire going. But it seemed incredibly far away.

Rex . . . ?

"Melissa!" he cried aloud, sensing that she was nearby. Whirling around to look for her, he realized that his brief flight with the beast had taken him closer to the railroad tracks.

"Rex!" a cry answered.

Following the sound, he saw a sheet of blue sparks through the branches and charged toward it. He was unprotected by the flare now, and the looming shapes in the trees were moving toward him. His ankle throbbed with every step, and the metal on his boots sparked as crawling slithers struck at his legs. But Melissa was so close.

The blue sparks glowed through the trees again, revealing the silhouette of a great cat raised up on his haunches. The creature was young and eager for a kill, full of the fervor of Samhain. Then Rex spotted a human form just past the darkling: Melissa tossing up handfuls of metal, hurling the bolts and screws that Dess had created into the cat's face, driving it wild with fury. It let out a cry, swiping a claw at the tiny missiles.

Then it dropped into a crouch, ready to launch itself at her.

Rex felt his body changing, transforming more than it ever had before, the full fury of the beast inside him unleashed at last. Suddenly his injured foot seemed beside the point, the great cat's size and strength meaningless— nothing mattered but saving Melissa.

He found himself crashing through the trees with a hunting scream, taking a wild leap onto the back of the darkling. He plunged Animalization into its shoulder, and the creature let out a howl. Its coiled muscles exploded under Rex, a jump that carried both him and the beast straight up into the air.

It twisted beneath him, trying to bring its powerful

claws around. But Rex hung on with a wild, inhuman strength, his metal-encircled boots sparking against its flanks. He and the darkling spun around each other in midair like some bizarre rodeo ride.

The taste of Melissa entered his mind . . .

Get off it, Rex!

It made no sense, letting the beast free to shred him, but this was *Melissa*, and his human half obeyed the frantic demand without thinking. He pushed away with all his strength, leaving the knife embedded in the darkling, trying to shield his face from its flailing claws.

Rex fell hard on the damp ground, battered ribs letting out a *crack*, his ankle screaming with the pain he'd ignored. The beast inside him had faded a little. It had wanted to fight to the death, but he'd listened to Melissa instead. . . .

He struggled to his feet with empty hands spread wide, defenseless.

The darkling lay a few yards away, its paws twitching like a dreaming cat's. Then it let out a horrifying scream. For a moment Rex didn't understand, until he saw the metal shaft protruding from its flank: some kind of spear, its steel still sizzling with blue fire. The creature twitched once more, then stopped moving.

Melissa emerged from behind its bulk, looking stunned, her hands black with the creature's blood.

"Uninterrupted Vivisectional Preoccupation," she said.

Rex blinked. She had set the spear on the ground and let the darkling fall on it.

"Thanks for distracting it," she said.

Rex heard slithers flapping away from them in all directions, momentarily scattered by the dying howl of the great
cat. He took a painful step, put a gloved hand on her shoulder. "No problem. But what are you *doing* out here?"

"I got bored of waiting and figured you needed some
help." She held up a backpack. "I brought fireworks. So,
um . . . where's the fire?"

Rex looked back the way he'd come; the red glimmer
was just visible in the distance. "That way."

A puzzled expression crossed Melissa's face. Her eyes
closed for a moment. "You left our only fire with a couple
of *thirteen-year-olds*?"

He nodded. "Pretty much."

Melissa shook her head with disgust. "Daylighters in the
secret hour." She sighed, tossing him a long metal shaft
marked with spirals of solder. The steel burned even
through Rex's gloves, but its heft felt good in his hands.

"Thanks," he said. "How's Jessica doing?"

"Don't worry about her; worry about us." She lifted
another spear onto her shoulder. "There's a lot more darklings on their way."

They crashed through the trees toward the bonfire's glow,
swinging their spears at the slithers that struck through the
air. Every step shot through Rex's injured foot and his
throbbing ribs, but the pain had faded into a mindless blur.
He had reached Melissa, and his human half was willing to
let the beast take over.

The bonfire ahead was building, the smell of smoke

swirling through the forest. More of the four-armed dark-lings thrashed at the trees around it, as if trying to batter it into submission. But the wind of their wings only seemed to drive the fire brighter.

As they grew closer, the slithers stopped coming at them, wary of the whirlwind of sparks and burning leaves.

"Cassie! Beth!" Rex shouted.

"Rex?" came a cry. He saw Cassie silhouetted against the flames, the highway flare still sputtering in her hand.

"We're coming!" he yelled back.

"What about them?" Melissa asked, coming to a halt.

As she spoke, the bloated forms of five huge darklings rose from the forest floor. Their mouths glistened, and the clusters of eyes that dotted their bodies glowed dully in the purple light of the rip. Their long, hairy legs were splayed like the bars of a cage around the fire.

"Spiders," Melissa said. "Your favorite."

"Not a problem." Rex held out his hand. "Give me the backpack."

He unzipped it and dug his hand in, feeling a collection of bottle rockets, Roman candles, and firecrackers threaded in long strings. "Any highway flares?"

"Sure. At the bottom."

His hand closed on the flares, and he handed three to her, keeping another for himself. "One for each of us. After I deal with those things, we'll light up and make a run for the tracks."

"There's *five* of them, Rex. And they're just standing

there, staring at that fire like it's no big deal. They're not going to be afraid of *you*."

Rex smiled, feeling the beast well up in him. "They should be."

He turned, spear in one hand and backpack in the other, and limped toward the great spiders. They stood impassively, eyes aglitter with firelight. They were old, he could tell now. As he grew near, Rex felt their minds moving through him, the taste of ash and sour milk coating his tongue.

Abomination. You will die tonight.

"We'll see." He broke into a painful, ungainly run.

The spear left his hand first, shooting through the air toward the closest darkling. Two of its arms rose to ward it off, flailing like hairy tentacles. The spear glanced off one of them, coming to rest in the soft earth at its feet.

But the still-unzipped backpack was already soaring over the darkling's head. It traveled in a long arc, over Cassie and her sputtering flare, its contents already spilling from it as it flew. It all landed with a burst of sparks and smoke in the center of the bonfire.

Watch this . . . he thought at the darklings.

A moment later the scattered fireworks began to explode, balls of fire spitting out in all directions, the shriek of long strings of firecrackers expelling clouds of smoke, rockets bouncing among the branches. The burning tongue of a Roman candle reached out to ignite one of the spiders, and the beast screamed in pain as flame spread across its hairy surface. One of the winged darklings caught a bottle rocket and began to flail its wings, then crashed into the beast beside it, the two creatures wrapping around each other in a frantic, blazing embrace.

Beth and Cassie dropped into the wet leaves, hands over their heads. The great spiders shifted, their arms shuddering, their terror washing through Rex's mind with an electric taste.

He rolled under the nearest darkling, pulled his spear from the ground, and thrust it into the beast's belly. A foul smell spilled from the wound as the beast reared up, its mouth opening wide, its teeth as long as knives.

As Rex raised his spear, a squadron of rockets skittered randomly across the ground in the corner of his eye. Then one hit his shoulder, leapt into the air spinning head over tail, and shot into the gaping mouth of the darkling. The creature made a choking sound as Rex rolled toward the bonfire, rising to his knees to scrabble over to where the girls huddled.

"Are you okay?"

"Those *things* . . ." Beth sobbed.

"Don't worry. They're leaving." He looked up.

The beast behind him was trying to transform, wings sprouting from its back as the legs were sucked into the body. But then Rex heard a huffing sound—the rocket in its gut exploding—and tasted the beast's panic in his mind. Its glittering eyes dulled, and a gout of flame burst from the spear wound in its belly. The wings began to crumble. . . .

Rex covered his head as the creature exploded, a mighty rush of scorching heat, the light blinding even through his slammed-shut lids. The earth bucked beneath him, a roar like a jet taking off filling the air.

And then the sound was fading, until all he heard was the screams of midnight creatures retreating in all directions.

When Rex opened his eyes, he saw Melissa kneeling nearby, lighting the highway flares from the remains of the fire. Burning leaves were spread far into the trees, but a few glowing embers and a broad dark patch of ground were all that was left of Cassie's efforts.

"They're gone, Rex," she said. "Looks like you ruined their Samhain."

He nodded, his vision swarming with glowing spots. "Yeah. I guess bonfires have gotten a lot nastier since their day."

"We can do even better with the stuff back at the tracks. And we need to get there fast." She stood, two hissing flares in each hand.

Cassie was already standing, pulling Beth to her feet. They were covered with ash and wet leaves, their faces blank with shock. But Cassie took the flare that Melissa handed her. "Are they all gone?" she asked.

Melissa closed her eyes. "Not hardly. We have to run, girls." She pointed toward the tracks. "There's tons more fireworks waiting for us that way."

"Just give me a minute," Rex said. His torso was bruised all over, his ankle aching, his vision and hearing swarming with echoes of the explosion. His lungs felt scorched, as if he'd inhaled too much bonfire smoke.

He didn't hear Melissa's words at first.

"*Rex?*" Her hand pulled at his jacket.

"Just a second."

"We have to go *now*."

"I can barely stand."

"Look." She reached up and bare fingers brushed his neck, her mind entering him in a wild rush. He saw what was coming. . . .

"Oh, crap." Rex shuddered. He'd been a fool, all his plans empty gestures. "I never knew."

Melissa took her hand away and lifted his weight onto her shoulder, pulling him forward. "We can help Jenks, anyway."

They set off through the trees, Rex's battered body responding once more to the commands of his will. He didn't bother to look back, but the jittering of the branches ahead showed that the girls were following, their flares casting wild shadows through the forest. The tracks were only a few minutes away, but it all seemed futile. . . .

Rex shut his eyes and ran, ignoring the pain, trying to erase the image that Melissa had given him. A flood of darklings, a wave that darkened the sky, a vast horde beyond anything in the lore. Their fireworks would present nothing but a trivial detour to the onslaught.

Jessica Day was their only hope.

31

LIGHTNING

They bounded down the railroad tracks, following the rip. It stretched out before them, a red arrow pointed at the heart of Bixby.

"Can we make it in time?"

Jonathan nodded. "It's clearing the way for us, knocking down the frozen rain as it goes. But watch out when we get ahead of it. Water sucks."

"Jonathan!"

A man stood on the tracks ahead of them, dressed in a bathrobe and wearing an expression of disbelief. They took an extra-high jump so as not to hit him, and his pale face lifted to watch them pass overhead.

"Okay, that was weird," Jessica said.

"There are more of them. The rip is getting crowded. And not just with humans."

As they neared Bixby, houses became more frequent. They saw more people wandering around, first alone or in twos and threes, then in crowds gathered on the street. Some of them stared up in wonder at Jessica and Jonathan, but many didn't even noticed as they soared overhead, too dazzled by the blue-red world around them.

"You think Rex is right?" she said. "Can we really stop this?"

"If he isn't, most of these people are in big trouble. They're just standing here, right in the middle of the rip."

"At least the darklings aren't here yet."

He pointed ahead. "Some of them are."

Before them was another of the creatures made of wispy, grasping tendrils. It hovered over a small group gathered in the backyard of a house, what must have been a Halloween party going late. Everyone was in costume— knights and devils and cowboys and even a white-sheeted ghost all standing almost motionless. The darkling thing had a tendril wrapped around each of them, and Jessica saw that their hands were shaking, as if each was trapped in their own silent, private horrors.

"My God, should we stop?"

"No time," Jessica said. They had to halt this invasion. All of it, everywhere, not just in this one backyard. "But slow down a little."

She pulled a flare from her pocket and put one end into her mouth, yanking the top off. Then she banged it against the friction pad clenched between her teeth, sparks flying into her face, the first hiss of the flare burning her eyebrows before she could whip it away.

At the top of their next bounce she threw the flare down into the matted center of the thing. It ignited, the scream echoing across the blue time, its tendrils beginning to slip from the costumed people.

Jessica looked over her shoulder as they flew onward and saw that the crowd had sprung to life and were pulling at the thing's arms with a sudden and terrifying madness, as if trying to rip it apart.

"There's more," Jonathan said softly.

Ahead of them two of the old darklings were stretched across the railroad tracks, like hovering spiderwebs.

"Go around them?" he asked.

"They move too fast." Jessica pulled out another flare, then realized that it was the last one she was carrying. "Crap."

She yanked off its top with her teeth, managing to light it without burning her face this time. She thrust it out before them as they soared into the joined webs of tendrils.

At the touch of the flame the two darklings screamed, but Jessica felt cold feathers brushing her legs, her arms, her neck—slithering around her waist for a fleeting moment. Fear welled up in her again, a paralyzing horror that she had made the wrong decision. It was crazy leaving Jenks defenseless, her sister doomed. And suddenly she knew: the darklings had opened up the blue time because of her, because they hated Jessica Day so much. . . .

The end of the world . . . it's all my fault.

Only the feeling of Jonathan's hand in hers kept her

from giving in to the awesome despair that racked her being. He wouldn't abandon her, she knew. But they were wrapped around Jonathan as well; she had to fight.

Jessica gritted her teeth and slashed with the flare, carving into the matted tendrils, ripping herself free.

One by one, the fears fell away.

Then the feeling vanished, and she was filled with weightlessness again. The tracks reared up, and she reflexively took another bounding step. She glanced backward; the two darklings lay in a smoldering wreckage, scattered along on the tracks.

"No!" Jonathan yelled, his hand wrenching hers.

"Ow! What's wrong?" she cried.

"Huh?" He looked at her, dumbfounded. "Wait a second. I caught you . . . ?"

"Caught me? I wasn't falling."

"But I thought . . ." He stared at their joined hands.

"Oh." Jessica's eyes widened. "Is *that* your worst nightmare, Jonathan? Dropping me?"

He blinked. "Of course. But . . ."

Jessica felt a smile spread across her face. "That is *so sweet!*"

They landed and launched themselves into the air again. Jessica saw a glowing red boundary rising up before them. "What the—?"

"It's the front end of the rip," he cried. "Get ready!"

Jessica started to answer, but a wall of water struck her in the face.

She'd never flown through frozen rain before. Her first time in the secret hour, Jessica had walked around in a midnight shower, a magical experience no worse than dashing through a sprinkler in summer. But at seventy miles per hour, hitting the motionless storm was like having a fire hose trained on her.

The water soaked her already damp clothes, filled her mouth so she could hardly speak or breathe, and reduced their path to a blur before them. The highway flare sputtered in her hand, hissing like an angry snake. She could hardly see the ground rushing up at them.

She took a blind jump, and they began to spin.

"Stop! I can't see anything!" she shouted into the wall of rain.

"Can't stop for long—the rip's too close."

Jessica looked backward, which shielded her vision from the water. A huge sheet of red was streaking across Bixby, moving almost as fast as they were.

Turning back to face the deluge, she found she could finally make sense of the watery blue chaos. Through slitted eyes Jessica saw that they were entering downtown. On their next jump they bounded up onto the roof of a six-story building, then jumped higher.

Before her the tallest building in Bixby waited, a huge and winged shape glittering at its summit.

"Is that . . . ?"

"Don't you recognize Pegasus?"

"Wow." She had seen the giant horse from up close before, but never illuminated like this. A long finger of lightning reached down from the heavy clouds above, wrapping the sign in a thousand bright filaments.

They came down on another rooftop, skidding to a halt across wet black tar. Her soaked sneakers stumbled through a clutter of small shapes.

"Yo! Watch the fireworks!"

Jessica wiped water from her eyes. "Oh. Sorry, Dess."

"Where's Rex and Melissa?"

"Long story," Jonathan said. "We're on our way up there." He pointed at the lightning-sheathed Pegasus sign.

"What the hell for?"

"Rex thinks we can seal the rip."

"What, with *lightning*?" Dess swore. "You *do* know Rex is crazy these days, right?"

Jonathan looked at Jessica, who felt doubts rising in her again.

But she set her teeth. "We can't let this go on. We have to try."

"Don't ask me. But can I have that?" Dess pointed at the hissing flare. "Just in case you guys are crazy too?"

"Sure." Jessica handed it over.

"Come on." Jonathan was already perched on the edge of the roof. "The rip's right behind us."

"Good luck," Dess said.

"You too." Jessica ran to Jonathan and took his hand. She looked up at the glittering winged horse above them.

"Let's try to make it in one jump," Jonathan said.

"Can we get that far?"

"I hope so. Three . . . two . . . one . . ."

Jessica pushed off as hard as she could, and they soared into the air. At the peak of their arc, she was almost at eye level with the giant horse, higher than she'd ever flown before. But as they came closer, she realized that they were falling short.

"Uh-oh."

"We'll make it!" Jonathan flailed against the rain like an injured bird, then reached out one hand, and as they hit the building, his fingers found the edge of the roof. Jessica smacked into the wall below him, bouncing off and outward. For a moment the canyon of the street below yawned beneath her, and her hand seemed to be slipping through Jonathan's wet fingers.

But his grip remained firm, and he managed to cling to the building, letting her almost weightless body rebound in a circle over his head. She landed on the building's edge and pulled him up behind her.

"Made it!" he cried.

She looked back the way they had come, and her eyes widened. "Jonathan . . ."

The rip was barreling toward them, taller than a skyscraper now, wider than a football field. As the boundary of red time struck the rain, it released vast sheets of water, like a huge crimson tidal wave plowing through downtown Bixby's streets.

In its wake flew a horde of darklings, a thousand winged shapes of every size, vast whirlwinds of slithers glittering red and black, screaming their rat-squeak cries. A knotted mass of the tendril creatures flew at the center of the horde, their appendages intertwined like braided hairs.

"Rex didn't make it," she said softly. "Beth . . ."

"No, look." Jonathan pointed. Miles away, a tiny plume of fire rose into the sky over Jenks, showers of sparks and explosions in every color. "He and Melissa must have stopped some of them. Maybe there are more than we thought."

Jessica nodded slowly. Their carefully prepared plan had been woefully inadequate—a few fireworks against an army of monsters.

She tore her eyes away, dropping Jonathan's hand and running toward the giant horse. Its lowest hoof reached down almost to the rooftop—a strand of the arrested lightning wrapped around its metal support, bright and humming with contained power.

She reached toward it, her palm out, like testing the heat of a fire. Huge energies moved inside it, the hairs on her arms standing upright, her whole body tingling. It was like the glorious buzzing feeling when she'd first brought white light into the blue time, but a thousand times more intense. It made her heart pound harder, her vision swim.

Frozen or not, this was really *lightning*, she realized. An awesome force of nature, inconceivably deadly. Like sticking her hand in a light socket, but a million times more powerful. What was supposed to happen to her when she reached into it?

All she knew was what would happen if she didn't: thousands dead, the old ones feeding on their victims freely, humanity at the mercy of its oldest foe.

"I have to do this," she said softly.

"Are you sure?" Jonathan was right behind her.

"Stand back."

He shook his head, reaching for her, pulling her into a kiss. Jessica felt it in her lips then, the energy of the trapped lightning all around them mixed with the dizzying glow of Jonathan's midnight gravity. Her skin seemed to tighten, its surface running with wild currents and heat.

Jonathan pulled away, stepping back from her. "Okay. Be quick now."

"Farther, Jonathan."

He nodded, leaping to the edge of the roof. Behind him the crimson wave was almost upon them, a towering sheet of falling water and screaming predators.

Suddenly a hissing squadron of rockets rose up to meet them, bursting into showers of white light. Darklings wheeled and spun to avoid them.

"Dess," she whispered. The other building, only one jump away, was now inside the rip.

Jessica Day thrust her hand into the lightning. . . .

The frozen storm surged through her like an explosion. Thunder filled her ears, and wave after wave of pitiless energy rolled through Jessica until her body seemed to disappear and she could feel nothing but the primordial power locked inside that one instant of lightning. It built inside her, white spots flooding into her vision, her ears popping, the taste of metal skating across her tongue.

She felt like it was going to tear her apart.

Then the white heat burst out in a flood, shooting toward the approaching wall of the rip, cutting through its face and into the hordes of darklings and slithers, fire spreading from one midnight creature to the next in a mad zigzag pattern.

The mass of flying beasts began to wheel and howl.

Another torrent of lightning erupted from Jessica, then two more—four lines of fire radiating in the points of the compass, coruscating across the frozen darkness of the blue time.

Finally she felt the wild energies inside her body lessen, falling away like the shriek of a kettle picked up from the stove. The blinding light began to fade, and Jessica could feel her own breathing again and hear the beating of her heart.

The rip was almost gone, folding upon itself to make a narrow beam of red. The darkling horde was cut into fragments, reduced to scattered clouds of slithers and a few maddened darklings fleeing back toward the desert.

Jessica looked around; four streams of soft white light flowed from her, cutting into the distance toward the north, south, east, and west. The energies in her body dwindled further as she felt them spreading out across the entire globe, wrapping themselves around the earth in some sort of pattern.

Something Dess would want to see, she thought hazily.

But her consciousness was fading away.

Then she saw it through the supports of the giant horse, heading toward them from the east. The light of normal time, sweeping across the world like dawn. The dark moon overhead was falling fast.

Samhain hadn't lasted a whole day, not even an hour. . . .

"Jessica." Jonathan was walking toward her across the roof. "You're . . ."

"Be careful," she said weakly. White heat still burned in her hand. She lifted it heavily before her eyes and stared into the trapped lightning there.

But why was the midnight hour over already?

She pulled her eyes away from the fire pulsing in her palm and looked out at the horizon. She saw the storm unfreezing, the blue light of midnight swept out of the world.

Just as normal time reached her, Jessica felt herself fading. . . .

"Oh, no," she said, casting one last glance at Jonathan's stupefied face.

An interrupted peal of thunder rolled as midnight ended.

And then everything was gone.

32

EPILOGUE

The car slid to a halt in front of the house across the street, setting the neighborhood dogs barking wildly.

Nice move, Flyboy, Melissa thought. Dess had told him to keep it quiet tonight. Her parents were still in major curfew mode since the Great Bixby Halloween Hysteria.

He waited for a moment, then reached to honk the horn.

"Don't," Melissa said. "She's coming."

He glowered for a moment, his impatience bitter in the air. Of course, there was plenty of time before midnight to get to Jessica's house and still make it out to Jenks. But Jonathan was in a hurry to get tonight over and done with. It was all too emotional, and underneath his tension Melissa sniffed a sliver of fear. . . .

"Don't worry, Jonathan. She won't change her mind about leaving."

He looked at her, bristling, then sighed.

"She better not, anyway," Melissa said. "I don't think I can live with my parents much longer. Not with Rex's new rules on mindcasting." Her parents had never been psychos like Rex's dad, but the subtle web of deceits she had woven around them over the years was beginning to collapse. Melissa had spent the last sixteen years shrinking from their very touch; she doubted she was ready for any heart-to-heart talks about her private life.

In particular, they'd started asking about her missing car. It was definitely time to get out of town.

Dess appeared, slipping from her window and crossing the threadbare lawn at a deliberate pace. Melissa felt her annoyance at Jonathan's noisiness and saw her taking her time.

"Hey, Flyboy." Dess pulled the back door open and slid her backpack across, then jumped in herself. She didn't say hello to Melissa, but there was no real animosity in it, only habit.

Jonathan glanced over his shoulder at the backseat. "You really think we'll need that stuff? I mean, are there even any darklings left?"

Melissa found herself defending Dess. "A few got away. And the really cautious ones never even showed."

"Sure," Flyboy said. "But they're not in Bixby anymore. And the four of us will be there."

Dess shrugged. "When dealing with midnight, better safe than sorry."

Jonathan gave her his new wounded stare. "Guess that makes me sorry."

Melissa scowled as the sour milk taste of guilt rolled out of his mind. Two weeks later and he was still wallowing in the idea that what had happened to Jessica was his fault.

She sighed softly, wondering what it was going to be like to deal with Flyboy all alone for twenty-four hours a day.

Maybe without Rex around to challenge his freedom, he'd chill out. . . .

At the thought of leaving Rex behind, Melissa shivered a little and pulled her mind back to the present. The future could sort itself out now that they actually had one to look forward to.

Jonathan pulled out onto the street, swinging the car into a wide one-eighty that kicked up dust on Dess's dying lawn. Then he shot down the unpaved road, tires spitting gravel and sand. As usual these days, he wasn't in the mood to talk or watch out for cops.

Melissa settled into the front passenger seat, casting her mind across the empty spaces on the edge of town, staying alert. Since the Hysteria, curfew had a whole new meaning here in Bixby.

The official story was, of course, a big joke. A freak collision of air masses over eastern Oklahoma had caused a record number of lightning strikes and brain-rattling waves of thunder. Power had been knocked out across the county, and random electrical fields had disrupted even battery-operated devices and cars. These natural phenomena—along with statistical spikes of heart attacks, fireworks thefts, and costumed Halloween pranks—were the official reasons for the panic.

None of which explained the mutilated body of the camper found in outer Jenks or the seventeen people still missing. But it was a good enough rationalization for anyone who hadn't been awake and inside the rip that night.

Of course, a few conspiracy types had much better theories. Melissa's favorites were an electromagnetic pulse from an experimental plane using the new Bixby runway (which wasn't even built yet) and psychedelic mushrooms growing in the town water supply.

It was all part of a need to understand or, more accurately, to explain away what had happened. Anything not to have to face the truth—that the unknown had come visiting.

One certainty remained, though: Halloween would never be the same in Bixby again.

They reached Jessica's house just before eleven.

All the inside lights were off, both cars sitting in the driveway. There was no For Sale sign on the lawn yet or any other way to distinguish the Day house from the others on the street. But it looked different somehow, even before she cast her mind inside. Sadder.

"Are they really moving?" Dess asked.

"That's just a rumor at school," Flyboy said. He looked to Melissa for confirmation.

She nodded, her mouth filling with the burnt-coffee taste of anguish that still clung to hope. "They don't really know. Still waiting for some kind of hard evidence, I suppose."

"Waiting sucks," Dess said, and Jonathan nodded.

And then they waited.

She made her way out the window about fifteen minutes later, dropping ungracefully into the bushes. Her jacket looked too big on her, and she walked hunched, her hands jammed all the way down into the pockets.

When she was halfway to the street, Jonathan flashed his headlights once. She spun toward the car, and a sudden jolt of fear shot through the air. For a second Melissa thought that she was about to chicken out and crawl right back into her bedroom.

But a moment later she was at the car window. Her anxiety pulsed in Melissa's mind, her suspicion almost hiding the tight ball of grief in her stomach. Suddenly Melissa realized how brave Beth was to have agreed to this at all.

"Hey," Jonathan said.

"That's Dess, isn't it?" the kid said.

Dess nodded. "Yeah. How'd you know?"

"You look just like Cassie's picture."

Dess didn't answer, giving off the prickly taste of a lump rising in her throat.

"You cut your hair," Beth said to Melissa.

The mindcaster pushed her fingers through her one-inch buzz, a nervous habit she'd learned from Rex. "It's what I get for playing with fire."

Beth got into the back with Dess, sitting on the backpack with a *clink*.

"Ouch!"

"Just give it here," Dess said.

"What's *in* there?"

"Magic stuff."

Jonathan turned to give Dess a death glare, but the kid handed over the backpack with the utmost care.

★　　★　　★

Rex limped up the stairs of Madeleine's house, trying not to think of what was going on in Jenks. There were bigger issues to consider, lots of questions to be answered before the others left. He clutched his latest letter from Angie and its accompanying sheaf of photocopies—biface spear points from a museum in Cactus Hill, Virginia. She was research- ing Stone Age culture there, helping Rex search for a link to ancient finds in southern Spain. Rex had serious work to do tonight, more important than watching over ritual farewells.

Besides, Madeleine needed feeding.

In his other hand he carried a thermos of hot chicken soup. Not too hot, of course; she could drink on her own now, but like a baby, she didn't know enough not to burn her lips. Fortunately Rex knew a lot about caring for invalids.

He didn't mind taking care of Madeleine, actually. Here inside the crepuscular contortion that had protected her for fifty years, the human presence of the outside world didn't bother him as much. No cable TV, no cordless phone filling the air with its buzz. The place stank of thirteen-pointed steel, but rust had long ago consumed the alloy's bite. The midnighters who had named those weapons were all dead, except for Madeleine.

Not merely alive: Melissa said that her mind was slowly repairing itself, rebuilding from what his darkling half had done to her, a survivor to the last.

When he opened the door to her room, Rex was surprised to see her sitting up, a gleam of intelligence in her eyes. The smell of weakness and death had lifted a little.

"Madeleine?"

She nodded slowly, as if remembering her name. "What day is it?"

Rex blinked. The dry, rough-edged words were her first in a month. "Samhain has come and gone. The flame-bringer stopped it."

She let out a rattling sigh, a smile fluttering on her lips. "I knew that girl was special. I was right to call her here to Bixby."

Rex couldn't argue with that. Since Samhain he had been forced to admit that Madeleine's manipulations over the years had saved a lot of lives. Her orphaned set of mid-nighters had done more for Bixby than all the previous generations put together. However broken the two of them were, they could congratulate themselves on that.

He sat down next to her, twisting the top from the thermos.

"Where is Melissa?" she croaked.

"She's leaving." The two simple words sent a spur of pain through him. But of course it was the only way.

"Where?"

He shrugged. "Eat."

She took the thermos in trembling hands, held it to her lips, and drank. Rex watched her wrinkled throat move with each greedy swallow. Apparently rebuilding her damaged mind was hungry work. He looked down at the spear points, reading the lore symbols in Angie's cramped handwriting. It was easier on his brain than modern letters.

Melissa found it maddening how much he enjoyed the letters from his new pen pal.

Finally Madeleine rested the thermos in her lap, catching her breath. "You're a fool to hate me, Rex."

"I don't hate you. I pity you when I bother to think about it."

"I did it all for you, Rex. Don't you see?" Her eyes gleamed, and he could see what remained of her colossal egotism. "I wanted to make Bixby as it was in the old days."

He shook his head. "That Bixby was a nightmare. It's our day now."

She snorted. "What would you know about it? A half-darkling, half-midnighter and so concerned with *daylighters*. It's perverse."

Rex smiled, glad to hear her diagnosis. She could see that the beast inside him was under control, subservient to his human side. Maybe she wasn't the only one repairing herself.

"Did you say Melissa was leaving?"

He nodded.

"But why? I cowered in this house for fifty years rather than leave the contortion. She'll be blind and deaf out there, without a hint of taste. A daylighter, Rex—a *nothing*."

"No, she won't be."

He swallowed, fear moving through him again at the thought of her leaving. It wasn't Melissa he was worried about, of course. It was Rex Greene. Would he still be able to hold himself together once his oldest friend was gone? Maybe he should join the others, leaving Dess all alone in

Bixby, leaving his father and the old woman to die. They deserved whatever they got, and without Melissa's calmness of mind, without her touch . . .

Rex shook his head, steeling himself. He took the thermos from Madeleine's hand and wiped stray soup from her chin. Perhaps Melissa was right, and it was tending to his father and an old woman that had kept him sane all along. His cares kept him human.

Madeleine hadn't heard him; she was still mewling. "Why, Rex? Why would she leave? This is *Bixby*, after all."

He drew himself up and gave her a predatory smile, knowing that the news would silence her.

"Because Bixby isn't special anymore."

They reached Jenks without any trouble, and Jonathan drew to a halt in the same field that Rex had raged across in his mother's pink Cadillac. As the four of them made their silent way toward the rip, he stared down the railroad tracks, which still bore the scars of Halloween—a few cross-ties were blackened from burning oil and rocket exhaust, and the soggy relics of firecracker-red paper clung to bits of gravel everywhere.

But the surrounding grass had recovered from the rip's strange light, Jonathan noticed, a healthy green again. Maybe the dark moon wasn't so tough after all.

There wasn't much left of the rip anymore, just a sliver. A few more nights and it would fade into the lore completely. When they reached it, Dess pulled out Geostationary and began to make a small, precise circle of stones.

Beth stood close to him, watching her. "What's that thing?" she said softly.

"A GPS device," he answered. "It's not magic or anything."

"What's it supposed to do?"

"It's for finding places. You have to be in exactly the right spot for this to work."

Beth looked at him, her stare suddenly fierce. "I've got my mom's cell phone, you know."

He blinked. "That's . . . good."

"So you guys better not try anything weird."

Jonathan sighed. What they were about to try was, pretty much by definition, weird. "Don't worry, okay? We're all friends here. You said you wanted to do this."

Beth only swallowed and for a moment looked like she was about to cry.

"She wants this too," Jonathan added, wishing he were somewhere else. He'd been the one to break the news to Beth, to argue against her suspicions, her angry disbelief. After the hours spent convincing her to come out here, Jonathan was all out of words. He reached out and put his arm around her, drew her closer.

"Really?" she said, her voice breaking. "And this is for real?"

He smiled. "Well, I ain't dreaming." She felt unbelievably small and fragile, shivering in the cold.

"Come on," Dess said. "Stand right here."

Jonathan guided Beth up onto the tracks and into the circle of stones. The frightened expression on her face made something loosen in his throat, and his voice grew hoarse. "Don't worry. It'll be okay."

He stepped back, waiting, hoping that this would work.

Midnight fell a few moments later, the moan of the cold wind switching off like a light, the blue time sucking the color from their faces. Jonathan felt the awful weight of Flatland lift up from him.

Same old midnight—damaged, unleashed from its proper boundaries, but not destroyed.

For a moment Jonathan wondered if they'd waited too long to try this and the rip had faded out. Beth just stood there in her circle of rocks, as motionless as any stiff.

But then her eyes blinked. "That was weird."

"No kidding," Jessica said from behind her little sister. She'd asked them to face the kid toward Bixby and had wisely chosen not to be standing in Beth's view. She kept her right hand in her jacket pocket as well.

It still freaked Jonathan out how Jessica always *folded* out of the air as midnight fell. Even darklings and slithers had to escape from the sun, hiding in caves or burying themselves. But the flame-bringer had become something altogether different, a whole new kind of midnight creature.

She wasn't frozen during daylight . . . she simply *wasn't*.

Rex called it "temporal dependence." Jonathan didn't know what to call it. During the day it felt like Jessica was gone, like that first night when he thought he'd lost her to the lightning. He'd searched the roof for hours before trudging down the twenty-six flights of stairs to the ground floor, exhausted by Flatland, crushed by grief. It had been a whole terrible day before midnight had fallen again and he'd flown back up to Pegasus, hoping to find some kind of sign.

And she was standing there . . . still in shock, not realizing a whole day had passed without her. Alive.

But his joy had faded when midnight had ended again and they realized that Jessica was trapped now inside the secret hour.

Jonathan looked at her, feeling that fractured rush of relief again. For the last two years his life had been split in half, between glorious midnight and the crushing gravity of daylight. These days it was even worse: Flatland was much flatter without Jessica and the secret hour suddenly more precious.

Midnight stretched across the whole world now, after all. They could fly anywhere . . . in their one hour.

Beth turned around slowly, huddling in her jacket as if the air were still cold. She stared at Jessica.

"Come on, Flyboy," Dess said. "Let's give them some privacy."

He caught Jessica's eye, and she nodded.

Walking away felt like a kick in the stomach, giving up these minutes with Jessica. *This* was what he'd always tried to avoid since the day his mother had departed and not returned: this feeling that if you lost someone, your world could come crashing down. And it had happened again.

But at least Jessica hadn't disappeared completely. She was only gone for twenty-four hours a day. And Jonathan knew he would hold on to that one hour left to them for as long as he could.

"Jess?" Beth said in a small voice.

"Yeah, it's me." Jessica felt tears on her face. She'd known the exact spot her sister would shimmer into view, but it still made her breath catch.

"You're really . . . here."

Jessica nodded. She wanted to gather her little sister into a hug, but for these first fragile moments she'd decided to keep her right hand in her pocket. "Yeah. I've been here all along."

"Why didn't you come home?"

Jessica bit her lip. "I can't. I'm stuck here."

"What? In *Jenks*?"

"No, in midnight. I only exist for an hour a day. I'm part of midnight now." Jessica shook her head sadly. Maybe she'd been part of midnight since she'd woken up that first time in the secret hour. It had nibbled away at her life since then, until only this one sliver was left.

She felt a mental nudge from Melissa, standing close by, and stood straighter, swallowing her self-pity. Jessica had made her choice on that building top, after all, knowing that sticking her hand into the bolt of lightning would change everything.

"Why didn't you *tell* me what was going on?" Beth said. "The whole time, you could have let me know."

Jessica was ready for this. "Are you going to tell Mom and Dad?"

"Tell them . . . ?"

"About this. Are you going to tell them you saw your missing sister appear on some railroad tracks in Jenks?"

Beth thought for a moment, then shook her head. "They'd probably send me to a shrink."

"Exactly." Jessica nodded. "So you have to keep it secret. Like I did. That's just the way it works. But Beth, at least you'll know I'm . . . somewhere."

"*Somewhere* isn't good enough, Jess! You're leaving me all alone."

"I'm not. You've still got Mom and Dad."

Beth clenched her teeth. "Mom cries all the time. She thinks it's because she was working so much that you disappeared. And Dad's an even bigger zombie than before."

Jessica closed her eyes, her tears hot on her cheeks in the cool of the blue time. The thought of her parents missing her, not knowing what had happened, was too much to bear. "They need you, Beth."

"They need *you*. Maybe they could come here and stand here like I did. I'll think of some way to get them out to Jenks. I'll *make* them come. . . ."

"No." Jessica took a step forward, put her left arm around Beth. "The rip is fading. And besides, I won't be here anymore. Jonathan and Melissa and I are leaving Bixby."

Beth kicked at the gravel, tears appearing in her eyes. "You *are* leaving me."

"Midnight's spreading, Beth. There are going to be more people like me, waking up and finding themselves in the blue time."

"And lying to their little sisters?"

"Probably, at first." Jessica nodded. "Right now they need our help."

"*I* need you too, Jessica." Beth was sobbing now.

"I know." She drew her little sister into a left-handed hug and sighed. "I'm so sorry, Beth. Maybe it wasn't fair, bringing you out here."

Beth shook her head.

"But you'll have to keep everyone in the dark, just like I did," Jessica said. "You'll have to lie about it."

Beth raised her head. "Not to everyone. There's Cassie."

Jessica nodded slowly. "That's right. She saw the rip, anyway. I guess you could tell her about me too."

Beth sniffed once. "Already did."

"What?"

"When Jonathan was trying to convince me to come out here. I had her spend the night, and she hid in my closet. And listened."

A momentary wave of annoyance, all too familiar, went through Jessica. But then it turned into a feeling of relief and she let out a chuckle. "You little sneak."

"There have to be more people in Bixby who know about all this, who've figured out how it works." Beth pulled away a bit, staring fiercely into her sister's eyes. "And believe me, Cassie and I are going to find them. Don't think you've gotten away from us yet."

Jessica looked down at her little sister, a smile spreading across her face, suddenly certain that Beth was going to be okay, with or without her big sister around.

★ ★ ★

Dess let herself wander along the tracks, looking into the trees, searching for any sign of life. It was almost too quiet these days; she wouldn't mind the sight of a slither among the leaves. Certainly she was safe enough, between Counterfeiter in her pocket and the flame-bringer a few hundred feet away. Jessica hadn't tried out her new, softly sparkling right hand on any darklings yet, but Dess was pretty sure she didn't need a flashlight anymore.

Dess hadn't slain anything herself in ages now. Why had they *all* run away? Darklings were like tigers, she figured. You didn't want them eating you, but you didn't want them going *extinct*. The world was less interesting without them.

Of course, after a few thousand years in one crappy town, Halloween had probably looked like Christmas to the darklings who'd survived.

When Jessica had sealed the rip, the energies built up along Bixby's fault line hadn't disappeared—they'd spread across the globe.

Dess shook her head. After all her work on the geography of the secret hour, it seemed a shame to throw out all those maps. Still, she couldn't wait for Jonathan and Jess to start exploring the 36th parallel, finding out how far midnight stretched in the aftermath of Samhain.

Did it extend along the whole 36th parallel? And the 12th, 24th, and 48th as well? Was it wrapped around the entire globe, or did it only pop up at the intersections of multiples of twelve?

Or was midnight simply *everywhere* now? Were lucky midnighters waking up in every city and town, amazed at the blue and frozen world?

Dess heard the crunch of gravel and turned. Flyboy was bouncing along behind her, looking unhappy, like he needed someone to talk to.

She sighed. "So when do you three leave?"

"Probably soon." He pointed his chin back toward the girls. "Now that this is over and done with."

"It's going to be lonely, only seeing Jess an hour a day."

"It's already lonely."

Dess shook her head, wondering if he'd bothered to do the math on that little conundrum. Jess lived only one hour to his twenty-five, which meant she'd be hitting her nineteenth birthday just about the same time Jonathan was dying of old age. And sometime *way* before that, things were going to get . . . icky.

"Oh, well." Dess smiled wryly. "You've always got Melissa to talk to."

He looked up from the tracks. "Why do you still hate her? She saved Jessica that night, you know. *And* Beth. Maybe everyone in the world."

"I don't hate her." As the words left her mouth, Dess realized it was really true—her hatred of the mindcaster had quietly expired. "Still, she's not exactly road trip material."

"Maybe not." He smiled. "But without her, we'll never find all of them."

"*All* of them? Flyboy, there's lots more than you think."

Jonathan looked at her, then shook his head. "Any idea how all this happened? I mean *why* it happened?"

Dess just snorted at that one. Let Rex bury himself in the lore, still trying to figure that stuff out, how the time-quake and the lightning had chosen the same moment to strike. But Dess knew that was nuts. Not that she was against doing the math—explaining why and how things happened was the credo of the Discovery Channel, after all. But sometimes the numbers would never add up, no matter how hard you calculated.

After all, the chances of a bolt of lightning hitting the center of Bixby on the exact stroke of midnight on Halloween were . . . rather low. And if you thought for too long about why it had happened in exactly that way, you weren't doing your brain any favors. In which case it was better to leave the math the hell alone.

She looked into the sky and saw that the dark moon reached its apex. "Come on, Flyboy. Time for your party trick."

"Okay." He swallowed. "You really think this will help?"

"Of course it will." Dess led Jonathan back toward where the other three stood. She knew the two sisters had more stuff to work out, but sometimes apology math was funny: no number was ever high enough, and you just had to get over it.

They were holding each other, as if already out of words. Melissa stood off to one side, eyes closed. Prompting? Controlling? Or just eavesdropping? Dess wondered if this new non-evil style of mindcasting really helped or was just another crock.

Dess waited until she caught Jessica's eye, then pointed at Jonathan.

Give the poor kid this much at least.

Jessica nodded back and pulled away. "Come on. I want to show you something about midnight. Something not horrible. It's a little weird but . . . trust me?"

Beth made a choked little sound, wiping at her face, then said softly, "I trust you."

Jonathan stepped forward, holding out both his hands. "You saw us do this, right? On Halloween?"

Beth nodded, taking his hand carefully. As her smaller fingers closed around his, a look of surprise crossed her face.

"It's . . . dizzy."

"It's a lot better than dizzy," Jessica said, smiling. She pulled her right hand from her pocket; white sparks fluttered upward from it. The bracelet she wore glowed, its tiny charms aglitter. Dess squinted at the light.

Beth stared at it openmouthed. "What *is* that?"

"Don't you remember? It's a present from Jonathan . . . plus some lightning." Jessica took Flyboy's hand.

At first they took a weenie, ten-foot hop. Then a longer one took them to the middle of the field. Finally they opened up big time, heading for the motionless Arkansas River. Jessica's right hand sparkled in the distance, its trail of white light coruscating across the blue horizon.

Dess felt a smile spread across her face, and she was

suddenly much less depressed. Beth had seen the blue time again; she'd gotten to fly.

"Yeah, I know," Melissa said.

Dess let out a sigh. Alone with the bitch goddess one more time.

"I'm still sorry, you know. For what I did to you."

Typical mindcaster trick, catching her off guard and getting all sentimental. Dess heard herself saying, "Whatever. It's probably not your fault, the way you are."

"We saved Rex that night."

Not so sorry after all? Dess thought. But she couldn't argue with Melissa's logic. "You'll miss him, won't you?"

Melissa nodded. "I already do."

Dess sighed again. Maybe there was one darkling left in Bixby.

They stood there in silence for a while, waiting for the others to come back.

"So how many more of us are out there?" the mindcaster finally asked.

Dess took a breath, glad to be talking about math instead of all this emotional crap. "Well, let's say you have to be born within a half second of midnight, right? That would be one out of every eighty-six thousand four hundred people."

"In a big city that's a lot, isn't it?"

"In New York about a hundred. In the world . . . a hundred *thousand*."

"Crap," Melissa said softly, like she hadn't thought through the scale of their little road trip yet.

Amazement radiated from the mindcaster, a tingle

that shot down Dess's arms into her fingers, bringing back her smile. Even being stuck here in Bixby with crazy Rex and crazier Maddy, even with no darklings left to slay, even living in a major curfew zone for the next two and a half years, Dess couldn't complain about the cards she'd drawn.

Once the midnighters had gone their separate ways, Dess would no longer be stuck between the two couples, hemmed in by the constant clash of egos. And eventually she would be free of Bixby itself. No longer a fifth wheel.

After high school, Dess knew, she could get a job anywhere. Computers, spacecraft, all kinds of cool stuff that hadn't even been invented yet—all of it needed math. And with midnight spreading across the globe, thousands of polymaths would be waking up. Finally she'd have people to talk to with minds like hers, math geniuses in a frozen time where math kicked ass. Together they could map the expanded secret hour, have whole conversations in tridecalogisms, try to figure out how time itself worked. Change the world, maybe.

Screw the lore, with all its propaganda and lies and bitter history. Dess was going to be the one to write the axioms of midnight, the first principles of Dessometrics.

Inexhaustible. Unsmotherable. Extraordinary. That was her.

It was way cool, being the one who did the math.